THE COMMITMENT

THE UNBROKEN SERIES: HEAVENLY RISING

SHAYLA BLACK
JENNA JACOB

DREAM WORDS LLC

The Commitment

ONE BRIDE. TWO BACHELORS.
TOTAL COMMITMENT?

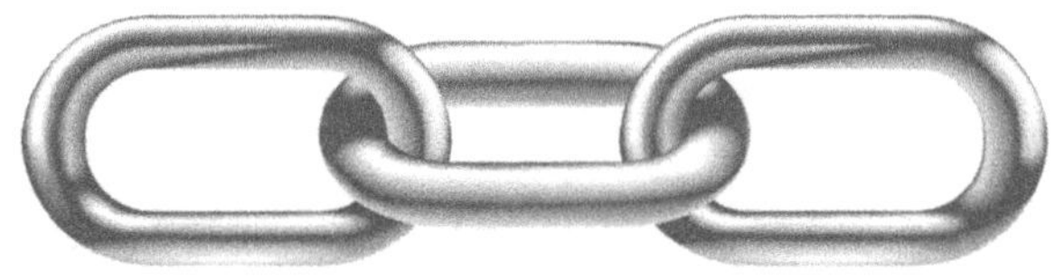

THE UNBROKEN SERIES: HEAVENLY RISING FOUR

NEW YORK TIMES BESTSELLING AUTHOR
SHAYLA BLACK
USA TODAY BESTSELLING AUTHOR
JENNA JACOB

THE COMMITMENT
The Unbroken Series: Heavenly Rising (Book 4)
Written by Shayla Black and Jenna Jacob

ISBN: 978-1-956445-14-5

This book is an original publication by Shayla Black and Jenna Jacob

Cover Design by: Rachel Connolly
Edited by: Julie Barney and Shayla Black
Proofread by: Mallory Black

AUTHORS' NOTE

THE UNBROKEN SERIES: Heavenly Rising saga is a serialized succession of novels that MUST be read in order. If you've purchased this book and have not read the others in the saga, here is the reading order:

The Choice
The Chase
The Confession
The Commitment

We hope you enjoy reading these stories
as much as we did writing them.

Happy Reading!

Shayla Black
Jenna Jacob

ABOUT *THE COMMITMENT*

One Bride. Two Bachelors. Total Commitment?

Seth Cooper must decide between growing a future with Heavenly Young and Kenneth "Beck" Beckman or losing them forever. His heart says yes...but his head knows that if he has to mourn his loved ones again, he won't survive. He chooses Heavenly and Beck—swallowing the quiet terror that their commitment might be the thing that shatters them all.

Then, Seth's devoutly Catholic mother's wedding compels the trio to New York. To preserve her happy day, he asks Heavenly to pose as his fiancée, while reducing Beck to platonic friend. The charade is temporary…but it quickly tears them apart.

When the trio's plans for the future become terrifyingly real, a new discovery forces Seth to confront an old threat—exposing a betrayal he never saw coming and dragging them into the very risk he feared most. With everyone he loves—along with his secrets—in jeopardy, Seth must stop the killer or history will repeat itself in blood. Because surviving the danger is only possible if they fight for it together.

** Series must be read in order **

Chapter One

Los Angeles
September 7

"What the fuck is wrong with me?"

Raking a hand through his hair, Seth Cooper sank onto the bottom step of the house he shared with Kenneth Beckman and their girlfriend, Heavenly Young. The riser creaked beneath his weight. His lungs felt as if they'd collapsed. Each breath was a conscious effort as he sat frozen, the weight of his choices —past and present—crushing him like a vise.

The two most important people in his life were upstairs, waiting for him so they could start their happy future…and he was down here, choking on his own bullshit.

He had to think. Had to breathe.

Their last conversation replayed in his head.

You're going to get her pregnant. Seth had hurled the words like an accusation.

Beck hadn't blinked. *God, I hope so. You can be a part of that, but you've got to decide if your past is more important than your future. If it is, well… You know the way out.*

The thought of intentionally impregnating Heavenly dredged up memories Seth had spent years burying. They crashed past his barriers and drowned him with regret. He could see it all now: pulling up to his house, pieces of his wife's car still smoldering on the neighbor's yard. Flames shooting out from the busted windows while Autumn and their infant son burned inside. Tristan's pacifier melted to the concrete. A singed blue bootie in the gutter. The teddy bear his boy had slept with every night since birth burning as the December ice beneath it melted.

Seth pressed the heels of his hands against his eyes, but that didn't stop the images from coming. The baby blanket his mother had lovingly handcrafted, caught in the branches of the bare oak tree, edges blackened and curling with the heat. The smell—god, the smell—of melting plastic from the car seat his baby had been strapped into. And the terrible note the killer had left for him: MERRY FUCKING CHRISTMAS.

He'd stood there, helpless, knowing the only person he could ultimately blame for Autumn and Tristan's murders was himself. If he hadn't been so reckless, so stubborn and arrogant in pursuing the case that had gotten his father killed nearly a decade prior, they would still be alive.

That's what he was running from now. Not just losing his wife and son, but the terror that history could repeat itself.

The logical part of his brain—the investigator, the problem solver—kicked into gear, sifting through evidence.

Their killer is dead. Eight years ago, Seth had made damn sure he'd slaughtered the bastard who had murdered his young family—in the most violent way possible. For four days, he'd tortured Silas Nichols in his disgusting South Bronx apartment, feeding off the man's screams before putting a bullet between his eyes. That monster was rotting now, six feet under and serving as maggot food.

No one had ever connected Seth to Silas's death. No one ever would.

And in the years since, had there been even a whisper of a threat? Nothing. Not a goddamn thing. So why was he still living like everyone he dared to love had a target on their back?

"Because you're a fucking coward," he whispered into the awful silence, the words burning his throat.

Despite becoming an edge-walking, gun-toting badass, his father would've admonished him for being afraid of a boogeyman he'd already vanquished. Fear had never stopped Michael Cooper from living, from loving, or from fighting for what mattered.

Seth curled his hands into fists. He was going to lose them. Beck's patience had run out. And Heavenly, his sweet angel, had walked away from him tonight. Not physically, but emotionally. He'd seen it in her eyes. Heard it in her trembling voice.

I'm sorry, Seth. I won't sacrifice having a family because you're too scared to make one.

Her quiet devastation had cut deeper than her anger ever could.

Then, while he'd been clutching his figuratively kicked-in balls, Beck had heaped more truth onto him.

If you were actually trying to help yourself, we'd gladly give you all the time you need. But you're not. Heavenly and I have waited for months. We're done. We're starting our future tonight.

Seth bit back a curse. What was he fighting so hard to avoid? More loss? More pain? He'd lived through both. It had nearly destroyed him, but he'd survived…though he hadn't really healed. Instead, he'd weaponized his grief, using it like a shield against any potential heartbreak. As if loss could be prevented by refusing to truly live. If he didn't get his shit together, he'd let his past—and his fear—fuck his future for good.

And he'd have no one to blame but himself.

The realization slammed into him like a wrecking ball. He couldn't put off this decision. They intended to start their tomorrows tonight. Right now. So he had to choose: stay paralyzed by fear and lose everything…or step into uncertainty and fight for the life he wanted?

Because he *did* want it. All of it. Beck's steady strength. Heavenly's endless compassion. Their morning coffees and midnight confessions. The brash yet stoic way Beck always had his back. The sweet sound of Heavenly's laughter and her soft smiles.

Seth scrubbed a hand down his face. How could he ask the woman who had already put her life on hold for her dying father to wait again because he was scared shitless? How was it fair to deny her motherhood because he feared what *might* happen?

It wasn't…but neither is them expecting me to get over eight years of grief in the next three minutes.

He sighed. *Hell, maybe I'm just dragging them down, and they're better off without me.*

Seth tried to picture himself walking away. Beck and Heavenly would move on. They'd be happy without him. A clean break would hurt less in the long run, right?

No. This goddamn doom-and-gloom was nothing but cowardice dressed up as nobility. Fuck that.

He surged to his feet. He wasn't giving up without a fight.

Maybe he'd never really overcome this gutting terror. Maybe he just needed to find his balls, spit in fear's face, and get the fuck on with his life.

But what would he tell his mother? She knew about Heavenly…but he hadn't dared to whisper a word about Beck. How the hell would the three of them attend her wedding in New York in less than a month? Grace Cooper would faint if she figured out that he shared Heavenly with the good doctor. He couldn't see her ever approving. But he also couldn't see her ever turning her back on him. And a grandchild? She'd be over the moon, no matter the circumstances.

Mom's disapproval was an issue…but not the one that kept him from committing. That stumbling block was all in his head.

How was he going to get past all the fucking loss he'd endured? Almost no one could comprehend what he was going through.

But there was *one person…*

Beck's younger brother, Zach, who was staying in his old apartment should be drowning in grief. His wife and daughter had been brutally murdered five months ago. By all rights, the guy should be falling apart, struggling against the past threatening to swallow him whole.

Instead, Zach was already beginning to move on—and actually starting to live.

How?

Seth heaved a sigh. He didn't know, but *if* he was going to take this leap, he needed to do it right. Not as a reaction. Not because Beck had cornered him. Not even because Heavenly deserved his all, though she did.

He needed to do it because he was choosing their future over his fear. Eyes open. No half measures.

And if he couldn't, he needed to get the fuck out.

Seth took the stairs two at a time, his heart hammering against his ribs. Before he even reached the bedroom, he heard Heavenly's muffled sobs. Through the crack in the door, Seth could see them: Beck reclined against the headboard, Heavenly curled up against him, her shoulders shaking as he stroked her pale halo of curls.

The sight was like a knife between his ribs. He'd done that. He'd put her pain there.

Seth eased the door open. The pair turned. Their eyes locked on him—one set blue and desolate, the other dark and angry.

"Give me an hour." Somehow, his voice sounded steady, despite the earthquake rumbling through his chest. "Please."

Heavenly sat up, wiping tears from her cheeks and faced him with more of that heart-rending disappointment. "An hour to what, Seth? To decide if you want me forever? If I'm worth it?"

"What the fuck will an hour change?" Beck's voice sounded low, dangerous. The quiet before the storm.

Seth swallowed hard as he looked at them both, willing them to understand. "It would be easy to say yes and fuck the consequences, but I want to be sure. Not just go along to get along. I want—" He sighed. "No, I *need* to deserve you two."

They exchanged a silent glance. A wordless judgment. Their hesitation pierced his chest like a blade. But he'd earned that.

Finally, Beck looked at his watch, his expression cold and decisive. "One hour. The clock is ticking. If you're not back by then, we're starting the future without you."

Each word was like a hammer sealing shut the nails of his coffin.

Seth's stomach dropped, but he nodded. "Understood."

Beck tightened his arm around Heavenly's shoulders and focused on her upturned face, pleading for comfort. Seth hated that he couldn't give it to her now.

"C'mon, little girl. I'll run you a bath," the surgeon murmured.

Seth watched as Beck gathered Heavenly in his arms, lifting her as if she weighed nothing. Even now, with everything falling apart, the tenderness of the gesture twisted Seth's gut.

Beck carried her toward the en suite, shouldering past Seth without a glance and kicking the door closed behind them. The sound of running water followed, then murmured voices too low to hear.

Seth's temporary reprieve was ticking down. He glanced at his watch. Fifty-eight minutes left to fight his way out of this mental prison he'd walled himself in eight years ago. Fifty-eight minutes to save the bonds that mattered most. Fifty-eight minutes before his future started without him.

As he bolted down the stairs, he jerked his keys from his pocket, then slammed the front door behind him. His SUV roared to life, tires squealing as he tore from the driveway.

He knew exactly where he needed to go.

The door slammed with such force that Beck felt it in his bones. Heavenly flinched, a fresh sob escaping her. She trembled as she bit back the sound while he settled her on the edge of the oversized tub.

"Shhh," he murmured. "Let me take care of you."

He turned the taps, adjusting the temperature of the water until steam rose. It gave his hands something to do while his mind raced.

Seth had one fucking hour to get his shit together—or Beck was done. Done waiting. Done hoping. Done putting their future on hold.

After months of vying for Heavenly's heart, Seth had become like a brother to him—closer in many ways than his actual brother. He and Seth understood each other. Two men of action. Two protectors. Both willing to do whatever it took to keep Heavenly safe.

Why couldn't they agree on how to make her happy?

"I'm worried," Heavenly whispered.

"Don't borrow trouble, little girl."

"What if I'm not enough? What if he doesn't come back?" She lifted tear-filled eyes to him that wrenched his fucking heart. "What if he won't take another chance?"

Beck crouched closer. Her cheeks were mottled. Mascara tracked dark paths down her face—remnants of the elegant makeup she'd worn to Raine, Liam, and Hammer's wedding earlier that evening.

"Stop," he insisted gently, reaching for a washcloth. He doused it and carefully wiped away the black streaks, leaving her fresh-faced.

Even with swollen, red-rimmed eyes, she was the most beautiful thing he'd ever seen. "Seth has to wrestle his demons. You can't do it for him. Neither can I. This is about what's in his head; it has nothing to do with you not being enough. You are, and he knows it…or he wouldn't be struggling. Seth has to choose to overcome his fear."

He reached for the zipper of her dress. Once he'd lowered it, she lifted her arms automatically, helping him. Such trust. Such soft surrender.

"What if he doesn't? What if he…can't?"

Her ragged question broke his heart, and if Seth wasn't dealing with an implosion of his own shit, Beck would have beaten the hell out of him. Now, all he could do was comfort their girl.

"When we talked the night Raine's twins were born, you said you were ready to have kids." He unhooked her bra as she stepped out of her panties. "But you wanted to wait for Seth."

"Yeah," she murmured as he helped her into the water.

"If that's not possible…if he doesn't come back, do you want to stay, knowing I'll be the one to get you pregnant?" He swallowed hard and forced himself to ask what he feared most. "Can you be happy with just me?"

Losing his first love, Blessing, had hurt. Dissolving his marriage of convenience to Gloria had been bittersweet. But losing Heavenly would destroy him.

In the steaming water, she drew her knees to her chest, her voice breaking. "Since Dad died, I've realized how important family is. How precious. How quickly they can be gone." She blinked up, sadness filling her eyes. "I want both of you. I always have. But we can't wait indefinitely. I know that. It's not fair to you."

Beck lathered the washcloth and stroked her back. "Don't worry about me. I want to know what you're feeling. What you want. And before you make any decision, I want you to be sure."

She twisted her hair into a makeshift bun, nibbling on her bottom lip. "I'm young. I have time to have kids. But I understand. You want to start a family while you're young enough to enjoy them."

"That's true, but that isn't what I asked. You're still focusing on me. I'm asking what *you* want."

Heavenly closed her eyes with a sigh. "It's not that simple. My head is a mess. I can't even think straight, and—"

"Let's break it down, then. If Seth doesn't come back, what about us? Just you and me?"

Her eyes sprang open, and she rushed to reassure him. "I love you. I'm not leaving."

The relief filling him nearly stole his breath. If Seth couldn't pull his head out of his ass and embrace their shared bliss, it was his fucking loss. Beck would do everything in his power to give Heavenly the strength, guidance, passion, and joy she needed.

"I just can't picture what life would be like if Seth left for good. We'd figure it out, I'm sure, but…" She heaved a shaky sigh. "When we finally got together, I thought our relationship would look more like Raine, Liam, and Hammer's. That we'd all share this love. It might take more than a night for me to change my vision of the future."

"I get it. Changing mine will require an adjustment, too. But if Seth forces us to do that, lean on me. We'll work through it together. I'm not going anywhere, little girl."

She lifted her hand from the water and squeezed his. "I needed to hear that. I rely on you both so much. But if we're going to have kids, I'd like to get married. Maybe that's old-fashioned but—"

Beck couldn't help the smile that broke across his face. "I'll marry you tomorrow. My divorce from Gloria has been final for months. I've been waiting ever since to put a ring on your finger."

"I'm ready. For a while, I thought I wanted to travel and explore first…but not more than I want family, love, and permanence. We can travel later, right?"

"Of course. Whenever and wherever you want. We'll definitely have a hell of a honeymoon."

She gave him a wobbly smile before her gaze skittered to the rippling bath water. "But what if Seth stays? What if he asks for more time? If he's not ready for kids, is he even ready for marriage? Or commitment in general?"

These were the conversations they'd skirted for months, dancing around them like landmines. He cupped water in his hands and let it trickle down her shoulders. "Listen, Heavenly. We—"

"I'm not done. All these questions keep swirling through my head. So many possibilities… What if you get me pregnant and then Seth comes back?"

"We'll cross that bridge, but if he comes back for good—to commit —I'd welcome him."

"But would he accept our child? And if he comes back, and *he* gets me pregnant, would you accept his?"

"I can't speak for him. For me, any child you have by one of us belongs to all of us," Beck assured her. "But you're trying to 'what if' every possibility, and I don't have the answers. No one does—except Seth. We just have to wait and see. Whatever he decides, we'll handle it *together.* That much, I promise."

With a teary nod, she rested her chin on her knees and blinked up at him. She looked so young and too fucking vulnerable.

"Where are you in your cycle?" He was pretty sure he knew since he'd tracked her for months.

"In the middle." She blushed. "I felt ovulation pains yesterday."

Beck's pulse quickened. His cock stiffened. After tonight—if things went as he hoped—there was a real possibility she would be pregnant. That they'd start a family. That he'd be one step closer to everything he'd longed for.

"Yeehaw…" he drawled, his voice rough.

A little smile peeked through her tears. "Beck…"

He stroked her cheek, his fingers leaving damp trails on her skin. "In all seriousness, I'd rather have Seth with us, but I'm not putting off our happiness anymore. He can either join us…or walk away."

"You're right," she said so softly, he almost didn't hear. So sadly, it nearly broke him.

Beck ached to pull her from the bath, tumble her into bed, and let nature take its course. But she needed tenderness and reassurance that he could—and would—handle whatever came their way. He'd be her anchor, whether Seth was beside him or not.

"It's okay. Just relax." He took his time, pampering her, washing her body with gentle, almost paternal care. When the water began to cool, he helped her stand and wrapped her in a fluffy towel. Then he lifted her into his arms, nuzzling her softness against his chest as he carried her back to their bed.

There, he settled against the headboard and unwound her hair from the loose knot, calming when she sighed and cuddled against him, full of trust.

The minutes ticked by on the bedside clock, each one seemingly longer than the last. Forty-three minutes left. Then forty-two. Then forty-one.

"I love him," Heavenly whispered into the silence, looking bereft and lost.

"I know." Beck pressed his lips to her crown. "I care about him, too." And he did. Seth understood him, had his back. The big former cop had been one hundred percent behind him when the religious zealots he'd once called family had come. Beck wasn't sure any of them would have made it out alive if not for Seth and his tactical know-how. "But there comes a point when you have to protect yourself—and the people you love—even if it hurts."

Outside, a car drove past, the sound of its engine rising and falling. Not pulling into their driveway. Not Seth's SUV returning.

"What if he never comes back? Never even speaks to us again?"

A cold knot formed in Beck's gut. He tightened his arms around her. "He wouldn't do that. But if he chooses not to stay, we lick our wounds. Then we move forward. Together."

The question she didn't ask, the one buzzing through his head, hung between them, impossible to answer: Would she truly be okay without Seth?

The ticking of the clock seemed to grow louder with each passing minute. Thirty-eight. Thirty-seven. Thirty-six.

Beck clenched his jaw. His fingers twitched and tightened around Heavenly, betraying the calm he fought to project. If Seth didn't walk through that door in—he checked the clock again—thirty-five minutes, her world could implode. His, too.

And it would make the agony of waiting feel like nothing.

Chapter Two

Seth pounded on the door of his former apartment, each knock an urgent echo of his racing heart. He checked his watch. Forty-two minutes left.

No answer.

"Zach?" He knocked harder, ignoring his throbbing knuckles. "It's Seth! You there?"

The peephole darkened before the door swung open, revealing Beck's youngest brother in sweatpants and a plain white T-shirt. His bushy beard and flannel shirts were long gone. He no longer looked like a stranger from another century, but modern and at ease in secular surroundings. Still, Seth saw the same haunted expression in Zach's eyes that reflected back at him when he looked in a mirror.

Zach scanned him up and down, frowning. "It's late. Is something wrong?"

"I need to talk to you. Can I come in?"

"Sure." Zach stepped back. "What happened? Is Beck all right?"

"Fine." Seth kicked the door shut behind him. "But he and Heavenly gave me an ultimatum, and I have forty minutes left to decide if I'm willing to commit to them—marriage, kids, picket fence—the works. Or if I'm out. For good."

"Ah." Zach's expression softened with understanding as he gestured Seth to the couch before easing into the nearby armchair. "And you're struggling to practice what you preached at the wedding reception earlier tonight?"

Seth nodded. Fear had burrowed inside him like a parasite, feeding on every potential happiness and hope. He didn't know how to stop it.

"Fuck, I can't think straight." Seth sank onto the sofa and raked his fingers through his hair, noting that the pictures of Zach's late wife and daughter that had once dominated the mantle were gone. "I came here because…"

How could he put this into words?

"I'm the only one who truly understands what you're going through?" Zach finished. "Because, despite your big speech earlier, you're worried history will repeat itself?"

"Aren't *you?*"

"Sure. But after our talk tonight, I decided that I can't keep running in place. On my way home, I called Hannah, a woman I met in my religious order survivors' group, and I asked her out. We're having our first date. I'm picking her up at five."

Seth's head snapped up. "Tomorrow? That's fast."

But maybe that explained why Zach had tucked away Faith's and Joanna's pictures.

"So I should drag my feet?" He raised a brow. "I've been thinking a lot. Tonight, you gave me even more to consider. I've slept with a lot of women since I left the Chosen. Felt good…at first. But once you've known love, sex with strangers feels empty. Hollow. I want more."

"And you've decided Hannah can give that to you? You barely know her."

"You're right. But she's the *kind* of woman I can see myself marrying someday. We've talked. She understands where I came from, what I've been through. The cult, the grief—all of it. She's been there, too."

"So you're ready to risk everything again? Just like that?" Seth snapped his fingers. "You're not fucking afraid?"

"I'm terrified. But what's the alternative? I'm thirty-one. I have a lot of life in front of me. Should I stay frozen in place?" Zach scoffed. "That's just a slower way to die."

That truth hit him like a punch to the jaw. Zach was already thinking about building a new life, while Seth still felt paralyzed by fear. The realization was a bitter pill. His chest tightened. It felt uncomfortably like shame. He'd been hiding behind his grief like it was a shield. Zach was facing his future head-on.

Seth checked his watch again. Thirty-seven minutes.

"My therapist told me that we should honor those we've loved and lost by living, not by dying with them. Would your late wife have wanted you to bury yourself with her?"

Seth clenched his jaw. "It's not that fucking simple."

"It is. You're just complicating it with fear."

"But what if something happens? What if you married Hannah and lost her someday, too? Could you survive that?"

"What if I choose fear and then nothing happens? I'll have thrown away decades of happiness," Zach countered. "What if you abandon Beck and Heavenly and you end up spending the rest of your life alone? Think that won't hurt? That you won't be bitter?"

His words shot Seth right between the eyes with pinpoint accuracy.

Zach continued on in the silence. "According to my therapist, it's tempting to cling to fear and keep everyone out, so you'll never feel pain again. But that's a lie, an illusion of control."

"But I can't go through that kind of agony again. I fucking can't."

"You're already in pain, just a different kind."

Another bullet. Another killing blow.

Seth stood abruptly, pacing the small living room. "You don't understand."

"You came here because I do, and we both know it. Loss comes; pain follows. Then we all face the same choice: stay half dead or risk living again."

Seth stared at him, anger broiling in his chest. He wanted to argue, to tell Zach that his situation was different somehow. Special. But the words died in his throat because deep down, he knew Zach was right. They were mirror images of each other—both broken by loss, both hamstrung by guilt, both facing the same impossible choice. The only difference was that Zach was choosing to move forward while he was standing still, letting fear dictate his future.

"I had a devoted wife and a perfect son." Seth's voice cracked. "And I got stupid. I pushed too hard on a cold case. They paid for my arrogance. They got fucking blown to pieces because of me."

"I lost the family I loved because I tried to protect my daughter from a predator—my own brother. Jedediah had my wife and daughter killed. You think I don't blame myself every single day?"

Seth clenched his fists. "But you're already resolved to start over. How?"

Zach was quiet for a long moment. "I haven't told anyone…but before the raid at Messiah City, I found Faith's journal. She was afraid the elders would come for her and Joanna if they ever figured out what I was up to. If the worst happened, she wanted me to move on. Find happiness again. She didn't want me to feel guilty for trying to do the right thing. She knew what could happen. And I'm sure Autumn was well aware of the risks of being married to a cop who worked dangerous cases."

"She did…and she didn't. We talked more than a few times about the possibility of something happening to *me.* Never her or Tristan."

"All right, but if you could talk to her, do you think she'd want you to give up your chance at a happy future to spend your life alone?"

Shit. If Autumn could see him now, she'd be disappointed.

Seth's shoulders fell as he sank back onto the couch, his fight draining away. He'd kept his body coiled tight since the day of the explosion. Now, all that seemed to dissipate, leaving him hollow but blessedly lighter.

"Fuck. You're right. I've been using fear as an excuse to avoid risking my heart again." Seth checked his watch. Twenty-four minutes. "I should go."

"Home?"

Even though it was scary as hell… "Yeah."

"Good. Choose Beck and Heavenly. Choose to live. Choose to love."

"When the fuck did you get so wise? Because I know it had nothing to do with Jack and Connor. They're dumb as dog shit."

"They're not that stupid." Zach sent him a faint smile. "But once I thought about it, I realized I had nothing left but the truth."

That made sense. He understood that. "Thanks. Good luck tomorrow with Hannah."

Seth stepped into the hallway, closing the door behind him. In the silence that followed, Zach's words echoed in his head.

Choose Beck and Heavenly. Choose to live. Choose to love.

Seth intended to. If he was being honest, he'd made his decision the moment he'd walked out of the house, determined to find answers. The question wasn't whether he wanted a life with Beck and Heavenly. He wanted that more than his next breath. The issue had always been finding the courage to embrace that want without reservation or retreat.

If the past had taught him anything, it was that nothing in life was guaranteed. Not safety. Not tomorrow. Except, perhaps, regret. And his biggest one would be walking away from Beck and Heavenly and the love they shared forever.

Seth gunned the engine. Eighteen minutes left.

Just enough time to cut out that motherfucking parasite, get home, and show them that he refused to let fear win.

Seth floored the gas, pushing his SUV well past the speed limit. His eyes flicked between the road and the clock on his dash. Seventeen minutes left. He'd make it. He had to.

The wheels ate up the pavement as he replayed Zach's words in his head. *Choose to live. Choose to love.* Simple in theory… Hard as hell in practice. Still, he couldn't be a coward anymore. Otherwise, Heavenly and Beck would cut him loose and go on.

And that scared the shit out of him.

But even as he did his best to embrace Zach's logic, dread sat heavy in his stomach. Knowing something intellectually didn't magically rewire eight years of terror. He wished that was possible, but no pep talk could flip the magical switch in his gut. His fear was still there, lurking beneath his resolve like a cancer. That part of him still flinched at the thought of holding a tiny, vulnerable bundle and knowing its safety was in his hands. He'd push through it and say yes to conceiving a baby because losing Beck and Heavenly wasn't an option. And maybe by the time the child actually came, he'd have figured out how to feel what he knew was right.

The surgeon's desire for kids was hardly surprising. He was on the downhill slide to forty, and he'd been without family for decades. Of course he wanted roots.

Seth had family—his mother and his four younger brothers, whom he'd basically raised—but for years he'd been too mired in the past to care about any sort of future. He'd hooked up and whipped subs and called that a life.

Until Heavenly.

In retrospect, her desire for a family, especially after losing her beloved father, should have been obvious. He felt like a fucking idiot for not realizing it sooner.

Brake lights flashed ahead. Seth cursed as traffic slowed to a crawl. Red and blue lights pulsed in the distance.

"Fuck. No!" He slammed his fist against the steering wheel, craning his neck to see past the sea of stopped vehicles. An overturned semi blocked two lanes. Emergency vehicles crowded the scene.

He glanced at his watch. Thirteen minutes.

"Son of a bitch!" He scanned the area for escape routes, but he was hemmed in on all sides.

Panic seized him.

If he didn't get there on time, he'd have to watch their happiness from the outside. And how the fuck would that feel, watching the two of them have kids and build their happy life without him?

He'd never realized how terrifying that notion was until now, as it was threatening to slip through his fingers.

Finally, the cars inched forward. A police officer waved traffic through a narrow gap.

Nine minutes left.

Seth weaved between lanes like a madman, cutting off a delivery truck and earning a blare of horns. He ignored them. Nothing mattered except getting home.

The digital clock on his dash mocked him as the minutes slipped away. Eight. Seven. Six.

Fuck!

When Seth finally skidded into their neighborhood, almost turning a corner too fast, he had three minutes to spare. He slammed on the gas, praying no cops were around to witness his flagrant disregard for residential speed limits and his California stop.

The garage door seemed to rise in slow motion. Seth didn't wait for it to open fully before pulling in, the roof of his SUV clearing the rising door by mere inches. He killed the engine, grabbed his keys, and bolted for the entry.

Two minutes.

Slamming into the house, he tossed his keys on the hall table, not caring when they skittered across the surface and clattered to the floor. He took the stairs two at a time, shedding his suit coat as he climbed.

One minute.

At the top, Seth paused only long enough to draw a deep breath.

This was it. He was about to commit to something that still scared him shitless, betting everything on the hope that his head would catch up to his heart. But what choice did he have? Lose them for certain…or take the leap and pray he could fake it until he felt it?

He shoved the bedroom door open. Instantly, two heads snapped in his direction.

Tissue in hand, Heavenly perched on the edge of the bed, eyes red, face blotchy from crying, clutching the lapels of her silky robe. Beck stood by the window, shirtless, dressed only in sweatpants, shoulders tensed as if ready to defend Heavenly against whatever Seth might say or do. They both looked his way with a mixture of wariness and hope. Chest heaving, he met their stares.

No one spoke.

Seth tossed his suit coat onto a nearby chair, then approached Heavenly, sliding onto his knees beside her and taking her hands. "I'm sorry, angel. I never wanted to hurt you or make you doubt my love."

She swallowed. Her lips quivered as if she held back more tears. "I know your past is rough. I understand having fears. Even knowing they aren't logical doesn't make them any easier to overcome. We all have them. But we've all leaned on each other to get beyond them. You just…cut us out."

Seth nodded, his throat tight. "You're right. I let fear choke me. I didn't know how to let it go."

Beck turned, his expression somewhere between closed and inscrutable. "And now?"

Pressing a kiss to Heavenly's palm, he released her and stood. He knew what the surgeon was asking. "I'm in. All the way. Let's do this."

He began working at the buttons of his dress shirt, toeing off his shoes at the same time. "Tonight."

"Really?" she whispered. "Now?"

His fingers dropped to the fly of his dress pants. "Right now."

"Hold up," Beck barked, shifting to put himself between Seth and Heavenly. "After weeks of balking, you're ready? Just like that?"

Seth froze, fingers pausing. Yeah, he should have known Beck would want guarantees. "You gave me an ultimatum. I'm giving you an answer. So yeah. Just like that."

Beck's eyes turned hard, searching. "You're totally in…or just for the night?"

"Totally in," Seth replied, zero hesitation.

"You swear on your father's grave?"

That pissed him off. "Leave my father out of this. I said I'm in. Accept it or not."

"You're a stubborn son of a bitch. Capitulation isn't your style," Beck pointed out. "Where did you go? What changed your mind?"

Jesus, he'd turned himself inside out in an hour and given in without stipulations or conditions. And Beck wanted to challenge him? "Does it matter? I figured you'd rather get Heavenly pregnant than play twenty questions. Did you change *your* mind?"

"Don't fuck with me. You know the stakes. Once we go down this path, I don't care if you get scared again. You can't back out. You get that, right?"

"Of course I get it. I've been a father."

Beck nodded slowly. "And if Heavenly wants marriage?"

"Absolutely. I'm not sure how that will work with my mother or the law, but committing isn't my issue. I've wanted that since day one. It's the fear of something happening to Heavenly or our kids that scares me." He swallowed hard. "After Autumn and Tristan, I lived for revenge. Offing Silas gave me a hollow victory, not the closure I expected. After that, I plodded through one numb day after the next. When well-meaning people like my mother asked, I'd swear I was fine and reassure them with plastic smiles and counterfeit laughs. I didn't think about the future because…what did I have left? I'd defined myself by my roles for so long. But I wasn't a husband, a father, or a cop anymore. I lost most of my friends…and all of my self-respect. I was fucking alone—except the two tons of guilt on my chest, slowly suffocating me.

"Then…I saw you, Heavenly. At the hospital the terrible morning Raine killed Bill. One glance, and I not only fell, but I had purpose again."

Beck snorted. "Yeah. Fighting with me for the right to touch her."

"That kept me so blinded, I didn't think about what the future looked like." Seth cupped Heavenly's cheek. "You asked me earlier if you're worth it. Angel, you're beyond worth it, and you should know that. I uprooted my existence and left my family to be with you. I'd lay down my life for you. I'm facing all my fears for you."

"I know." Tears sprang to her eyes as she nuzzled into his hand. "Thank you."

She pulled away with a kiss to his palm before she sent Beck a beseeching glance. The surgeon sent a sharp nod back, and she flashed him a smile.

Thank god they'd accepted his explanation. Seth nearly sagged with relief.

Heavenly shouldered her way between them and laid a soft hand on his chest. His whole body tightened as he gave in to his urge to draw her closer. "Angel?"

"I know another tragic loss isn't impossible, but your job, that case… That's not your life anymore. You're here now—different line of work, different coast, different people. This time, you have Beck and me, not to mention all our friends. Since they risked their lives to protect us when Beck's family attacked, I know they'd do anything to keep our children safe."

She was right. Whatever came next, whatever problems they had, his circumstances had changed. And he wasn't alone. He had Beck and Heavenly, and they'd face everything together.

Seth looked at Heavenly—really looked—taking in the hope and love radiating from her, despite the tears she'd shed for him. "No more roadblocks. No more hesitating. I'm here—if you're sure." He paused, memories of Autumn's collapse under the weight of motherhood flashing through his mind. "And you're aware that a baby will change your life forever. School will be harder. Growing your career may take longer. That travel you wanted—"

"We'll make it work." Her soft voice carried conviction.

"A baby will change everything between us, too."

"I know," she assured him.

But did she? Did either of them? "I've been a parent. Autumn and I…" He hesitated, not wanting to seem as if he was grasping for more excuses. "She wasn't ready for that responsibility. It strained everything between us."

Heavenly's eyes softened with understanding. "I'm not Autumn, Seth."

"You're right; you're nothing like her," he acknowledged. "You're strong and incredibly independent. But I need to make sure you understand that a baby isn't just a cute addition to our lives. It's a lifetime commitment. It's endless nights without sleep. It's arguments about who's more exhausted. It also means less time for us." He glanced between them. "And right now, what we have is…pretty close to perfect."

Beck stepped forward. "Perfect doesn't mean complete, Cooper. Life moves forward or you're not really living."

Seth nodded. "I know. I'm not pushing back again. I wish Autumn and I had realized some of these things before Tristan was born. I'm making sure you both understand what we're walking into."

Heavenly placed her palm against his cheek, the gentle touch steadying him. "The difference is you won't be trying to take care of both the baby and me. The three of us will face this together."

True. Being a parent wouldn't be the same this time. With Beck and Heavenly, it would be something different. Something new.

Her soft voice carried gravity. "I've been thinking about this—our future—for a while. And I want a family with both of you."

Heavenly would make an amazing wife and mother.

Seth held her gaze, feeling the last of his resistance evaporate. He'd made it home—physically and emotionally—with seconds to spare. He was choosing to live. Choosing to love. Choosing *them,* just like Zach said. Just like Autumn would have wanted.

Heavenly was on board, but…

He turned to his partner in her pleasure—and hopefully, in the rest of their lives. "Beck?"

Chapter Three

The other man studied him for a long moment. Then he heaved something that sounded like a cross between a growl and a sigh. "Don't fuck this up."

Seth nodded. He wouldn't. He couldn't. Not unless he wanted to be alone and miserable for the rest of his fucking life.

"So…are we done talking?" Heavenly's soft voice hung in the air between them.

"I am," Beck drawled. "Seth?"

His name—a single question that carried almost infinite weight. His answer would change his future. *Their* future.

But what more did they have to say?

Tonight, they would take Heavenly without barriers or protection. As conflicted as he'd been, he now grasped that he could either share his tomorrows with the people he loved or fucking spend them alone.

"Nothing left to say, except…" He tore his dress shirt from his shoulders impatiently. "She needs to be naked."

"Hell, yes, she does." Eyes darkening, Beck moved behind her and cupped her shoulders, his gaze meeting Seth's over her head. "Just like she needs to be fucked. To be bred."

That *word.* It ignited him, sparking fantasies he hadn't even realized were burning in the back of his brain. Logic told him he should be terrified…but even the idea set him on fire. Fuck, Seth had sworn he'd never cross this line again, but he was choosing this. With Heavenly's eyes pleading and his head feeding him images of her taking him bare and deep…

He had no fucking prayer of resisting.

"Now," he demanded.

Together, he and Beck lunged for her, Seth tearing at the tie around her waist. The instant it gave way, the doctor yanked the garment from her body, unwrapping her with the unabashed enthusiasm of a kid at Christmas.

Holy shit. She gleamed, pale like a pearl in the low, golden light. He'd seen her naked countless times…but she always stole his breath —lush tits, soft hips, slender thighs. And those eyes, the way she blinked up at him, looking so innocent and sweetly vulnerable. For months, he and Beck had been ruining her. Corrupting her.

That wasn't enough anymore. He ached to cement his place in her life, to imprint himself on her and bind himself to these two forever.

"Isn't our little girl perfect?"

"She is." He dragged a hand up her body, skating over her breast, skimming her beaded nipple until he settled a finger under her chin and forced her to meet his stare. "I've never not wanted you, angel. From the moment I laid eyes on you…"

Her breaths turned short, her pulse banging at her throat. Because he was touching her? Because she was aware of the significance of what they were about to do?

Beck grabbed his arm and settled Seth's palm over her flat middle. "Imagine her pregnant, ripe and round with our child. Our ultimate mark on her."

Suddenly, he could picture it. *So* easily. She was the most beautiful woman he'd ever seen, but if she was breeding for them? His earlier fears aside, the primal part of him relished the idea with a visceral, almost deviant thrill. That twisted part of him had loved taking her bare at the lodge last spring.

At the thought of sliding his naked cock into her again, Seth swallowed. His blood surged. His veins caught fire.

"You can see it, can't you?" Beck's husky whisper slid into his ears like a provocation, unleashing more filthy fantasies. "And we can make that a reality right now…"

Seth watched, mesmerized as Beck cupped Heavenly's breasts and thumbed her distended nipples, alternately pinching and caressing them until they turned a dark rosy red. Heavenly's eyes slid shut, her lashes fluttering as she melted between them.

Her breathless surrender threatened to unhinge him.

It didn't make sense, but he couldn't wait to fill her, fuck her…and release deep against her unprotected womb.

As if Beck read his every dirty thought, he lifted her breasts to Seth in offering. "Once she's pregnant, her hormones will be raging. These nipples will be so fucking sensitive. We can suck them for hours, torment her until she begs us to fuck her."

Yes. God, yes... He couldn't wait to see her pleading and desperate for their touch.

"We'll never say no." Beck's lips skimmed the side of her neck before settling against her ear. "We'll be inside you every fucking day."

"And all fucking night." Seth took her other breast in his palm.

"Please..." she breathed out.

As he dragged his thumb over her pebbled nipple, he watched Beck stimulate the other. She gasped, tossing her head back, looking like a goddess.

"We'll put her between us, naked and wet. We'll pleasure that pretty pussy and stuff that gorgeous ass until she screams, until we wring her out, until she wails for mercy." Beck's eyes turned hot. "Will we have any?"

Seth's cock jerked. He began to sweat. When the fuck had he ever been so aroused he could feel desire thickening the air? Taste it on his tongue? Burning his skin? "Not one bit."

"I know that's right." Satisfaction deepened Beck's voice. "What do you think, little girl?"

"Yes. Please." She shivered helplessly. "Please..."

"She's being such a good little girl for us. Listen to her beg." Beck hummed. "So sweet. So futile."

Seth clamped his fingers around her nape, then twisted them in her hair. "Beg us more."

Heavenly lifted heavy lids to him. "I'm melting. I need—"

"We know what you need." Beck glanced at Seth as he tugged Heavenly's arms behind her back, thrusting her breasts forward. "Isn't she pretty? I'll hold her still while you suck those sweet little nipples."

Seth fused his gaze on her, his blood heating. She looked like a deliciously helpless sacrifice, a beautiful vessel for his desire.

Arousal whipped him hard. Fuck words. Fuck everything except getting his tongue on her tits.

He dropped his chin, parted his lips, and latched onto one tempting breast. Sweet. So goddamn sweet he growled and sucked her deeper, drawing her stiff tip against the roof of his mouth.

Heavenly's breath caught. She jolted. Her little whine burrowed in his ears and crawled into his brain, feeding the possessive beast inside him that demanded he penetrate her. Impregnate her. Now.

With a rough groan, he laved his tongue over her flesh, capturing her swollen nub again. This time, he caught her nipple between his teeth and gave it a stinging tug.

Heavenly cried out again, louder, sharper, urging him on, driving him to glide his tongue across her velvety skin so he could lay siege to the other.

"Now imagine her feeding our baby with those beautiful, milk-swollen tits while we watch." Beck dragged his hand over her hip, fingers skimming her ass. "Tell me that doesn't turn you on."

Seth couldn't lie. Every word out of the doctor's mouth burned him with heat so intense he could barely breathe. Lust sizzled in the air, scorched his veins. He strained against the urge to toss Heavenly onto the bed, shove down his zipper, and fuck her mercilessly. "It does."

Beck smiled. "Can you smell her cunt?"

He sucked in a breath, nostrils flaring. "It's driving me insane."

"I think our little girl is wet for us. Don't you?"

Heavenly whimpered, the sound high-pitched and desperate.

Beck answered into Seth's silence. "I'll check."

Seth grunted his approval while continuing to lave, bite, and suck her nipples—back and forth.

The surgeon secured her wrists at the small of her back in one hand, then snaked the other around her waist and parted her legs with his feet. "No coming."

The scent of Heavenly's arousal perfumed the air, sharper and stronger than before. It filled Seth's head, seared his senses, and fucked with his sanity.

He knew the instant Beck slid his fingers between her folds by the way Heavenly cried out and bucked her hips.

"Mmm," Beck moaned. "She's hot and slick. Dripping."

Seth wrenched from her nipple and stared down her body with

wild eyes. The sight of the surgeon's glistening fingers rooting in her saturated pussy nearly dismantled him.

As if reading his mind, Beck slowly withdrew his fingers. Heavenly mewled pitifully as the surgeon lifted his digits toward Seth's lips, her drugging scent hanging between them.

"Taste?" Beck taunted.

Seth didn't care where her flavor came from. He needed it now.

He gripped Beck's wrist and plunged the man's fingers in his mouth. Her warm spice ignited his taste buds.

And the last of his patience tapped out.

With a feral roar, he seized her lips, swallowing her gasp before tumbling her to the bed. He followed her down, never breaking the kiss. Beneath him, she writhed, jacking up his primal need. No doubt, her pussy was swollen and pink, desperate to be filled.

Heavenly spread her legs. Blood slammed into his cock. Urgency screamed through his system.

He stared into her eyes as he yanked down his zipper and tore off his pants.

Beside him, Beck kicked out of his sweats. Seth barely noticed. He was too busy hovering over Heavenly like a predator claiming his prey.

His heart pounded as he gripped his aching cock and aligned it against her slick folds. The moment was here, and he burned as he wedged his swollen crest into her tight slit. A feral groan ripped from his chest.

"How good does she feel?" Beck pinched and plucked her sensitive nipples.

"So. Fucking. Good." Seth groaned, eyes nearly rolling to the back of his head as he sank deep into her. "*Holy shit.*"

"Yeah?" Beck drawled, watching intently.

"Jesus, she's so fucking tight around me. I can feel..." Seth shuddered as he railed her with one insistent stroke after another, like he'd never get enough. "She's killing me. Hot. Slick. Soft." He withdrew, then slammed inside her once more as he laved his way up her neck. "God, the way she smells..."

"Sweet?"

"Fuck, yes." He gripped the headboard and spread her legs wider with his knees before driving inside her faster and harder than ever. "I can't. Stop. Fucking. Her."

Under him, Heavenly surrendered every part of herself. It nearly destroyed his carefully constructed restraint.

She tightened her thighs around his hips. Her keening cries filled his ears. Seth's rhythm grew more urgent...more demanding. Heavenly lifted her hips to meet every driving thrust. Electric need skipped down his spine.

"That's hot," Beck muttered thickly. "Fuck, yes... Pound her. Come deep inside her. Don't hold back."

"You're not helping," Seth bit out.

"We have all night. Finish her." The surgeon cupped Heavenly's chin. "You come hard for him, little girl. Then you'll take me. Understood?"

"Yes!" she keened, mindlessly bucking against the battering ram of Seth's cock.

Her hoarse cry threatened to shred the last of his self-control.

Seth gripped her ass, pinning her in place as he slammed deep, the force of his thrusts banging the headboard against the wall. The sound rang in his ears and drove him higher, along with her wails of passion.

"Oh..." She gripped his biceps, nails digging into him. "Oh, *god!*"

The pinpricks stung. Seth hissed, but didn't break his shuttling rhythm into her clasping, clinging cunt.

"*Yesss,*" Beck hissed. "Fuck her hard."

Heavenly's silky pussy and the blistering friction of his strokes torched every cell in his body. Her quivering walls softened. Panic flashed across her face. She was seconds from shattering.

So was he.

"Look at me," he growled as he seated himself deep inside her, to the hilt.

She did, her eyes glassy and unfocused as their gazes fused. She mewled, the desperate sound ringing in his ears, burning down the last of his restraint.

Heart chugging, Seth shuddered, shaking the bed with every thrust.

"I-I need… I can't…stop it," she shrieked.

Thank fuck. "Come, angel!"

He bottomed out inside her again as ecstasy pulled her under. She tossed her head back and screamed, bearing down as she clenched and clamped on him, milking him while she shattered.

Stars flashed behind his eyes. He couldn't goddamn breathe. Blackness narrowed his vision. Tingles burst under his skin.

Fuck, fuck, fuck.

One last time, he drove as deep inside her as possible. Then he stilled, his body quaking against his will. The top of his head threatened to blow off as he unloaded everything inside her with a feral roar, showering her with his seed in what felt like an endless geyser.

Holy motherfucking christ. Best. Orgasm. *Ever.*

Finally, the grip of ecstasy that had overtaken him began to loosen. Breath returned. The languid liquid opium of satisfaction wound through his veins, spreading to every part of his body.

As they rode out the aftershocks together, something shifted inside him.

He hadn't totally exiled his fears; that might never happen. But what he felt now was something stronger: Hope. Love. Faith in their future.

The contradiction didn't escape him—how could he be so fucking aroused by the idea of breeding her when the thought of actually holding a baby again made his chest tighten with dread?

"Fucking amazing." Beck twisted Heavenly's face to his and pressed a demanding kiss to her mouth, swallowing her trembling exhalations. Then he peered back at Seth with a hot grin. "So…was it good for you, honey?"

Despite everything, Seth laughed. "Fantastic, darling."

Still clinging to him, Heavenly giggled.

Beck began stroking his cock. "Don't fall back to earth yet, little girl. I'm not done with you."

Seth eased from her snug cunt with a hiss, earning another moan from Heavenly. She was still engorged and, no doubt, throbbing.

Seamlessly, he rolled away. Beck settled on the mattress, sliding down her body and dragging his tongue over her clit. He sucked it into his mouth until, wide eyed, her back arched and she wailed for more.

He lifted his head from between her legs with a dirty grin. "Arms above your head, little girl. You're at my mercy now."

As Heavenly complied, Seth didn't miss the spark in her eyes or the shiver rippling through her body. He cinched a hand around her wrists and pinned them to the mattress. She blinked his way in surprise, arching and twisting, lifting her sweet tits against his lips.

With a groan, Seth flicked his tongue across one stony peak while Beck surged up her body, compounding her torment with a lick to the other. Simultaneously, they each sucked deep. She moaned, spreading her legs wider with a wordless plea.

No way would Beck decline that invitation.

The doctor backed down her body, bracing himself on his knees between her splayed thighs. As he peered at her, he gripped her waist in his big hands and hoisted her onto his legs. Then he leaned over her, aligning his weeping crest against her swollen pussy. "I'm going to fuck you fast and hard."

"Yes… Please!" Heavenly rolled her hips.

Beck clenched his jaw. A low growl rumbled from deep in his chest as he slammed inside her. She sucked in a wide-eyed gasp, back bowing, as he brutally impaled her. Together, they held her down, forcing her to take each and every one of the doctor's ruthless strokes.

She bucked, an almost incoherent stream of moaning and begging filling the air. Seth watched with hot eyes, gripping her wrists tighter as he sucked her distended nipple onto his tongue.

As Beck shuttled in and out of her, balls deep, he watched their girl with laser focus, jaw clenched.

"More!" she moaned, the sound something between a wail and a demand.

Beck slid his hands down to her hips, exerting more control. And instead of giving her what she begged for, he withdrew. Then slowly… so slowly, he began feeding inch after inch inside her clasping pussy.

The good doctor was purposely holding back. Seth smiled and bent to devour Heavenly's nipples again.

How long could the poor bastard hold out? No doubt the hungry beast snarling to mark and breed their girl clawed at Beck to spill deep inside her.

With a tortured groan, Beck violated her silky cunt, ratcheting up the pace just enough to intensify her torment…but never letting her fall over.

"Beck. Beck…" She tossed her head. "Please! I can't… Oh, yes. Right there. I'm…*oh!*"

"Oh?" Seth slid his fingers to Heavenly's clit, toying with her swollen nub as she flushed and writhed. "Something you want to say, angel?"

She nodded frantically, her chest rising and falling with every breathless pant. "Now. Please. I'm…dying."

"Are you sure you want more, little girl?" Beck taunted, his grin turning downright evil.

"Yes." She thrashed wildly. "God, *yesss!*"

"Hear that?" Seth muttered. "She's so pretty when she begs. We should do this every day."

"At least once. Maybe she'll get to come. Maybe she won't…"

Heavenly struggled to break Seth's grip on her wrists as her entreating stare bounced between them. "No, please. I'm a good girl. I'll be better. I'll—"

"Do whatever we say?" Beck drawled.

"Yes!"

"Pinky promise?" Seth teased.

"Pinkies. Fingers. Toes. Whatever you want. *Pleaseee…*"

"Since you begged so sweetly, I'll show mercy—this once." Beck gripped her hips even harder, pistoning in and out of her pussy. "I'll give you all you can handle."

He did. Sweat glistened across Beck's back and beaded at Heavenly's temples. Their bodies strained. Their need spiked.

Fuck, Seth had already come explosively inside her, but Heavenly's whimpers morphed into keening cries that echoed off the walls, driving up his desire again. His cock was unbelievably hard and throbbing, as if he hadn't already come.

He more than wanted this woman. He loved her like he'd never loved anyone. And he knew the doctor felt the same.

"Beck!" she wailed, struggling against Seth's grip. "Give me… everything. Yes!"

Eyes locked on their woman, Beck clenched his jaw and slammed deep inside her one last time. "Come now!"

Seth lifted from her breast and pinched her stony clit between his fingers. Heavenly twisted, bucking hard, every muscle tight and trembling.

As she and Beck shattered together in a cacophony of heady shouts, Seth could *see* their tomorrows so vividly. For the first time in eight years, he felt completely and truly alive.

But as the passion faded, the shadows lurking in his head reappeared. The worry. The fear.

He shoved them aside, refusing to give them more of his energy. This was his future. Fuck the past.

With a gratified groan, Beck withdrew. Heavenly closed her eyes with a sigh, sinking into a satisfied sleep almost instantly. She looked ethereal in the soft lamplight, her pale hair fanning across the sheets, her skin gorgeously flushed. Something fierce and possessive stirred in Seth's chest.

Mine.

No, ours.

He and Beck exchanged a glance before the surgeon grinned. "That was fucking amazing. Nice not to have to worry about condoms."

Seth couldn't argue. "Amen."

Glancing down at Heavenly, Beck cocked his head as if studying the situation. "Maybe this won't help, but…"

He shoved a couple of pillows under her hips. Then his grin became a big smile.

Seth scowled. "Are you serious?"

"Hey, why not give our swimmers the best chance possible? A little gravity, and…you never know."

"You're bent as fuck."

"Nah, just hopeful. Speaking of…" He crawled off the bed and donned his robe.

He pressed a soft kiss to her forehead, his lips lingering for a moment before he straightened and caught Seth's eye. With a subtle bob of his head, he motioned toward the door.

Seth wasn't sure where Beck was leading him or why, but he pulled on his discarded dress pants and leaned down to brush his own kiss across Heavenly's damp brow. She barely stirred, lost in a deep, thoroughly satisfied sleep.

The primal satisfaction of taking her bare and filling her with his seed was still coursing through Seth's veins. He'd never experienced anything like tonight. Apparently, he'd been harboring a secret breeding fantasy. Where the hell had that come from? He'd never had that particular kink, even when Autumn had gotten pregnant. But the idea of marking Heavenly so fundamentally, of watching her grow round with their child, ignited something primal in him that he didn't fully understand.

Beck led him down to his home office, a sleek space lined with medical journals and expensive whiskey. Seth half expected him to pour them a drink or say something about what had just happened. Instead, he unlocked one of his desk drawers.

When he turned around, he was holding a small velvet box.

Seth's heart lurched when Beck opened it to reveal a stunning engagement ring. The oval center stone had to be at least two carats, surrounded by a brilliant halo of smaller diamonds that cascaded down the band in an intricate pattern. It was beautiful, elegant, and undoubtedly expensive.

"When the hell did you get that?" Seth demanded.

"A few weeks ago," Beck replied vaguely.

A few weeks ago? About the time Raine gave birth to the twins? When the subject of babies had been uppermost in their minds? When Heavenly had stood at that nursery window with tears in her eyes, clearly yearning for a baby of her own?

Part of Seth was furious that Beck had picked out a ring without him. They were supposed to be partners in their pursuit of Heavenly's heart. But the other part—the bigger part, if he was honest—understood completely. They'd been chasing her, either individually or together, for nearly ten months. Beck was ready for family and future.

Heavenly was, too. Seth couldn't think of a single reason they should wait for him to untangle his fucked-up head.

"Were you planning to propose without me?" Seth demanded.

"Don't be a cockbag. I wanted to be ready when the moment felt right. And after tonight..." His gaze flicked up to the ceiling, toward their sleeping angel. "Now that she could be pregnant? I'd say the moment is right."

Seth swallowed. "You want to do this now?"

"You got a better time in mind?" he challenged. "In the most biological way possible, we just committed to spending our lives together. What the hell are we waiting for?"

The doctor had a point. And if there was more pleasure like they'd just shared—if this was what their future looked like—then he wasn't waiting for a goddamn thing. Seth's earlier misgivings felt misguided, overly cautious. He wished the niggling worries would just go the fuck away.

"If she's going to carry our babies, don't you think she should have a ring on her finger?" Beck pressed. "She wants one. She told me that earlier."

"Then you're right. Let's do this."

Together, they fetched a bottle of champagne from Beck's wine fridge and three crystal flutes. The moment was important. For the second time tonight, they were about to change everything.

When they returned to the bedroom, Heavenly was still sleeping peacefully, the sheet now draped across her curves, making her look like a goddess recovering after being thoroughly worshipped. The sight sent another wave of possessive satisfaction through Seth.

They set the glasses and bottle on the nightstand, and he wondered if they should take her out for a romantic dinner, surround her with flowers, and make it the kind of proposal she'd probably dreamed about as a little girl. But he also understood Beck's urgency. After tonight, after crossing this irrevocable line, it felt right to cement their bond officially.

Beck knelt beside the bed. Seth joined him, positioning himself next to the surgeon, close to where Heavenly lay.

"Wake up, little girl." Beck caressed her shoulder.

Her lashes fluttered. When her eyes opened, they were soft and unfocused. But as she took in the sight of both men kneeling and holding the ring box between them, she bolted up with a gasp, her expression shifting from sleepy to wide-eyed.

Seth's throat went dry. His fingers trembled as he gripped his side of the velvet box.

"Heavenly Hope Young…marry us." Beck's voice was thick with emotion.

"Say yes, angel. We've come so far. We can conquer anything together."

"And we can't imagine our lives without you," Beck vowed reverently. "We want to marry you. Have children with you."

"Build a beautiful life with you." Seth's heart pounded as he lifted the lid of the box, the tiny hinges hissing in a soft whisper.

The diamond glinted as Beck plucked the ring from its velvet nest. "All you have to do is say yes."

For a moment, she blinked, just staring at them, her eyes filling with tears. Seth began to sweat as he held his breath. The silence stretched. His world teetered.

Was Heavenly having second thoughts? He hadn't even considered that she might turn them down. Goddamn it. Raine had refused to marry either Liam or Hammer for months, insisting that she couldn't choose one over the other. Fuck, had the princess rubbed off on Heavenly?

Finally, she let out a half laugh, half squeal before she tossed off the sheet and threw herself into their arms.

"Yes!" she gasped against Seth's neck, then pressed kisses to Beck's face. "Yes! Of course!"

Thrill crashed over Seth, nearly knocking him sideways. They kissed her feverishly, desperately, pushing her back to the mattress as Beck slipped the ring onto her finger with shaking hands. For a moment, the band caught at her knuckle before Seth assisted, helping the doctor slide it home. Something fundamental shifted in his chest, like a lock clicking into place. Then they adored her with their hands and mouths, whispering promises of forever.

When they finally came up for air, all of them breathing hard, Heavenly stared down at her hand in wonder. "It's beautiful."

"Not as beautiful as you," Beck murmured, pressing a kiss to her temple.

Seth traced the outline of the ring with one finger, marveling at how right it looked there. "Beck is right, angel."

Heavenly smiled. "Oh, my goodness. I can't stop looking at it. I couldn't have picked anything more perfect."

Guilt panged Seth. He hadn't had a fucking thing to do with picking out her engagement ring. He would offer to pay Beck for half, of course. But that wasn't the same as the two of them choosing it together.

Seth wanted to be annoyed the doctor had bought it without consulting him. Hell, without even talking to him. But he could only blame himself. Until an hour ago, the two of them had feared—with good reason—that he had one foot out the door.

"It looked like you." Beck pressed a soft kiss to her lips.

"Gosh, we're engaged! I guess we need to set a date." She turned to Seth. "But I don't want to upstage your mother's wedding."

"And we have to consider your schooling," Seth pointed out. "You've worked hard. We want you to graduate on time."

"I do, too, but if we keep this up, by the time I get my degree, I'll be pregnant. And if we get married after that, I'll have to waddle down the aisle."

All the talk about conception stabbed Seth with anxiety, but he pushed it aside. He'd not only crossed that bridge tonight, he'd burned it. There was no going back.

"Then we'll plan on getting married after Grace, something small and intimate before you're too far along to enjoy it," Beck suggested. "Unless... Did you have your heart set on a big wedding?"

She shook her head. "I don't have any family, and I don't need an elaborate production. I just want to marry you two."

Seth wanted that, too...but he'd have to explain the three of them to his mom. That stumbling block wasn't new, and he wasn't about to let that stop him. Grace would come around...eventually. "That works for me. Just...not December."

They both nodded, well aware that December would always belong to Autumn and Tristan's memory.

"We could always hop on a plane to Vegas tomorrow." Beck grinned.

"Um..." Heavenly winced. "I don't want Elvis marrying us."

Seth nodded. "Same. And if I got married without inviting my family, they'd kill me."

Beck shrugged. "Fair enough. January?"

"I'd be okay with that," Heavenly replied. "Are we having a purely symbolic ceremony? Or am I legally marrying one of you?"

Seth exchanged a glance with Beck before the doctor spoke. "Actually being married will make medical and legal stuff easier, not to mention bank accounts, insurance... And the caveman in me, wants you to tie the knot with one of us."

"You'll still belong to us both," Seth added.

She paused, her brow furrowing. "Okay...but how do we decide who I'm marrying?"

"We'll figure that out later. Maybe we'll flip a coin." Beck smirked. "For now, come here, our bride-to-be... We want to make sure you feel *really* loved."

The waggle of his brows suggested something a lot dirtier.

Seth was all too happy to join in.

As they made love again—slower this time, reverent and pulsing with their new commitment—Seth felt a deep sense of rightness. His future was set. His angel would be theirs, bound to both of them by choice and by love.

When he figured out how to break the news of their unconventional arrangement to his mother, she would love Heavenly. The whole family would. How could they not?

But even as he lost himself in Heavenly's soft sighs, reveling in the knowledge that they were engaged and might soon be pregnant, a small voice whispered in the back of his mind.

If his future was mapped out and everything was falling into place, why did he still feel so unsettled?

Chapter Four

Seth couldn't sleep. Even with Heavenly's warm body pressed against his side and Beck's steady breathing filling the room, he couldn't shut off his brain. The primitive satisfaction of taking Heavenly without protection, of potentially filling her with their child had been mind-blowing. The memory sent heat coursing through his veins.

But beneath his primal triumph, Seth was haunted by nagging fears that only grew louder in the bedroom's silence.

Jesus, Cooper. Get your shit together.

Careful not to wake either of them, Seth slipped from the bed and padded to the dresser. He pulled on a pair of gym shorts and grabbed his phone, casting one last look at the tangle of limbs on the bed. Heavenly's hair spilled across Beck's chest, their faces peaceful in sleep. He was where he belonged; he knew that. So why did his chest feel tight with something that wasn't quite panic…but still too close for comfort?

He needed to move. To sweat. To give his restless energy an outlet.

The tri-level house was quiet as Seth made his way to the bottom floor and into the large home gym. He scrolled through his phone until he found his workout playlist—driving rock that would help him focus on something other than the circular thoughts consuming him.

The punching bag hung in the corner like a patient enemy, waiting to absorb whatever he dished out. Seth wrapped his hands quickly, muscle memory from years of training taking over. The first punch landed with a satisfying *thwack,* vibrating up his arm and clearing some of the mental fog.

One-two. One-two-three.

Each combination felt better than the last, his body falling into the familiar rhythm. Sweat beaded his forehead as he increased the intensity, letting the physical exertion burn away the confusing tangle of emotions.

He was deep in the zone when his phone buzzed, the ringtone

cutting through the loud music. Seth glanced at the screen and frowned. Liam O'Neill's name flashed across the display.

"What the hell?" Seth muttered, pausing the music and answering the call. "Liam? It's your wedding night. Shouldn't you and Hammer be doing unspeakable things to your bride right about now?"

Liam's rich laugh filled the speaker. "Well, hello to you too, Seth. And for your information, we just finished doing unspeakable things to her. Raine passed out, mate. Hammer's getting us water. And I felt compelled to call you."

Seth unwrapped his hands, suddenly wary. When his Irish friend felt "compelled" to do anything, it usually meant his psychic abilities were kicking in. "Why exactly are you thinking about me tonight, of all nights? That's either flattering or deeply disturbing."

"Bit of both, probably." Another chuckle. "But I needed to check on you. See how you're handling things."

Seth's stomach clenched. "Handling what things?"

"The choices you made tonight. With Heavenly. And Beck. But don't worry. I won't tell Raine and ruin Heavenly's surprise. Nice ring, by the way."

The words hit him like a blow to the gut. Seth sank onto the weight bench, his legs suddenly unsteady. "How the fuck do you—never mind. I don't want to know." He scrubbed a hand over his face. "So… who legally married Raine? You or Hammer?"

"Don't deflect," Liam returned. "But we've all vowed never to tell. Let people wonder. Adds to the mystique."

"You're all evil. And a bit insane."

"Says the man who just took turns with another guy to knock up his girlfriend." Liam's voice softened. "How does it feel, knowing Heavenly could be pregnant?"

Seth's heart hammered against his ribs. "*Could* be? You mean you don't know for sure?"

"No. Conception is a process, not an instant event. Right now, it's merely a possibility. I can see what *has* happened and what *could* happen, not what *will* happen." Liam paused. "But the potential is there. Strong potential."

"Shit." Seth leaned forward, elbows on his knees, his body caught between excitement and dread. Part of him thrilled at the possibility. But another part clenched with familiar terror. "I thought I was ready for this, that I'd worked through my fears."

"And you have, mostly. But it's natural to feel unsettled when you're standing on the precipice of everything you've ever wanted."

"Is it? Because I feel like I'm going to crawl out of my skin."

"Seth." Liam's voice carried that familiar tone, the one he used when he was about to drop a truth bomb. "What if you reframed this entire experience?"

"I'm listening."

"You've been thinking about fatherhood as something you lost, something that was taken from you. But what if it's actually about reclaiming your legacy?"

"My legacy?"

"As a Cooper. Think about your father—the man and parent Michael was. You've been so focused on protecting your heart from potential pain that you've forgotten the honor would be passing on the best parts of him to the next generation."

The words hit like a sucker punch. Seth's throat tightened as memories flooded back—his father teaching him to throw a curveball, showing him how to change a tire, explaining the importance of protecting those who couldn't protect themselves.

"Your father raised a good man, Seth. A fighter for justice. Those qualities shouldn't die with you."

"But what if something happens to Heavenly and the baby? What if I lose another family?"

"Then you'll grieve, and you'll survive, like you did before. But the alternative—living in fear, denying yourself love and family because of what *might* happen? That's not surviving. That's dying slowly."

Seth closed his eyes, Liam's words echoing in his skull. Zach had said something eerily similar hours ago, but this felt like an even harder-hitting mic-drop moment. "Fuck."

"Look, I know your past better than most. I was there; I saw your pain. But I've also seen your future—or at least, the potential one. And Seth? It's beautiful. Messy and complicated but absolutely beautiful."

"You really think I can do this? Be a father again?"

"I think you've been a father figure to your brothers for years. I think you have your father's heart and your mother's strength. And I think any child lucky enough to be yours will know exactly what kind of man they came from."

"Damn." Seth's chest loosened slightly, some of the crushing weight lifting. "You make it sound simple."

"It's not simple. Nothing worthwhile ever is. But it's right. For you, for Beck, for Heavenly."

They talked for another ten minutes, Liam sharing snippets of their time in Vegas so far, his voice a steady anchor. Just as Seth was feeling more centered, more grounded in his decision, Liam's tone shifted slightly.

"You know..." his Irish friend began almost casually. "Sometimes the things we think we've resolved have a way of resurfacing when we're on the verge of something new. Something that matters."

Seth froze. "What's that supposed to mean?"

"Keep your eyes open, mate."

A chill ran down Seth's spine "If you know something—"

"I don't. Just...be aware. That's all."

Seth waited for more, but Liam fell silent. The vague warning sat uncomfortably in Seth's chest. He'd already been through hell and come out on the other side. The past was behind him. He'd made damn sure of that. So whatever niggled at Liam couldn't be worse than what he'd already survived.

"Thanks for the cryptic warning," Seth said dryly. "Really helpful."

Liam chuckled. "Sorry. Sometimes I get feelings about things, but I can't say for certain what they mean. Probably nothing. Just...take care of yourself, yeah?"

"Yeah," Seth promised before they hung up.

But as he darkened his phone and left the home gym, that familiar doubt crept back in. He'd made the choice, taken the leap, and committed to their future. If the rest of his tomorrows were mapped out and everything was falling into place, why did he still feel like he was holding his breath, waiting for the other shoe to drop?

It's just nerves, he told himself. *Anyone would feel unsettled about committing to a whole new life in one night.*

As Seth let out a deep breath and headed for the stairs, he couldn't quite shake the feeling that something was waiting in the shadows. Something he hadn't accounted for.

Seth was halfway up the stairs when his phone buzzed again. He glanced at the screen, expecting a follow-up text from Liam. Or a message from a client with a cheating spouse. Instead, his mother's name popped up. He froze.

Shit. It was three-fifteen in the morning in New York. After all the upheaval tonight, he didn't have the emotional bandwidth to juggle a crisis three thousand miles away.

But Grace Cooper wouldn't call at this hour unless something was seriously wrong.

"Mom?" Seth answered, sinking onto the stairs. "What's going on?"

The sound that came through the speaker was something between a sob and a gasp. "Thank goodness you answered. I'm sorry to call so late. I didn't know what else to do."

"Hey, hey. Take a breath. Tell me what happened." Seth's protective instincts kicked in, and he shelved his own turmoil. "Are you okay? Is someone hurt?"

"No. But…" Her voice broke again. "Carl and I went away for the weekend. He got sick, so we came home early. We walked in…and found Jack and Connor. Sleeping…with the same girl."

Fuck. Seth closed his eyes and pinched the bridge of his nose. He'd feared this day would come. After the twins had spent last summer with him in Cali, he'd gotten an eyeful of their proclivities. He hadn't expected them to change, but he thought they'd be smart enough not to fly their freak flag around their deeply Catholic mother.

"Mom, I'm sure that was shocking, but—"

"Shocking?" Grace's voice climbed an octave. "It was... it was disgusting. Sacrilegious. Where did they even get that idea? How could they do something so...so deviant?"

He flinched, his fingers tightening on the phone. *Deviant?* If only she knew what her eldest son had been up to earlier this evening. Hell, for months.

Grace continued, her voice thick with tears. "When I confronted them, they admitted they've been sharing women all along. Why would they do that? How did I not know?"

His mother had often been willfully blind to her younger sons' more colorful exploits, chalking up their antics to "boys being boys" rather than acknowledging the depth of their wild streaks.

"What did we do wrong?" she wailed on.

Because she didn't know what to do and wanted him to fix the problem.

What a clusterfuck.

"Mom, I know you're upset, and that you don't approve. But Jack and Connor are grown men. They can make their own choices, even if we don't agree with them."

"But what they're doing…it's *sinful*. Terrible. It goes against everything we raised them to believe. Against God's plan." She was crying harder now.

"I know that's how you feel. But they aren't fifteen anymore."

"That makes it worse! This isn't just teenage wildness. And I can't…" Another sob, this one louder. "You have to help me."

"I don't know what you want me to—"

"Come home. Please… You have to talk to them. I can't make them see reason, but they respect you. You can make them understand."

No, he couldn't. He had zero moral high ground here.

Seth's stomach twisted. The hypocrisy was glaringly obvious… Here he was, fresh from making love to his fiancée bareback before he watched another man—his partner in her pleasure—do the same. And his mother was asking him to lecture his brothers about the sanctity of traditional relationships?

"I…" Seth swallowed hard. What could he say?

"I know you're busy. I know it's a lot to ask, but I'm at my wit's end. Carl doesn't know what to say to them either."

Seth wasn't surprised, and it was probably for the best that his mom's future husband wasn't wading into family drama. The new man in their mother's life wasn't going to have any sway with the twins.

If anyone had any prayer of smoothing over this situation, it was him.

His sigh was full of resignation. "All right. I'll come home for a few days. But don't expect miracles. Jack and Connor are—"

"Really? Thank you," she gasped out as if she hadn't heard his warning at all.

This was going to be a shit show. "I'll be there soon."

"I really am grateful. You've always been such a godsend." Grace's voice brightened slightly.

She wouldn't say that if she knew the truth.

"Any chance Heavenly can come with you? You two have been together for months. I'd love to finally meet the woman who captured my son's heart and made him start living again."

Seth froze. Bring Heavenly to New York? To meet his devoutly Catholic mother who was currently having a meltdown over his brothers' sexual preferences? When he himself was doing what she would undoubtedly consider worse?

Yes, he'd planned to bring Heavenly to the wedding, but that would be different—Grace would be distracted, and Beck would just be a friend who happened to be in town.

"She can't. She just started her final year of nursing school. It's really intense, and she can't afford to miss classes."

He wasn't lying…exactly. Heavenly's schedule *was* demanding. But the real reason was far more complicated. How could he explain that bringing Heavenly meant excluding Beck? That the three of them were a unit, bound together by more than just convenience or sex, but a love they'd chosen to share?

And what would happen when his mother started asking about his future with Heavenly? About settling down? A wedding, grandchildren, and a picket fence? Questions he wasn't ready to answer because he didn't know how to explain that any children Heavenly had would belong to Beck as much as him.

"I'm disappointed, but I understand," Grace murmured. "School is important. Maybe it's not the best time anyway. The twins' behavior is…so embarrassing. I don't want her getting the wrong idea about our family. But I'll be meeting her at my wedding next month, right?"

"Yes," Seth promised. "Mom, about Jack and Connor… I'll talk to them, but I can't force them to change. You know that, right?"

"I know. I just… I don't understand. Did I fail them that badly? I tried to be a good influence, but—"

"You didn't fail them." Seth's voice was firm. "People's sexuality… They like what they like. It isn't really a choice. Maybe…that's just who they are."

The words burned his throat. He was talking about himself as much as his brothers.

"No. They didn't have to do this. They *chose* to," Grace insisted. "And it needs to stop. I know you'll help. When can you be here?"

"Probably Tuesday. I just need to…" *Explain to Heavenly and Beck why I'm running across the country in the middle of her fertile window.* "Rearrange my schedule. I'll send you my flight information once I've made my reservations."

They talked for a few more minutes, Grace gradually calming. By the time they hung up, she still sounded shaken, but more like herself.

Seth darkened his phone and sat on the stairs, his head spinning. What the hell was he supposed to tell Jack and Connor? That sharing women was wrong? That they each needed to find a nice girl and settle down?

The hypocrisy would be laughable if it weren't so fucking tragic.

The truth was, Seth understood his brothers. The high of sharing a woman was undeniable. And the way some people fit together didn't always match societal expectations… It just was. He couldn't condemn them for following their hearts when he'd done the same.

But he also understood his mother's shock, her horror at discovering her sons engaged in behavior she saw as immoral. Grace Cooper was a good woman, but she was also a product of her generation and her faith. The idea that love could exist outside the narrow confines of one man, one woman, one marriage was simply incomprehensible to her.

Seth cursed. His lies were piling up, creating a house of cards he feared would come crashing down. He could only deflect for so long before he'd have to tell his mother the truth. Somehow.

And speaking of deflecting… He had to convince Beck and Heavenly that this trip didn't mean he was backsliding after they'd just committed to their future. He feared the fragile peace they'd negotiated was about to be tested.

Beck wouldn't be happy. And Seth couldn't blame him. If their positions were reversed, he'd be furious.

He was also unsettled by the thought of Beck and Heavenly alone while he was gone. Not because he was jealous, but because he wanted to be *with* them, a part of whatever happened next. What if Heavenly conceived while he was gone? What if Beck got her pregnant while Seth was three thousand miles away?

The irony wasn't lost on him. He'd spent months terrified of getting Heavenly pregnant, and now he was worried about missing his chance to knock her up.

He sounded like he needed a shrink. Or a lobotomy.

Seth stood slowly, every muscle suddenly feeling like it weighed a thousand pounds. Somehow, he had to work through his fears about fatherhood while navigating the complex web of family expectations, religious beliefs, and social conventions. *That's not a tall order at all,* he thought sarcastically.

As he climbed the last of the stairs toward their bedroom, Seth feared that this trip to New York was a disaster waiting to happen.

He paused outside the door and took a deep breath. Inside, Heavenly and Beck still slept peacefully. He wanted to join them…but somewhere in the back of his mind, Liam's cryptic warning echoed: *Sometimes the things we think we've resolved have a way of resurfacing…*

Seth wasn't sure what his friend meant, but as he quietly slipped inside the bedroom, he couldn't shake the feeling that he was about to find out.

Chapter Five

The next morning, Heavenly woke to sunlight streaming through the bedroom window and the gentle weight of her engagement ring on her finger. She lay tangled in their sheets, savoring the memory of the night before—Seth's desperate return, the intoxicating pleasure they'd shared, then the moment they'd knelt beside the bed with their hearts in their eyes, holding her beautiful ring and asking her to be their wife.

I'm engaged. She stared at the extravagant diamond, dazzling in the morning light. Warmth fluttered in her chest.

But as awareness fully returned, she realized she was in the bed alone. She'd expected to wake surrounded by them. The silence felt off-kilter.

Frowning, she glanced around the room. Beck's wallet still sat on the dresser, where he usually left it at night, so he hadn't been called to the hospital. But where was Seth? After everything they'd shared, everything they'd committed to...was he pulling away again? The thought made her stomach clench. She'd pushed him hard last night. Beck had, too. What if, in the cold light of day, it had been too much, too fast? What if he'd awakened regretting everything?

That worry niggled her as she climbed out of bed and pulled on her yoga pants and a tank top. Seth emerged from the bathroom in a cloud of steam and aftershave, hair damp from a shower. His smile was warm when he saw her, but she saw shadows under his eyes and tension in his shoulders.

He hadn't slept. He didn't when he was stressed.

"Morning, angel," he murmured, taking her in his arms and kissing her softly before he pulled back to thumb her ring. "Last night wasn't easy, but I'm beyond grateful you took me back. And that you said yes."

Relief flooded her...but she still had questions. "Of course I said yes. You should have known I was going to. We've talked about it enough. And you know I love you both." She studied him more closely. "If you're happy I accepted, why didn't you sleep?"

"You can tell, huh?" He huffed out a laugh. "You know me. Just…a lot on my mind." He brushed a strand of hair from her face. "Other things, not us. It's not bad…just shit to deal with."

Heavenly didn't like the deflection. "Work?"

He shook his head. "I'll explain. Hang tight, okay?"

With a few words, she went from mild concern to growing anxiety. "You'll tell me soon?"

"Oh, angel…yeah. In ten minutes. It's nothing you need to worry about. Promise."

Why didn't that make her feel better? And since she didn't quite believe him, what did it say about their trust?

Heavenly took a breath and asked the question she didn't dare put off. "I'm glad you're happy about the engagement, but what about… the rest? Do you have any regrets about last night?"

He cupped her face and smiled, but something in his eyes… They closed up. "Not for one second. You're stuck with me now, angel."

"And if I get pregnant?"

The grin he flashed her didn't look quite genuine. "Wasn't that the point?"

It had been, but he hadn't actually explained his feelings. He'd seemingly been all in last night, but… Maybe he was just tired or anxious about what he had to say. Maybe she was the one making a mountain out of a mole hill.

She smiled back and tried to loosen the knot in her chest as he took her hand and they headed downstairs for coffee.

"I can't wait to tell Raine about our engagement," she said.

"Since she's probably somewhere over the Atlantic on their way to honeymoon in Paris, maybe you should wait to call until they get back. No need to interrupt…things and piss off her grooms." Seth smiled and tapped her on the nose.

He was probably right. After everything Raine and her men had endured, they deserved a romantic getaway.

At the bottom of the stairs, they stopped short at the sight of Beck leaning against the granite counter, talking to Pike, of all people. He looked thoroughly disreputable and out of place in their pristine kitchen, dressed in head-to-toe black—T-shirt that showed every muscle, leather pants that cupped him in all the places he wanted to show off, and big, scuffed combat boots. Why was he dressed like that before seven a.m. on a Sunday morning? Then again, other than her father's funeral, he was always dressed that way.

"Cooper," Pike said stiffly as he turned toward them, maintaining a careful distance from Seth. Then he nodded her way. "Heavenly."

"Pike," Seth returned with equal coolness, squeezing her hand protectively.

"Morning, Cullen." She tried to lighten the mood. "Coffee?"

"He was just leaving." Beck clapped Pike on the shoulder and hustled him to the foyer. "Good to see you, man. Thanks for stopping by."

Then, with a slam of the door, he was gone.

"What the hell was that about?" Seth demanded the moment Beck returned.

Heavenly crossed her arms. "Please tell me this doesn't involve Madame Zelda and Clovis."

Beck sent her a wry smile. "No donkeys or rubber sheets, I promise. Club business. You know Hammer left me in charge of Shadows while he's gone, and I wanted to touch base with Pike since he's DMing."

"Gotcha." Seth relaxed.

She didn't understand. "DMing?"

Beck pulled at the back of his neck. "Yeah, he's been a Dungeon Monitor for years. He watches everyone at Shadows, making sure they're playing safely—"

"And putting a lot of scenes in his spank bank," Seth quipped.

Heavenly swatted his shoulder. "Don't put that visual in my head. Please."

They all laughed before Beck went on. "And since Pike was here, I picked his brain for something…special."

Seth raised a brow. "Ideas from *Pike?* Since that man's idea of 'special' involves livestock and bodily fluids, no thanks."

"I used his extraordinarily bent fetishes for good this time," Beck assured, turning back to finish cooking breakfast. "I think you'll like this. I'll explain while we eat. Come here, little girl."

Heavenly smiled and crossed the floor to kiss Beck's cheek. He caught her around the waist, and the quick peck she intended became something raw and passionate that made her knees go weak.

"I need caffeine and food before any of that, mister." She wriggled free with a grin.

They all laughed, but as they sat with their plates, Seth's nervousness ticked up.

Beck's sharp gaze missed nothing. He slammed his coffee mug on the table with a clatter. "Whatever's up with you, man, spit it out."

Seth set down his fork and heaved a long sigh. "I know this is the worst fucking timing ever, but..." He recounted the call he'd received from his mother and her horror at finding the twins sharing a woman. "She wants me to fly back there and, um...talk some sense into those 'deviants.' Yes, the ridiculousness of her request isn't lost on me."

It wasn't funny...but it kind of was. It was also deeply concerning. If Grace thought Jack and Connor were deviants for sharing the same girl, what would the woman think of her? Heavenly couldn't help but fear Grace would see her as the harlot who had corrupted her son. Would the woman ever accept Seth's relationship with her and Beck?

"So let me get this straight," Beck drawled with characteristic snark. "Your saintly Catholic mother wants *you*—the poster boy for debauchery—to preach about one-man-one-woman wholesomeness? Should I start the slow clap now or wait for the encore?"

"Like I said, it's peak irony. And completely futile. Those leopards aren't changing their spots. I tried."

"Of course they're not. You gave them that speech when you caught them over the summer. It failed spectacularly."

Seth winced. "She doesn't know that, and I can't tell her. She'd *freak* that I didn't come clean."

"Because if you had...the twins would rat you out about us." Beck winced. "Gotta love it. So you're supposed to fly to New York to tell them to 'Just say no?'"

"This isn't you running away again, is it?" Heavenly had to ask.

Seth's stare snapped to hers. Hurt flashed across his features before he shook his head. "I'm not, angel. Since my mom called, I've been wondering how I could turn this situation to our advantage. I have an idea."

Beck glanced her way, then raised a brow at Seth. "We're listening."

"If I can get Mom to admit she'd never care about her sons any less for being with whoever they love, that any grandchildren would be welcome no matter the circumstances… Maybe I can lay the groundwork for her to accept us."

Relief swirled with hope in Heavenly's chest. Not that she wanted Seth to leave or for the twins to be out of their mom's good graces, but he was onto something. "That might actually work. Appeal to her heart."

Seth's voice carried conviction now. "Exactly. It won't be easy, and her attitude won't change overnight. But Mom asking me to come fix this situation could be a blessing in disguise."

Beck pondered Seth for a protracted moment. "All right. But you come home to us. No matter what happens back there."

"I will. I told her I'd fly out on Tuesday, but I have to be back by the weekend." Seth lifted her hand and pressed his lips to her palm. "I want you to know, I put off leaving for an extra day because you're still in your fertile window."

Heavenly felt a flutter of relief in her belly. His words melted away some of her lingering concerns.

"Good thinking," Beck said, pushing back from the table. "My thoughts were on a similar path. That's another reason I called Pike this morning and asked him to stop by. I wanted to arrange something special for us tonight. A celebration. Well, a kinky one."

Heavenly's pulse quickened. "What are you up to?"

With a wicked grin, he reached under the table. "All the inches I'm going to stuff you with later, but I digress. This is an adventure. Can you two get free this evening? We need to leave about an hour before dusk."

Maybe Heavenly shouldn't be, but she was excited. "I just have to study some and finish a paper, but it won't take all day."

Seth shrugged. "I'm going to do my laundry for the trip and touch base with River, let him know I'm jetting out. Other than that, I'm good. So…you going to tell us what you have in mind?"

"Nah. But I think you'll really enjoy it. We all will." Beck's eyes glittered with mischief as he looked at Heavenly. "I suggest you rest up today. Oh, and I hope you can run."

Hours later, Heavenly fidgeted anxiously in the front seat of the SUV. All afternoon, she and Seth had pelted Beck with questions about their *surprise*, but her sexy surgeon had remained tight-lipped, refusing to give either of them the slightest hint.

Why would she be running? She could, of course…but as quickly as Beck? And Seth was even more athletic. They'd both run circles around her.

And…what would happen if they were faster?

Dressed in head-to-toe black, Beck navigated the vehicle out of the city. The sun hung low in the horizon, painting the sky in shades of gold and crimson. It looked pretty, but Heavenly was too nervous to appreciate it.

She'd be less apprehensive if Beck had "picked" someone's brain other than Pike's. The taciturn, tattooed loner had proven his proclivities prowled a dark, freakishly twisted trail. Was that the reason Jasmine kept him in the friend zone?

As Beck turned off the main road and onto a gravel lane, Heavenly stared out the windshield at their rapidly changing surroundings. Through the few-and-far-between gaps in the trees, she spied a towering chain-link fence, topped with razor-wire.

Where the heck was Beck taking them?

Seth, also wearing unrelieved black, scowled from the back seat. "Are we visiting a prison?"

"No." Beck laughed. He was keeping them both in the dark—and he was enjoying it.

Heavenly huffed. "Then what is this—"

"Patience, little girl."

The next five minutes dragged on, feeling like half of forever before he stopped in front of an unassuming rustic lodge, almost completely surrounded by trees. The crude wooden sign above the door read THE WILD STALK.

"A hunting lodge. Is that what we're doing?" Seth's question was laced with intrigue, as if he suddenly understood tonight's activity.

Heavenly didn't want to hurt Beck's feelings, but…what had he been thinking? "I-I don't know anything about hunting."

"You don't have to." Beck reached over the console and patted her thigh.

Maybe he'd meant that touch to be reassuring…but it seemed a lot more sexual, given his lingering palm and wandering fingers.

"In fact, it's better if you don't." Seth grinned enthusiastically as he unbuckled his seat belt.

Heavenly turned in her seat to frown at Beck. "Okay…but I'm *not* killing Bambi. I-I can't."

Sending her a tender smile, he threaded his fingers through hers, then softly kissed her knuckles. "We're not here to kill anything, little girl. I promise. Come with me. You'll see."

Suddenly eager, Seth hoisted up the duffel beside him and hopped out of the back seat. Before she could even reach for the handle, he opened the passenger door and held out his hand.

His wolfish grin told her he grasped what Beck had planned. As she slid her hand in his and eased from the SUV, she studied his face for clues, but his expression didn't tell her anything—except that he was impatient.

Seth gripped her tight while Beck settled his palm at the small of her back. Together, they surrounded her as they led her up the stairs. She could feel excitement pinging off them.

When they entered the wooden building, a forty-something bearded man lifted his head and studied them with a sharp, assessing stare. "Beckman?"

"Yes."

A little frown burrowed between his graying brows. "Are you waiting for other hunters…or is this your whole party?"

"This is it," Beck confirmed.

The proprietor shrugged. "Sure. Usually, hunting packs are bigger, but...whatever. You're paid up for four hours. Don't be late. There's a midnight hunting party booked after yours." The man handed them each a release form. "These are standard waivers. If you want to play... sign away."

Play? Play what?

Beck and Seth stepped in close, flanking her as Heavenly scanned the document. Words like *pursuit scenario, safe words,* and *consensual adult role-play* jumped off the page. She tensed. Her pulse quickened. The air grew thick.

Beck stroked her arm while Seth skimmed his fingers down her spine.

"What exactly are we hunting?" Her gaze bounced between them.

But there was one obvious answer. And the way they both stared, eyes hot and hungry, made her tummy knot and her blood pool even lower.

"You're not hunting, little girl. Seth and I are. And we'll be hunting *you,*" Beck murmured against her ear.

The Wild Stalk.

I hope you can run. She finally understood Beck's cryptic comment.

She gaped at him. "You're...serious?"

He didn't reply, but his grin turned into a wicked smile that made her womb clench.

On her other side, Seth's entire body tightened as he leaned closer. "Oh, yeah. We'll even give you a head start."

They want to chase me. Hunt me like prey.

A tremor of fear and yet contradictory excitement quaked through her. "And...if you catch me?"

Their smiles turned positively feral.

"We claim our prize...however we want." Beck winked, his eyes full of dark promise.

Heavenly could barely breathe. Their game was twisted, barbaric. She should be afraid, feel revulsion. She should refuse. But the incessant throbbing between her legs told her the last thing she felt was disgust.

She fidgeted, pressing her thighs together to quell the ache. No such luck.

"You game, angel?" Seth chivalrously gave her an out. "You don't have to do this."

"No. I-I want to." Unable to contain her excitement, she caught her hand trembling as she signed.

The guys both did the same, then Seth set down the pen with a decisive *clack*.

"Your website indicated there's a room where she can change?" Beck said to the bearded man in the plaid shirt as he lifted the black duffel.

"In there." The proprietor pointed to a door on the far side of the room.

"Perfect."

Heavenly's heart kicked up another notch. "What am I changing into? What's wrong with what I'm wearing?"

Beck grinned as he guided her into a room lined with tall metal lockers, Seth following behind. "It will be more fun if you wear this…"

He plucked a gauzy white nightgown from the duffel.

She stared at the garment, her mind racing as she blinked up at him. "It's…transparent."

Seth's expression turned downright dirty. "It is."

Nibbling her bottom lip, Heavenly considered the situation. The fence suggested the property was private. The weather was perfect, a mere hint of a breeze to ruffle the temperate evening. She only had one question.

"Will anyone else see me wearing this?"

"We're the only guests here tonight," Beck promised.

That was a relief. She wouldn't want to run into other strangers "hunting."

She took the nightgown from his grasp. "Do I just put my things in the locker?"

"Yep. And, um…leave your shoes here, too." Beck nodded to her sandals.

She frowned. "I'll be barefoot."

"Oh, you will," Seth drawled as if he liked that.

Her eyes narrowed. "But…won't I be at a disadvantage?"

"That's the idea." Beck smiled deviously.

Heavenly licked her lips. "You don't play fair."

Together, the guys laughed before Seth dropped his hand to her waist, then slid it down to her backside. "You're just now catching on?"

"Don't worry, little girl," Beck added. "You'll be screaming later, but not because you're angry about the rules."

She could just imagine all the ways they'd make her scream.

Heavenly blushed. "I'm marrying perverts."

Again, they both laughed before Beck dropped a kiss just beneath her ear. "You already knew that."

She did. "I need to have my head examined."

"So..." Seth drawled. "Is that a yes, angel? You'll play with us? Wear the nightgown and let us hunt you?"

Even his words made her quiver with a thrill she didn't understand. "Yes."

She whispered, but they both heard. The approval in their eyes matched the lust pinging between them.

"We'll wait for you out there."

He and Beck both disappeared back to the main office, shutting the door behind them. Shaking, she tugged off her clothes and slipped the flowing white gown over her head. She glanced at herself in the full-length mirror behind the door—and her jaw dropped. Trimmed in bows and lace, the nightie almost looked girlishly innocent...except she could see her dusky pink nipples, the indention of her waist, the hint of shadows between her legs, and the outline of her thighs—all of which proved she was a woman.

No doubt, they'd love this get-up. And because she was learning well what turned them on, she grinned as she pulled free the ponytail holders she'd used to secure her messy bun, then braided her hair into neat little pigtails.

Satisfied, she stepped out the door, staying in the shadows and away from the proprietor.

Beck and Seth both turned to her. Instantly, heat lit their eyes.

"Hmm. You look gorgeous, angel." Seth skimmed his fingers down her cheek before settling the locket he'd given her over the tiny pearl buttons nestled between her collarbones.

"Beautiful," Beck added, his voice husky.

Seth ducked into the changing room, shoved their duffel into one of the lockers, then slammed the metal door before pocketing its key. Then he returned to their side. "Ready?"

His wolfish grin said he was. Beck, too.

She nodded bravely. "As I'll ever be."

"What's next?" Beck asked the man behind the counter, standing in front of her to block his view. Seth joined him, creating a wall of man between her and the proprietor.

"Just need to go over a few things before you start." The guy behind the counter handed each of them a map. "There are five buildings on the property, all with a specific theme. Locations are completely stocked with condoms, lube, scenario-appropriate toys, costumes of all sizes, and a bed…of sorts. As you can see, we have our barn. That's the Obedience Corral. The school is our Headmaster's Office. Then there's the church, The Ministry of Sin. Not to be outdone is our medical center, St. Merciless General. And last, our ever-popular Love-Shackled Cottage."

Every word sent more heat spiraling through her. The thought of being dragged into one of those themed rooms and left to Beck and Seth's mercy…

Anticipation permeated every cell in her body. The map jostled in her trembling fingers. Goose bumps peppered her skin as the man cleared his throat. "I need to talk to your girl."

Beck and Seth exchanged a glance before Beck peeled off his windbreaker and draped it around her, covering the essentials. Seth studied her. Seemingly satisfied, they both stepped aside.

"I'm here," she murmured.

The man behind the counter pinned her with a solemn stare. "First, you'll have a five-minute head start before the men begin hunting you. Do you understand?"

Five minutes wasn't long, but Heavenly hoped that gave her enough time to find a good hiding place. "Yes."

"Secondly, you signed the waiver, but I also need verbal confirmation. Are you here of your own free will?"

"Yes," Heavenly assured.

"And you understand that all sexual activity on premises is deemed consensual in the course of play. If you no longer consent, you change your mind, the scene becomes more than you can handle, or you have any sort of emergency, each building is equipped with a small panic room. You simply step inside and push the red button on the wall. The doors will slam shut. Every employee in the compound and I will extract you promptly. Understood?"

She couldn't imagine a scenario she'd need to physically flee from Beck or Seth. "Yes."

"You've all noted on your forms that her safe word is *freedom*, correct?"

"Yes," they answered in unison.

"We don't record any audio or visual activity on the premises, but we do have sensitive microphones throughout the property. I've entered her safe word into a special computer program. If she says that word, cameras and mics will turn on and begin recording. It will also alert me…here." He tapped a black receiver tucked in his ear. "If either of you fail to honor her safe word, my employees and I will descend on your location and escort you off the premises. You'll be banned for life. Clear?"

"Crystal," Beck and Seth assured in tandem.

"The other employees I've mentioned are situated inside the compound. They're dressed in camo. They strive to remain invisible to enhance your experience. Don't be alarmed if you happen to see one during your hunt, but it's unlikely since they're discreet and your hunting party is so small."

"That's the second time you've mentioned our party having fewer members than normal." Beck cocked his head. "How many usually join a hunt?"

The man grinned. "Last night, we had ten hunters."

"How many prey?" Seth arched a brow.

"Just one."

Ten on one? The mental image of that stole her breath—being overwhelmed, outnumbered, completely at the mercy of *ten* hungry men. Her core clenched involuntarily. She'd never want that for herself; she loved Beck and Seth too much to take on anyone else. But…she could imagine how excited last night's "doe" must have been.

"I don't know what all they did to her." The man shrugged. "But they had to carry her out."

She couldn't even walk?

Seth grinned devilishly. "If things go as planned, we'll be carrying out our fiancée tonight as well."

Seriously? Heavenly bowed her head as her cheeks caught fire.

The man merely chuckled, then stepped from behind the counter before handing Beck and Seth each a pair of night-vision goggles. "Any other questions before we begin?"

"None from me," Beck replied.

"I'm good," Seth seconded. "Angel?"

"No questions." Her voice quivered—not from fear, but from a heady mix of arousal and anticipation humming through her veins, leaving her short of breath and a little dizzy.

"Then follow me, and we'll get the hunt started," the bearded man instructed.

Heart pounding and blood pumping, she handed Beck his windbreaker. He and Seth each cinched an arm around her waist. Together, they followed the man down a long, narrow hallway before pausing at a wide, sliding-glass door.

Darkness was settling over the densely treed landscape. Everything was black except the ambient footlights lining a dirt path to a tall wooden gate.

"This is as far as you gentlemen go…for now," the man announced, then smiled Heavenly's way as he opened the glass door. Cool air, heavy with the scent of earth, wafted over her face. "Ready?"

Her pulse jackhammered. Her breaths shortened. "Yes."

"We'll see you soon, little girl," Beck promised roughly, eyes hungry.

"And when we find you?" Seth growled. "We'll remind you exactly what it means to be owned by us."

Her pussy quivered. Heavenly tried to swallow, but her mouth was too dry. After a last clinging gaze, she turned and scurried out the door.

"Better run fast!" Beck called out after her.

Neither of them would ever hurt her, but this game got into Heavenly's head, pumping nerves, anxiety, and clenching need all through her body.

The bearded man followed her along the path until the glass door snicked behind them, enclosing them together in the shadowy hall leading to the wooden gate. "One more thing. You've signed a waiver and given me verbal consent, but I need to ask one more time...*alone.* Are you consensually engaging in this hunt?"

She crossed her arms self-consciously over her breasts, but he wasn't looking. "I am, willingly and gladly."

He sent her an approving smile. "Once you enter the compound, I'll begin the timer. You'll have five minutes before I...release the hounds, so to speak. Good luck."

"Any hints? Best places to hide?"

Grinning wryly, he shook his head. "I've explained the five major locations on the property. If you want to get caught, choose one you know will appeal to your hunters. If you want to make this last, pick a place you don't think they'll look. And if you really want them to work for it...one of the locations—I won't say which—has an underground hidey-hole. You just have to find it."

As jittery as she was, would she be able to? Did she even want to? "Thank you."

He nodded. "We're here if you need anything. Safety is most important. But...have a good time."

Nervously fingering the locket Seth had given her, Heavenly hurried to the gate, pushed it open, then paused. She glanced back once more to find Beck and Seth bathed in light, watching her through the sliding glass door with matching predatory stares.

They were coming for her...

Heart thundering in her ears, she sucked in a ragged breath. Then, with a whimper, she ran...

Chapter Six

In the rustic office, Beck's pulse thudded hard in a tense, anticipatory beat. Seth stood beside him, tension vibrating off him in waves. Both men fixed their hungry stares on the wooden gate where Heavenly had vanished into the darkness.

The bearded proprietor glanced at his watch. "Four minutes, thirty seconds."

Time was crawling by.

With a sigh of impatience, Beck dragged his gaze to the map in his hands. Seth followed suit, leaning close. The compound's layout was deceptively simple—five buildings scattered across what looked like twenty acres of wooded terrain.

"We should strategize. Where do you think she went?" Beck murmured, eyeing the schematic. He had to admit, the names of the structures on the property were clever…

"Since I don't think she's eager for us to toss her to the ground and do her under a bush, she'll run straight to one of the locations."

"Absolutely."

Seth tapped on the icon for the Love-Shackled Cottage. "Here. It's her style—romantic, intimate…with a bit of bondage. She's likely to feel most comfortable there."

"Probably." Beck eyed the other options. "But let's be tactical. If she's not there, where should we search next?"

"Since the cottage is the furthest building on the property, I say we work our way back toward the front." Seth traced a suggested path with his finger across the map.

"Makes sense. So, our next stop would be, St. Merciless General?"

"Yep."

"God, I hope she doesn't go there. I work in a medical facility; I don't want to play in one." Beck grimaced. "Then again, our girl might think it's funny to make me chase her through a fake hospital."

"I wouldn't mind giving her a thorough exam, like we did in San Diego." His smile was sly. "Good times."

"Oh, the night she wore the pearl panties and we made her walk back to our villa after dinner? *Great* times." Even the memory ratcheted up his lust.

"I'm down for a repeat."

"Same, but *not* in a medical environment. Next time, though, I'll swipe you a lab coat...*Dr. Cooper*."

"Deal." Seth chuckled, then quickly sobered as his finger swiped across the page to The Ministry of Sin. "I fucking hope she doesn't pick the church. Between our priest and my mom, I'm already carrying enough Catholic guilt."

"With my past, you know I hope she chose somewhere else." Beck consulted his map again. "Obedience Corral and the Headmaster's Office are about the same distance from the church. I can guess which one flips your switch."

"The Headmaster's Office." They chuckled in tandem.

"You said she got off on that game of 'master and maid' you played with her last spring."

"Oh, she loved the power dynamic." Seth's rough voice dropped an octave. "And the thought of her playing naughty student to our very stern principals..."

"That doesn't turn me off. But...maybe she'll surprise us and choose Obedience Corral. We've introduced her to a few different kinks, but she's always curious about more." Beck had never shown her his single-tail skills, and his cock stirred at the thought of cuffing Heavenly to a cross and sending her to subspace.

"True that. It will be interesting to see where we find her. At least we have a game plan when that goddamn timer finally goes off. How much longer?" Seth asked over his shoulder.

"Two minutes," the proprietor announced.

Beck groaned. Each second crawled, stretching his nerves thin. That sounded like two goddamn years.

"I'm impatient, too. But not much longer." Seth clapped him on the shoulder as they tucked away their maps.

Anticipation coiled in Beck's chest. When Pike had mentioned this place, Beck had known Seth would be all in. And he'd jumped at the opportunity to see how Heavenly took to primal play. Though their girl was still innocent in some ways, she had a dirty heart. He'd bet most every dime, she was going to melt and scream—and love every minute of this.

As soon as they found her.

God knew he relished the chance to hunt her and make her theirs in the most intrinsic way possible as she surrendered to them completely.

"When you're done for the evening, gentlemen, mark one of your maps with whatever buildings you used and leave it with your goggles on the counter on your way out," the proprietor said. "We've got to clean and sterilize everything for the midnight hunting party booked after you."

He and Seth nodded, their focus on the wooden gate as the seconds ticked down.

Beck felt like a caged animal, every muscle ready to spring into action. Beside him, Seth's breaths came short and fast, his hands flexing and releasing at his sides.

They exchanged a glance, a moment of understanding. They were partners in this hunt, united in the pursuit of their woman. In finding her. In dragging her beneath them. In heaping every sensation and pleasure possible on her.

Impatiently, he glanced back at the bearded man. When would that fucking timer go off?

Finally, a shrill ding cut through the silence.

Liquid fire surged through Beck's bloodstream as the proprietor yanked open the glass door with a knowing smile. "Happy hunting, gentlemen."

A cool evening breeze rustled through the trees as the silvery moon rose in the sky. Beck and Seth pulled on their night-vision goggles in perfect synchronization and sprinted down the dirt path, now a landscape of green through the lenses. Dimly glowing footlights flared like bright white orbs. Shadows shifted at the edges of his vision, every rustle fanning his hunt instinct.

After last night, he and Seth were bound to Heavenly. They'd overcome so much, and tonight felt like a celebration. A claiming. A sealing of their commitment.

The crunch of Beck's boots against the packed earth mingled with Seth's, drowning out the sounds of chirping crickets and humming cicadas as they charged through the wooden gate and burst into the open compound.

Beck scanned the area. No sign of Heavenly among the foliage, which suggested she'd already hidden somewhere. Smart girl.

"The cottage is dead-ahead, nearly against the far perimeter fence." Seth led him along the path bisecting the hunting grounds.

Silent minutes later, they reached the Love-Shackled Cottage. Between the adrenaline and the run, Beck was already panting, his pulse kicking hard. She had to be here.

Together, they raced up the wide porch steps, dashing past the cozy bench swing and tearing off their goggles before they burst through the door. Their rapt stares combed the almost dreamlike interior for signs of Heavenly.

The place glowed warmly from a cozy fire crackling in the stone fireplace. Scented candles filled the air with vanilla and jasmine. A large four-poster bed dominated the center of the room, draped in flowing pale fabric and sprinkled in rose petals. Silk ties were attached to each corner of the frame. An innocent white, see-through lace camisole decorated with pink bows lay draped across the mattress like an invitation. Beck's cock jerked at the sight.

Baskets lined the shelves along one wall, filled with condoms, lube, butt plugs, vibrators, and more. An ornate vanity against the opposite wall held more tiny bows, lace gloves, ornate masks, velvet cuffs, and flavored massage oil. Next to that, a bottle of champagne chilled in an ice bucket.

"Are you here, angel?" Seth yanked open the closet door and peeked inside.

"Come out, come out, wherever you are, little girl," Beck taunted as he bent and checked under the bed.

They searched every nook and cranny—behind curtains, inside

wardrobes, even the bathroom. She was nowhere to be found. Was she evading them? Toying with them?

Yes, and the idea of finding her, pinning her, claiming her made his blood kick harder.

Beck settled his specialized goggles back over his eyes as they stepped outside again. "Looks like she's decided to be more adventurous."

"Or more devious," Seth drawled.

Either option shot thrill down Beck's spine. "But it's almost a shame she's not here. The thought of violating our girl in that flimsy little nightie makes me fucking hard."

"Your bow fetish is showing, doc."

He shrugged. "Sue me."

"Nah. I dig it, too." Seth laughed, as they jogged the path through the clear, crystal night.

Minutes later, St. Merciless General came into view. They removed their eyewear again the moment they stepped inside. The space was well-lit, clinical, and sterile, lined with cabinets and one narrow closet. The sharp antiseptic scent hit Beck's nostrils, so familiar he'd swear he was about to step into the operating room. A hospital gown was draped over a padded exam table complete with stirrups and cuffs. A metal stand held a tray containing condoms and lube, along with rubber gloves, a silver speculum, bottles of alcohol, cotton gauze, and a package of play-worthy needles.

"You hiding in here, little girl?" Beck called.

Total silence.

Seth checked the narrow closet near the door. "You know, I'm surprised you picked vascular surgery over gynecology."

"I didn't ever want pussy to get boring." Beck, who had been methodically opening cabinets, slammed the last one shut. "She's not here."

Seth glanced around one final time. "You're right. Let's head out."

Back under the moonlight, they donned their lenses again.

Unease crawled under Beck's skin as they trekked to The Ministry of Sin. The moment they stepped inside the church-like structure, his stomach rolled.

Organ music played softly from overhead speakers. The massive space stretched before them—a long aisle bisecting rows of wooden pews. At the front, four stairs led to a wide altar where massive golden candelabras stood beside a slab of pristine marble, carved to cradle a body and draped in white silk. More pews encircled the slab for voyeuristic pleasure. Rolls of silk rope and a transparent gossamer gown waited on a golden tray alongside the obligatory condoms, lube, and anal plugs.

Memories of Zach recounting how, as a boy, their twisted father had forced him to watch while he violated his child bride Blessing—and Beck's first crush—on their "wedding night."

His stomach pitched violently. "I-I can't stay here. If you find Heavenly, just…bring her out. We'll decide where else to take her."

On the front steps, Beck filled his lungs with cool night air and fought back the nausea. Through the open doorway, he watched Seth methodically search the pews.

"Heavenly, if you're in here, show yourself." Seth's voice echoed in the vast space. "We can't do this here."

Nothing.

Seth gave the place one more cursory search before closing the door behind him. He met Beck's stare and shook his head.

"Thank fuck." Beck dragged a hand through his hair. "I'm sorry for freaking out. It's just—"

"You don't have to explain. I was having flashbacks, too. Not like yours. Mine were of every Sunday growing up, pulling at the tie strangling my neck and listening to a solid hour of mass in Latin while sitting, standing, kneeling, standing, sitting, kneeling, sitting, kneeling… You get the picture."

"So the thought of fucking in a 'church' doesn't turn you on either, huh?"

"About as much as a prostate exam," Seth quipped as they pulled on their goggles again and headed down another lit path. "So…the Headmaster's Office or Obedience Corral?"

"Let's try the BDSM barn first. It would be a golden opportunity for us to teach her about new styles of play."

"Exactly." Seth tipped his chin toward the rustic building on the next rise. "Maybe she'll be here so you can dish out some pain."

"I'll dish out plenty of pleasure, too…eventually. And don't tell me you wouldn't enjoy lighting up her sexy ass."

"I would," Seth conceded. "But…I also don't hate the idea of interrogating our girl in the Headmaster's Office."

Same, but… "I just want to find her and get her all kinds of filthy."

Anticipation spiking, Beck eased open the door of the weather-worn barn. As he entered beside Seth, their jaws dropped. Heat flared through his veins. This wasn't a musty old service building, but a pervert's paradise.

A massive black gothic four-poster bed dominated the center of the room, topped with a thick blood-red tufted leather mattress that matched the walls. Silver cuffs dangled from O-rings attached to the frame. A sexy red leather corset and shiny red stilettos sat atop a black padded bondage table near the bed. Mirrors lined the ceiling and warm hardwoods covered the floor. One wall displayed an impressive array of paddles, whips, floggers, crops, quirts, and every other impact implement imaginable. Along another, various weights and textures of rope lay coiled on hooks. A polished St. Andrew's cross stood in one corner, a thickly padded bondage table in the other, with a padded spanking bench positioned between them. On a table, he found rows of vibrators, anal plugs, and nipple clamps of all varieties.

Beck squeezed his throbbing cock as he began searching for her. "We need a room like this at home."

Seth did the same as he explored the interior. "Totally. We'll have to soundproof it, though. Don't want to scare the neighbors."

"Just imagine all the agony and ecstasy we could heap on her anytime we want…"

Seth sighed like he was picturing just that and it excited the hell out of him.

Beck checked under the bed and stood with a curse. Empty. They'd searched every possible hiding spot. "She's not fucking here."

"Next time we come…" Seth suggested with a dirty grin.

Beck clapped him on the shoulder. "I like the way you think."

"So…by process of elimination, she's at the Headmaster's Office." Predatory hunger gleamed in Seth's green eyes.

"I know handing out corporal punishment doesn't break your heart."

Seth rubbed his hands together in anticipation. "Let's go *teach* our angel a thing or two."

They donned their goggles again and made their way to the final building. Instead of bursting through the door, they circled the perimeter of the little red schoolhouse, knocking on walls and tapping windows, letting Heavenly know they'd run her down.

"We've found you, angel," Seth taunted. "We're coming for you…"

Beck got into the spirit. "Your principals are here to deal with their naughtiest little pupil. I hope you're ready…"

After circling the building, they stepped under the portico and removed their lenses. Then Seth eased open the door, its squeaking hinges shattering the silence.

Inside the well-lit room, a single 1950s-style school desk sat in the middle of the beige tile floor. The gauzy white gown Heavenly had been wearing was draped over the back.

Bingo!

He and Seth exchanged a knowing smile as they cased the room. Maps and colorful posters hung on the walls. A bank of low cabinets lined the back of the room, while a long, polished teacher's desk dominated the front, complete with black leather-padded cuffs dangling from each corner. Behind that, beneath a cursive alphabet border, a large blackboard held a tray with a black felt eraser and several sticks of chalk. Various paddles and rulers hung from nearby hooks.

One wall featured cubbies filled with condoms, lube, and every penetrating toy known to man. A nearby bookshelf was lined with baskets of even more sexual supplies. In one corner sat a huge bed, complete with a stark white fitted sheet and bondage straps designed to thrill any pervert's twisted heart.

A tall storage closet contained an empty hanger. What costume had Heavenly donned? If she was wearing a little pleated plaid skirt… Hmm, he got harder just thinking about it.

"We're here," Beck shouted. "And you've been a bad, bad little girl."

"You *know* what's going to happen when we find you? Principals Beckman and Cooper will give you a thorough interrogation and mete out the punishment you deserve."

From the front of the room, a feminine gasp floated through the air.

He and Seth fist-bumped before Beck ambled toward the row of cabinets and whispered, "You start on that end. I'll take this one." He opened the first of the doors. "Once we find her…we'll decide how we punish her."

"The first time, you mean?" Seth grinned as he opened another cabinet door.

Ignoring the little whimper from the front of the room, they took their time, building the anticipation as they prowled through every storage closet and cubby.

"Where could our naughty little pupil be?" Seth drawled.

Beck dragged in a deep breath. "She's here somewhere. I can *smell* her."

"Me, too. But all this searching has worn me out." Seth strode toward the teacher's desk and clasped the back of the chair with a wink. "I need to sit."

Beck eased behind him as Seth rolled the chair from under the desk. Together, they bent and peered into the alcove below. Heavenly sat curled in a ball, blinking at them, looking both deliciously pure and afraid.

"There you are. Come out." Excitement roughened Seth's voice. "And face us."

Swallowing, she crawled out from beneath the desk and stood, fidgeting nervously. Beck looked her up and down—her little schoolgirl outfit straight out of his fantasies—and he forgot how to breathe.

God, she was beautiful, wearing a minuscule plaid skirt and a white blouse—at least two sizes too small. Her golden braids, now adorned with pretty pink bows, fell over her shoulders, framing her barely contained breasts. The skirt brushed the tops of her thighs and left the bottom half of her luscious ass bare. Pink ruffled ankle socks with more gratuitous bows hugged her feet, along with glossy black Mary Janes.

Possessive heat spiked through his bloodstream.

"Sirs?" she breathed.

Beck's cock lurched. A low growl vibrated from the back of his throat.

"Fuck me." Seth stood frozen like a statue, his hot stare raking their girl.

Heavenly blinked up at them with an expression so innocent, Beck's whole body lurched—and he started making a mental list of all the unspeakably dirty things he intended to do to her.

"I-I waited after class, like you said." She sent them a wide-eyed, little-girl-lost stare. "Why am I in trouble?"

She wants to role-play? Beck's cock nearly burst through his zipper.

"Did you finish your assignment, angel?" Seth asked, arching a brow.

She bowed her head in a sweetly submissive gesture. But Beck couldn't miss the twinkle of mischief in her big blue eyes. "I did, but..."

"But what?" Seth bit out impatiently.

"Um...my dog ate it?"

"You don't have a dog."

"I-it was the neighbor's dog."

Beck smiled. He had to give their little vixen props. She played her role perfectly.

"Why was the neighbor's dog at *your* house?"

"It wasn't. My neighbor invited me to his house."

"His?" Beck growled, gleefully joining in.

"Uh-huh. He's a really nice man."

Seth's eyes narrowed. "You're too young to be alone with a man. You were supposed to be home studying for your test."

"The test is *today*?" Nervously, she nibbled her lip.

"Right now," Beck clarified, voice thick with lust. "It's going to be a *doubly hard* test, too."

Heavenly let out a quivering breath. "Oh, no..."

"Answer me, Miss Young." Seth barked, plucking a ruler off its nearby hook. "What were you doing alone with your neighbor at his house?"

"Well, I-I was outside watering my flowers, then—"

"Dressed like that?" Beck interrupted.

She nodded. "I'd just gotten home from school, and this *is* my uniform."

He and Seth exchanged a look of feigned disapproval.

Clutching the ruler, Cooper settled it under her hem…then slowly lifted the front of her skirt. The sight of her bare pussy nearly took Beck out at the knees.

The ruler in Seth's hands quivered. "Where are your panties, Miss Young?"

Heavenly panted, her luscious breasts threatening to fall out of her too-tight blouse. "I must have forgotten to put them on this morning."

Scowling, Seth tucked his finger beneath her chin and drew her upright again. "I'm running out of patience, young lady. Answer my question. *What* were you doing alone with your neighbor at his house?"

"Watching a movie."

Their little actress wasn't purposely pushing their buttons; she was pounding them, and his guess? She loved every minute of it.

"Which one?" Beck demanded, impatient to start dishing out her funishment.

"Something I'd never seen. *My Big Fat Greek Weiner*."

Beck clenched his jaw, mostly to stop himself from laughing.

Seth closed his eyes and pinched the bridge of his nose. Yeah, the big guy was struggling to hold in his mirth, too. Finally, he lifted his stare and seared her with a manufactured glare. "You were watching *porn*?

Beck joined in, brow raised. "Alone with a grown man?"

Heavenly's eyes went wide. "Is *that* why they didn't have clothes on and were doing those…things?"

"You've been very naughty, and you deserve punishment."

"For that and her missing homework." Seth nodded. "Did the dog eat it while you were being a very bad girl and watching that very bad film?"

"Yes. I-I wasn't paying attention. The dog snatched it off the table and chewed it up. By the time I realized—"

"Enough!" Seth tossed the ruler onto the nearby desk and dragged her close, eating up her helpless little yelp as he bent her over the desk, exposing her luscious ass. "So not only did you watch an inappropriate movie alone with a horny older man, you failed to turn in your homework *and* you forgot your panties."

"You're racking up the punishments, little girl," Beck added, enjoying this game far more than he'd thought.

"You also lied," Seth heaped on.

"I didn't." She sounded beautifully distressed.

"The dog didn't eat your homework, did it? You didn't bother doing it." Seth's tone condemned her. "Tsk. Tsk."

"We can't let that go." Beck greedily eyed her pressed against the wooden desk, her pale ass exposed and waiting.

Heavenly peered over her shoulder, her face full of guilt, eyes swimming with tears. "I-I meant to, but…"

"I don't want to hear any more excuses or lies," Seth barked.

"Since you've been a very naughty little girl, we have to punish you." Beck ran a hand up her thigh.

"How?" Her terrified expression might have been convincing, if not for the hunger in her eyes.

"However we want. And in every way you deserve," he growled.

"Exactly. You've left us no choice. Lift your skirt to your waist." Seth snatched a thick wooden paddle off the wall.

Pretending to bite back a terrified gasp, Heavenly flipped the hem of her plaid skirt onto the small of her back with dramatic flourish.

Easing in behind her, Beck skimmed his palm over her ripe, round ass. Visions of her creamy white skin all red and bruised crowded his brain. His mental pictures were so real, he could almost taste her trembling pain.

"Spread your legs, Miss Young." Seth dragged the paddle up the insides of her thighs. "Wider. Now grip the edges of the desk."

She quivered as she complied. The pose put her pretty pink pussy on display. The scent of her arousal crashed over Beck's senses. He itched to tap out of this interrogation and latch his mouth over her swollen cunt before he tongue-fucked her into oblivion.

Seth held the paddle tighter. "So, in addition to your other transgressions, you admit that you lied about your homework, too?"

"Yes, Sir. I-I'm sorry."

Beck knew what was coming, and he took a step back.

Sure enough, Seth landed the solid wood across her pale cheeks with a ruthless *whack*.

Heavenly gasped. Her tits slid across the desk with the force of his blow. Beck's cock surged.

A wide band of pink marred her flesh as a cry tore from Heavenly's throat, the sound deliciously rife with suffering. Then she arched and writhed, already beginning to pant.

"Breathe through it." Seth sailed his palm over her heated flesh. "Rise above the pain."

So Seth had a sadistic streak, too? *Hot damn.*

"Not much of a warm-up," he observed.

"Does she deserve one? Her behavior is unacceptable." Seth handed Beck the paddle.

"True. Her transgressions can't go unpunished," he agreed.

"I'm sorry," Heavenly whimpered, reaching back with both hands to cover her ass. "Really. I'll never do it again, Sirs. I promise."

Seth seized her wrists, dragged her arms over her head, and pinned them to the desk.

"Too late. You're at our mercy now, little girl." An evil grin tugged Beck's lips as he swung the paddle.

When he struck her ass, another high-pitched wail tore from her throat. A fresh strip of pink darkened her pale skin, sending a shudder of need up his spine.

Blood surging, Beck wrapped her braids around his fists and lifted Heavenly's head from the desk. Tears slid down her cheeks as she continued riding the pain.

"Have you learned your lesson yet?" He laved her cheek and drank in the crystal drops.

"Yes! I promise."

Seth scowled, every inch the stern headmaster dishing out corrective punishment. "I'm not convinced."

Beck offered him the paddle, but Cooper shook his head and released Heavenly's wrists. Then he smiled.

What did the cagey bastard have in mind?

"H-how can I convince you?" Heavenly sniffled, doing her best to sound contrite.

"Go to the chalkboard and write 'I will not lie' a hundred times."

Nodding miserably, Heavenly made her way to the blackboard. Beck tugged the big guy's sleeve and whispered, "What the hell? That's going to take forever and be boring as shit. Let's strip her down and get her between us."

"Patience. This is the part she likes best. Watch..."

While Cooper strolled up behind her, Beck eased onto the edge of the desk and watched. As Heavenly wrote the fifth sentence across the blackboard, Seth heaved a disapproving sigh. "You forgot to dot the letter I."

"Oops." Contrition skipped across her face before she rushed to correct her error.

She scrawled out two more sentences before Seth growled again. "Are you purposely trying my patience, Miss Young?"

"No, Sir. What did I—"

"You failed to cross the letter T."

"My apologies. I'll correct it and—"

"No." Seth shook his head. "You'll erase it and write it again."

She shot them a look so genuinely tearful, Beck almost believed her. But when she fidgeted, pressing her thighs together to quell her ache, he knew better.

"Go on. Or are you incapable of completing this exceedingly simple task?" Beck arched a disapproving brow.

"I can't concentrate. You both keep looking at me, and it makes me nervous. And when I get nervous, I..."

"You what?" Seth's eyes narrowed.

"I-I get...wet."

Beck's cock throbbed worse than a toothache.

Seth raised a disapproving brow. "Is that another lie?"

"No. I swear. I-I can't help it."

"I don't believe you. Raise your skirt. Show us."

Heavenly bit her bottom lip and lifted her hem, exposing her pussy again. Sure enough, she looked even juicier.

Shoving down his desperate hunger, Beck moved in. "Spread your legs and beg him to *feel* for himself."

The pulse point at her neck kicked up. Her breathing shallowed. His little girl was turning them inside out.

Seth darted him a furtive I-told-you-so smirk before settling a weighty stare on their "pupil."

"He's waiting." Beck knew he didn't sound patient.

She eased one foot a scant few inches from the other. "Please—"

"Wider," Beck demanded. "Enough for him to get his big hands between your quivering little-girl thighs."

Heavenly gasped as she widened her stance.

"Good girl." Beck nodded approvingly. "Principal Cooper will continue. I'll supervise."

Heavenly cast a nervous glance at Seth. "I'm not lying. Touch me, Sir. You'll see for yourself how wet I am."

"So pretty." Seth dragged his fingers through her saturated folds and over her clit. She bit her lip and quivered, her heavy lids sliding shut. And when he plunged his fingers inside her, she tossed her head back with a wail of pleasure.

"She's telling the truth, Principal Beckman. She's drenched. I think you should check, too." Seth withdrew his glistening fingers and licked them clean. "Just to be sure."

The scent of her arousal hung in the air, driving Beck out of his mind as he approached. With a moan, he petted her. When she whimpered, he speared her with two fingers.

"Yes…" Heavenly pushed back, grinding against his hand.

Beck laved his way up her neck. "She's not just drenched; she's gushing."

"She is," Seth agreed with a groan in his voice. "But we still have a problem with Miss Young's concentration."

"Help me. I-I can't focus when you touch me like this."

Beck loved the way her eyes begged.

"Do you want to disappoint us?" He massaged her G-spot as he dragged her back to the chalkboard, delighting in the way she frantically shook her head. "No? Then keep writing, little girl."

She gripped the chalk with shaking hands and closed her eyes with a moan.

Seth glowered. "Do I need to take the paddle to your pretty white backside again?"

"No, Sir."

"Resume your punishment. No mistakes this time, Miss Young," Seth warned as he began strumming her clit.

The squeaking of the chalk over the slate was nearly drowned out by Heavenly's broken and pitiful whimpers.

"Start writing. Faster," Beck commanded as he dragged his thumb through her juices, then slid it past her tiny rosette.

"Oh. Oh!" The chalk slipped from Heavenly's fingers and shattered.

He and Seth tore their hands from her and cast her reproachful glares.

She clutched Seth's shirt, even as her stare pleaded with Beck. "No. Don't stop!"

They both ignored her. Seth cupped her jaw. "Pick it up."

Heavenly blinked, her pupils beyond dilated. "Please…"

"He said… Pick. It. Up." Beck landed a sharp, stinging slap to her ass. "Now."

With a yelp, she bent at the waist, giving them a spectacular view of her reddened ass and so-swollen pussy.

Impatience clawed at Beck's composure. He needed inside her now.

Slowly, she gathered the bits of chalk, sniffling for effect. As she rose, her breasts spilled from her too-small blouse. One look at her berry-hard nipples…and Beck swallowed a groan.

"Oops." She folded her arms over her breasts, but she couldn't quite hide them. In fairness, she didn't try very hard.

Tsking, he shoved her arms to her sides and filled his palms with her warm, lush tits.

Somehow, Seth barely managed to slide his stoic mask back in place. "You just destroyed school property. That's forbidden."

"Please, Sir." She dropped to her knees, her beseeching stare begging as much as her voice. "Don't spank me again. It hurt. Is there another way I can pay for breaking the chalk? And atone for lying about my homework?"

Her gaze dropped to the erection straining behind Seth's zipper before skittering over his. Then she blinked up, all innocence.

There sure as fuck is, little girl. Beck reached for his fly.

Seth scowled down at her, every inch the exacting headmaster. "Why should we let you atone by sucking our cocks?"

"I'll do my best to make you both feel good, Sirs."

"I don't know if your best will be good enough. Have you ever actually sucked a big, hard cock, Miss Young? Licked it with your tongue and swallowed it down?" Seth dragged the pad of his thumb across her bottom lip. "Let a man come down your throat?"

"No, but I'm a quick learner, and I saw them do it in that movie. See?" Heavenly sucked Seth's digit into her mouth and swirled it with her wet pink tongue.

A rough groan tore from his lips as a visible shudder rolled through him.

Beck's patience snapped.

Game fucking over.

He yanked down his zipper, hissing as his cock burst free—bouncing, weeping, and throbbing. "I'll accept your apology, little girl. But not with your words."

Slowly, she released Seth's thumb with an audible pop, then peeked up at him from beneath her thick lashes. "Yes, Sir." She tipped her gaze back to Seth. "Was I doing it right, Principal Cooper?"

"Not exactly. You need to apply yourself. Principal Beckman will instruct you. Be a good angel and listen."

"I will, Sir." She batted her lashes. "I'll do my very best."

"You better. Your actions have placed us in a very *hard* situation, Miss Young," Seth lectured. "If not? Well…our discipline will have to be far stricter until you learn to obey."

"Open your mouth and stick out your tongue," Beck breathed, stroking his cock.

She did, then she lavishly laved his crest.

As he bit back a groan, Seth grabbed her braids and tugged. "You sure you've never sucked cock before?"

"Never."

God, she'd never looked so fucking innocent—even when she had been a virgin. It bent Beck's brain and sent his primal urges soaring.

A dark, dangerous chuckle rolled off Seth's lips. "You better be telling the truth. Principal Beckman will administer your *first* lie detector test, and if we think you've been less than honest…"

The threat hung in the air as Seth stepped back. Beck surged closer and wrapped his hand around her nape. "Stop talking and stick out your goddamn tongue."

"Yes, Principal Beckman." She sounded breathy and deliciously penitent. "I'm sorry."

"If you want to convince us you're sorry, you'll have to take all of it, little girl," Beck bit out in a raw, raspy voice.

"Of course, Sir."

Slowly, seemingly reluctantly, she complied. He slid his angry purple crest across her lips, then shoved deep, filling her hot, silken mouth.

His heart sputtered. His cock roared.

Enveloped in her soft, slippery heat, he pressed all the way to the back of her throat with a groan that bounced off the walls. Opening wider and panting through her nose, she sucked him deep, bathing his cock with strong pulls, punctuated by her fluttering tongue.

"Yes," Seth ground out, his voice low and filthy as he yanked down his zipper and wrapped his fingers around his stiff length. "That's it, Miss Young. Worship his cock. Show us just how sorry you are."

Her answering whimper sent shock waves up Beck's shaft. His eyes rolled to the back of his head as a feral growl ripped from his chest. She was killing him.

Fingers clamping on her tighter, he fucked her mouth, savoring each blistering inch he shoved himself across her velvety tongue.

He increased his tempo, watching her lips stretch as he thrust in and out of her tight little mouth.

"It appears she really *is* a fast learner," Seth murmured thickly. "So she didn't lie about that?"

Too strung out to speak, Beck just grunted, his stare never leaving their sweet little girl and her obscenely parted lips.

Her familiar feminine musk—already branded in his psyche—seared his lungs. Her muffled whimpers called to the beast caged inside him. He plunged onto her tongue faster. Harder, shuttling in and out of her puffy mouth, then slamming to the back of her throat like a wild animal.

Seth crouched beside her, settling his lips at her ear and slid a hand between her legs. "You look so pretty on your knees with a mouthful of cock. I think you're enjoying this. Aren't you, Miss Young?"

Heavenly quivered and cried out. The sound reverberated down Beck's cock before ricocheting through him, threatening to splinter his restraint. Teeth gritted, he tightened his hold on her jaw and held her in place, now savagely fucking her mouth.

"She must be very nervous. She's even wetter, now spilling into my palm," Seth taunted, slowly rubbing her clit. "Yes… Keep sucking his big cock like a good girl."

Jesus, between Seth's lewd words and the sinful pull of Heavenly's mouth, Beck was about to slam headfirst into ecstasy. No chance of finding the brakes. And as much as he would love to explode down her throat, there was nothing like their girl's pussy. And there was an outside chance that her fertility window was still open…

With a feral roar, Beck tore from Heavenly's mouth, panting as Seth's fingers dragged from her an anguished chorus of whines and whimpers. "Time for her second test."

"She proved she's a fast learner. Your assessment, Principal Beckman?"

"A-plus."

"Excellent." Seth flashed a dirty grin as she frantically ground her pussy against his seeking fingers.

Cock still hard as steel and throbbing like a bitch, Beck fisted himself and watched. The sight of her heavy, half-lidded eyes, swollen lips, and straining thighs stole his breath. Her broken sounds became desperate cries.

"She's too close," he warned.

Seth pulled free of her cunt, licking his juice-soaked fingers.

"No. Please!" Heavenly wailed, trying to press her thighs together to relieve her ache. "Don't leave me like this."

"But you look so beautifully helpless."

"Just imagine how beautifully desperate she'd be if we edged her all night," Beck added with a sadistic smile.

"No, please...no," she begged, grabbing at their shirts. "Don't. I... hurt. I *need*."

"You haven't learned yet who's in charge, Miss Young." Seth tsked.

"Indeed." Beck nodded to the black leather-padded cuffs and the four long chains fastened to each leg of the desk. "Let's remedy that."

"Right now." Seth gripped her waist and hauled her to her feet. "Time for her next evaluation."

Chapter Seven

Together, they stripped off the last of her costume and lifted her sideways across the flat surface. Her splayed thighs and pigtails dangled off each edge. Then Seth rounded the desk, pausing at her head to secure her wrists while Beck positioned her feet flat against the wood and cuffed her ankles.

"I-I know you're in charge, Sirs." She sent them an almost-convincing expression of panic.

"We'll make sure you don't forget," Beck growled.

"You're at our mercy, Miss Young." Seth placed a finger under her chin and tilted her head over the edge of the desk. "There. Now you're in the perfect position." He dragged his crest over her rosy lips. "Be a good little angel and suck my cock."

Instantly, she obeyed. Seth cupped her cheek with an anguished groan as he pressed his thick crest onto her tongue.

Ignoring his own screaming cock, Beck plopped down in the teacher's chair, rolled between her legs before he clutched her hips, then dragged her ass to the edge of the desk. He stared at her swollen cunt, hunger twisting his gut.

"Where are your manners, little girl? You're leaving a puddle on the desk."

"Ruining school property again?" Seth admonished in a tight voice while he worked himself down her throat and tormented her engorged nipples.

"She's so naughty. I'll take care of that." Beck grinned.

Parting her slick folds with his thumbs, he leaned in and latched his entire mouth over her succulent pink cunt. Sucking, spearing, laving, and lapping like a starving man, his taste buds exploded as her flavor slid over his tongue. Bucking wildly beneath his ravenous onslaught, Heavenly's muffled shrieks filled the room.

A primal roar tore from Seth's chest as he thrust deeper into her mouth. The sounds of her gasping and slurping nearly unraveled Beck.

"Take every fucking inch of me," Seth snarled, driving past her lips, balls deep.

Beck plunged two fingers into her silky cunt and sucked her stony clit between his teeth, earning him a frantic shriek from Heavenly. She thrashed and writhed, helplessly tugging against her restraints. Her futile struggle made his perverted heart stutter and his cock ache.

Fuck. He was dying to get inside her and spill against her unprotected womb.

"I can't wait." Beck jumped to his feet and kicked away the chair.

"Be quick, I'm getting too close."

"We all are." Beck gripped her lush hips and aligned his crest against her saturated slit. "You ready to take my cock, little girl?"

With a muffled moan, she arched her hips, twisting and spreading her legs wider, wordlessly begging him. No way was he turning that down.

Heart thundering in his ears, he cinched her hips even tighter. Tomorrow, he'd surely see pretty bruises on her soft, pale skin. Fuck, if that didn't turn him on more.

Then with a single guttural roar, he drove into her tight pussy in one savage thrust.

Below him, Heavenly's eyes flashed wide. Her spine twisted, tugging against the cuffs, this time accompanied by an ear-piercing wail of need. He stroked her clit, ramping her up higher. Her silky walls fluttered, clutching and clamping on him while Seth bit out a sibilant curse, sweating and ruddy and trying like hell to hold on.

Beck's sadistic side swelled, but he wasn't merely excited about making her suffer. He loved that they were drowning her in bliss.

He and Seth established a familiar rhythm. Beck drilled her with harsh, grinding strokes, shoving her body forward, forcing Seth's cock deeper down her throat with each thrust.

He picked up the pace, relishing in her ragged breaths, her flushing cheeks, and the pleasure playing across her face.

"I warned you that your actions put us in a very *hard* situation," Seth managed to bite out.

"Fuck, yes." Beck drove even deeper into her slick, swollen pussy. "Is this *hard* enough for you, little girl? Have you learned your lesson?"

She answered with a pitiful wail, tears rolling from the corners of her eyes.

Seth wrapped his fists in her braids. "You keep screaming around my cock like that, and I'm going to come all down your pretty little throat."

"Wouldn't you rather breed her?" Beck gasped out, despite the barreling semi of his orgasm coming straight at him.

As if he'd flipped a switch, Seth clenched his jaw. His green eyes darkened and narrowed. The air between them turned electric, crackling with a tension Beck had never felt. Desire thickened. Need dripped. Reckless determination twisted Cooper's face.

Seth pulled from her throat with an inhuman growl, stroking his angry cock as he shouldered his way beside Beck, watching him plunder her gripping, grasping pussy. "Yes. Finish so I can. Hurry."

A distant voice told Beck he should psychoanalyze the shit out of Seth's frenzied behavior. But later. Because all he could concentrate on now was the mounting friction of Heavenly's sweltering cunt. The pressure built, strong, surging, urgent.

"Come hard, little girl. Scream and shatter!" he commanded, rubbing her stiff clit.

"All over his cock. Do it!" Seth barked, still stroking himself and watching with feverish eyes.

Heavenly stiffened and held her breath, her skin going from rosy to red as she bore down on every inch he'd shoved inside her with clutching, quaking contractions. That was Beck's cue.

He stilled, panting, his lungs working hard. But it wasn't enough. His head swam dizzily. His heart chugged like a runaway train. Lava seared his veins. Holy shit, this was going to kill him—and he wanted it so fucking bad.

Beck clenched his jaw as the shattering orgasm hit. He bared his teeth and fucked her like a madman. Sweat dripped. His heart drummed in his ears. He was on fire, gripping her hips so tight, his fingers went numb. But the rest of him… Gone. Disintegrated. Dust. The wave of pleasure didn't merely roll over him; it pulled him under, taking out his knees—along with his sanity. He fucking drowned in her, spilling all his seed and his soul, leaving them inside her.

Fuck, he'd never love any woman the way he did Heavenly.

She was still panting and quivering when Seth began strumming her clit again. "You're not done yet. You need to come for *me*."

"Yes…" she gasped out.

Struggling to breathe, Beck grudgingly eased from her clamping cunt and stepped aside for Seth. "Flood her, man."

"Fuck, yeah," he groaned raggedly as he slammed deep in one ruthless thrust. "Goddamn… She's so hot. Tight. Wet. I'm not going to last."

After the blowjob he'd gotten while he'd watched Heavenly get fucked? "No need. She's there."

Grunting and sweating, Seth seemingly focused every fiber of his being on hammering her sweet cunt like his life depended on planting his seed in her womb. His face transformed as he drove into Heavenly over and over. His desperate hunger wasn't merely lust; it was the same breeding fever that had consumed them last night.

Whatever reservations Seth had previously harbored about attempting fatherhood again? Those seemed to have burned away. The man fucking their girl wasn't holding anything back. And if Seth still had hidden reservations? Well, Beck had no trouble ruthlessly using Seth's perversions to his and Heavenly's advantage. In the end, when they were holding their child, they'd all benefit.

Beck rounded the desk and stared at their beautiful girl, her pretty blue eyes glassy and unfocused. Her lips looked red and well-used. Her swollen nipples pouted, hard and straining, as her chest heaved with each audible breath. She was still riding the high, bucking and keening for that next pinnacle. He helped her along, pinching her distended tips, rolling them between his fingers and thumbs. Then he leaned closer, whispering against her ear.

"You ready to take his seed, little girl? To splinter into a million pieces while he floods your hot cunt?"

"Yes!" she wailed as she thrashed wildly. "Oh, god. Please…"

"Hear her? She's begging you, man," Beck taunted, peering across the desk at Seth. "She's ready. She wants it. Give it to her."

"Fuck!" Cooper let out a strangled moan. His rhythm faltered, but he quickly recovered and sucked in a deep breath. "Now. Come, angel!"

Goose bumps broke out all over Beck's body as he watched them shatter together in a deafening, body-quaking crescendo of cries. He had no clue if either of them would be lucky enough to impregnate her, but he fucking hoped so.

Breaths sawing, Seth slumped forward, covering Heavenly's body and lowering his face to her neck. As he whispered soft endearments to her, Beck released the cuffs.

"Let's move to the bed and put her between us," Beck suggested. Their girl had earned plenty of aftercare.

"Yeah," Seth managed to get out before he slipped free and zipped his pants. Then he lifted her boneless body against him and carried her across the room, gently placing her in the middle of the mattress. Quickly, they both stripped and climbed in beside her, hugging her close.

"We've got you, angel," Seth cooed. "You okay?"

She lifted heavy lids. "That was…amazing."

Brushing away errant strands of damp hair that had escaped her braids, Beck murmured, "Rest. We'll head home soon."

"Mmm, 'kay." Her eyes slid shut again.

Beck smiled and pressed his lips to her forehead. Seth followed suit with a kiss to her nose.

Together, they lavished Heavenly in aftercare—tender kisses, languid caresses, and soft whispers. She curled between them, warm and sweet, trusting and accepting. Happy.

Beck began drifting off when the alarm on his watch dinged. He silenced it with a sigh.

Seth jolted awake. "Time's up?"

"Yeah." Beck gently extricated himself from their tangle of arms and legs.

Seth did the same, and they dressed quickly before Beck retrieved Heavenly's gown from the school desk.

"Angel?" Seth stroked her cheek. "Time to go home." When she didn't budge or even whimper, he chuckled. "I'm no doctor, but I think she's in a coma."

Beck beamed with pride. "Looks like we'll need to dress her and carry her out."

"On it." Seth lifted her, supporting her body while Beck slid the filmy gown over her head.

Once she was covered, the PI dragged the key to the locker from his pocket. Beck took it and extracted his map. While Seth gathered her sleeping form into his arms, Beck scrounged a red crayon in one of the cubbies and circled the schoolhouse before he grabbed the night-vision goggles and held the door.

"We need to do this again," Seth announced as he carried their girl out to the dark, starry night and trekked their way to the front of the compound.

"Hell, yes."

Once they approached the front of the compound, Beck pulled open the wooden gate. Inside the office, Seth shielded Heavenly's breasts with his arm. Beck darted into the locker room, fished out the key, and retrieved the duffel.

Behind the counter, the bearded man looked up, arched a brow, and grinned. "Looks like you three had a good time."

"Better than good," Beck agreed. "Hell of a place you've got here."

"We keep busy. You boys impress me. The two of you accomplished what it took ten men to manage last night."

"We're over-achievers," Seth quipped, looking mighty pleased.

As Beck placed the marked map and their goggles on the counter, a group of seven men strolled through the door, surrounding a lone woman whose eyes looked fever-bright with excitement. She took one look at Heavenly sleeping peacefully against Seth's chest, and she smiled. "I want what she had."

As the growls around her promised all that and more, Beck pushed out to the parking lot and opened the back door for Seth before settling into the driver's seat of the SUV. Cooper slipped in beside Heavenly, then pulled her onto his lap. She slept on. In the rearview mirror, Beck watched Seth stroke her hair with reverent fingers, the gesture so tender it made his chest tight.

This was what their future looked like. The three of them, sated and content, bound together for good. The diamond glittered on her finger even in the near dark, and the thought that she might already be carrying their child filled him with fierce satisfaction.

As they pulled onto the main road, Seth's phone buzzed once. Then again. Beck caught Cooper's grimace as he silenced it with a curse.

"A case?" Beck asked quietly.

Seth's jaw tightened. "My brother, Matt. He just ran into the twins at a bar...with the girl they've been fucking. He wants to know if he should tell Mom. I'll deal with it later."

Beck nodded, but unease crept in. In thirty-six hours, Seth would be three thousand miles away, talking Jack and Connor out of the same lifestyle the three of them had just celebrated. And despite Seth's promises, the engagement ring, their shared plans... Beck couldn't forget that, mere days ago, Seth had almost walked away.

He won't leave this time, Beck told himself firmly. *Not after we've come this far.*

But as Heavenly stirred and unconsciously pressed closer to Seth, Beck gripped the steering wheel tighter, dreading the big guy's departure.

"Ladies and gentlemen, please ensure your seat belts are fastened. We've begun our descent into LaGuardia and will be arriving shortly," a flight attendant announced over the plane's intercom.

Seth stared out the window, his stomach churning with more than the turbulence.

After Beck and Heavenly had given him the ultimatum, he'd spent most of Sunday and Monday taking her bareback every chance he got. That damn breeding kink he hadn't know he possessed was both shocking and inconvenient.

What if she's already conceived? The possibility made his chest tight. He wanted that...even as it scared the hell out of him. Last month, he hadn't been able to hold Raine's newborn twins without breaking into a cold sweat. Was he really ready for his fiancée to have a baby come summer?

Interminable minutes later, the plane touched down with a jolt.

Seth ignored the knot in his stomach and grabbed his carry-on from the overhead compartment. He had four days to begin laying the groundwork for his mother to accept his relationship with Beck and Heavenly. If Grace thought Jack and Connor sharing a woman was deviant… Christ, her reaction to learning that her eldest son wasn't just having a three-way-fling, but working with another man to marry and impregnate Heavenly—not necessarily in that order—would be apocalyptic.

Somehow, he had to bring her around. That was his uppermost thought as he made his way through the terminal, toward baggage claim. He spotted his mother before she saw him.

Grace Cooper looked every one of her fifty-four years today, standing with a tissue pressed to her red-rimmed eyes. Her usually pristine appearance was disheveled. She'd pulled her cool blond hair—the same shade he'd inherited—back in a severe twist, rather than wearing it loose and curled, as she had been recently.

"Mom." He approached, dropping his bag to pull her into a hug.

She clung to him, her shoulders shaking. "I'm so glad you're here. I don't know what I would have done if you hadn't been able to come."

"I'll always be here when you need me. But since it was such short notice, I can only stay until Saturday."

"I understand, and I know you dropped everything to help me. I appreciate it more than you know." Grace pulled back, dabbing at her eyes with the tissue. "I just don't know what to do with those boys anymore."

Guilt plunged into his chest like a knife. Could his promise to reason with the twins be any more hypocritical?

"Have you talked to them since…?" Seth probed as they walked toward the exit.

"Talked, no. I screamed. And I made damn sure they put on their clothes and got that girl—apparently, her name is Gia—out of my house."

Four-letter words almost never crossed Grace's lips. Her swearing now was a testament to her upset. "Then what?"

"I tucked Carl into bed with cold medicine, then I lit into those boys. They said they met her at NYU and that she's 'sweet', but…"

Grace's voice dropped to a mortified whisper. "I have another name for the kind of girl willing to go to bed with two men at once."

And it wasn't flattering. Seth tried not to wince.

If he was going to start changing Grace's mind to help the twins and facilitate his own future, he had to figure out how to approach this situation. He had an idea...but first he needed to talk to his brothers and understand exactly what was going on.

"Do the twins know I'm coming?"

She sniffed. "And give them a chance to hide? Of course not."

Once upon a time, Jack and Connor would totally have gone underground to avoid him. Now...he'd bet they didn't have a lick of fear. All they had to do was threaten to rat him out to Mom. Mutually assured destruction, goddamn it.

Finally, they reached Grace's pristine white SUV, sitting under the afternoon sun. Once they were both buckled in, she turned to him. "So, I've been thinking..."

Never a good thing... "What's that?"

"Well, since Heavenly couldn't come with you, maybe we can Face-Time with her this week? I'm dying to finally meet the woman who captured my son's heart." Grace's smile was the first genuine one he'd seen since he arrived. "Carl has been teasing me about interrogating her, but I'll behave. I promise."

Fuck. The last thing he needed was his mother cornering Heavenly via video chat and asking pointed questions he hadn't coached her how to answer. And if she happened to be wearing the engagement ring Seth hadn't confessed yet to slipping on her finger...

Yeah, he had to avoid that until he was ready to come clean.

"Honestly, her schedule is really crazy right now—clinical rotations, studying for boards, working at the hospital. She barely has time to sleep." *And she's probably still walking funny after our evening at The Wild Stalk.* "Besides, she's a little shy, especially at first. But I know you. You're so welcoming, and once you meet her, you'll bring her out of her shell." The lies were coming easier now, which only made him feel worse. "But I swear you'll love her. She's warm, funny, and incredibly sweet."

Crap. The same word the twins had used to describe Gia. Freudian slip?

Grace's expression fell. "Oh. I was really hoping… But I suppose I can wait until the wedding."

Seth's stomach clenched as he pictured trying to navigate that minefield. How was he supposed to sit beside Heavenly while Beck was seated in another pew and at another table, pretending to be nothing more than a friend who happened to be in town for a few days? How would the surgeon manage to keep his hands—or his stare—off Heavenly? Asking him to felt unfair. And he already knew it pissed Beck off.

"Speaking of the wedding," he said, desperate to steer the conversation toward safer territory, "how are the plans coming along?"

Grace's demeanor brightened. "Wonderfully! Father Heasley will marry us in the Church."

Of course. The one place where he couldn't marry Heavenly since Beck would be beside him. The Church would never recognize their union. Would his mother?

"Where's the reception?"

"A garden pavilion overlooking the Hudson. It's perfect. The event will be fairly intimate, just immediate family and close friends. About forty people total."

"I'm so happy for you. You love him?"

"So much." Her smile turned wistful. "I never dated because I never met anyone who made me feel the way your father did…until Carl. Now, I can't imagine life without him. His kids are thrilled he's happy again, years after losing his wife to breast cancer. I haven't met them yet, but they're both coming to the wedding. His son is a couple of years younger than you. He's currently living in Tokyo. His daughter was an oops baby. She just turned nineteen, and she's going to Notre Dame."

So she was a good Catholic girl. Figured...

"And while you're here, I was hoping you could get fitted for your tux. I know your general sizes, but I want everything to be perfect. You're still planning to walk me down the aisle, aren't you?"

"Of course. I wouldn't miss it for the world."

"Thank you." She squeezed his hand and sent him another misty smile. "I need to finalize seating arrangements. I'm putting Heavenly beside you."

"Perfect." Seth's belly clenched with nerves, but his mom had given him the perfect opening. "Do you have room for one more? My friend Beck will be in the city that week on business. Rather than leaving him alone in his hotel room, I'd hoped you wouldn't mind if I invited him. I'd love to introduce him to everyone."

She frowned. "Hammer's friend? Wasn't he pursuing Heavenly, too?"

Shit. He'd forgotten he'd told his mother about Beck when they'd been fighting over their girl. "It was a misunderstanding. We're good now. In fact, he's one of my best friends."

"Then of course he's invited. Would you like him to sit with you and Heavenly?"

"That would be great." Seth couldn't miss the irony. His mother wanted to honor Beck by seating him with family, not realizing that he actually *was* family in every way that mattered. "I appreciate it. When he said he was scheduled to speak at a medical conference in the city the same week as your wedding, inviting him just made sense."

"Oh, he's a doctor?"

"Yeah. A vascular surgeon. Pretty renowned."

"Is he single?" Grace perked up even more. "If he is...Mary Hagaman's daughter, Celeste, isn't married."

That didn't surprise Seth. Celeste had always been bat-shit crazy. And his mom trying to hook up his future co-husband to Heavenly with another woman was priceless.

"Mom, they live on opposite coasts. And Beck is far too busy for a serious relationship."

"You never know..."

"Actually, I do. We've talked. He's not looking."

"Well, Heavenly is all yours. That's what's important." His mother beamed. "So...any plans to make her more than your girlfriend? Do I hear wedding bells in your future?"

Seth's chest tightened. He had to be careful. "Proposing to her has crossed my mind."

Grace's eyes widened, then filled with happy tears. "Really? You're ready to get married again?"

"Maybe." What else could he say since Heavenly was already wearing an engagement ring? He fucking hated having to lie to his mother, but it was temporary. "She's everything I never thought I'd find. She's nothing like Autumn."

That would be a relief to his mother, who had never truly liked his wife.

"Does Heavenly know?" Grace asked, her voice gentle but pointed. "About your first wife. About Tristan?"

"Yeah. Since April. It was a lot for her to process at first. But she knows how much losing them affected me. She's very supportive and understanding."

"That tells me everything I need to know about her. If she can handle your past with such compassion, she must be very special."

"She is." Seth's voice was thick with emotion—and guilt. Time to change the subject. "So…are Jack and Connor back at their apartment near campus?"

"I assume so. I threatened to stop paying their tuition if they don't focus on school and curb their…behavior." Grace's grip tightened on the steering wheel. "I only have so many ways to influence them these days. I mean, they're twenty-one. But I still pay their bills, and I can make their lives more difficult if they don't walk the straight and narrow."

Seth tested the waters carefully. "But…what if they really care about this girl? What if she cares about them both?"

"Care?" Grace's voice pitched higher. "That's not care. That's perversion. And it doesn't justify breaking God's laws, Seth. It's supposed to be one man, one woman, joined in holy matrimony. If they keep thumbing their noses at that, I'll have no choice but to disown them."

The words hit Seth like a physical blow. *Disown*? His mother—who'd cried for weeks when he'd moved to California, who still sent care packages and called frequently—was willing to cut her youngest sons out of her life?

Seth's mouth went dry. If his mother couldn't even entertain the possibility that love might take different forms without threatening to rip apart their family, how the hell was he supposed to find an approach that would save his own relationship with her?

They pulled into the driveway of his childhood home, the familiar two-story colonial looking exactly the same. For a moment, he was thirty-two going on seventeen.

"But hopefully, it won't come to that," Grace said, turning off the engine. "Those boys will listen to you. They always have."

Not anymore. But she didn't know that. He wasn't changing his life to please his mother, and he could hardly coerce or browbeat the twins into doing the same.

"Like you pointed out, they aren't kids anymore. I'm not sure how much they'll listen to me."

"Just do your best. That's all I can ask."

As they gathered his bag and headed toward the front door, Seth couldn't shake the feeling that he was walking into a trap of his own making.

He had four days to begin changing his mother's mind about non-traditional relationships, while hiding the fact that he was living the life she found so abhorrent. Four days to figure out how to bridge the gap between the family he'd grown up in and the future he'd chosen. Four days to figure out how not to lose his mother's approval, despite the love he shared with Beck and Heavenly.

If he failed, would she disown him, too?

As Grace unlocked the front door, her fingers still trembling with emotion, that worry nearly knocked Seth off his feet. He'd already lost his father and his first family. Could he survive losing the rest?

Chapter Eight

A breeze blew through the September morning as Seth stood beside his mother in Lower Manhattan, at the edge of South Pool, listening to the names being read aloud in the hushed reverence that always marked this somber anniversary. Years had passed since the fall of the Twin Towers, but the weight of that morning still pressed against his chest like a stone.

Grace dabbed at her eyes with a tissue as the ceremony continued. Around them, families clutched photos and flowers, their grief raw, despite the passage of time. Seth found himself scanning the names etched in bronze around the memorial's perimeter, recognizing far too many brothers in blue. Heroes who'd run toward the danger when everyone else had run away.

He watched a young woman trace her finger over a name and murmur, "I miss you, Daddy."

Seth clenched his jaw. *Life is too fucking short to waste on fear.*

His recent idiocy smacked him in the face. Here he was, surrounded by reminders that this precious life could change in the blink of an eye…while he'd spent too many days terrified of the very future he wanted most.

When the ceremony concluded, a somber hush fell over the crowd at the memorial. He and his mother began walking toward the street, neither speaking. If he remembered some of the fallen officers and firefighters from his childhood, Grace had known many of them personally through his father. That day had been not only an attack on the country, but a deep scar gouged into New York. It still showed in his mother's withdrawn expression and the trembling of her pale hands.

He wrapped an arm around her shoulders in silent comfort and guided her toward the car. Halfway there, a familiar voice called out.

"Seth?"

He turned to find Tony Marconi approaching. His former beat

partner looked a bit older now at thirty-one, but he still carried himself with that unmistakable cop swagger from their patrol days.

"Tony. Good to see you, man." Seth held out his hand.

His former partner shook it. "Likewise." Then he turned to Grace. "Hi, Mrs. Cooper."

At Tony's respectful nod, she smiled. "Nice to see you, Tony. You two catch up. I'll wait in the car."

"I won't be long," Seth promised.

Once his mom disappeared, Tony relaxed. "I didn't know you were here. I heard through the grapevine that you'd moved to California."

"I did. Los Angeles. Just here for a few days."

"SoCal, huh? I can't picture you there. You were always a New Yorker, through and through. But I gotta admit, that tan looks good on you. You like the West Coast?"

"Mostly. It's an acquired taste. Weather's great. Traffic sucks." Seth shrugged. "It's definitely different. But I've got some good friends out there. And…a girl."

"Yeah?" Tony clapped him on the shoulder. "Good for you. Is it serious?"

"She's the reason I moved out there." He and Tony had been tight once. Back in the day, he might have said more about Heavenly, maybe even fessed up about sharing her with Beck. But now? Tony still knew some of the same people his mom talked to. He couldn't risk that information getting back to Grace.

"Wow, good for you, man." Tony smiled.

His former partner hadn't liked Autumn much. He'd called her whiny and clingy. At the time, Seth had been pissed off. He and Tony had exchanged words. In retrospect, his friend had been right.

"You still in the PI business?" Tony asked. "I know your brother Matt took over here."

"Yeah. I put out my shingle in Cali. You still at the Two-Four?" He scanned Tony's passable off-the-rack suit. "Looks like you made detective."

Tony's expression darkened. "Yeah, but the precinct isn't what it used to be. Politics and bullshit. Trust me, be glad you got out when you did."

Seth had sensed the tone shift at the precinct even before he'd left. "You still single?"

"Not for long. I met a girl online. Crazy, right? Her name is Megan, and we're getting married in March."

"Congratulations! That's fantastic." Seth glanced at his watch. "Hey… I hate to run. I've got an appointment in Yonkers, so I've got to get going." Not that he was looking forward to getting fitted for a tux with his mother's fiancé, whom he barely knew. "But it was great seeing you, man."

"If you've got time later, I'd love to grab a beer. Maybe hear more about how you made the successful switch from homicide detective to PI?"

Because Tony was thinking about doing the same?

"Maybe next time? I'm only in town for a few days, but I'm back next month. It would be great to shoot the shit." Seth wanted to hear more about the change in the precinct, especially if it was making Tony re-think his direction in life.

"You got it. Take care of yourself out in La-La Land." He clapped Seth's shoulder.

After they parted ways, Seth headed for Grace's car and found his mom waiting patiently. He couldn't help but feel a pang of nostalgia for the old days, mixed with relief that he'd left when he had. Some chapters in life were meant to close.

The drive home was quiet after the somber ceremony. It wasn't until they were sitting in traffic that Grace spoke again.

"Do you ever miss police work?"

"Sometimes. But not enough to re-join the force."

"California really is your home now, isn't it?"

"Yeah." Because that's where Heavenly and Beck were.

After dropping Grace off at the house, Seth arrived at the formal wear shop to find Carl Mahoney waiting. He was a bear of a man with reddish-brown hair and a matching beard tinged with gray, weathered hands that spoke of years in construction, and gentle eyes.

The tailor bustled around them with measuring tape and pins. In the awkward silence, Seth found himself searching for something to say.

"So, Mom says you're in construction," Seth offered. "What kind?"

"Commercial mostly. Office buildings, a few residential developments. Been doing it for thirty years." Carl shifted as the tailor adjusted his collar. "Grace tells me you're doing well with your PI business out in California."

"Can't complain. It's steady work, even if the hours sometimes suck, and I get tired of cheating spouses."

"I'm sure."

Their conversation lagged again until Carl cleared his throat. "You know…your mother misses you. Talks about you all the time. She's so proud of how you held the family together after your father passed. That couldn't have been easy. You were still a kid."

Seth felt his throat tighten. "Someone had to step up, and I was the oldest."

"She says you made sure your brothers stayed in line, that the yard work got done, and that the house didn't fall apart around her. That's not something many teenagers could manage. You were basically a father to the other boys when you were still growing up yourself." Then Carl's smile turned wry. "And Jack and Connor's romantic life aside, they turned out just fine."

Seth grimaced. "They're good men. They just…need to grow up."

"I'm sure you worry about your mom, especially after the way you and I met." Carl winced, clearly still embarrassed that Seth's first introduction had been when he'd walked in on Carl fucking her on the kitchen table. "Our relationship may have seemed sudden to you, but she waited a long time to open her heart again after losing your father…"

"A very long time."

"I understand. I lost my wife to breast cancer eight years ago. I thought I was done with love."

"But it wasn't done with you." Seth understood. When he'd lost Autumn at twenty-four, he hadn't planned on ever getting involved, much less married, again. But he was living proof that things changed.

"No. I resisted my attraction to your mother for weeks, but the more I tried…the more I fell for her. She made me re-think everything. She's a good woman."

"The best. And if she finally said yes to you after all these years, she must be sure."

"How do you feel about that? Danny, Matt, and the twins have all accepted us, but…in hindsight, I should have asked for your blessing before I proposed to your mother."

Seth softened. "Mom has always been her own woman. If you make her happy, that's all I need. I'm actually glad she won't be spending the rest of her life alone. She belongs with someone who knows how special she is."

"She is, and I don't know how I got so lucky. I can't wait for her to meet my kids."

"You've got two, right? Mom said your son lives in Japan and your daughter is going to Notre Dame."

Carl nodded as the tailor pinned his sleeve. "My son Blake is thirty. He works construction management in Tokyo. My daughter Catherine —she prefers Cat—just turned nineteen. She's a sophomore."

Seth raised an eyebrow. "She must be smart."

"Too smart. She gets that from her mother. Cat is pre-med. Wants to be a pediatric surgeon. Anyway, they'll both be flying in for the wedding. Blake is excited to have brothers. And after my wife passed, our house was awfully quiet, so Cat is looking forward to having big holiday celebrations again."

That tracked, but Seth had other things on his mind. If he had to spend "quality time" with his mother's fiancé, maybe he should make the most of it and gather some intel.

"Can I ask you something?"

"Sure." Carl stiffened. It was subtle, but impossible not to notice.

"When Mom asked me to fly out here and talk to Jack and Connor about their behavior, she was hysterical. She seems calmer now, but she's threatening to cut those idiots out of her life. I'm trying to keep the family together." Seth watched Carl's face carefully. "You were there. What's your take on this mess?"

"You know Grace's upbringing. Her faith. She sees the world through a very specific lens, so she was shocked."

"I know. But how do *you* see it?"

Carl hesitated, glancing around to make sure the tailor was out of earshot. "I'm...more of a lapsed Catholic. Honestly? I've experienced enough to accept that happiness doesn't always look the way we expect."

True that. If it did, Seth wouldn't be sharing Heavenly with Beck. But now he didn't want his future any other way.

"Look, that girl between Jack and Connor might have been screaming, but..." A sly grin flirted at Carl's mouth. "She definitely wasn't protesting."

His answer gave Seth a spark of hope. "So...you don't have a moral problem with it?"

"Not my place. I know Grace never pictured the twins sharing a woman, but they're grown men—well, mostly—and Gia is an adult. If that's what they want, who are they really hurting?"

"No one," he agreed. "I'll talk to them about being more circumspect...but I won't have the family torn apart over this."

"I doubt Grace actually wants that." Carl paused. "Jack and Connor aren't my boys, so I've stayed out of it. If they're just having fun...who can blame them? But I don't think they're mature enough for a relationship that complicated."

Seth had to chuckle. "Oh, after the summer they just spent with me, I *know* they're not."

"I understand your mom's concerns. If it was one of my kids, I'd be worried, too. But she can't tell Jack and Connor how to live their lives anymore. She's just not ready to accept that."

"That's where my head is, too." Even more than Carl could possibly know.

"Would it help if I talked to Grace? Gently, of course."

"Would you?" Seth felt a surge of optimism. "She might listen to you."

"Sure. Her happiness is my first priority. But she's going to have to soften her attitude and accept that the twins seemingly have a... different approach to romance. If she severs the family, she'll regret it."

"We all will." He clapped Carl on the back. "I appreciate your help."

Seth had never expected his mom's fiancé to become an ally, but he just might be the only person who could bridge the gap between his mother's beliefs and her sons' desires.

"Of course. Your mom has a good heart. She just needs help seeing that 'normal' isn't the only way to be happy."

"Exactly."

The rest of the fitting passed with companionable small talk, and Seth decided he liked Carl. The man would fit well in their family.

After he waved goodbye to his future stepfather, he climbed into Grace's SUV and headed back to her house. Along the way, he pulled out his phone and dialed the office.

"Cooper Investigations West, this is River. If you're dying, hang up and call 911."

Seth laughed. "Charming phone manner as always, Kendall."

"Thank fuck you called. I've been busier than a one-armed paper-hanger trying to juggle everything."

"I've been gone twenty-four hours. What the hell happened?"

"The computer backup system exploded, two potential clients called to hire us right this instant, and I'm pretty sure something died in the break room refrigerator. Other than that, I'm peachy."

"Sounds like it. How's everything else?"

Raine's brother sighed bitterly. "Oh, fantastic. Dean dumped all my shit on the porch last night and changed the locks while I was out on surveillance. Apparently, his new roommate is some law enforcement buddy. I don't know his name, but I hear he's Dean's new wingman. They're hitting the bars together. He was my best fucking friend, and now he's pretending I never existed."

"That sucks." Once, River and Dean had been like brothers.

"Yeah, well, the asshole bought me out of our house. We signed the papers yesterday. I've got the check in hand, so at least I'll have cash to find a new place…when I get time. For now, I'm sleeping on the office sofa, and it's about as comfortable as a pile of rocks."

Seth winced. "I've slept there, too. I know. You need somewhere to crash? Liam and Hammer would—"

"No. Raine and the guys have twins, and they just got back from their honeymoon. Last thing they need is me ruining their romantic bliss. Besides, I don't want to see or hear the things they do to my sister. That would scar me for life."

He tried not to laugh. "Have you asked Heavenly to help you find a place? She might have some ideas."

"Already did. But your girl has gone crazy. She suggested I talk to Pike, of all people, about renting a room in his Beverly Hills mansion. Ha! That will be a cold day in hell. I told her I'd rather sleep on your office sofa."

"Are you sure? Pike lives just down the street from where Jasmine takes care of that elderly couple. She's, like, three blocks away."

River hesitated. "I didn't think about that."

"Pike met her in the neighborhood. They were both walking their dogs. Living there might make it easier to 'accidentally' run into her."

"Huh. I fucking hate you for being right."

"No, you don't. You love me for being a brilliant strategist."

"I'm hanging up now before you talk me into something else I'll regret."

"But you're calling Pike?"

"If I can figure out how to get the fucker to talk to me? Yeah."

After a bit more small talk, they ended the call. Seth found himself chuckling despite everything as he walked into the house.

"Everything go all right?" Grace asked.

"Yep. Tuxes acquired, and I put off some office drama. It can wait until I get back to LA."

Grace kissed his cheek. "I know today was busy. Are you planning to talk to the twins tomorrow?"

Seth didn't see how he could put it off. "Yeah."

"Thank you. Since you're here, I'm making your favorite pot roast for dinner. Everyone's coming. Well, except Jack and Connor."

Because they'd refused to come…or because they hadn't been invited?

He chewed on that unsettling worry until the Cooper house began filling with family. Matt arrived first, carrying a bottle of wine and looking like a successful New York PI in his tailored suit. Danny and his wife Maggie followed with their baby girl, Anna, who immediately commanded everyone's attention with her chubby cheeks and infectious giggles.

"Matt." Seth caught his brother's arm as Grace bustled around the kitchen. "Can I steal you for a minute? I wanted to talk…business."

"Sure." Matt followed him into the den, closing the door behind them. "You really want to talk about shit at the office? Or the twins? I know Mom asked you to talk some sense into them since she's apoplectic. But, honestly…I don't think the twins are going to change."

Seth didn't think so, either, but he wanted to hear Matt's side of this. "Because?"

His younger brother winced. "Um, I've known for a while that Jack and Connor share girls."

"Yeah? Since we're confessing, I found out this past summer, when the twins crashed with me in Cali. I kept my mouth shut because I knew Mom would lose her mind. How long have you known?"

Matt rubbed the back of his neck, looking guilty. "About three years. I heard rumors, so I followed them. And…yeah. I didn't say anything for the same reason you didn't. So…got a plan? Know what you're going to say to them?"

"No, and now Mom is talking about disowning them."

Matt's expression darkened. "Shit. She's that serious?"

He nodded. "That can't happen."

"It can't." Matt leaned in, dropped his voice. "Especially over something like this. Hell, I've shared a woman with another guy once or twice. Who am I to judge?"

Seth blinked in surprise, then felt a laugh bubble up. "Seriously?"

"Why do you seem shocked? It was in college. Me and my roommate both had a thing for the same girl. She dropped by one night, we opened a bottle…and one thing led to another." Matt grinned. "Best night of my life—at least at the time. Don't knock it until you try it."

"I have. More than a time or two." Seth felt guilty for not telling Matt about Beck and Heavenly, but he wanted to break the news to the family all at once. Though he couldn't before he'd primed his mom.

Shock crossed Matt's face, then he laughed. "Of course you have. Anything I've done, you've done more."

"And better," Seth teased. "Any suggestions on how we keep Mom from tearing the family apart over this shit?"

Before Matt could answer, the door opened, and Danny poked his head in. "You two discussing the twins, by chance? You're holed up in here, whispering like a couple of conspirators, so I figured…"

Seth and Matt exchanged a glance. "We are."

Danny stepped inside, closing the door again. "Them sharing girls isn't new. I've known since they were seventeen. I caught them at a house party."

Seth's jaw dropped. "And you never said anything?"

"Who was I going to tell? Mom would have had a stroke. Matt was finishing college, and you were busy with your PI business. Besides, I didn't see the harm." Danny shrugged. "I shared a woman or two with other guys before I married Maggie—not that she'll ever know. That would blow her modest little mind."

"Looks like we all have." Seth clapped his brothers on the shoulder. "This kink must be genetic."

They all burst into laughter.

Then Seth sobered. "I talked to Carl today. He agrees that Mom needs to let this go. He's going to try talking to her before she carries out her threat to kick Jack and Connor out of the family. I'll do the same."

"Good. I'm not losing my brothers because Mom can't handle their love life."

Danny nodded. "And she can't cast us all out of the family."

"Amen," Matt seconded.

Seth felt a surge of relief so strong it nearly knocked him over. When the time came to tell the family about Beck and Heavenly, he'd have his brothers' support. Mom would have to cave when she realized all her sons stood against her, right?

Grace called them to dinner, interrupting his thoughts. The three brothers agreed to share intel before they headed to the dining room.

Dinner that evening felt like stepping back in time. The table was crowded with family, full of laughter and conversation, though he was keenly aware of the twins' absence.

"So…California treating you well?" Matt reached for another

dinner roll while Anna tried to grab his glasses off his face from her high chair.

"It is. Weather's perfect, work's steady, and I've made some great friends. And so far, no major earthquakes." He laughed self-deprecatingly.

"Still can't believe you left New York for good." Danny speared another morsel of Grace's famous pot roast.

"LA is home now."

"Because of Heavenly?" At his nod, Maggie smiled. "Tell us more about her. I'm dying to meet her. Grace said her father died in April. Did you get to meet him?"

Seth felt his chest tighten. "Briefly, right before he passed away. Heavenly and Abel were really close. Losing him broke her heart."

Grace reached over and squeezed his hand. "Oh, that poor girl."

"What about Heavenly's mom?" Maggie pressed gently.

Every time he thought about the woman, he got angry. "She left when her dad got his diagnosis... Heavenly was fifteen, and she hasn't had any contact with her mom since. She doesn't even know where to find the woman."

If Heavenly ever wanted to know, Seth would find Lisa Young. But honestly? He hoped she didn't.

Grace frowned. "You never told me that. Bless her heart. She's endured so much loss."

"She has, but she doesn't like to talk about it, especially after losing her dad."

"That's terrible," Maggie murmured. "She have any siblings?"

Seth shook his head. "She's an only child, and she has no other family to speak of."

Maggie gaped. "So she was alone when you came along?"

Except for Beck. "More or less. The minute I met her, I wanted to protect her."

Among other things...but I can't share my other urges with the family.

"Sounds like she's been through a lot for someone so young," Carl observed.

"She has. But she's stronger than she knows."

So unlike Autumn.

As the evening went on, filled with conversation, baby giggles, and the familiar rhythms of family dinner, Seth felt an ache settle in his chest. He loved these people. Loved the chaos, the warmth, the sense of belonging.

But he loved Beck and Heavenly more. And he was secure in the knowledge that moving to LA, pursuing Heavenly, and building a life with her and Beck had been the right choice. The *only* choice for his heart.

The question that haunted him as he laughed at Danny's terrible jokes and watched Carl clear the table was simple: Once his mother knew the truth, would there be any more easy family meals like this? Or would the life he'd chosen force everyone to draw battle lines and shatter the close-knit Cooper clan?

After arriving at the twins' apartment on campus, Seth climbed the narrow stairwell of the converted brownstone, stepping over a pile of takeout containers someone had left rotting on the third-floor landing and trying not to inhale the stench of secondhand weed. The building reeked of stale beer, puke, and irresponsibility—exactly the kind of place college kids ended up when their parents were footing the bill but wanted to teach them about "real-world budgets."

Fortunately—or not—it didn't take him long to find his youngest brothers. Were they in their apartment studying? Or atoning for last weekend's fuck fest under Mom's roof? No. They were loitering in their open doorway, taking turns kissing goodbye a petite blonde in short shorts.

"Text me." The barely legal girl smiled before hurrying toward the elevator, her athletic shoes squeaking across the nuclear-war-proof industrial carpet.

Both twins leaned, watching her ass sway down the hallway, completely oblivious to Seth's approach.

"When you're done eye-fucking your way into more trouble, think you can invite me in so we can talk?"

Both brothers jolted and spun around like they'd been electrocuted.

"Seth?" Connor's face went pale. "What the hell are you doing here?"

"Well, look what the California breeze blew in," Jack drawled, his trademark smirk sliding into place. "You're here to lecture us, right? That means Mom called, and you came running. Son-of-the-year recipient right here, folks…"

"Can the sarcasm. Someone has to be the adult in this situation." Seth pushed past them into the apartment and immediately understood why they'd taken Gia to Grace's house.

What a fucking disaster. Granted, he was a neat freak, but holy hell. Empty pizza boxes littered the card table that served as their dining room. Their couch looked as if it had survived more than a few frat parties and possibly a small war. The kitchenette consisted of a mini-fridge, a hot plate, and a sink full of dishes that might qualify as a biohazard. But hey, the TV was state-of-the-art, currently flashing a collection of photos of scantily clad bikini babes.

"Charming place," Seth said dryly, settling into the only chair that didn't look like it would stain his pants. But he sure as hell wouldn't want to take a blacklight to it.

"It's not that bad," Connor mumbled, but his face said he knew better.

Seth snorted. "Sure. That's why you took Gia to Mom's instead of… impressing her with this palatial penthouse. Speaking of your girlfriend, is that who just left?"

"No." Connor looked pissed. "After Mom started her fire-and-brimstone routine, Gia was done."

"She wanted nothing to do with our 'family drama,'" Jack added bitterly, making air quotes. "Having your boyfriends' psycho mother scream about eternal damnation kinda kills the mood."

Seth felt a stab of sympathy. He remembered being young and stupid, thinking physical chemistry equaled love. Laura Clarke and the summer he'd turned fifteen came to mind… "So the blonde I just saw wasn't Gia?"

"No. That's Hannah. Or Holly. Something with an H." Jack shrugged like it didn't matter, but Seth caught the slight tightness around his eyes. "Met her in Physics. I put her in my contacts as 'Horny'. She's… uncomplicated."

Seth tried not to roll his eyes. "Were you two ever serious about Gia?"

Both brothers stared at him like he'd spoken in tongues.

"Define serious," Jack shot back with a bit less bite than usual.

"Were you in love with her? Seeing a future? Ready to fight for her?"

Jack huffed. "Dude, we're twenty-one. We're supposed to be having fun, not planting white picket fences."

"Besides," Connor added, "if she couldn't handle one bad episode with Mom, what kind of future would we have?"

There it is. The fundamental difference between his brothers' casual approach and the love he'd found sharing Heavenly with Beck. When Grace inevitably lost her shit about their relationship, they wouldn't run. They'd stand with him, their hands in his, and weather whatever came.

"You know why I'm here, right?" Seth braced his elbows on his knees and glared their way.

"To give us another lecture about responsibility and discretion?" Jack's snark was back full force. "Save your breath. We heard your little 'Do as I say, not as I do' lecture the first time."

"Not well enough, or I wouldn't be trying to talk sense into you now."

Connor gulped. "We thought you'd be too busy playing house with Beck and Heavenly to come."

"You mean you hoped. But here I am…"

"Nobody's making you stay," Jack shot back.

"Don't be a disrespectful shit. I can still put you down with one punch." Seth studied his brothers' faces—near replicas of his a decade ago, but filled with a wariness that hadn't been there last summer. Beneath their defensive postures, he caught glimpses of the boys who used to climb into his bed during late-night thunderstorms.

Connor stomped to the fridge and snagged a couple of beers. "Want one?"

Seth shook his head. "No, thanks. Tell me precisely why you two rocket scientists decided to take Gia to Mom's house?"

"She and Carl were supposed to be away all weekend," Connor explained. "We wanted more room so we could spread out. At home, the TV is bigger, the beds are more comfortable, and the kitchen is prime."

"Yeah, Mom always stocks the good food," Jack added. "We figured we'd throw some steaks on the grill and make a weekend of it. No harm, no foul. Until Mom came home early."

Seth stared at his brothers, seeing so much of his younger self in their cavalier attitudes. Before Autumn and Tristan. Before he'd learned that the universe could rip away everything he held dear in a single heartbeat.

"I'm here because Mom isn't just upset. She's threatening to disown you both."

Seth's announcement seemed to suck the air from the room. Connor, clutching his beer, actually staggered back. Jack closed his eyes and cursed.

"Seriously?" Connor demanded. "Would she really—"

"In a heartbeat. No more tuition, no more rent money, no more grocery allowance. Kiss your degrees goodbye unless you can suddenly afford to finance the rest of your senior year yourselves." Seth gestured around the apartment. "And judging by this disgusting place, you don't seem responsible enough."

Jack's face had gone parchment white. "She's that pissed?"

"She's that *ashamed*," Seth corrected, watching the twins flinch. "Every time she replays what she walked in on, she worries about nosy Mrs. Patterson from church finding out. Or Father Heasley asking pointed questions about her sons' moral character."

Seth paused, the weight of his own hypocrisy settling in his chest like a stone. When he eventually came clean about Beck and Heavenly, Grace would face the same gossip he was warning the twins about. The same whispered conversations after church, the same pointed looks from neighbors with moral sticks up their asses.

"Jesus, it's not like anyone got hurt," Connor protested.

"You were hurting *her*. When you flaunt your arrangement in public, you're risking her reputation. Her standing in the community —which she's spent decades building. While you two are picking up your flavor of the week, Mom's at home weighing whether or not to pull the plug. Unless you do something fast, you'll be on your own."

"What the fuck…" Jack began to pace.

"Look, I know this sounds hypocritical coming from me." Seth frowned. "When I tell Mom about my situation, she'll have to deal with the same shit. But at least I'm giving her time to adjust gradually, not blindsiding her all at once. And maybe by then…" He shrugged. "Who knows? We'll be discreet during our visits here. Maybe she'll be so focused on potential grandchildren that the neighborhood gossip won't matter as much? I don't know. But Beck, Heavenly, and I will figure it out together." He met the twins' stares. "The plan isn't perfect. But it's better than the alternative, which is losing our family. Sometimes in life, like now, you have to choose between bad options and worse ones."

The apartment fell silent except for the sound of a neighbor's TV bleeding through the thin walls.

"What do we need to do?" Jack's voice finally sounded devoid of its usual cockiness.

"Yeah." Connor nodded. "How do we fix it?"

Seth had never seen his brothers look so genuinely rattled. Good. Maybe now they'd *finally* understand the gravity of the situation.

"No more PDA. No more taking girls to Mom's house—*ever*. And your sex life needs to be completely underground. Matt and Danny have both caught you in public with other girls over the years." When their eyes bulged in shock, he skewered the twins with a stare. "So if you want to share, do it where *no one* can see."

Connor looked ready to cry. "But you're asking us to hide who we are."

"No, I'm telling you to grow the fuck up." Seth's voice turned sharp. "You're playing at relationships like they're video games, moving from one level to the next without any real investment."

Jack's jaw clenched. "That's rich, coming from *you*."

Seth sent them an imposing stare. "What the fuck is that supposed to mean?"

"We *caught* you and Beck putting Heavenly between you two in the backyard, remember?" Jack's voice carried an edge of challenge. "We kept our mouths shut, but you're every bit the pervert we are. So, don't lecture us."

"I appreciate you not running to Mom," Seth said carefully. "But what I told you this summer still stands. What I'm doing is different. I'm not just looking for a quick piece of ass. What I have with Beck and Heavenly isn't a game or a thrill or something I do for kicks. I'm in a relationship with people I'd fucking *die* for."

Connor blinked, eyes round with shock. "No shit?"

"No shit. And it's a good thing, because when Mom finds out and threatens to disown me? I'll be fucking sad. But I'll still choose them without hesitation." Seth's voice was rough with emotion. "They're *everything* to me—my air, my heartbeat, my reason for existing. And if you can't understand the difference between that and putting a hot piece of pussy between you for a few hours, you'll never know true happiness."

The twins stared at him, something shifting in their expressions.

"I'm planning to come clean with Mom after the wedding," Seth continued. "If you two can keep your heads down for a couple of months, maybe my confession will pave the way for whatever you do next. No promises; she might disown us all. But that's a chance I'm willing to take for the people I love."

"You'd really choose them over family?" Connor all but whispered.

"Every time. Without question. Without regret."

Jack swallowed hard. "We've never felt… I mean, no girl has ever…"

"Then you've never been in love." Seth shrugged. "Hopefully, one day you'll find a woman worth fighting the whole world for. When you do, you'll understand why I can't walk away from Beck and Heavenly. Why I won't."

Seth paused as the twins seemed to absorb his words. "I talked with Matt and Danny last night. I even had a sidebar with Carl while I got fitted for my tux yesterday. None of them give two shits what you two do in the privacy of your bedroom. While they don't agree with the way Mom is reacting, they understand. They've offered to try and help broaden her admittedly narrow-ish mind."

A flicker of hope lit up his brother's faces.

"Don't get too excited. There's no guarantee any of us will be able to chisel through her strict Catholic upbringing. But they're willing to try."

"What should we do until then?" Connor's voice quivered.

"Go to the house and apologize to Mom. Tell her you're truly sorry. That you never meant to shock or upset her. And that you've learned your lesson, that you'll be more responsible from now on."

"What if she asks if we're still…" Jack shifted uncomfortably. "You know."

"Sharing? Don't lie to her. Remind her that you're adults. That you don't ask about her sex life, so you'd appreciate it if she didn't ask about yours. But do it nicely. Respectfully. Maturely."

"So…basically a 'Don't ask, don't tell' policy?" Connor asked, brows furrowed.

"Exactly."

"Seth?" Jack's voice was smaller than Seth had heard it since they were kids. "What if we never find our *one*? What if she's not out there? What if we're just…broken somehow?"

The question hit Seth square in the chest. He turned back to see both his brothers looking scared in a way that had nothing to do with Mom's threats.

"You're not broken," he said quietly. "You're just…not ready yet. It'll happen. When it does, when you meet the woman who makes your chest feel like it's going to explode every time she smiles, you'll know. And all the fun and games you two are having now will feel completely pointless."

The twins sat silently, looking as if he'd just turned their world upside down. Hopefully, he had.

Seth stood, hugged them both, then left them in their disaster of an apartment. As he walked back down the narrow stairwell, he couldn't shake the weight of his own words—or the certainty in his voice that had surprised even him. For months, he'd been paralyzed by the fear of choosing between love and family. But somewhere in that conversation, he'd drawn his line in the sand. He'd just sworn he'd choose Beck and Heavenly without hesitation. Now all that remained was proving he had the courage to follow through when Grace forced his hand.

Chapter Nine

When Seth returned home he found Grace exactly where he expected—in the kitchen, meticulously wiping down spotless counters. Her movements were precise but restless, the kind of nervous energy that came from trying to stay busy while waiting for news. She glanced up the moment she heard his footsteps, her eyes immediately searching his face for answers.

She set down the dishrag and began fidgeting with the edge of her apron. "Did you talk to them? Did they listen?"

Seth chose his words carefully. "They're no longer seeing Gia."

Grace's face lit up like Christmas morning. "Oh, thank God. I knew you'd be able to talk sense into them. What did you say to make them change their minds?"

The hope in her voice was a knife to his gut. Seth rubbed the back of his neck, already dreading the coming letdown. "I'm not sure I did, Mom. Gia left on her own because she didn't want any part of our 'family drama.' The second you started lecturing them about morality, she was out the door."

"Well, good riddance. Maybe now they can find a nice girl. Each of them, individually."

Seth felt the familiar weight of responsibility settle on his shoulders—the same burden he'd carried since he was sixteen and had suddenly become the man of the house. "Like I've said before, they're adults. You might not like their decisions, but they have the right to make them. And if they're mistakes..." He shrugged. "That's on them."

Grace's face darkened like a storm cloud. "Not with my money paying for their education, their apartment, their food. If they want to act like heathens, they can figure out how to support their deviant lifestyle themselves."

"You can't cut them off, Mom."

"Oh, I can." Her voice was steel. "I'll call their school tomorrow and cancel the tuition payments. They can find jobs and see how long their little arrangement lasts when they're flipping burgers."

With a heavy sigh, Seth sat at the kitchen table, the same scarred oak surface where he'd done his homework as a kid, where Grace had bandaged countless scraped knees, where the family had shared thousands of meals with and without his dad.

"Mom, do you love one of us boys more than the others?"

Grace scowled, hands on her hips. "What kind of question is that? Of course not."

"So…it's possible to love more than one person at a time, right?"

"If you're talking about children, then yes." Grace's eyes narrowed.

"What about a partner? A girlfriend or boyfriend?"

"A single partner is perfectly fine. Normal. Natural. But not some girl who gets passed around like a…" Grace's face reddened. "Like a sex toy. Besides, it doesn't matter now that Gia is out of the picture, thank the Lord."

Seth took a deep breath, knowing he was about to step into a minefield. "What if one day, down the road, Connor and Jack find someone new? Someone they both love? Someone who loves them back? Someone who wants to build a future with them?"

"You mean another easy woman who'll let them—"

"I mean someone who *chooses* to be with them in a loving, committed relationship. Someone who wants what they're offering." Seth leaned forward, his voice gentle but firm. "Are you really going to disown your children because they love differently than you expect them to?"

Grace's face closed up, but her voice got quiet. "I didn't raise immoral brutes."

"You didn't, but you can't expect grown men to let their mommy dictate the rest of their lives. Since Dad died, you've considered me the father figure around here. I was happy to try to fill those shoes for the other boys—while they were kids. But I won't disown them for thinking or wanting something different. And I don't want you to destroy our whole family over a disagreement." Seth's voice cracked slightly. "You've spent too many years and sacrificed too much to keep us all together, to keep us whole. Dad would—"

"Don't." Grace's voice was sharp as a blade. "Don't you dare bring your father into this. He would be just as ashamed of what those boys are doing as I am."

"Would he? Or would he trust that he raised them to know their own hearts?"

Grace turned away, but not before Seth caught the shimmer of tears in her eyes.

Sensing that she was getting overwhelmed, he quickly changed tactics. "I know you don't approve, but what gives you—or any person—the right to define what love is? Or what love is acceptable? And before you say God, remember—He's the one who gave us the capacity to love unconditionally and without end. He's the only one with the true authority to judge us."

Grace didn't answer, just stared at him with a mixture of hurt and fury.

"Love doesn't follow rules, Mom. It might not look the way you think it should. It might not fit society's norms or whatever preconceived notions we carry up here." Seth tapped his temple. "And whether you're ready or not, when love comes your way—when you find your person—it doesn't really matter if it fits some predetermined mold or not."

Grace's voice was suddenly small. "I don't want them to be ridiculed. Embarrassed. Hurt. Ostracized."

Seth studied his mother's face, seeing past her righteous anger. "No, Mom. That's what *you're* afraid of."

The words hit their mark. Grace flinched as if he'd slapped her.

She sank into the chair beside him. "Their morality—or lack thereof—is a reflection of me as a mother, as a person, and as an upstanding member of the church. What will people think? What will Father Heasley say when he finds out I raised sons who share women like… like animals?"

"Do the opinions of others really matter that much? Do you care about that more than your own sons, especially when the fallout for their actions are on them, not you." Seth reached out and took her hand. "Listen, Jack and Connor are still young, and they have a lot of growing up to do. But they're the ones who have to decide what their lives will be. You let them pick their school and their majors, the fields they're pursuing and their friends. If you trust them with those decisions, why can't you trust what's in their hearts?"

"Because it's wrong."

"In *your* opinion. Not in theirs." Seth squeezed her fingers. "Do you want Jack and Connor to be happy?"

"Of course, but—"

"No buts. If they change their 'wicked ways' to make *you* happy—to keep you from being appalled or shunned by others because their love doesn't look the way you think it should—will *they* ever truly be happy?"

"Seth…" she mumbled, shoulders sagging.

"They won't. And they'll resent you for the rest of their lives. If sharing their love with one woman is what they want, who am I, you, or anyone else to say it's wrong? That they should be forced to conform to someone else's wishes? Who are we to shame and disown them for following their hearts?"

Grace sent him a pleading stare, her carefully constructed composure finally cracking. "But the Bible… God… The church…"

Seth felt his heart break a little at the genuine anguish in her voice. "*Your* God. *Your* Bible. *Your* church, Mom. What about other religions? Take fundamental Mormons, for example." Mentally, he excluded the sect Beck had grown up in; they were crazy. "Those men take multiple wives and have dozens of children. Do you think they believe God sees them as perverts?"

"No," she grudgingly admitted.

Seth took both her hands now, feeling how they trembled. "Mom, you can't make the twins choose between you and whoever they love. If you do, you'll lose them forever. Can you honestly imagine not having them in your life anymore? And what if one day, once they've chosen a wife, they have babies with her? I know you. You would never reject your own grandchildren."

The tears Grace had been holding back finally spilled over. She shook her head, unable to speak.

"Even though none of us boys are innocent anymore, we're still your babies, Mom."

Grace choked out a laugh through her tears. "Yes, you are. I just... I don't know if I'll ever understand how or why the twins could desire the same woman. It seems so…"

"You don't have to understand it." Seth's voice was soft but firm. "You just need to keep loving them."

Grace wiped her eyes with the back of her hand. "I do. I love all you boys. I always will. I'll work on trying to accept…the life they're pursuing. Just…don't expect me to get there overnight."

She was thinking. That was a step in the right direction. "I can't ask for more now. Just…try to see this from their perspective, too."

Grace sniffled. "I'll do my best."

Seth stood and lifted Grace from her chair, hugging her tightly. For the first time since arriving in New York, he felt a glimmer of hope. Maybe, just maybe, when the time came to tell her about Beck and Heavenly, she'd remember this conversation. Maybe the groundwork he'd just laid would make his eventual confession a little easier to swallow.

Grace wiped her eyes and blew her nose, then checked her watch. "I'm babysitting Anna for a few more hours. She's sleeping upstairs. I was planning to make lasagna for dinner, but I need to run to the store for a few things. Would you mind staying here in case she wakes up?"

"Not at all." Seth smiled. "Do what you need to do."

Grace grabbed her purse and keys, pausing at the door. "Seth? Thank you. For everything. Your father would be so proud of the man you've become."

As the door closed behind her, Seth sagged into his chair. He'd just argued for his brothers' unconventional love life…while hiding his own. The hypocrisy was killing him, but everything he'd said about Jack and Connor held true for him, too. If she wanted her oldest son to be happy and remain in her life, and if she wanted to know his kids, then she needed to accept that love didn't always fit into a neat box.

Seth bounded upstairs to his childhood bedroom, so he'd be close enough to hear Anna if she woke. Inside, he kicked off his shoes, then put them in the closet when he spied the cardboard box that represented his biggest failure in life. He'd shoved it away and tried his best to forget, but some things he couldn't bury.

His hands trembled as he reached for it and lifted the lid.

Inside, he found his father's case files, filled with everything about the drug ring he'd been investigating before he'd been killed. Manila folders, newspaper clippings, photographs, and a notebook filled with pages of his father's careful handwriting stared back at him. The contents of the box had consumed years of Seth's life—and had ultimately cost him his wife and infant son.

The conversation he'd had with Liam less than a week ago echoed in his head.

"Sometimes the things we think we've resolved have a way of resurfacing when we're on the verge of something new."

Seth still didn't know what that meant, but he couldn't open this goddamn can of worms again. He hated leaving his father's murder unsolved, hated letting whispered suspicions about Michael Cooper being on the take tarnish his otherwise sterling legacy. But Seth had once given everything short of his own life to figure out whodunit. He couldn't fall down this rabbit hole again. The past was a fucking graveyard—and if he didn't walk away, it would bury him, too.

He shoved the box back into the depths of the closet and closed the door with more force than necessary. If he didn't dredge up this cold case, the past couldn't come back to haunt him. Besides, like Beck and Heavenly had pointed out, he wasn't the same man he'd been then. He didn't have the same job. He wasn't chasing the same demons. He was on a different coast with different priorities, like building a happy future with the ones he loved.

Who'd bother coming after him eight years later?

"No one," he bit out as a soft cry sounded from down the hallway.

Seth bolted out the door and rushed to Danny's old room, now a cheerful nursery with pastel yellow walls, stuffed animals galore, and the usual rocking chair, changing table, and baby bed.

"Hey there, sweet girl." He lifted his nine-month-old niece from her crib.

For a heartbeat, his breath caught—the familiar weight of an infant in his arms, the trust in her little grip. As Anna blinked up at him with wide, curious eyes, his chest tightened. He'd avoided holding babies since—

He severed the thought and forced himself to focus on his niece, who gurgled and reached for his face with her tiny, perfect fingers.

Dragging in a bracing breath, he carried her to the changing table. "I know I'm not Grandma Grace. But unlike your Uncle Matt, this isn't my first rodeo. I'm admittedly rusty, but I know the routine… Wet diaper off, wipies everywhere, clean diaper on, then snap the onesie back in place. See, I can do this."

The motions came easily—like riding a bike. When he lifted her again, Anna's tiny fist gripped his shirt and she curled up against his chest, her heartbeat a steady rhythm against his.

He eased into the rocking chair and fell into the gentle sway of the glider, cradling her protectively in his arms.

Anna's downy hair tickled his neck as she settled against him, trusting and perfect. He breathed in that sweet baby scent—powder and milk and innocence. This he remembered. And to his shock, he'd actually missed these tender moments.

Seth closed his eyes and began humming some half-forgotten lullaby. Whether he meant to calm her or himself, he wasn't sure.

As he carried the tune, he stared down at her, so small, so fragile. He held her safety, her existence, in his hands.

The realization was both humbling and terrifying.

She cooed, her little legs pumping. And he froze. Tristan had babbled these same sounds, made the same motions.

As memories slammed into Seth, his world tilted sideways.

Suddenly, he was in the past, his three-month-old son falling asleep in his arms after a 2 a.m. feeding, exhaling that same contented sigh. Giving him that same unguarded trust.

A week later, Tristan had burned alive in his car seat.

Seth's breath stuttered. Sweat broke out across his back. He tightened his grip on Anna as his heart hammered against his ribs—right where her tiny body pressed against him, warm and alive and so goddamn vulnerable.

He forced himself to breathe.

Jesus christ, what the hell was he doing? He couldn't even hold his niece without freaking out, yet he'd sworn to Beck and Heavenly that he was ready to start a family. He'd stripped off his condom, buried his cock inside Heavenly, and convinced himself his choice meant he'd healed. That plowing ahead was the same as being emotionally prepared for the consequences.

But sitting here, holding Anna, feeling her absolute trust and fragility, he knew the truth he'd been avoiding. He wasn't ready—not even close. He hadn't been honest with them. Hell, he'd even fucking lied to himself.

All that crap about working through his fears, about choosing their future over his past—it had been well-meaning lies. Bullshit. He hadn't worked through a fucking thing. He'd shoved his terror into a box, slammed the lid shut, and hoped that by the time Heavenly handed him their newborn, he'd magically be ready.

That sounded logical...but it was unrealistic as hell.

The terror was still there, just as vicious as it had ever been. Maybe worse, because now he knew what it meant to lose everything.

What if Heavenly was already pregnant? What if, right now, their baby was growing inside her? The thought that should have filled him with joy made him break out in a nervous sweat.

Anna stirred in his arms, her tiny hand flexing against his chest. Seth looked down at her happy face. She was so perfect. So innocent. She had no idea that the man holding her was a fucking coward who couldn't protect the people he loved. Who'd gotten his wife and son killed because he'd been too arrogant, too reckless, too convinced of his own invincibility.

What the hell are you going to do?

The question ricocheted around his skull, brutal and unforgiving.

He couldn't tell Beck and Heavenly that he was having second thoughts, that he'd committed to starting a family before he was ready, that the thought of being a father again scared the fuck out of him. They'd waited for him to get his shit together. Beck had drawn a line in the sand. Heavenly had walked away. They'd barely given him one last chance, and he'd promised he was all in. But what else could he have done? Losing them would destroy him.

And what would having a baby do?

If he didn't want to lose them, he only had one option: figure out how to get over this shit before their baby arrived. Force himself past this terror—somehow. Fake it until it became real. He'd white-knuckle his way through Heavenly's pregnancy and delivery, and when they put that baby in his arms, he'd scrape together the will to be the father they needed him to be.

Even if the fear never left. Even if every moment was hell. Even if he had to pretend for the rest of his fucking life.

The familiar sound of the front door shutting jolted him back to the present. Anna squealed as Seth stood, his legs unsteady, and carried her downstairs, projecting a calm he didn't feel.

"Hi." Grace set the grocery bags on the kitchen counter. "When did she wake up?"

"About fifteen minutes ago. I've changed her, but she might be hungry." It gave Seth an excuse to hand the baby to his mother, who took her with a smile. His relief was almost as intense as his fear had been.

He took a calming breath and began putting the groceries away. "Hey, Mom. Can I get the key to my old house? I want to clean it out and put it on the market. I think…it's time."

"I've been wondering, going over there every so often and keeping it up." Grace's expression softened. "But I think you're right."

He might be mixed up about wanting kids, but he was committed to moving forward…whatever that looked like. "I need to close that chapter of my life."

And to figure out the next.

His mother's smile was full of relief and pride. "The key is upstairs in my jewelry box. I'll get it for you."

He put the last of the dry goods in the pantry. "I'll grab it. You've got a precious armful."

"I do." She grinned down at Anna, making faces and laughing at her little-girl giggles.

When he returned moments later, he clenched the key in his fist. "Got it. Thanks."

Gentle understanding filled his mother's face. "I know it won't be easy, but you're doing the right thing."

If she knew the truth, she'd undoubtedly tell him he was making the biggest mistake of his life. Seth wasn't convinced she'd be wrong.

After waving goodbye to his mom and baby Anna, Seth pocketed the key and slid into Grace's SUV, fighting the rising dread. Traffic was shitty, but that wasn't his problem.

He hadn't set foot in this house in eight years, and he was under no illusions. It was going to hurt.

Gripping the wheel tighter, Seth blew out a heavy sigh and shoved away the tragic memories of his past.

When he turned into the subdivision, he was startled by how much the neighborhood had changed. It looked older. The fences weren't quite as straight and white. The oak trees that had been saplings when he and Autumn had moved in now towered over the sidewalks, their branches creating a canopy of green. A few houses showed signs of neglect—sagging roofs and overgrown weeds—while others gleamed with fresh paint and colorful flowers. The Hendersons' blue colonial was now a cheerful yellow.

Yet in other ways, everything looked the same. Same winding lanes. Same front doors. Same suburban vibe.

Seth turned onto his former street, vaguely wondering if Mrs. Vacarro—the crazy cat lady—still lived in the corner house. He remembered the way Autumn had saved leftover chicken for the strays, then sneaked out to feed them when she'd thought he wasn't looking. A melancholy smile tugged at his lips.

Rolling past the Whitaker's place, he arched a brow at the bright red tricycle, turtle-shaped sandbox, and the assortment of toys scattered across the front lawn. Either the contentious couple who used to have screaming matches regularly—often involving the cops—had worked out their issues or a different family lived there now.

Seth saw subtle changes everywhere. Grimly, he realized that while he'd spent the last eight years frozen in the aftermath of that grisly Christmas Eve, the rest of the world had kept on spinning.

When his old house came into view, a sudden arctic wave swept up his body, chilling his veins. Conversely, he started to sweat.

The craftsman-style ranch looked eerily preserved—exactly as he remembered. Fresh paint kept the exterior a warm cream. The gutters were clean. The lawn neatly trimmed. But the flower beds Autumn had once spent hours tending no longer exploded with riotous color. Instead, practical perennials his mother must have chosen dotted the beds—low-maintenance, sensible.

It looked like a house. Not a home.

As he pulled into the driveway, he saw faint scorch marks on the street and sidewalk. Dark stains that no amount of time or weather had been able to erase. Wounds that never quite healed…

Like me.

Drawing in a ragged breath, he stopped the SUV and killed the engine. He stared at the house—so familiar, yet so foreign.

Seth gripped the wheel with trembling hands and dragged in a rough breath, trying to gather his courage to leave the safety of the car.

When he finally managed to step from the SUV, his legs felt filled with lead. Each step toward the front door was a battle, raging between the part of him that needed to move on and the part of him that wasn't ready to face his past. Or his future.

Ruthlessly, he shoved aside the memories and bit back a curse, wiping the sweat beading his brow as he tried like hell not to hyperventilate.

Focus. You have to fucking focus.

With that admonishment rolling through his head, he fished the key from his pocket. His hands were shaking so badly he fumbled it, nearly dropping it on the weathered porch boards.

Christ, get it together.

He steadied his grip and lined up the key with the lock. It scraped against the plate—once, twice. His heart hammered against his ribs. Sweat trickled down his spine despite the cool September air.

Third try. The tumblers finally turned.

Seth gripped the knob, his palm slick, and pushed the door open.

The hinges creaked—a sound he'd heard a thousand times but had forgotten until this moment. He stepped inside, and the door swung shut behind him with a soft click that seemed to echo in the stillness.

He froze.

Holy fuck.

The air was thick and stale, undisturbed for years. Dust motes drifted in the slanted light filtering through the curtains Autumn had picked out—cream with delicate blue flowers. The Christmas tree and presents he remembered from that final night were gone, packed away by someone who'd cared enough to erase the holiday but not enough—or maybe too broken—to change anything else.

The floors were clean. No dust on the furniture. His mother had meticulously maintained this place, preserved it like an exhibit of a life that had ended.

But everything else remained exactly as he'd left it.

Tristan's baby swing still sat in the corner of the living room, its bright primary colors now faded with time. The bassinet was beside the couch where Autumn had often curled up to nurse him while watching late-night TV. A toy basket brimming with stuffed animals sat at the base of the coffee table—toys his son never had the chance to outgrow.

Seth forced himself to move deeper into the house, his footsteps hollow on the hardwood. He needed to assess what repairs were necessary. Check for water damage. Note what furniture could be sold or donated. Make a list.

Stay clinical. This is just a job.

He forced himself to look at the house with a cop's eye instead of a grieving man's. The caulk around the front door had cracked. A faint water stain spiderwebbed near an air vent in the hallway ceiling. He added roof inspection to the list. The couch and chair could be donated.

In the kitchen, the fridge still hummed when he opened it, but it needed a good cleaning before listing the place. Tristan's bouncy seat still sat on the table, the cheerful jungle animal pattern now sun-bleached where the light had hit it year after year. Seth could see it so clearly—Autumn moving around this space, singing off-key while she cooked dinner. Tristan kicking his chubby legs in that very seat, making those soft baby sounds, looking up at him with wide, trusting eyes.

Like his daddy was his whole world. Like his daddy would protect him from anything.

Seth's chest constricted. His vision blurred at the edges.

No. Hold it together, goddamnit.

He turned away, forcing his legs to carry him down the hallway. The nursery door was closed. He should open it. Check for mold, water stains, structural issues.

His hand hovered over the knob.

He couldn't do it. Not yet. But he'd have to deal with Tristan's things…later. Somehow. But he couldn't picture dismantling his boy's nursery, couldn't imagine removing a few keepsakes from his past life and walking away for good. That's what needed to happen but…

Fuck.

For now, he moved to the master bedroom. The bed was made, the room neat. The closet door stood ajar, and he could see Autumn's clothes still hanging there. Dresses she'd never wear again. Shoes she'd never slip into.

In the corner, near the window, sat the rocking chair where he'd held Tristan those first exhausting nights home from the hospital. The image slammed into him with brutal clarity: Autumn in her pink dress with the daisies, exhausted but glowing, watching him cradle their son wrapped in that soft blue blanket. The weight of Tristan in his arms. The fierce, terrifying love that had consumed him.

The promise he'd made to keep them safe.

He could see it so clearly now—carrying Tristan through that front door for the first time. Autumn trailing behind, her hand on his arm, both of them giddy yet anxious. Tristan had been oblivious to the momentous occasion, fast asleep beneath the blue blanket Grace had knitted for him. Seth remembered unlocking the door, thinking he was the luckiest bastard alive, as the September sun warmed his back.

September.

Seth's heart stuttered.

Tristan would have turned nine next week.

The realization sucker-punched him in the chest, stealing the air from his lungs. His hands wouldn't stop shaking.

Nine years old. His son would have been old enough for little league, soccer, football. Old enough to enjoy skateboarding, riding his bike, playing video games, building Lego cities with those small, careful hands.

What would he have looked like? Would he have had Autumn's dark curls or Seth's own dusty blond hair? Would he have been tall, like the Coopers? Or short and small-boned like his mother? What would he have dreamed of being when he grew up—an astronaut, construction worker, professional athlete, or a cop like his father and grandfather?

When would he have cut his first tooth? Taken his first steps? Spoken his first word? Gone to his first day of school?

He'd never know. All the answers to his questions—along with every memorable milestone—had been brutally and heartlessly stolen from his life.

Because of me.

Seth's chest caved in. His knees buckled.

A strangled sound tore from his throat—half sob, half roar. The room spun. He couldn't breathe. The walls were closing in, the air too thick, too heavy with ghosts and guilt and the suffocating weight of everything he'd lost.

He had to get out.

Seth stumbled backward, his shoulder hitting the doorframe. He barely felt it. His vision tunneled as he lurched down the hallway, past the nursery he couldn't face, past the kitchen with its cheerful bouncy seat and memories of off-key singing.

His hands slammed against the front door. He wrenched it open and burst onto the porch, gasping for air like a drowning man breaking the surface.

He needed to fucking leave here. Right now.

With impatient hands, he locked the house as if it could lock away his memories. Then he hauled ass to the SUV, shoved the key in the ignition, started the engine, and peeled out of the driveway. Tires squealing, he barreled down the street, out of the neighborhood, and out of the little town he'd once thought was perfect.

By the time he reached the highway, the small measure of progress he'd felt while holding Anna—the fact that he hadn't completely freaked out—felt meaningless now, crushed under the weight of his oppressive guilt.

He wasn't over his fucking past.

He was still broken, still fucked up, still mired in grief and guilt and whatever was making him unable to move on.

And Beck and Heavenly... Christ, what had he been thinking? How could he risk putting them through the horrible end that Autumn and Tristan had suffered? How could he be selfish enough to want a family when he'd already proven he couldn't protect them?

The blades of doubt that had plagued him before taking Heavenly without protection sliced through him again, each one sharper and cutting deeper. What if his past caught up to them? What if his love destroyed them? What if history repeated itself?

Mentally trapped in a loop of what-ifs and should-have-beens, he careened through the city. The future that had seemed possible mere hours ago now felt like a beautiful lie he'd told himself to avoid facing the truth.

Some wounds never healed. And he'd been a fool for thinking otherwise.

"Have you heard from your sister or her new husbands?" Heavenly glanced at River, currently sprawled behind his desk, rearranging Seth's client files by date and priority.

He watched with obvious amusement. "I got a text from Raine yesterday. According to her, the Louvre was 'educational' and the Eiffel Tower was 'romantic.' I'm calling bullshit. I bet they've barely stopped fucking long enough to leave their hotel room."

Heavenly's cheeks heated as she turned back to the filing cabinet. "You're terrible!"

"I'm honest. They may be honeymooning in Paris, but you actually think they're sightseeing? Trust me… They're getting plenty of something, but it's not culture."

Heavenly laughed. "Maybe. But I'm excited for them to get back on Sunday. I can't wait to hear about the sights they *did* see. Have you checked on Liam's sisters? I called Tuesday, and they seemed to be juggling those adorable baby girls."

"Talked to them this morning. Meg said everyone is fine. Ciara and

Catronia are handfuls, but nothing some rocking and burping can't fix. Aisling called it 'enjoyable chaos.' I told them to call me if they need anything."

Heavenly grinned as she rearranged the stack of invoices on Seth's credenza. "Liam's sisters are sweet, and they adore their nieces."

"Like I do. But don't tell anyone," he said in a stage whisper. "I might have to give up my man card."

She rolled her eyes as she began dusting Seth's desk. "I don't think anything could make you give that up."

River laughed, then gestured her way with his coffee mug. "You know you don't have to stress-clean Seth's office. He won't blame you if there's a pen out of place."

"No, he'll blame *you,* so you're welcome," she quipped. "Honestly, I'm just eager to get him home tomorrow and hear about his visit with his family. Since my last class got canceled today and he's been under so much stress, I thought I'd lighten his load."

Was the pressure the reason he'd been quiet yesterday when he'd called? Something was on his mind; she could feel it. Whatever it was, he'd glossed over it. That worried Heavenly.

"It's never easy running a business. Then…Jack and Connor shocked his mom with that Gia girl in her family room. And Grace is getting married in a few weeks…" River shook his head. "It's a lot to juggle."

"He loves her, but her reaction to the twins sharing a girlfriend…" Heavenly winced.

"She doesn't know about you three, does she?"

"No, and he's trying to figure out how to tell her, but not until after her wedding."

"Seth said you three were attending together. As…what? Friends?" River snorted. "I'd love to be a fly on the wall for that."

"Everyone thinks I'm his girlfriend, so we're sticking with that story."

"Girlfriend or…fiancée?" River cast a meaningful glance at her engagement ring.

Heavenly jerked her gaze down to her finger, then looked up with a blush. "Fiancée."

"They asked?"

"Yes, after they both got down on one knee. It was really sweet." Never mind that they'd all been naked. "But you can't tell Raine yet! Please…"

"You want to tell your bestie. Got it." He grinned. "Congratulations. I'm happy for you three. So…Beck will be attending the wedding as a friend?"

"Who happens to be in town, yes. It's not perfect, but it will work for a few days. I hope."

"Isn't family drama a bitch?" he drawled.

Heavenly nodded. "Speaking of drama… Did you call Pike about renting a room? He's got that swanky Beverly Hills mansion all to himself, and since I heard Dean bought you out of the house—"

"I haven't called Pike yet." River scrubbed a hand down his face. "But I gotta do something. I'm back to staying in a sketchy rent-by-the-week place starting tonight because the office sofa"—he pointed to the sleek black leather tufted couch—"doubles as a torture rack. It's destroying my back. But I'm not sure living with Pike would be better. I mean, the guy knows performers who put on a sex-donkey show." He shuddered. "I'm a pervert, but seriously. I don't want to know what the fuck goes on in his house."

Heavenly tried not to laugh. She hadn't liked Pike…until she'd spoken to him one-on-one about Jasmine. Then she'd seen a more respectable side of him. "You still need somewhere to live. And he might surprise you."

"Doubtful. Besides, I tried living with a 'friend' and look how that turned out. Granted, I took his sister's V-card. But how the hell was I supposed to know he was related to Jasmine? That didn't matter; Dean still screwed me over. So the idea of living with someone who's *not* my friend?" River's laugh was bitter. "Pass. And how awkward would it be living with the *other* guy pursuing Jasmine?"

"When you put it like—"

The office door crashing open startled her into silence. The glass rattled before it abruptly slammed shut. Furious footsteps clomped up the stairs to the office. Heavenly exchanged a glance with River, who stood, imposing and ready to take on their intruder.

A teenage boy with a mile-wide chip on his shoulder stormed to the landing and stopped, pinning them with a glare.

Heavenly stared at his face and gasped.

He was a younger carbon copy of Seth.

Head spinning, she catalogued him. He had Seth's sculpted cheekbones, his rugged jawline that could cut glass. The same sandy-blond hair, which caught the afternoon light streaming through the windows. But it was his eyes that really startled her. She already knew those shimmering green eyes could go from warm as summer grass to—like now—cold as a winter frost.

Her heart stuttered in her chest as the bottom dropped out of her stomach. Seth didn't have a brother younger than Jack and Connor, so… *Oh. My. Goodness.*

Was this Seth's…*son?*

Chapter Ten

Heavenly stared at the boy. Gaped. Seth had told her and Beck about Tristan. Surely, he would have told them if he had another son. Unless…

He didn't know.

The thought hit her like a sledgehammer.

He was going to blindside Seth. There was no way she could call him in New York and drop the bomb about his long-lost son.

How old was this kid? Seth was thirty-two, so logically his son shouldn't be older than thirteen or so. But another scan of the teenager told her he definitely was.

With a backpack over one shoulder and a bulging duffel dangling from his fist, the young man stared back, his eyes almost accusing as he swept the office.

"Holy shit," River muttered, seemingly frozen in place.

The teenager's gaze peeled from her as he dropped his luggage on the floor with a thud and glowered at Seth's junior PI. "I need to see Seth Cooper. Now."

His voice stunned Heavenly all over again. It was so shockingly like Seth's—timbre, inflection, even accent.

"Um…he isn't here," Heavenly replied, proud that her voice sounded steadier than she felt. "What's your name? Maybe I can help."

His eyes narrowed, his expression laced with barely controlled fury. "When will he be back?"

She darted another glance at River, not quite sure what to say.

"I'll…ask Beck if he knows." River shot Heavenly a meaningful look as he pulled out his cell phone and dashed off a text.

Good idea. He should know about this shocking development. What were they going to do? Say? Seth wouldn't be home for almost twenty-four hours.

"Who's Beck? And who the hell are you?" The teenager demanded.

"I'm River. I work with Seth." Before he could say more, his phone dinged in response. He glanced down to read the reply, leaving Heavenly the sole focus of the kid who wore Seth's face like an accusation.

The more she looked at him, the more she knew her suspicions were right. She saw Seth in the way the stranger held his shoulders, straight and proud. In the stubborn set of his jaw, which she'd seen on Seth countless times. Even the way he scanned the room, taking in every detail with sharp, assessing eyes.

All pure Seth.

"I didn't catch your name."

The teen scowled at her, eyes flashing with suspicion. "You his secretary or something?"

Panic fluttered in her chest. She had no roadmap for handling this situation. But if the kid wasn't even willing to tell her his name, she refused to divulge Seth's secrets—especially given his attitude.

"No, I'm just helping out today," she said finally. "But if you'll tell me who you are, I can help find him."

"Fine. I'm Hudson. When can you get him here?"

Since the truth would only make him angrier, she groped for an answer that might pacify him.

"Hey, don't grill her. She's just trying to help," River snapped. "I'm working on it."

Heavenly was grateful for his intervention. "Would you like something to drink while you wait? A soda or water?"

Grudgingly, Hudson accepted a bottle of water. She grabbed it from the small refrigerator, then watched him ease onto the leather couch, perched on the edge as if ready to bolt. In the background, River's phone dinged once. Twice.

Their unexpected visitor fixed on the stairway, as if expecting Seth to materialize at any moment. The tension radiating from his tall, lanky frame was palpable.

Heavenly tried to guess his age. Fifteen? Sixteen? Where had he come from? Based on his accent, somewhere back east. Where was his mother? And why did he look *so* ready to burn the world down?

His gaze shifted, and he studied her with the same sharp intensity, though his voice softened. "What's your name?"

"Heavenly." She lowered herself onto the chair across from him, trying to appear nonthreatening and approachable.

Finally, something besides anger flickered across his features. "That's…fitting."

Was he…hitting on her?

"That's enough," River growled.

"It's not like I fucking jumped on her. Geez…" Hudson bristled, then bobbed his chin at River. "What is he, your daddy?"

"I told you to watch your mouth. Heavenly is my sister's bestie."

"Yeah?" He scanned the office again, then turned back to her. "If you don't work here, how do you know Cooper?"

"Seth and I are…friends."

The words felt inadequate, almost like a betrayal of everything they meant to each other, but it was the safest option until she knew what Seth wanted to tell Hudson.

"Yeah, the naked kind." Hudson gave her another once-over. "Lucky him."

"Can it." River saved her from sputtering a reply, then turned to her. "Beck was already on his way over. He'll be here in a minute."

Thank goodness. Heavenly sighed in relief.

"I don't know who Beck is, but I didn't come here for a party." Hudson leapt to his feet. "Tell me when you expect Cooper. I'll come back then."

Since Seth wasn't going to magically walk through the door, she needed to keep Hudson talking until Beck arrived and they figured out what to do. "Wait! Beck might have more information."

Hudson hesitated, then slouched back onto the sofa. "If he doesn't, I'm out."

The awkward silence descended again. The ticking of the wall clock was audible in the hush. Heavenly glanced at the device. Almost five. Now what?

Her thoughts pinged like a metronome, back and forth, as she tried to sort through this surreal situation.

Eyes narrowed, River eased into his desk chair, still sizing up Hudson, who fidgeted on the sofa.

The sound of bounding footsteps on the stairs had everyone turning. Beck rushed into the room and skidded to a stop. He took one look at Hudson and his eyes flared wide, the same shock still ringing through Heavenly written all over his face.

"That's my cue." River stood and approached Beck, sending him a sympathetic grimace. "I'm going to…grab a sandwich. I'll be back."

Beck nodded, never taking his eyes off Hudson. "Yeah."

A second later, the door slid shut again. They were alone—with a secret big enough to tear Seth from their lives.

Shaking, Heavenly stood and approached him. "Beck, this is Hudson."

"Is Cooper with you or not?" The teenager glowered at Beck.

Beck's mouth opened, then closed. For a moment, his stare flicked between Hudson's face and her own. "Let's talk about this."

The kid huffed and got to his feet. "Fuck that. I'm out. Tell me when the hell he'll be back."

Heavenly watched Beck processing the same thoughts still racing through her head. Did they dare tell Hudson that Seth wouldn't be back until tomorrow? He'd disappear to God knew where. She didn't want to lie, not when the teen possessed Seth's stubborn streak. And he'd probably see right through them. But since he was carrying luggage, he was probably far from home. Did he have anywhere to sleep tonight?

"Here's the deal: Seth is visiting family. He'll be back soon." Beck slowly approached Hudson with careful, non-threatening movements. "How do you know him?"

"How do *you?*"

"We're friends."

"Like her, huh? The naked kind." Hudson sneered. "So he'll fuck anything with a pulse."

Beck's jaw clenched. "Watch your mouth. You talk like that in front of your mom?"

Hudson snorted. "All the time, and Blondie there is *not* my mom."

Heavenly tried to jump in and diffuse the situation. "Why are you looking for Seth?"

The kid hesitated, both wary and determined to control the situation. "That's between me and him."

So he didn't want to admit the obvious. Unless he did, she and Beck couldn't either.

Her stomach twisted anxiously. Until Seth returned, how were they supposed to handle this? And how could they possibly prepare him for finding a son who looked exactly like him?

As if sensing her spiraling thoughts, Beck caught her eye and sent her the slightest nod. *We'll figure this out.*

"Well…" Beck turned his attention back to the teenager. "Since we're waiting for Seth, tell us where you're from."

"Connecticut." Hudson's answer was clipped, but at least he was talking.

"You've come a long way. How did you know where to find Seth?"

"Called the office in New York. Some guy named Matt told me he was working out of the LA branch." Hudson shrugged like it was no big deal, but Heavenly could see the tension in his shoulders.

"Matt is Seth's younger brother," Heavenly volunteered. "He has four of them, actually." She wondered how much he knew about the Cooper family.

Hudson's laugh was bitter. "Why should I care?"

Oh, this poor kid. He must think Seth didn't want him—had never wanted him. No wonder he was so angry.

"Just making small talk. I thought you might be interested to know that Seth is really close to his family."

Hudson's expression flickered—surprise, maybe?—before the mask of anger slammed back into place. "Good for him."

Beck moved in closer, eyes fixed on Hudson. "Let's cut the shit and address the elephant in the room. You're here to meet Seth because he's your dad, right?"

Hudson's shoulders went rigid, his expression belligerent. Heavenly feared he would bolt.

"I never said he was my dad."

"You don't have to," Beck drawled. "You look—"

"Exactly like him. So I've gathered." Hudson rolled his eyes with the practiced disdain only teenagers could master.

"You do," Beck confirmed.

"So much," Heavenly seconded softly. "How old are you, Hudson?"

He shifted uncomfortably. "Sixteen."

That meant… No. Impossible.

But Hudson standing in front of her proved it wasn't.

She bit back a gasp. Beck, now beside her, didn't look any less shocked.

"When's your birthday?" she managed, her voice shaking.

"April twentieth. You mathing, Blondie? I'll save you the calculation. He was fifteen when he knocked my mom up."

Seth had been a child when this boy was born. After losing Tristan so tragically, how would he feel about having an almost-grown son? Would it be more than he could take?

Another glance at Beck told her he was wondering the same thing.

Beck frowned. "Is your mother…Mary Jo Bartkowicz?"

Hudson frowned. "Who?"

Heavenly shot Beck a quelling stare. It was logical to wonder if the first girl Seth had ever had sex with had been the one to bear this child. But she was grateful that Hudson seemingly hadn't been conceived in the men's room at the White Castle.

"No one important," she supplied.

"Look, I'm going to shoot straight with you," Beck jumped in. "Seth is in New York. He'll be back in LA tomorrow. Do you have someplace to stay tonight?"

Hudson cursed under his breath. "Not your problem. I'll figure it out."

"Stay with us," Heavenly offered. "We have a guest room, and it's free. You won't have to find a hotel—"

"Us? You live together?" He looked between them speculatively. "You banging Blondie, too?"

"That's *none* of your business. And watch your fucking mouth. If you don't have family to go to, you're staying with us."

"Why?" Hudson's tone suggested the idea was ridiculous. "You don't give a shit."

"We do," Heavenly insisted. She hated him thinking that no one cared.

"And you're a minor," Beck added. "So you're coming home with us. End of conversation."

"You can't make me."

"Me? No, but I can call the cops, have them track down your mother, and send you home tonight."

Hudson cursed again, uglier this time.

Heavenly sent Beck a reproachful stare, then softened when she looked Hudson's way. "Seth would want us to keep you safe."

Especially since he'd already lost one son. Losing another—for any reason—would devastate him. The thought of this boy wandering around Los Angeles alone made her chest tight with panic. How had he gotten here from Connecticut? Had he traveled across the country alone?

"You'll have a room with a flat screen. There's a pool and a gaming system. I'll feed you..." The words tumbled out as she did her best to convince him.

"All right. I guess, if I have to wait..." Hudson rose from the couch with a fluid grace that reminded her painfully of Seth and grabbed his bags.

She glanced Beck's way, unable to shake the feeling that their lives had just changed irrevocably. Tomorrow, Seth would come home expecting to pick up where they'd left off. Instead, he'd walk into a reality that would challenge everything he knew about his past—and his future.

Beck drove them home in his Mercedes. Tense silence filled the car. He worked mentally through the reality of this new development while he kept one eye on Hudson in the rearview mirror. The kid slouched, arms crossed over his chest in an I-don't-give-a-fuck pose, barely controlled fury radiating from every line of his body. But he cast a side-eye out the window, seeming to take it all in.

He and Heavenly needed to find out what Hudson had been told, then figure out how to handle this situation when Seth returned.

Because one thing was crystal clear: Hudson had traveled three thousand miles to meet Seth, and that was going to change everything.

"Here we are." Beck pulled into their driveway, noting the way Hudson's eyes widened slightly at the size of the house before his mask of indifference crashed back into place.

"Nice," Hudson muttered, grabbing his bags. "Seth must be doing all right for himself."

Beck didn't tell the kid that, legally, it was his house. First, it wasn't any of Hudson's business. Second, they didn't owe him an explanation about their living arrangement. And third, Beck refused to give the sarcastic teenager any more ammunition to use against Seth.

With a sigh, Beck killed the engine. Heavenly slid out of the car and gestured Hudson to follow. "Come inside. We'll show you around."

Hudson shrugged, quickly banking his flash of curiosity. "Sure. Whatever."

Beck unlocked the door and stepped aside, then trailed the duo into the house. "Living room over there." He pointed straight ahead to the breezy white sofa with the modern tufted black leather chairs. "Up the stairs are more bedrooms and the home office. Down leads to your guest room with attached bath. There's also a home gym, game room with a big screen and Xbox, and the wine cellar. The last one's off limits." He trekked deeper into the house, past the stairs. "Dining room is to the right." A few more steps. "Family room. And kitchen on the left." He gestured to each space before nodding to the sliding glass doors at the back. "Patio and pool are out there."

Hudson assessed his surroundings with a dissecting stare. When he spied the framed photos hanging on the wall—pictures of Beck, Seth, and Heavenly together at various events, including one where she was smiling from ear-to-ear while both men had their arms wrapped around her, each kissing one of her cheeks—his jaw tightened.

Beck could practically hear the questions rolling through Hudson's brain.

Thankfully, he didn't ask, and Beck didn't volunteer.

"Cozy," Hudson said finally, his tone carefully neutral.

"We like it here." Beck intentionally didn't comment on the photos. "You'll have plenty of privacy in the guest room downstairs."

The kid continued scanning the place. Though he tried to bank his expression it was a bit too wide-eyed to be anything but impressed. Beck wondered what Hudson's situation was. What would prompt a sixteen-year-old across the country to meet a dad he'd already decided he hated?

They descended the stairs, Heavenly chattering nervously about the house's features while Hudson remained largely silent. Beck saw her anxiety building. She was trying so hard to make the boy feel welcome, probably because she was terrified he'd bolt before Seth got home. But Beck knew the kid would stick around. In fact, he'd bet every last dime that Hudson didn't have much he considered meaningful to go back to.

"Here we are." Heavenly pushed open the guest room door. "Fresh towels are in the bathroom, and there's a mini-fridge if you want drinks or snacks."

Hudson dropped his backpack and duffel on the hardwoods before swiping his fingers across the pristine white duvet covering the queen-size bed. Slowly nodding in approval, he scanned the spacious room, flat-screen TV, cozy sitting area, and floor-to-ceiling windows. "This'll work."

"Are you hungry?" Heavenly seemed reluctant to leave him alone.

Beck smiled. Her trying to mother a kid seven years her junior was cute. What wasn't cute? The way Hudson kept checking her out.

He shrugged. "I could eat, I guess."

"Pizza or Chinese?" Beck asked. Hudson's sudden appearance had given Heavenly enough to deal with. She didn't need to cook, too.

The kid sneered. "Doesn't matter. We do it better back east."

Heavenly smiled. "Your dad says the same thing. And I'll let you in on a secret. When he first moved out here, he was afraid of earthquakes."

Hudson frowned. "Bullshit."

"She's serious." Beck nodded. "He still is. We rib him all the time."

That made the teenager smile, like he was happy to have some dirt on the dad he'd never met.

"I'm in the mood for Chinese, if that's okay with you," Heavenly said.

"Even if it will suck? Sure."

She dropped a soft hand to his shoulder. "Why don't you get settled? We'll be upstairs in the kitchen. Just come find us when you're ready."

Heavenly shut the door behind them. Together, they ascended the stairs and made their way to the family room. Heavenly poured them each a glass of iced tea. While Beck lowered himself into the chair by the window and ordered Chinese from one of their favorite places, she eased onto the sofa. After he tucked his phone in his pocket, they looked at one another. For long moments, neither spoke, as if they had a ton to say, but didn't know where to start.

Beck broke the ice. "Crazy shit, huh? Finding out Seth has a long-lost son wasn't on my bingo card."

"Mine, either."

"He's going to be so fucking shocked."

She hesitated. "I'm terrified what this news will do to him."

Beck understood her fear. Hell, he shared it. Seth had endured so much, and he'd just committed to starting a family with them. Finding out he already had a sixteen-year-old son was going to rock him to his core.

His expression softened, and he took her hand, folding it in his. "I know, little girl. But we'll figure it out together. All of us."

"I hope so." She sighed. "I don't think we should tell Hudson about our relationship."

"We can't. Seth will be home in less than twenty-four hours. Then he can decide. Hudson isn't stupid; he already suspects. But until our other half weighs in, we just need to zip it."

"I don't like lying, but you're right."

"Which really sucks. I wanted to make you scream tonight." He wagged his brows at her with a levity he didn't feel, but he wanted to lighten her mood. "All night."

She rolled her eyes at him. "Behave. Hudson already thinks the worst of Seth."

"Yeah, he's got his work cut out for him if he's going to have any kind of relationship with that kid."

Heavenly opened her mouth to respond before loud footsteps

stomped up the stairs. A moment later, Hudson appeared now dressed in a pair of basketball shorts and a tank top with big, bare feet. He was tall and lanky, lean with muscle. Just like his dad. Jesus, the resemblance was uncanny.

"Food will be here in thirty minutes," Beck told the kid.

Plenty of time for the inquisition.

"Have you eaten today?" Heavenly offered, rising. "Do you need a snack to tide you over until dinner comes?"

"Do you wait hand and foot on dear old dad, too?" Hudson eyed her.

"She asked you a yes or no question," Beck snapped.

"No. I had a sandwich a couple of hours before I found you."

"Have a seat." Beck head-bobbed to the chair across from him.

"I'll stand."

"It wasn't a request."

"Son of a bitch," Hudson muttered. "You looking to bust my balls?"

"Only if you make me. I want information. We can do this easy or hard—up to you."

The teen sighed as if the whole situation was one giant imposition and plopped into the chair. "What?"

"So you live in Connecticut?" Beck did his best to keep his tone conversational.

"Cromwell," Hudson confirmed. "Shitty little town south of Hartford."

"You're a long way from home," Heavenly clucked like a mother hen. "How did you get here?"

Beck suppressed a smile. His little girl was both feeling her maternal streak and playing peacekeeper, smoothing over what she probably saw as his too-direct approach. But someone needed to cut through Hudson's shitty attitude.

"Well, I didn't fucking walk," Hudson drawled. "Of course I bought a plane ticket. Duh."

It took all of Beck's restraint not to grab the kid by the throat and squeeze. Instead, he got in Hudson's face. "Don't talk to her like she's an idiot, or we're going to have problems. Are we clear?"

"Yeah, yeah. Sorry." He crossed his arms over his chest. "This is just awkward as fuck."

"You're not making things any better by mouthing off. How did you pay for your plane ticket?"

"I had a job over the summer. I saved some money," Hudson said defensively.

"What kind of job?" In Beck's experience teenagers with unexplained cash usually had sketchy side-hustles.

Hudson's expression shuttered completely. "Student by day... gigolo by night."

Beck raised a brow. "Sure you are, smart-ass. Try again."

The kid's mouth quirked slightly—surprise, maybe, that Beck was keeping up verbally. "I was a lifeguard at the local pool, okay? Geez..."

"Better. We know you want to meet Seth, but what else do you want from him?"

"Closure? A relationship?" Heavenly asked, her voice a feather compared to his anvil.

Hudson's laugh was sharp enough to cut glass. "I don't want a damn thing except to put a face to the name of my sperm donor daddy."

Heavenly flinched, and dread settled in Beck's chest. The kid had clearly spent years building up his resentment, painting Seth as the villain in a story he only half understood.

Heavenly looked at him with pity. "Is your mom still alive?"

"Of course."

"Does she know where you are?"

The kid shrugged. "I doubt she cares. She's got a new husband and a new baby. She doesn't have time for a fuckup like me."

There it was. Beck recognized the pain behind the casual dismissal. Hudson felt sidelined since his mother had moved forward, so he was throwing out insults before anyone could reject him, building walls before people got close enough to hurt him. Beck had used the same defense mechanisms for years after escaping the Chosen.

"You should call her," Heavenly suggested. "Let her know you're safe."

Beck saw the *nope* all over the kid's face. "Call her. We're not harboring a minor without her permission."

Hudson rolled his eyes but pulled out his phone and dialed. "Hey, Mom." A pause, and even from across the room, Beck could hear a sharp female voice shooting rapid-fire questions that made Hudson hold the phone away from his ear. "Jesus, Mom. I'm fine. I'm in California." Another pause. "Yeah. I'm safe, okay?" A longer pause. "Fuck. School can wait. I have something more important to take care of." This pause was the longest yet as the woman on the other end of the phone screeched, then Hudson replied, "I came to meet Seth, okay?"

Beck winced as the woman's voice rose to near-shrieking levels.

Heavenly stood and approached, her face full of sympathy. "Hudson, would you like me to talk to her?"

The kid looked relieved to hand over the phone. "Good luck."

"Hello?" Heavenly's voice was warm and soothing as she activated the speaker. "I'm Heavenly Young, a…friend of Seth's. He'll be home tomorrow. Hudson is welcome to stay with me and his doctor friend until then."

"I'm Hudson's mother, Laura Clarke. I can't believe he flew across the country alone. Is he really okay? He's been missing since this morning, and I was about to call the police."

"He's fine," Heavenly assured her. "Probably tired from traveling, and we're about to feed him Chinese. He has his own guest room. It's quiet here. He'll be safe until he and Seth can talk."

Beck was impressed by how smoothly his little girl handled the conversation, setting the woman at ease while protecting Seth's privacy.

"You're sure?"

"Absolutely."

"Thank you," Laura breathed. "If…if things don't go well, will you make sure my son gets safely on a plane home?"

"We will," Heavenly promised. "Let me give you my number so you can reach us, just in case."

After exchanging contact information, Heavenly handed the phone back to Hudson, who shifted uncomfortably and disengaged the speaker. "It's me. I don't know when I'm coming home. We'll talk later, okay?"

He ended the call and tossed the phone aside, clearly annoyed. "Happy now?"

His dismissive tone didn't fool Beck. The kid was desperately trying to maintain his armor, but he was scared.

"Tell me about this invisible father of mine." Hudson stuck out his chin. "What's he really like?"

"He's a good man," Heavenly insisted. "I already told you he has four brothers. He grew up in New York. His mom is getting remarried next month, actually. His father was a police officer who was killed in the line of duty when Seth was sixteen. He stepped up and helped raise his younger brothers after that."

Beck watched Hudson's expression flicker at that information—surprise, maybe curiosity—but the kid quickly buried it under an indifferent expression.

"For a while, Seth was a cop, like his dad and grandfather," Heavenly went on. "But he left the force and started his own private investigation business. He's successful, honest, and he cares about people. Especially family."

"Sounds like a real saint." Hudson sneered. "If he's so awesome, why did he kick his pregnant girlfriend to the curb?"

Beck's jaw tightened until he could practically hear his teeth grinding. "What makes you think he did?"

"What other explanation is there? Mom gets pregnant, dad disappears. Typical shit."

Beck leaned forward, his voice deadly calm. "Is that what your mom told you?"

"Not in so many words," Hudson admitted, his posture defensive.

"So you're making assumptions?" Beck pressed. "I'm one of his best friends. I'm telling you now, I don't think Seth ever knew your mom was pregnant, so stop assuming he's a steaming pile of—"

Heavenly's hand on his arm stopped him mid-sentence. He glanced her way, at the plea in her eyes for him to dial it back. He sighed. She was right. Hudson's attitude was annoying as fuck, but he was just a lost kid.

Like Beck had once been.

Heavenly sent Hudson a soft stare. "Beck is right. I don't think Seth has any idea you exist."

"Whatever," the boy drawled, but Beck caught the way his shoulders sagged slightly, as if some of the fight had left him.

The doorbell rang.

They settled around the kitchen table with their takeout containers. Beck watched Hudson try not to look impressed by the spread—orange chicken, lo mein, fried rice, and spring rolls.

"So," Heavenly said, breaking the silence. "What kind of music are you into?"

Hudson shrugged, digging into his orange chicken. "Rap mostly. Travis Scott, Kendrick, some drill music."

"Seth likes classic rock," Beck offered. "But I've heard him listen to hip hop."

"Hmm." Hudson shrugged like he didn't care, but Beck bet he was filing away the information.

"What about sports?" Heavenly asked. "Do you play anything?"

"Football and baseball. Made varsity teams in both as a sophomore." There was a hint of pride in Hudson's voice before he caught himself. "I'm a decent pitcher and an all-star receiver."

"Do you have a favorite pro team?" Beck asked.

"The Yankees. Obviously." Hudson shot him a look like he was an idiot. "Best team out there."

"Seth is a Yankees fan too," Heavenly said with a smile.

Hudson's fork paused halfway to his mouth. "Yeah?"

"When he lived in New York, he went to games with his brothers. He moved to LA this past February. I'm sure he's sad he missed this season."

Beck watched something flicker across Hudson's face—interest, maybe even longing—before he banked it.

"Cool," Hudson mumbled. "I guess."

"Got friends back home?" Beck asked.

"A few. Most of those kids are fucktards."

Heavenly did her best to hide her grimace. "How about…a girlfriend?"

Hudson snorted. "Fuck no. The girls in Cromwell are either stupid, skanky, or boring as fuck. No thanks."

So the kid felt like an outsider. Beck changed the subject again. "You have your license?"

"Yeah." Hudson's expression turned sullen. "Had to take the test twice though. Parallel parking's a bitch."

After that, quiet fell. They ate, the earlier tension starting to ease. Hudson even helped himself to seconds, though he tried to be casual about it.

"This is…actually pretty good," he admitted grudgingly. "Almost as good as the Chinese place back home."

"Seth agrees but swears New York pizza is *way* better," Beck said. "He prefers West Coast Mexican food, though."

Hudson's smile was quick but genuine this time. "Yeah, our Mexican sucks. No spice."

"You like spicy food?"

"Love it. Nothing like a super-hot Thai dish."

"Seth and I both love that. Her?" He thumbed at Heavenly. "Not so much."

She swatted his arm. "I'm from Wisconsin! I'll take cheese curds any day over that."

"What the hell is a cheese curd?" Hudson asked.

As she explained and finished eating, Beck studied the kid. Beneath the angry armor, Hudson was trying so hard to be tough, to not care. But Beck was beginning to see the cracks.

The question was: what would Seth see when he looked at Hudson tomorrow—a second chance at fatherhood? A gift he'd never expected? Or another son he could lose if he failed to protect him?

Seth had just committed to starting a family with them, but Hudson wasn't some hypothetical future child. He was real, almost grown, and carrying sixteen years of baggage about the father who'd never been there for him.

"So," Hudson interrupted Beck's thoughts. "What time is Cooper supposed to be back tomorrow?"

"If his flight is on time, he should be here by two," Heavenly supplied.

Hudson nodded as if he couldn't wait for the confrontation.

"Listen," Beck said carefully. "I need you to understand something. Seth's been through a lot. Lost people he loved. Finding out about you is going to be a shock."

"What are you saying?" Hudson's voice was deliberately casual, but Beck heard the real question underneath: *Will he want me?*

Beck exchanged a glance with Heavenly. How the hell was he supposed to explain to the kid who'd come all this way to meet his father that the man might not be emotionally ready to be a dad?

"Just don't judge him by his initial reaction," Beck said finally. "You've known about him for...how long?"

"Most of my life."

"Yeah, you're going to blindside him. It's not your fault. Just...give him a hot minute to catch up, okay?"

Hudson's jaw tightened. "If he doesn't want me around, I'll just go home. No big deal."

Wrong. It absolutely was a big deal, and they all knew it. The kid had waited years for this moment. If Seth rejected him tomorrow, it would destroy what was left of Hudson's already fragile sense of belonging. And Beck didn't know how to brace either of them.

All he could hope now was that Seth was strong enough to handle what fate had just dropped in his lap.

Chapter Eleven

Once most of the Chinese food had been consumed and the conversation fell into a lull, Hudson pushed back from the table. "Dinner was decent. Thanks. I'm going to crash."

Already? Then Heavenly realized it was after ten pm on the East Coast. "Sure. There are extra pillows in the closet if you want more," Heavenly called after him.

"And help yourself to the Xbox," Beck added. "Seth has a collection of games down there, mostly first-person shooters and RPGs."

"I play those, too. Cool," he said before he disappeared down the stairs.

She waited until Hudson's door closed before tossing the last of the takeout containers in the trash, while Beck wiped off the table. When they finished, he took her hand. "Come on. Let's go upstairs and talk, little girl."

"I think we should. There's…a lot."

Once they reached their bedroom, Heavenly wrapped her arms around herself as she stared out the window, into the backyard. The pool lights cast rippling blue shadows across the water, but she barely saw them.

"Tell me what you're thinking." Beck's voice was soft behind her, but she heard his concern.

She turned to find him leaning against the doorframe, his dark hair mussed from running his hands through it. The stress lines around his eyes had deepened since Hudson's bombshell arrival, and she wanted nothing more than to smooth them away.

"Seth was fifteen when Hudson was born. Just a kid himself. I don't know how he's going to take this as an adult."

He joined her at the window, wrapping his arms around her waist. "I don't, either."

"Just as I thought our lives were coming together…they're going to get really complicated."

"Nothing about our lives has ever been simple, but we've made it work. Don't worry, little girl, we'll figure this out, too." As he turned her to face him and pulled her in close, she melted against his chest, breathing in his familiar musky scent.

"Hudson is so angry. That 'sperm donor daddy' comment was awful and heartbreaking at the same time."

Beck stroked her hair, clearly trying to soothe her. "His whole life, Hudson has believed that his father knew about him and just didn't give a shit."

"Seth finding out he has a sixteen-year-old son he knew nothing about will be shocking enough, but when he realizes the kid hates him…"

"Yeah." Beck nodded. "It's going to shock the fuck out of him."

"Totally. And what will this news do to his relationship with his mother?" Heavenly closed her eyes. "If it's already strained, that will make him telling her about us even harder. What if she never accepts us?"

That might kill him.

"Don't borrow trouble, little girl."

They stood in silence, their concerns hanging heavy in the air. She closed her eyes and imagined how Seth would react when he walked through the door, expecting some sort of normalcy…only to be blind-sided by a son he never knew.

"You're right, but the timing couldn't be worse." She sighed. "Seth is still coming to terms with his guilt for Tristan's and Autumn's deaths, and it's like the universe is conspiring against him. Against us. What if he can't handle a teenager in his life? If he rejects Hudson? Or leaves us?"

"Shhh." Beck placed a finger against her lips. "Seth might shut down. But it's also possible that he'll take one look at Hudson and see all the opportunities he lost with Tristan. Then?" Beck gave her a sanguine shrug. "Knowing Seth, he'll get so overprotective he'll annoy the hell out of the kid."

"You're probably right."

"Seth may *need* the chance to be the father to Hudson he hardly got to be with Tristan."

Beck's observation made her throat tight. She loved that he had the ability to really see people and the insight to understand them.

"What if Hudson refuses to listen? What if he's determined to hate Seth?"

"The kid wouldn't have flown across the country just to tell Seth to shove it up his ass. He would have stayed in Cromwell, used the money he spent on plane fare to buy video games, and kept badmouthing his 'sperm donor dad'. He's going to lash out, but under all that anger? He secretly wants Seth to care about him."

"I hope you're right."

"I promise you, that boy is desperate for a father, even if he'd rather die than admit it. And despite whatever his mother told him, Hudson *needs* the truth." His voice was steady, certain. "We just have to make sure he gets it. The bigger question is, what happens next? Hudson brought more with him than a change or two of clothes. I'm not convinced he had any intention of going home. I don't think he has a lot to go back to—at least in his head."

She hadn't thought of that, but Beck had a point. The kid's backpack and duffel were both bulging, and his relationship with his mother sounded strained at best. Fair or not, he seemed to resent his stepfather and their new baby.

"You're right. He feels invisible there. Do you think he's hoping to...stay here?"

Beck shrugged. "That's my guess. He might not admit it, but he came to see if he could salvage anything with Seth. If not...I think he intends to strike out on his own."

Heavenly gasped. "Sixteen is too young."

"I managed at that age...but barely."

"If you hadn't found Gloria—"

"I'd be dead."

Heavenly's heart caught in her throat. "If anything happened to Hudson, it would destroy Seth. We can't let that happen."

But she was painfully aware that meant taking Hudson in. Parenting. Raising a belligerent, rebellious teenager. What would that do to their lives? What would happen when they inevitably had a baby? Would Hudson feel forced out again? Flee and put himself in danger?

"I should check on him." Heavenly started to pull away.

Beck held her tight. "Give him space tonight. Tomorrow will be soon enough for...whatever happens."

The urge to comfort the angry, hurting boy downstairs tugged at her. She'd always felt compelled to care for the people around her. It was one reason she was studying so diligently to become a nurse. But her father's death had taught her that she couldn't fix everything simply because she wanted to.

"You're right. I'm going to get ready for bed. It's early...but I feel exhausted."

"We should probably wind down since Hudson is on another time zone and may be up at the ass crack of dawn."

"Good point," she said as she began washing her face and brushing her teeth.

Beck stripped and hopped in the shower. She always enjoyed gawking at him. The people he worked with had no idea the muscles and tattoos he hid under his dress shirts and lab coat. But she did, and she loved every inch of him. Tonight, though, she had too much on her mind to do more than stare.

As he stood under the pelting spray, she patted her clean face dry—and a realization burned through her head. "Seth never called or texted us today."

Beck froze, then tried to shrug it off. "It's his last night there. He's probably just busy."

Maybe, but... "It's not like him. He almost always checks in, makes sure we're okay." Fear crept into her voice. "Do you think something happened in New York? What if...he's having second thoughts about starting a family?"

"If anything's going on with him, we'll deal with it when he gets home."

Heavenly hated to be negative, but avoiding the terrifying possibilities wouldn't solve anything. "What if he decides he can't handle all this?"

"We'll remind him how good we are together." Beck's voice was as fierce as his dark eyes, even through the steamy glass. "That we're worth fighting for."

She nodded, hoping that was enough.

Seth stared out the airplane's window at the patchwork of land below, his stomach churning with more than turbulence. The guilt and regret from yesterday's visit to his old house wouldn't fucking quit. Hell, he'd barely stepped through the door before the onslaught of memories had pulled him under, and he'd run. Less than five minutes, and he'd let the specters of Autumn's and Tristan's memories drive him out.

The house shouldn't still haunt him, much less hold this much power over him. The fact that it did terrified Seth.

Why the hell can't I get over it? What do I tell Beck and Heavenly?

They'd been so patient. Seth had convinced himself that the passing of time and embracing of his new life had allowed him to conquer his demons. But he'd been blowing smoke up his ass. One step into his past, and he couldn't deny that he was still spectacularly fucked up.

As much as Seth ached for a future with Beck and Heavenly, wanting and actually being able to were two entirely different things. He was learning that the hard way.

God, he fucking hated being right back where he'd started.

The flight attendant's voice crackled over the intercom, announcing their descent into LAX.

Seth clenched the armrests. Beck and Heavenly were at home, undoubtedly waiting to pelt him with questions—about the twins, about any inroads he'd made with his mom, about their future. And, of course, eager to keep trying for the baby they both longed for.

The baby that both excited and terrified Seth to the depths of his soul.

He closed his eyes, remembering Beck's face the last time they'd made love to Heavenly. He'd seen not just a primal satisfaction, but hope. And Heavenly—god, the way she'd looked at him afterward, like he was her whole world. They deserved better than his inability to control his fears and exorcise his demons.

He knew his misgivings were irrational…but that didn't change shit. Every time he thought about getting Heavenly pregnant, about holding *their* child, he was thrilled at the notion of claiming her so ultimately…even as panic clawed at him. What if he failed at fatherhood again? What if he couldn't protect this family? What if—

Stop. He shoved down his internal chaos.

What if a baby was exactly what he needed? What if holding their child would finally prove he *could* protect what mattered? What if getting Heavenly pregnant cemented their bond so completely that nothing could tear them apart?

When the plane touched down with a gentle bump, Seth's throat tightened. He'd missed Beck and Heavenly, but today…coming home felt as if he was being frog-marched toward a cliff.

An hour later, Seth pulled his SUV into the driveway and killed the engine. The house looked exactly the same—warm and welcoming in the late afternoon sun. A respite under the California sky.

He grabbed his bag from the trunk and headed for the door, key in hand.

Before he could unlock it, the slab swung open. Heavenly stood in the portal, her stare clinging to him. But she didn't throw herself into his arms. Her expression was surprisingly unreadable, her posture tense. Was she upset because he hadn't called last night?

"Welcome home." Her voice shook.

Shit. She was upset. Fresh guilt threatened him. He should have shoved down his freakout long enough to call them yesterday, reassure her.

"It's good to be home." He stepped into the foyer and set down his bag before he swept her into his arms and planted a soft kiss on her mouth. This was what he'd needed. "Angel… God, I missed you."

Beck appeared in the doorway behind her. "Glad you're back. How was the flight?"

His expression was too careful.

Seth's gut clenched. "Long. The whole trip was. I'm just happy to be home with you two. Everything okay? You both seem—"

"We should talk."

Seth's stomach did a free fall to his toes. Something was wrong.

Heavenly kept glancing at Beck, and the surgeon's usual confidence seemed strained.

Alarm bells went off in his head. "What's going on? Are you pregnant?"

Heavenly shook her head. "It's too early to know."

Beck led him through the house and into the family room, all but shoving him into an armchair. "Sit down. We need to tell you something."

"And we didn't think this was something we should say over the phone," Heavenly whispered.

His panic shot up ten notches before movement outside the sliding glass doors caught Seth's eye. Someone was in the pool—a man. No, a teenager, his body long and lean as he cut through the water with easy strokes. Whose kid was swimming in their pool?

Seth was trying to piece it together when the teen hauled himself onto the deck and grabbed a towel. The harsh afternoon sunlight caught blond hair and obscured his face. His fluid movements were like an athlete's, and his posture seemed familiar. Awareness pricked Seth, a realization just beyond his grasp.

The teenager toweled off, then loped toward the house, ducking under the shade of the patio cover.

Then Seth got a good look at the kid's face.

And his whole world tilted off its axis.

He froze, tingling from head to toe, his head spinning with shock.

"What the…" Unconsciously, he stood, mouth agape as his vision narrowed to the figure opening the sliding door.

The kid stepped inside and swaggered toward him, stare full of challenge. The closer he strode, the more undeniable the resemblance. Same height, same build, same green eyes, same stubborn jawline.

Seth felt as if he was looking in a mirror from sixteen years ago.

Holy shit, is this kid…mine?

"So I finally get to meet the infamous Seth Cooper?" The teen shot him a cynical brow.

Forcing himself to breathe, Seth raked a hand through his hair. "Yeah. What is… I don't…" He sighed. "Goddamn it, who are you?"

"Hudson." He lifted his chin defiantly, as if that name should mean something.

It didn't. Seth sucked in a rough breath, blinking as Hudson stood there.

"Are you..." The question stuck in his throat. He cleared it and tried again. "Shit. Are you my...son?"

"I'm sure as fuck not your daughter."

Seth ignored Hudson's snide delivery and gaped.

His *son*.

In an instant, everything he knew about his life crumbled. The room slanted, spun, turning his whole world upside down.

Fuck me.

He glanced at Heavenly, who looked pensive.

Then he darted a stare at Beck, who nodded. "He's yours."

No shit.

When? Who? How? A strobe of reckless teenage memories crashed through his brain. But Seth had done more partying and fucking around than he could remember, especially in this shocked moment.

"Who...who is your mother?" he managed to croak out.

"How many girls were you banging at fifteen?"

More than he should have been. "Answer me."

"Laura Clarke."

Seth felt the color drain from his face as memories of Laura dive-bombed his brain.

He'd never forgotten the stunning girl he'd worked with in the Catskills the summer he'd turned fifteen. She'd been nothing like the prepubescent girls who'd gone to his school. Laura had been a woman...lush breasts, curvy hips, pert ass, and a bawdy sense of humor. He remembered the daring twinkle in her blue eyes, her throaty laughter, her shameless flirting, and the intense thunderstorm the fateful night they'd shared shelter—and passion.

The walls of the past closed in around him. Seth began to sweat.

"Jesus, you don't even remember her," Hudson accused.

"I do. You're...sixteen, right?"

"As of April twentieth." Hudson pinned Seth with a long stare before he snorted. "Fuck. It's all over your face. You had no idea I existed, did you?"

"None. If I had, I would have been in your life from day one."

Hudson huffed. "Right… What kind of dad would you have been at fifteen?"

"Maybe shitty, but I wouldn't have been absent." Jesus christ, he couldn't believe he was talking to his son. "So…where's your mom? Is she okay? Does she know you're here?"

"Yeah. When I flew out yesterday—"

"From Connecticut," Beck broke in. "Without parental knowledge or consent."

"Seriously?" Seth exploded.

"I'm fine. He made me call." Hudson pointed to Beck. "Mom knows I'm safe. She talked to Heavenly, too. It's cool."

Seth stared at this angry, hurting boy who'd jetted alone across the country to find him. "Why did you come?"

"To meet my sperm donor. Why else?"

Seth heard his pain under the snark. The kid felt neglected, abandoned. Of course he was pissed. And Seth had a mountain of questions, but those were for Laura. Later.

"You want to know your father," Seth shot back, voice far steadier than he felt.

"No, I just came to tell you what I think of you."

"Bullshit. You were brave enough to find me, so why won't you be brave enough to be honest?"

"Fuck you." Hudson looked away.

"Fuck your attitude. What do you want to know?" Seth challenged. "Ask me anything. I'm an open book."

The kid stood there, staring. They were at an impasse. Seth half expected him to storm out, maybe for good. Instead, he shoved his hands on his hips. "How did you meet my mom? Her old letters didn't say."

"I used to spend summers in the Catskills with my grandparents. I met your mom working as a busboy at a swanky restaurant in one of the resorts." He could still picture it—the elegant dining room, the mountain views, Laura moving between tables with easy grace. "She was a waitress. I was fifteen, but I…told her I was heading to college in the fall, not my sophomore year of high school. When she learned the truth…" He trailed off, remembering Laura's fury when she'd confronted him. "She stopped talking to me. Within a few weeks, she was gone. I had no idea she was pregnant."

Hudson shifted uncomfortably. "She never talked about you. I had to dig up your name in her old stuff. How did you two…you know? How did I happen?"

Seth's thoughts drifted back. "We'd been flirting back and forth for a few weeks. One night the manager got sick and left Laura with the keys to lock up. By the time we finished cleaning, it was late. I didn't want to wake up my grandparents to give me a ride, so Laura offered to drive me home. But a massive storm hit. Lightning, thunder, hail, tornado threat—the works. We took shelter in the basement storage area that doubled as the manager's crash-pad. The power went out."

Seth glanced at Beck and Heavenly, both of whom were listening intently.

"I, um…found some candles, and we hunkered down to wait out the storm. We were both soaked and…" He met Hudson's eyes. "One thing led to another. We fooled around a few more times after that, but then Laura found out how old I really was from our manager. Wasn't long after that she quit without saying goodbye. I never saw her again."

But even as he said it, Seth reeled. What did Hudson's existence mean for his future with Beck and Heavenly? How was he going to tell his mother? His brothers?

Christ, he could barely handle the thought of having another baby, and now he had a teenage son who clearly had years of built-up resentment.

"That sounds like Mom. She's…not much for confrontations."

As far as Seth remembered, that tracked. "I need to talk to her. Give me your phone."

Hudson hesitated, then handed it over with a soft curse.

"Stay here."

"Should I bark like a dog, too?"

"Watch your fucking mouth," Beck growled as Seth stepped onto the patio.

The kid's attitude was a problem he'd have to deal with later. Now, he dialed Laura's number, his heart hammering. She answered on the first ring.

"Hudson? Are you coming home—"

"Laura? It's Seth Cooper."

Silence. He could feel her shock. "Oh, my god."

"Our *son* is sitting in my living room. You never told me."

"What was I supposed to say? You were *fifteen*. You couldn't support him. What were you going to do, drop out of high school to be his dad?" Her voice cracked.

She had him there.

"I haven't been fifteen for a long time."

She sighed. "You're right. I tried looking you up nine years ago, thinking you'd be an adult and that you might want to know about Hudson. But you were married with a baby on the way. I didn't want to blow up your life."

Seth's stomach clenched. "They both died that December. Explosion."

Laura gasped. "Oh, god. Seth, I'm so sorry. If I'd known..."

"It...was a long time ago. You been okay? It can't have been easy raising Hudson alone."

"It wasn't until I got married a few years ago. But my husband, Ted? He and Hudson butt heads, especially since our daughter was born last year."

That explained a lot. He could guess how a new baby made Hudson feel.

Where did that leave the kid? Where did he feel safe? Where did he belong?

Silence descended as Seth's head spun possibilities and scenarios—all of which meant change.

"You must be in shock," she finally offered.

"I'm...processing." Seth pinched the bridge of his nose. "Laura, do you know why he's here? What he wants?"

"Not exactly. He hopped on a plane without my permission. Since he finally called to tell me where he'd gone, I've been asking myself that. All he told me is that he wanted to meet you."

Seth hadn't talked to Hudson much, but his gut told him he wasn't here merely to satisfy his curiosity.

"What do you want me to do? Keep him for the weekend and send him home? He must have school…"

"When he actually decides to go. He's gotten so big and so rebellious, I can't make him do anything anymore. He's taller than my husband, and Ted doesn't want to get in the middle." Laura's heavy sigh carried across three thousand miles. "I've tried to be both mother and father, but I'm at the end of my rope. He's become impossible, Seth. So angry all the time. I'm hoping meeting you will give him some answers. Some closure…"

"He's more than angry." That was obvious. "I'm late in being his dad, but what can I do? What does he need?"

"Honestly? Structure and discipline. I keep trying but—"

"What if…he stayed with me for a while?" Seth blurted the question. He had no idea how he'd handle having the kid around, or if he was even ready for that. And how would Beck and Heavenly feel? But he couldn't let his own flesh and blood flounder or feel insecure. "I could get him in school and straighten him out." *I think.*

"What do you know about raising teenage boys, Seth?"

"The summer after we met, my dad was killed in the line of duty. Over the next decade, I raised my four younger brothers. They're all productive members of society now. Well, mostly. The verdict is out on my youngest two, the twins. They're seniors in college, and they're crazy…" He was rambling, and he made himself stop. "But if there's one thing I know well, it's teenage boys."

"You just met Hudson, and you would do that?" Her voice was thick with unshed tears.

"He's my son. That was obvious at a glance."

"No denying he looks exactly like you." There was almost a smile in her voice. "He's not a bad kid, but he's mouthy."

"He's sixteen. He's a normal teenage boy." But Hudson had other reasons to be angry and off-balance. Since Seth had failed Tristan in every way, he didn't want to compound that by letting Hudson down.

"Hormones, right?" she tried to joke.

"Yeah."

"You have room for him?"

"Plenty. I'm in a big house. Hudson could have his own bedroom and bathroom."

Laura let out a sigh of relief. "He needs privacy. Our place is only two bedrooms. Now that the baby is sleeping through the night, she really needs a room of her own..."

And what teenage boy wanted to share a room with his baby sister? "He'll have plenty of space and privacy here."

"Heavenly won't mind if Hudson stays? She seems very sweet, by the way."

Laura was fishing, and Seth didn't blame her. If his kid was staying with a relative stranger, he'd want to know who else would be hanging around. "Probably sweeter than I deserve. And she won't mind. We also live with a doctor friend. A vascular surgeon. He's good with it, too."

And Seth wasn't divulging more about his relationship than that right now.

"Wow, that's...amazing. You're truly willing to keep him for a bit?"

Everything felt so sudden, but what other decision could he make? "Yeah. But we'll need to call our lawyers. If my name isn't on Hudson's birth certificate, I need to be legally named as his father."

"It's not."

Seth swallowed back useless anger. "Fix it. We'll need a custody arrangement, too."

"You're right. I don't have a lawyer, but my mom had one who put her will together. I can call him tomorrow. If he can't do it, he'll give me a referral."

"Once you're in contact, have your attorney reach out. I'll put him in touch with mine, and we'll take it from there."

"Thank you." The tears in her voice were unmistakable. "W-would it be too much to ask for me to come out and visit him? I promise I won't be in your way and—" Her trembling exhalation told him this was hard for her. "I don't think I can go too long without seeing

Hudson. I love him so much, but he just…doesn't believe that right now."

Seth's heart hurt for her. She'd been a single mom for so long, and she was unprepared to handle a testosterone-laden man-child. "I'll be in New York next month. My mom is finally getting remarried, and I'll…probably bring Hudson with me to meet my family. You could visit with him then."

"Really? If you could bring him out, that would be great. I…can't tell you how much I appreciate all this."

He could hear the gratitude in her voice. "We'll get the details figured out. I'll be in touch."

"Thank you for…everything."

"Of course." Seth hung up.

What the hell had he just agreed to? This morning he'd been struggling with the idea of becoming a father to a hypothetical baby he might have with Beck and Heavenly. Fast forward a few hours, and he had a teenage son who needed him—right now. Seth had just volunteered to parent the defiant kid…whether he was ready or not.

Shit.

Heaving a sigh, Seth trekked back inside and tried to gather his words. He had to break the news to Beck and Heavenly. He had no idea how they'd take it…

How would Hudson? Probably with more attitude and pushback. That didn't bother Seth; he could handle that. But he had to prove to Hudson that he'd be there as a father. Even if this arrangement was temporary, blood was forever.

"All right," he addressed his son. "Your mom and I agree—you can stay here for a while. But there are conditions."

Seth caught Beck's eye over Hudson's head. Beck gave him the slightest nod. Heavenly was already looking at him with that soft, understanding expression. Somehow, they were on the same page without even a word. Thank fuck.

Hudson bristled. "I never said I wanted to stay."

"If you don't, hey. No sweat. I'll put you on a plane back to Connecticut tomorrow."

Hudson growled, shoulders stiffening. "I fucking hate Cromwell."

"Well, here or there are your only two choices. What's it going to be?"

"Jesus, you're way more of a hard-ass than Ted."

"I'm not your stepdad. He might treat you with kid gloves. I won't. Tell me what you want."

"Fuck." Hudson rolled his eyes. "Fine. I'm staying."

"Good. I don't know the situation at home, but here you have rules. You'll talk to your mother at least once a week. That's nonnegotiable. And if you're staying, you'll be going back to school. Also nonnegotiable. So is respect. You either knock that chip off your shoulder, or I'll do it for you."

"I'll help," Beck quipped.

Seth tried to repress a smile. "And you'll be especially respectful of Heavenly, or we'll have a major problem."

"Fuck, I've known you for thirty minutes, and already you're a buzzkill?"

"I'm not your bestie; I'm your father. And watch your mouth. You either fall in line, or you're going home."

Hudson groaned like Seth was torturing him, but they spent the next hour negotiating—curfew, chores, acceptable behavior, and expectations. Hudson pushed back, clearly unused to boundaries, but Seth held firm.

Finally, Hudson threw himself back against his chair with a dramatic sigh. "Okay. Whatever. Geez. At least going to school will be better than hanging around and watching Beck and Heavenly pretend they don't want to fuck each other constantly."

The room went dead silent.

Seth glanced Beck's way, then turned his stare on Heavenly. "They do, and I'm glad you noticed. Now we don't have to hide anything. Beck and I are both engaged to Heavenly. That a problem for you?"

Hudson gave him a long look, then pointed between him and Beck. "You two gay?"

"Would it bother you if we were?"

"No."

Seth didn't believe Hudson, but he figured there was no sense in yanking the kid's chain. His life had just been uprooted, too. "We're not gay."

"We don't...what's that phrase?" Beck put in. "Cross swords."

"Ever." Seth nodded.

"So you two...share her?" He tossed his head in Heavenly's direction. "Well, at least I know where I got my kinky streak."

Great. Another problem to contend with. Seth tried to keep the *oh-fuck* off his face. "Have you shared a girl?"

"No." Hudson grinned. "But I'm damn good with rope."

Holy shit. His teenage son apparently took after him in more ways than one.

Heavenly gaped. "You're only sixteen!"

Hudson's grin widened. "What can I say? I'm adventurous."

Beck clapped Seth on the back with a grin. "Well, like father, like son."

Seth dropped his head into his hands, then glared up at Beck. "You're not helping."

That just made Beck laugh.

He and Heavenly were being understanding, but Seth knew they must be asking themselves the same obvious questions he was. How was this going to change their dynamic? Their plans? Their future?

Seth had no fucking idea. All he knew was that his carefully constructed life had just been blown apart, and he was going to have to figure out how to put the pieces back together.

Chapter Twelve

Seth looked at his son—christ, that was going to take some getting used to—and felt the weight of sixteen missing years pressing down on him. But dwelling on what he couldn't change wouldn't help either of them move forward.

"Let me put on something more comfortable." He gestured to his travel attire. "After that, how about we hang out downstairs? Play some video games and talk."

Hudson shrugged. "Whatever."

Seth tried not to let the casual dismissal sting. The kid had every right to be guarded. Seth had his work cut out for him.

He grabbed his carry-on and headed upstairs, Beck and Heavenly following close behind. In their bedroom, Seth stripped off his button-down shirt. As he did, it felt as if he was shedding an older version of himself—one who'd boarded his flight this morning without knowing he was a father.

"I'll unpack for you," Heavenly offered, reaching for his bag.

Seth almost smiled despite everything as he kicked off his pants. "You're welcome to try, but you know I'll end up reorganizing everything."

She shot him a look. "I'm well aware, Mr. OCD."

"I'm not OCD, just particular." He pulled on a tank top and shorts, feeling more like himself already.

"Bullshit," Beck fake-coughed the word.

They shared a momentary laugh before Seth sobered. "Seriously, are you two really okay with Hudson staying? I wasn't misreading those nods downstairs?"

Beck leaned against the dresser. "The kid needs to stay. He's exactly like I was at that age—all attitude to cover up the hurt."

"He needs a *father*," Heavenly added softly. "And you need him."

They were right.

"Thank you. Both of you. I don't know how long Hudson will be with us, but I'm damn grateful for your understanding. Especially since I struggled with having your brother here." And didn't that make Seth feel like shit now?

"Totally different situation. And Zach is happier alone. It's all good. Your son is just a kid. He needs you now, but you've got us forever."

Those words made Seth's chest feel soft as a marshmallow. He brought Beck in for a shoulder-bump. "That's pretty fucking eloquent for you, man. Thanks."

"We'll do our best to make Hudson comfortable and happy," Heavenly assured, looking teary.

He pulled her close, closing his eyes and savoring her in his arms before he kissed her, sinking deep and savoring his sense of coming home. "God, I waited five long days to do that."

"It felt like you were gone half of forever. Was your trip all right? How did things go in New York?"

His New York problems seemed like ancient history now, but those issues were still waiting, poised to fuck up his life if he didn't handle them carefully. "On a clusterfuck scale of one to ten? About what you'd expect. I'll fill you in later. I really wanted to spend today with you two. I missed you so much. But if I'm going to build any kind of bond with Hudson…"

"You need to start now. Go," Heavenly insisted softly. "We understand."

Beck grabbed her hand. "Do what you need to."

Seth kissed her again, patted Beck's shoulder, then dragged in a bracing breath before heading downstairs to find his son.

When he ducked into the game room, he found a freshly showered Hudson already sprawled on the sectional, controller in hand. The massive flat screen showed the *Call of Duty* loading screen.

"Hope you're not shit at this," Hudson said without looking up.

"Dude, I've been playing video games longer than you've been alive." Seth settled beside him and picked up the second controller.

"Don't 'dude' me." Hudson glanced over, then did a double take. "Holy shit, is that—" Hudson pointed at Seth's right shoulder, where a small crescent-shaped birthmark was visible above his tank top.

"What? My birthmark."

"I have the exact same one. Same spot and everything." Hudson pulled his shirt aside to flash his.

Seth looked at his son's shoulder. Sure enough, he had an identical crescent mark. "I'll be damned."

"Guess you don't need a DNA test now, right?" Hudson's tone dropped and lost some of its edge.

"Never did. I knew at a glance."

"So did Beck and Heavenly."

That made Seth smile. "I'll bet they did. You probably shocked the hell out of them."

"Oh, yeah. That River guy, too. You should have seen their faces."

"You're lucky no one had a heart attack." Seth selected his loadout. "Now…you ready to show me what you got?"

"Bring it, old man."

"Watch that 'old man' shit. If we weren't on the same team, I'd wipe the floor with your ass."

They spawned into a team mission together, and Seth was immediately impressed by Hudson's skill. His son was a natural—quick reflexes, good tactical thinking, and he actually communicated during firefights instead of going rogue.

"Nice shot," Seth said as Hudson took out a sniper. "Cover me while I plant this charge."

"Got your six," Hudson promised, focused while he guarded the perimeter. "So, uh, Heavenly said I have a grandmother and four uncles?"

"Yeah." Seth lobbed a grenade around a corner. "I'm the oldest, then there's Matt—he runs the New York branch of Cooper Investigations."

"So when I called over there last week and talked to Matt, that was my uncle?"

Seth nodded. "Danny is a couple of years younger than Matt. He's married and has a baby girl. Jack and Connor, the twins, are finishing their senior year of college."

"They're not that much older than me, huh?"

"They're not." And that was a terrifying realization.

"Hey!" Hudson warned. "Watch that doorway. Hostiles incoming."

"Got it." They coordinated their attack seamlessly.

Once they'd defeated the squad, Seth grabbed a soda from the fridge and offered his son one.

"How do you think your family will react? You know, to me."

"*Our* family will love you. Fair warning though, the Cooper clan is loud and crazy when we get together. And your Grandma Grace will lose her mind. She's going to be so excited to meet you."

Hudson actually smiled at that. "Sounds better than spending time at my mom's place. There it's all awkward silence. Well, unless Ted is sneering at me about something or the baby's crying."

Seth hated the thought of his son feeling like he didn't have anyone on his side. "We're busy here, but when we're all home, there aren't many awkward silences."

"And no babies!" Hudson sounded thrilled.

Well, not yet…

The next mission loaded, and they jumped in, covering ground and taking defensive positions.

"What was it like growing up with all those brothers?" Hudson asked. "Being an only child sucked. Well, I thought it did until Emma was born. She's *loud*."

"It was chaotic and fun…and way louder than one baby. Trust me."

"Yeah? Did you share a room? Fight a lot? Play sports together?"

"Sometimes, yeah. When we were teenagers, we all had our own rooms, and we played on teams together…but none of that stopped the fighting." He chuckled. "Drove Grandma Grace nuts."

"Did you all compete with each other, too?"

"Constantly." Seth switched weapons as they moved to the next objective. "We were always trying to one-up each other. Once, I convinced Matt to jump off our garage roof with a bedsheet as a parachute."

Hudson looked shocked. "Oh, shit. Did it work?"

"Define 'work'? After a broken arm and a very pissed-off mother, I'll say no. We were reckless as hell." Seth paused the game and looked at Hudson seriously. "But even though I was a teenage jackass, I always loved and respected my mom. You running out on yours without a word? That's not cool, and that shit won't be tolerated here."

Hudson's jaw tightened, but he nodded. "Yeah. I get it."

"She was worried about you. You know that, right?" Seth picked off an enemy trying to sneak up on Hudson's flank.

"I know. Thanks for saving my ass."

"Happy to."

"It kinda blows that Mom never told you about me. We could have...I don't know, talked sooner and stuff."

"No kinda about it. It totally sucks, but it's not all her fault." Seth took advantage of the slight lull in the game. "Your mom tried to contact me once, but when she looked me up, she didn't say anything because I was married with a baby on the way."

Hudson frowned. "Where are they now? You divorced?"

"No." Seth's hands stilled on the controller. "They were killed in an explosion. Tristan was barely three months old."

The game continued around them, but Hudson stopped playing entirely. "Oh, shit. I'm sorry. That's... fuck. That must be why Beck told me to go easy on you. Because you've lost people."

"We all have." Seth resumed playing, needing the distraction. "Beck's family is gone except for his younger brother Zach, who you'll meet soon. Heavenly's mom abandoned her when she was fifteen, and her dad—whom she was really close to—died earlier this year. We're all dealing with grief and trying to figure out how to move forward."

Hudson was quiet for a long moment, focusing intently on the screen. "When my grandma died last year, I cried. I still miss her like crazy. She pretty much raised me, took care of me before and after school every day. We were close."

"I'm sorry you lost her, but I'm glad you had her," Seth said, and he meant it. "And I'm glad you'll have those memories. Thanks for sharing that with me."

They cleared the next bunker in comfortable silence before Hudson spoke again. "So what's the deal with you and Beck sharing Heavenly? That's got to be complicated as hell."

"At first. About six months ago, we finally worked it out. It took a while, not to mention a lot of head-butting, but..." He smiled. "She put us in our place."

"So you're admitting you're whipped?" Hudson grinned.

"You've seen her. Can you blame me?"

"Nope. You did all right. But I'll bet most people don't get the threesome thing. What does your family think?"

Seth pulled at the back of his neck. "It's…complicated."

His son raised a brow. "In other words, they don't know."

The kid just kept proving that he was smart. "They don't. Grandma Grace is very Catholic. She'll object the most, so I'm waiting to tell her until after her wedding next month. I don't want to upset her and ruin it." Seth speared Hudson with a serious expression. "Until then, I'd appreciate it if you'd keep this on the down-low. My friends here, like River, all know. You'll meet Raine, Liam, Hammer, and the rest soon."

"You're trusting me with information that could fuck you up?"

"I want our father-son relationship to work, Hudson. I care about you being in my life, and I'm hoping we can figure out how to get along and build something solid together." Seth's voice was steady, but he felt the weight of the admission. He was already attached to this kid, snark and all.

"Huh." Hudson seemed to digest that as they moved into a new area of the map. "Okay. Your turn to ask questions."

"I wasn't waiting for permission, but since you offered… You have a driver's license?"

"Yeah, got it on my birthday. Already told Beck that."

"You drink or do drugs?"

Hudson hesitated. "I drink at parties sometimes. Tried coke once but didn't like it, so I don't do that shit anymore."

"Good. It will rot your brain. I was a teenager once, so I get wanting to party. If you drink, it won't be out there, without me knowing. And it won't be behind the wheel. I get custody of your car keys. Deal?"

"Deal, I guess."

"Tell me about your childhood. Before your mom got married."

"We were pretty poor and lived in run-down apartments. We moved around a lot, but mostly stayed close to Grandma. I spent a lot of time with her when I was little. Mom didn't have any other family." In the game, Hudson took heavy fire, so Seth came with backup and blew his attacker away. "We didn't have to watch every dime once Mom married Ted, but..."

"But you don't like him."

Hudson gave a half shrug. "He's not a bad guy. A bit of an asswipe. He treats me like I might break something valuable." Hudson made a face. "But everything turned to shit after the baby came."

Seth could imagine that suddenly having an infant around was a shock. "Tell me about school. You have a favorite subject?"

"I like science and history. Math is okay. I make decent grades...but I could do better if I actually tried."

"Try." Seth slanted him a fatherly glare. "Sports?"

"I play football and baseball. Made varsity in both as a sophomore."

Of course Hudson would be athletic, like him. "Nice. Got a car?"

"No, but I want one." Hudson shot Seth a hopeful look.

"We'll see how you do with the rules first." Seth grinned. "You got a sex life?"

"Hell, yeah. That's not changing," Hudson said matter-of-factly.

Christ, the kid really was just like him. "You use protection?"

"Always." He frowned. "No offense. I don't want to be a teenage father."

"Smart. I didn't plan on that, either. Any idea what you want to be when you grow up?"

Hudson was quiet for a moment, concentrating on an incoming wave of enemies. "I always wanted to be a cop."

Seth nearly dropped his controller. The words brought back memories of his father in uniform, of his own years on the force before everything went to hell.

"Really?"

"Beck mentioned you used to be one. Like your dad."

Seth's throat felt tight. Grace would be shocked when she found out about Hudson, but learning he wanted to follow in the Cooper tradition of law enforcement? She'd be over the moon. And his father... God, his dad would be so proud that another generation wanted to carry on the legacy.

"If that's what you want, I'll help however I can," Seth managed.

They finished the mission in companionable silence, then started comparing likes and dislikes while loading into the next mission. They both loved spicy foods, action and sci-fi movies, and sports—especially the Yankees. They both hated beets, Brussels sprouts, and standing in lines. Seth was shocked to discover how much they had in common.

"You know," Hudson said during a brief lull in the action, "I came here planning to rip you a new asshole for running out on my mom. Wanted to find a whole bunch of reasons to hate you."

"And now?"

Hudson glanced at him sideways. "You're actually…decent, which is annoying because it would be easier if you were a dick."

Seth felt relief settle in his chest. "Whether or not you came to LA looking for a dad, you've got one now. I mean that, Hudson. I want to be involved in your life."

"Yeah?" For the first time, Hudson's mask slipped completely, revealing the vulnerable kid underneath. "Even though I'm already sixteen and probably more trouble than I'm worth?"

"Especially because of that." Seth bumped Hudson's shoulder with his own. "Coopers stick together."

It was too early, but Seth was already itching to make Hudson a Cooper legally. He'd have to see how things went, but the way everything stood now? He'd be talking to his son and Laura about that soon.

As they settled into the next mission, Seth's thoughts raced. In the span of a few hours, he'd gone from fearing hypothetical fatherhood to actually being a dad to a half-grown teenager. Part of him was terrified. But another part of him, the part that was already growing fiercely protective of this snarky kid, wondered if maybe this was exactly what he needed.

He just had to figure out how to be the father Hudson deserved without derailing his future with Beck and Heavenly in the process.

While Beck set the table, Heavenly called down the stairs, "Dinner's ready!"

Heavy footsteps bounded up from the game room, and Seth appeared, slightly out of breath. "Sorry, we lost track of time."

"No apology necessary." Heavenly kissed his cheek, breathing in his familiar scent as she whispered, "How did it go?"

"Better than I expected." Seth's smile looked both genuine and a bit surprised. "I'll fill you and Beck in later."

Hudson's slower footsteps announced his arrival.

"Wash your hands," Seth called over his shoulder to his son, head-bobbing toward the sink.

Grumbling, Hudson did, and Heavenly caught herself smiling at how naturally Seth had slipped into dad mode.

As they all settled into their chairs, Heavenly looked around the kitchen table. Having a teenage boy here—especially Seth's son—felt surreal. He'd been here for twenty-four hours, but she supposed that Hudson's presence would take some getting used to—for all of them.

As they each filled their plates with the pasta and salad Beck had prepared, Seth and Hudson immediately launched into good-natured ribbing about their gaming session.

"That last headshot was pure luck," Seth said, passing the garlic bread.

"Luck, my ass. I've got skills you can only dream of, old man." Hudson's grin was the first genuine smile Heavenly had seen from him, and it transformed his entire face. The defensive armor was still there, but it had definitely softened.

Beck caught her eye across the table. He'd seemingly noticed the change, too.

"Yeah?" Seth tossed back. "Who saved your scrawny ass more than once from incoming hostiles, whelp?"

"Bite me," Hudson groused.

Seth laughed, then turned his attention to her and Beck. "What did you two do while we went on a *Call of Duty* killing spree?"

"I slaved away in the kitchen like a proper housewife," Beck said dryly.

"I'm jealous. Cooking sounds like paradise compared to studying for Monday's Pharmacology test," Heavenly groaned. "I crammed all afternoon, and I still don't know if I have a prayer of passing."

"You're still in school?" Hudson frowned. "How old are you?"

"Twenty-three, and I'm studying to become a nurse. I just started my final year. It's getting harder—lots of memorization. Drug interactions, dosages, contraindications." She twirled pasta around her fork. "It's worth it, though. My dad was sick for so long with Guillain-Barré before he died, so I decided to devote my life to helping people."

The teenager seemed impressed. "That's actually…cool."

"It is, and she'll be a great nurse." Seth smiled her way before slanting Hudson a pointed stare. "Speaking of school…"

He rolled his eyes. "I know. You already told me I'm going."

"Damn straight. Every day."

"I heard you."

"Good." Seth turned to Beck. "What do you know about the schools around here? I need to get Hudson enrolled ASAP."

Beck shrugged. "I've never paid much attention. I know there's a local high school and a couple of private academies, but you might be better off talking to that retired teacher down the street or the folks next door who have three kids. They'll know which schools are actually good."

"I'll do that. I'm already leaning toward one of the private academies."

"Wait. Whoa…" Hudson shook his head. "Don't put me in a fucking all-boys school. Please."

Seth shot him a warning look. "Language."

The kid shot him a glare. "I'm serious. I'll lose my fucking mind."

Seth wasn't going to win the F-bomb battle, in Heavenly's estimation. First, he and Beck used the word constantly. Second, trying to change Hudson's habits—especially since Seth had functionally been his father for a handful of hours—seemed unlikely. And really, would cleaning up Hudson's language really matter that much in the long run? Breaking down his walls and making him feel like family were the far bigger issues.

Beck suppressed a smile. "Why would you lose your mind? I mean, academic emphasis. Focus on sports."

Seth joined in, also trying not to laugh. "Exactly. Lots of great connections. School spirit…"

"But there's no pus—" Hudson slanted a glance at Heavenly, then stopped himself. "Um, girls."

At that, they all burst out laughing.

"Hey, private schools aren't all bad. I went to one when I was about your age," Beck offered. "I turned out okay."

Seth snorted. "Did you, really?"

"Fuck off."

"You first."

"You're just jealous that I had a steady supply of pussy at his age." Beck nodded Hudson's way.

"I have living proof that I was getting busy at that age." Seth pointed at Hudson. "You only got laid because Gloria kept you dick-deep in hookers."

"Guys!" Heavenly protested. "If you don't dial it down, Hudson will need therapy before dinner is over."

"Nah, I'm good," Hudson swore, never taking his bulging eyes off Beck. "Hookers? Seriously? And who's Gloria?"

"My ex-wife."

"She hooked you up with…?"

"Prostitutes? Yep. She's a madame in Vegas. She 'adopted' me when I was sixteen. Well, actually we got married, but same difference."

Hudson's expression turned downright disbelieving. "You're making that shit up!"

"He's not," Seth promised. "But…maybe you shouldn't mention that to your mom just yet."

"Or the fact you're in a threesome?" Hudson raised a brow.

Seth winced. "Yeah. Don't mention that yet, either."

"Probably wise." Heavenly laughed.

"So…I heard you tell my mom that he's a doctor," Hudson said.

"A vascular surgeon," Beck verified.

"How the hell did you go from running away to banging hookers to getting an MD?"

Beck flashed him a devilish grin. "Private school."

They all laughed again before Hudson shook his head, eyes narrowed. "That's not bullshit?"

"No. But it was a lifetime ago. Now I devote my life to patching up patients. That makes me happy. So does being here with Heavenly and your dad."

"Damn... So how did you three actually meet?" Hudson looked curious. "I mean, your whole situation seems...complicated."

"It is, but less now than it used to be," Heavenly replied. "I met them at the hospital where I volunteer. On my first day, I'd been walking in circles for fifteen minutes, and Beck helped me. He offered to be my friend."

Hudson scoffed. "You believed him? Didn't you know that's code for 'I want to get in your panties?'"

Clearly, the kid was less naive than she'd been.

She sent him a self-deprecating smile. "I know that now... And Seth was with friends in the ER waiting room."

"Why didn't you just pick one over the other? I mean, I'll bet the sex is off the chain, but—"

"That's not why. I tried to choose, but you wouldn't believe the lengths they each went to win my heart."

"And get in your panties," Beck drawled.

Seth grinned. "That, too."

She slapped each of them on the shoulder. "Behave!"

"Why start now?" Beck winked.

"So how did you end up with both of them?"

Seth's expression grew serious. "Neither Beck nor I knew this, but Heavenly was half starving, and she was about to be homeless. Her landlord was demanding sexual favors instead of rent. We intervened."

Hudson scowled. "You beat the shit out of him?"

Heavenly flattened a smile. The kid really had no idea just how much like his father he was, even down to the protective streak.

"Let's just say I broke my Hippocratic oath that day, and now the son of a bitch eats through a straw," Beck drawled. "In prison."

"Good." Hudson clearly approved. "He sounds like a dirt bag."

"He was awful. Every time I talked to him, I got the heebies. But that place was all I could afford."

"She didn't tell either of us how bad her problems were, but when we finally realized, we stopped fighting each other and started taking care of her—together."

"And here we are." Heavenly reached for both men's hands. "It all worked out for the best."

They finished dinner with more good-natured banter and jokes. Heavenly had to admit that having Hudson here was far less awkward than she'd thought it would be. Certainly, more natural than it had felt even thirty minutes ago. He fit right in, and honestly, she didn't hate the idea of having another person to nurture, especially one who needed it so much.

Once they'd finished eating, they all rose. Seth looked at Hudson. "Help us clear the table and load the dishwasher."

"All right." Hudson didn't sound thrilled, but he didn't argue.

As far as Heavenly was concerned, that was progress.

They worked together, and she watched the easy way Seth and Hudson moved around each other. Their bond was tentative but growing almost before her eyes.

When the kitchen was clean, Seth sidled up to his son and bumped his shoulder. "Want to watch a movie?"

"Nah. I'm going to go to my room and chill, if that's cool. I've talked more today than I have in the last month."

"No sweat," Seth told him. "Set your alarm for six-thirty."

Hudson frowned. "In the morning? What the fuck for?"

"Starting tomorrow, we're working out together. Meet me in the home gym."

The kid froze. "You're serious?"

"As a heart attack."

His eyes narrowed. "Are you some kind of sadist?"

"No, that's my role," Beck bantered with a sarcastic wave.

Hudson didn't answer right away. "I'm not even going to ask."

"Better if you don't," Heavenly whispered.

"He's not kidding." Seth crossed his arms over his chest.

"Okay, then." The kid stepped back, hands raised in jest. "I'll just try not to think about the fact that I'm living with someone who gets off causing pain."

"He's harmless," Heavenly assured, but when Beck raised a challenging brow, she added, "Well, mostly."

"Nifty. You all have a good night. I'll…see you in the morning."

"If you need anything, just let us know," Heavenly called to his retreating back.

"Yeah. Thanks." Hudson paused at the top of the stairs, turning serious. "And thanks for…you know. Letting me stay."

"You're family," Seth said simply.

After Hudson nodded thoughtfully and disappeared downstairs, Heavenly followed Seth out to the back patio. Beck joined them. The warm evening air enveloped them as the guys settled into the outdoor sofa, pulling her between them.

This was where she belonged. And despite all the recent upheaval, this was where she felt safe. But now…they were alone, and she had so many questions.

"So…tell me about your time with Hudson downstairs."

"We had a really good talk." Seth's voice was rougher than usual. "It's early days, and I know that kid is going to test me. Hell, he'll probably test all of us."

"He will." Beck nodded. "I see so much of myself in that kid."

Seth nodded. "Same. But I'm thinking…this could work. How are you feeling?"

"I agree." Heavenly took his hand and squeezed it. "You're doing the right thing."

"You are," Beck agreed. "But I'm sure walking in and seeing him today was a hell of a shock. I give you credit for handling it so well. Seems like fatherhood is like water off a duck's back for you."

"More like riding a bike." Seth ran his hands through his hair. "But I'm still trying to wrap my head around everything, especially some stuff that happened my last day in New York."

She exchanged a glance with Beck before she turned back to Seth. "Is that why you didn't call last night?"

For long moments, he didn't answer. Then he finally blew out a harsh breath. "Yeah. Lately, I started thinking that if we're going to have a baby, we'll need a bigger house. One with fewer stairs, proper nursery space. Maybe a yard big enough for a swing set."

Heavenly's heart fluttered at the image he painted, at the future he envisioned. It sounded idyllic.

"I've been thinking the same thing," Beck added. "This place won't work long-term."

Seth nodded. "It's past time I sell the house I lived in with Autumn and Tristan, free up some cash to hopefully buy a new place. I hadn't stepped foot inside that place in eight years—until yesterday. I went there to see what work it needed before I put it on the market."

Heavenly blinked at Seth in shock. He'd never mentioned owning another house. In fact, he almost never talked about that part of his life.

"I'll sell this place, too," Beck said. "Together, we'll be able to afford something bigger and better. I have a patient who's an amazing realtor. She'll help us find exactly what we need."

"In a good school district," Heavenly piped in. "We'll need that right away, if Hudson stays. But we can't get too far from everyone's work."

"Exactly," Beck agreed, then turned back to Seth. "So what kind of work does your place need?"

Seth was quiet for a long moment before he rose, putting his back to them and staring out at the pool. "I don't know. I lasted less than five minutes in the fucking house before I ran out. I just...couldn't be there. Too many ghosts."

"Oh, Seth," Heavenly breathed, her heart hurting for him. She rose and approached him, smoothing soft hands over his shoulders.

"Everything was almost exactly the same as the day I left eight years ago. Autumn's knickknacks were still all over the house. Tristan's toys were still tucked into baskets in the living room. It was like walking into a tomb." His voice cracked. "Logically, I get why it affected me; I hadn't seen the place since they died. But running out made me feel like a fucking coward."

Beck approached and forced Seth to meet his head-on stare. "You survived something horrific, and confronting those memories isn't fucking easy, man. You dealt with trauma that would have broken most people."

"He's right," Heavenly reassured, reaching for Seth's hand. "Going there took incredible strength."

"But I tucked tail and ran." Seth raked a hand through his blond hair. "I want to move forward with you two. Start the future, get married, have babies, and build our family. I know it's important to you both, and I'm trying."

But could he give them what they craved? That thought terrified Heavenly. "We know you are."

"You don't. And I keep disappointing you. I just..." Seth trailed off, looking lost. "Mentally, I'm not where I should be. But I'm trying. And I'll keep trying. Today, talking to Hudson felt...good. Maybe it sounds crazy, but I feel like, if I can handle having a teenage son here, maybe...I'm not as broken as I thought. Maybe I can actually do this fatherhood thing again."

Clearly, he hoped that was the case. And maybe he was right, but Heavenly couldn't help but wonder... Would having a teenage son help Seth work through his fears? Or would it painfully remind him of what he'd lost when Tristan perished.

"One day at a time," she whispered. "It's not as if we're having a baby tomorrow. Just keep talking to us, okay?"

"Yeah. I'm sorry I didn't call, but I wasn't ready to talk last night. I needed time to process. And I didn't want my mom to overhear. She'd only worry."

"Keeping things to yourself might work with your mom. But don't fucking hide your feelings from us because you think we'll worry," Beck insisted. "That bullshit won't do any of us any good."

"I know. But sometimes, I feel like I'm drowning. I don't want to take you down with me."

"Ever think that we'd just throw you a life jacket?"

Seth chuffed. "I'm so used to rescuing myself—and everyone around me."

"Yeah?" Beck challenged. "Well, stop that shit. You have us."

"Exactly," Heavenly agreed softly, raising up on her tiptoes to press a kiss to Seth's lips.

He turned and took her in his arms, laying a desperate kiss over her mouth, lifting his head only when she was halfway to melting. "I missed you two so fucking much."

Heavenly knew that look on his face. He needed her, needed to be with them. Bond with them. Become one with them.

"We missed you, too. Come on." She took his hand and led him inside.

She and Seth checked on Hudson while Beck headed upstairs. The teenager was sprawled on his bed watching a sitcom in the dark.

Seth's expression grew soft as he looked at his son. "Sleep well."

Hudson nodded. "You, too."

Afterward, she climbed the stairs toward their bedroom, Seth directly behind her. At the top of the landing, he swept her into his arms, his eyes heating when he entered and caught sight of the bed turned down. Beck stood waiting, already shirtless.

Slowly, Seth set her on her feet, letting every inch of her body slide down his, including his stiff cock. "I need you naked. Now."

Instantly, Heavenly recognized his voice. Seth had gone into Dom mode.

She dropped her stare and kicked off her sandals. "Yes, Sir."

"Faster. Then lay across the bed, pretty legs spread so we can see that pussy that belongs to us. Beck, why don't you grab the rope?"

CHAPTER THIRTEEN

"Hell, yeah." Beck strode to the closet, dissecting the urgency straining Seth's voice. It matched the dominant energy pinging off his body.

The night they'd agreed to start a family, Seth had been so torqued up and impatient, he'd nearly ditched the bed and fucked Heavenly on the stairs. His mood now felt similar…but wilder, almost manic.

Beck completely understood why the guy was desperate to control something. He'd had an emotional reckoning in New York, then been blindsided by instant fatherhood the minute he'd returned to LA. But the edge—the demand—on Seth's face gave Beck pause.

He shelved his concern for now.

BDSM toy bag in hand, he stalked to the bed as Heavenly peeled off her pale pink tee beneath Seth's exacting stare. The big PI all but salivated as her breasts spilled from delicate lace. Beck set the bag near the bed and found himself following suit.

Heavenly glanced at the black duffel and blinked. "What's that?"

"Our bag of tricks," he quipped with a dirty smile.

"The fun kind." Seth yanked the zipper open.

"Which we should have introduced you to months ago," Beck drawled.

Heavenly raised on her tiptoes and lifted her chin, trying to peer inside.

"No peeking, little girl." He swatted her ass playfully.

When Heavenly yelped, Seth crowded closer, fisting her hair with a tug. "I said strip."

"Yes, Sir." Her voice quivered.

Slowly, he released her hair, squaring his shoulders and clasping his hands behind his back, eyes dark and watchful. Demanding.

She peeled off her yoga pants, revealing her slender legs—and the fact that she wore nothing beneath. Then she met Seth's Dominant stare and unfastened her bra. It floated to the hardwoods, leaving her naked.

The air seemed to leave the room. Her soft skin and rosy-hard nipples stole what was left of Beck's breath. His steely cock throbbed.

He flicked a glance at Seth, who raked Heavenly with hungry eyes and wrapped a hand around her throat. Command crackled in the air.

Fuck. He and Seth would drown her in orgasmic bliss, but Beck needed to make sure the big guy didn't turn savage.

"Angel… Five days without you felt like five fucking lifetimes."

Heavenly softened, as if sensing that Seth needed her to yield. "We missed you."

With a rough groan, he gripped her nape, tilted her face under his, and took her mouth in a bruising kiss.

"I think he missed us, too, little girl," Beck muttered thickly in her ear.

Her muffled whimpers torched Beck's blood. He couldn't keep his hands off her for another second.

With a growl, he pressed in behind her. While Seth devoured her like a Dom possessed, Beck brushed the hair off her shoulder and scraped his teeth up her neck. Heavenly melted between them with a satisfying shudder, arching her breasts against Seth's chest while shoving her hips back at Beck with a needy moan.

Seth tore his mouth from hers with a feral roar, eyes wild. He ripped off his tank and flung it aside. "Didn't I already tell you? On the bed. Legs spread. Now. Don't make me say it again."

Heavenly scampered onto the mattress. Her shallow breaths, coupled with the trust glowing on her face, made Beck's heart clutch.

She settled onto her back and parted her thighs shyly, barely exposing her glistening pink folds. At the sight, Beck hissed. His restraint began to dissolve.

Seth's nostrils flared as he inhaled the scent of her arousal. "Arms above your head."

Heavenly complied while he shoved a hand into the duffel. Moments later, the big PI yanked out a bundle of rope with glittering eyes. With lips flattened into a tight line, he began whipping the soft cord around her delicate wrists.

Concern pricked Beck. He knew Seth well—his non-con fantasies, his breeding kink, and harsh taskmaster games. But watching him fight not to lose his command was new. Beck would make damn sure Cooper didn't push their girl too far.

Seth knotted the rope, latching her to the headboard. All the while, Heavenly blinked up at him. Trying to understand the man's edge? His urgency?

Though the sight of her helpless surrender jolted him, Beck held back and gave Seth's beast more leash. For now.

He eased onto the bed beside her and dragged his tongue up her neck, pausing at the shell of her ear. "I'll be right beside you, but Seth needs to control you so he can center himself. It's a Dom thing. Can you give him that?"

A thousand questions swam in Heavenly's eyes. She didn't voice them, just gave him her trust wrapped in a barely perceptible nod.

"Good girl." He claimed her mouth with an incendiary kiss as he slid a finger under the rope to test the binding.

Despite Seth's desperate single-mindedness, it wasn't too tight. He'd put Heavenly first.

"Safe word?" Seth oozed impatience as he climbed between her thighs and shoved her legs wide.

"Freedom." Her breath hitched. "Sir."

Beck rewarded her by brushing his palm over her stomach, savoring the quiver of her skin beneath his fingers.

"Do *not* come without permission." Seth's voice was dark with warning.

"No, Sir."

"I haven't tasted your sweet cunt in five hellish days." He lowered his head until he hovered above her pussy, breathing hard. "Spread wider. I'm fucking starving."

As she obeyed, Seth clutched Heavenly's soft thighs and consumed her pussy. At the first touch of his mouth, she jerked against her restraints. Seth didn't respond except to gorge on her, showing no mercy.

Her feminine musk and kitten-soft moans went straight to Beck's cock. His skin prickled. Primal need stirred in his chest as he strummed her beaded nipples and watched Seth lash her clit with his tongue. As they drove her higher, Heavenly bucked and gripped the rope, her blue eyes heavy-lidded and dilated.

"You like Seth eating your cunt, little girl?" Beck taunted.

"Yes…" she mewled, grinding her pussy against Seth's unrelenting tongue. "Yes!"

The PI jerked his head up and slapped the swollen pad. "Did I give you permission to fuck my face?"

Heavenly blinked rapidly, as if trying to focus. "I-I… N-no, Sir. I didn't…"

"You did. Who's on top?"

"You, Sir."

"That's right. *I* control your pleasure. Forget again, and I'll leave you aching."

"I-I'm sorry, Sir."

"Ease up, man," Beck warned. "If you don't want her grinding on your face, keep it out of her pussy. Or give her some rules."

Seth's jaw tightened. Beck wondered if the big PI intended to lunge at him. But he dragged in breaths and stared down at Heavenly. Finally, he scrubbed a hand through his hair. "I was just trying—"

"To assert your Dominance. Yeah, I get it. We both do. But it's not fair to punish her for moving when you didn't tell her to stay still."

Seth caressed her hip with an apologetic grimace. "I'm sorry, angel. I didn't mean to bark at you. I'm just…on edge."

"I know. It's okay," she murmured.

"Let me make it up to you." He lowered himself between her legs again and glided his tongue through her slit.

Heavenly let out a long moan.

"That's it," Beck whispered. "Close your eyes. Focus on the pleasure we give you."

When he fastened his mouth over her breast, she nodded, her lashes fluttering shut with a soft sigh. He alternated sucking and laving her nipple, then compounded her sensations by pinching and plucking the other between his fingers. The berry tips hardened even more.

Seth lashed and sucked her clit with savage urgency while he eased two fingers inside her, slowly dragging them over her G-spot in torment.

Her gasps and groans as she arched between them drove Beck higher. He kept at her tits, one after the other, with his mouth and hands, teasing her swollen nipples, sparing an occasional breath to whisper something filthy in her ear.

Time lost meaning as they ramped her higher and higher. They'd learned Heavenly's body well, knew when her taut muscles began to quiver and her keening cries grew hoarse that they'd taken her to the brink. Neither he nor Seth was ready to end this sweet torture. If they wanted to deny her release, they needed to downshift.

Beck enjoyed edging subs, always had. But watching Heavenly struggle between clawing lust and her innate desire to please flipped every sadistic switch in his body.

Seth tongued her clit while pumping his fingers inside her, keeping her endlessly suspended between heaven and hell—while she cried for mercy.

They had none.

"You want to come, don't you, angel?" Seth muttered against her thigh before he nipped it.

"Yes!" Heavenly sobbed, her voice raw with need. "Please, I…I can't hold—"

"You better." Beck bit her nipple between his teeth. "You don't have permission."

He laved away the sting, sucking the bud into his mouth, then grazing his teeth over her sensitized peak. He repeated the process again, delighting as she twisted and shuddered, her expression a deliciously helpless plea.

Together, he and Seth kept her on a rack of blissful torture, keeping her orgasm just out of reach. Her body bowed. Her agonized shriek became a one-word litany on repeat. "*Please…*"

They ignored her and backed off. Her whimpered protests filled the room as they kissed her, whispering and murmuring against her skin, stroking and caressing her until she softened, caught her breath, and quieted her pleading.

Then they started in again, soaring her to the cusp of release with their hands and mouths until Heavenly strained against the ropes and an inhuman cry tore from her throat.

"Please. P-please..." Tears slid from the corners of her unfocused eyes. "I-I need to come. I c-can't take it anymore."

"You *can*. You still don't have permission," Seth scolded with an evil smirk.

"I-I know. But...I-I'm dying."

"We're just warming you up, little girl." Beck eased sweat-soaked strands of hair from her face.

"No. No!" She tossed her head from side to side. "I can't... I-I'm on fire."

"You have a safe word," Seth reminded, licking away her juices from his lips with a grin. "You can end your suffering right now."

"*Noooo*," she wailed. "Don't...s-stop. I need to...to come."

"But until you focus on *our* pleasure more than your own, you're not getting permission." Seth masterfully mind-fucked their girl.

Heavenly didn't argue. Hell, they'd annihilated her ability to reason, so she couldn't. And Beck relished it.

"Let's help her focus." He reached into the toy bag and retrieved a small rubber flogger—perfect for tickling or tormenting her pussy. He also extracted a pair of clover clamps—because the sadist in him wasn't finished torturing her nipples—along with a tweezer clamp for her clit.

Briefly, he thought about grabbing a ball gag, but the sweet sounds of Heavenly suffering was too erotic to give up.

"You're evil." Seth smirked. "That's one of the things I like most about you."

Beck chuckled, then sucked one of Heavenly's nipples back into his mouth. He drew deep, elongating the tip before releasing it with a pop. Then he squeezed the clamp open and aligned the tiny rubber pads on either side of her peak. With a grin, he released the metal hinge. Its jaws shut tight.

Heavenly's eyes flashed wide as she squealed and writhed, attempting to escape the pain.

"Breathe. Ride the sting. Rise above it," Beck commanded, capturing her other breast, and repeating the process.

Howling now, Heavenly tossed her head back, flailing and tugging at the ropes in vain.

Beck grabbed her wrists to keep her from rubbing them raw. "Don't fight, little girl. Let the pain flow over you. Become one with it."

"It *burns*."

"I'll fix that." Seth lowered his head and engulfed her pussy in his mouth, savagely pillaging her wet slit.

At the touch of his tongue, she jolted as if they'd hooked her up to a live wire. "Yes... *Yes!*"

They drove Heavenly to the brink again. Watching her was beyond mesmerizing, but they'd kept her poised on the edge of orgasm for so long, Beck wasn't sure she had the willpower to keep from shattering. She definitely hadn't had the practice.

Beck's cock swelled so painfully, he swore his skin would split. The want—no, the *need*—to slam balls deep in her slick cunt plagued him. He ached to feel her clamp around him as he released his seed against her unprotected womb.

A glance at Seth, still feasting, told him the PI was nowhere near done.

With a wicked smile, he flicked the little rubber flogger over the angry tips of her clamped nipples. Heavenly's glassy, unfocused eyes flew open. Beck's deviant heart skipped as she sucked in a ragged breath and pressed her head back into the pillow—arching her back and thrusting her breasts into the air. Another pain-drenched scream ripped from her throat.

"That sounds so pretty," Beck cooed. "Give us your agony."

"All of it," Seth muttered against her cunt.

Beck switched up the sensations, swirling the rubber falls over her nipples in a delicate, almost gossamer dance of tingles—a startling contrast to the bite of the clamps.

As he absorbed more of her thrashing and screeching, he looked down her body and met Seth's stare. His expression blazed. He tore from Heavenly's pussy with a growl, eyes rapt as he took in her torment. "Fuck. I have to be inside her."

Beck didn't object.

With shaking hands, Seth tugged down his zipper. His cock burst free. He shoved the denim around his hips and fisted his shaft, quickly positioning himself against her drenched opening. "Is she still fertile?"

Alarm bells gonged through Beck's brain. His stomach bottomed out.

What difference does it make?

Seth fucking knew the answer. They both did.

Are we back to square one?

Beck almost didn't want the answer to that question. If Seth couldn't bury his trauma in the past, where it belonged, it would eventually destroy their progress and prevent them from sharing a happy future.

Seth glared, waiting for an answer. Beck studied the PI's strained expression as he teased Heavenly with his crest. He nudged the tip just inside her before hissing, cursing, and pulling back. Then he started the process all over again. She cried out in pure torment as she lifted her hips, straining to engulf Seth inside her.

Last night, Heavenly had asked what they would do if Seth had changed his mind about starting a family. He'd promised he would remind his pal that they were worth fighting for.

The time had come to practice what he'd preached.

"Is she?" Seth snarled the question again.

"No," Beck finally answered.

"You're sure?"

"Positive. Her window is closed. Take her bare."

Palpable relief skidded across Seth's face before he flashed her an evil smile. "Do you want my cock, angel?"

"Yes. Oh, god… *Yessss.*"

"You don't sound pitiful enough, angel. You'll have to do better if you want me to give you this big, hard cock." He slapped his wide, weeping crest against her clit.

"Please, Sir! I need…"

"What?" Seth taunted. "Tell me."

"You," she gasped. "I need you."

"I'm right here, angel. Do you need my grocery list?"

"No!"

"My stake-out schedule?"

"*Noooo,*" she whimpered.

"Tell him you need his hard cock fucking your little pussy," Beck growled.

"*Yesss.*"

"Say it," Seth thundered.

"I need…" she panted, eyes rolling back in her head. "Oh, god…"

"Say it," Beck dragged the rubber falls over her clit, gratified when she shivered.

"I-I need your…cock. Please!"

"Where?" Seth pulled back to watch her.

"Inside me."

"Your *mouth?*" Beck taunted, landing the flogger against her cunt.

Heavenly jolted with a strangled cry. "Inside my…my pussy."

"This sweet, tight pussy?" Seth pressed his wide crest through her narrow slit.

Then he stopped.

"Oh, god… Yes!" Heavenly gripped the ropes, panting and struggling.

Seth reared back, hissing as he shoved forward, filling and stretching her with inch after hard inch. Heavenly rocked under him, her hips surging up to take more.

Before Cooper could reprimand her again, Beck flattened his hand over her quivering stomach and slapped the flogger across her pussy with the other. "Stay still."

Eyes glassy, Seth nodded and eased from her tight cunt, his withdrawal like molasses. Heavenly cried out, her plea hoarse and wordless. God, she looked so flushed and aroused. So sensual.

Beck couldn't resist adding to her torment. He trailed his fingertips down to her clit and stroked her slowly, rhythmically. She tensed. Her eyes slammed shut. Her toes curled. She wailed in anguish.

He loved every second.

"Fuck. Do that again," Seth choked out, face contorting as he slammed inside her again, slick and savage until he bottomed out.

"With pleasure."

When Seth pulled back for his next stroke, Beck was prepared. He met Heavenly's unfocused stare with a smirk—and lashed her pussy with the falls before he gave it another rub.

She gasped and jerked. Then Seth thrust into their girl again, his harsh strokes measured, designed to scrape every nerve ending in her pussy and drive her higher. Jack her up to unbearable heights.

Then, to the chorus of her mewls, he reared back as if he had all day. Beck landed the biting little flogger on her clit again, yanking her from the edge of ecstasy.

As if they shared the same degenerate mind, he and Seth found their rhythm…

Seth thrusted. Beck whacked. Over and over and over.

Thrust. *Whack.*

Thrust. *Whack.*

Thrust. *Whack.*

Heavenly's cries—an anguished fusion of misery and bliss—melded with the thudding flogger and slapping flesh like an erotic symphony.

"You like his fat cock fucking you?" Beck nipped her lobe.

"*Yesssss…*"

"What about these?" Beck flicked the nasty clamps compressing her nipples. "Do you like them?"

Heavenly sucked in a startled gasp and arched, thrusting her tits in the air. Hungrily, he plucked at one before he covered her mouth with his, swallowing her scream of pain.

When she quieted, he eased back with a feral growl and sipped the tears leaking from her eyes.

"Beck? Beck…" Heavenly stared at him, beseeching, as if he alone could save her.

He could. But he wasn't going to. Not when he was enjoying her agony so much. A glance at Seth's face said he was, too.

"You're suffering so sweetly, little girl," Beck murmured.

"It burns." She strained against the ropes, wriggling and clamping down on Seth's cock, still driving into her with slow, bulldozing strokes.

"Fuck, yes," Seth hissed, sweat sliding from his brow. "Burn for us, angel. Don't come."

"Yet," Beck taunted. "We're enjoying your delicious agony. Give us more."

A pitiful wail tore from her lips. Beyond the lone afternoon she'd asked Beck to whip out his belt and unleash his inner sadist, he'd never explored pain with her, much less driven her to the edge of her tolerance with Seth.

Beck wasn't even inside her yet, and already this might be one of the most delicious fucks of his life.

"Please!" She shook her head violently from side to side.

"More? Harder?" He flashed her a subversive grin. "Happily."

Seth's wolfish smile said he agreed and relished the opportunity to heap more torture on her.

His thrusts became ferocious, almost barbaric, each punctuated by the headboard hitting the wall. Then Heavenly's whimpers became jumbled pleas for mercy, followed by Seth's bellows-like breaths. Beck stayed in sync with their rhythm, landing blow after blow with the flogger on her enflamed cunt. He watched in fascination as it turned rosier and redder with each thrust and every strike.

Heavenly, trapped between pain and pleasure, glistened with a fine sheen of sweat. She begged with her big blue eyes while her chest heaved with every panted breath. Pleas spilled from her lips, sharp with desperation.

"How does her pussy feel?" Beck demanded.

"Too fucking good." Seth shoved out the words between clenched teeth.

"Please!" Heavenly's voice hitched on a sob. "*Pleaseee.*"

"You want him to come inside you, little girl?" Beck cajoled.

"Yes!"

"Beck," Seth snarled, his thrusts uneven. "Fuck! I can't…can't fucking, hold—"

"Wait!" Beck barked.

Seth stilled instantly, muscles straining and trembling as he held back. "What?"

Beck didn't reply, simply grabbed the tweezer clip and secured it to Heavenly's swollen clit.

Seconds later, her shrill screams pinged around the room, splitting the air.

Beck moaned. "Fuck, you look so pretty in pain. No coming, little girl. Understand?"

"No," she all but sobbed, licking her suddenly dry lips. "Don't do this. Don't leave me to—"

"Suffer? That's the whole point." He turned to Seth with an evil chuckle. "Flood her cunt."

The PI didn't hesitate, just cursed, then rammed inside her, establishing a driving, dizzying rhythm. Heavenly clawed at her ropes and sent him more of those beautifully helpless stares.

Then Seth shouted and stilled, every muscle in his body tense as he shuddered and tossed his head back. With a thunderous roar, Seth came, releasing every drop of his seed inside her as he rode out his searing climax.

When he finished shuddering and growling, Seth tore free and rolled away, panting wildly. Heavenly twisted in protest. Her hips rose in unfulfilled need as her thighs splayed even wider.

Beck didn't wait for an invitation. He tore off his jeans, hissing as his weeping cock sprung free. Fisting his throbbing shaft, he hurtled himself between her thighs and stared at her swollen cunt.

"Beck…" She blinked at him, begging.

"You still don't have permission." He wedged his wide crest against her opening.

"But—"

"The more you protest, the longer we'll make you wait. Now take my cock, little girl." He reveled in her trembling sounds as he gripped her hips and began submerging one throbbing inch at a time inside her.

As he bottomed out, Beck's eyes rolled to the back of his head. Then he pulled back until only his swollen crest teased her fluttering walls.

Jesus…

He wrapped a mental death-grip around his resolve and slammed balls-deep inside her, reveling when Heavenly bucked under him with a cry.

As Beck set a hard rhythm in and out of her molten pussy—controlling each plunge and pull—Seth sank a fist in her hair, forcing her to look at him. "Is he stretching that tight pink cunt? Does it still burn?"

"Yes," she gasped.

"You feel him all the way inside you? Where I just fucked you?"

Heavenly nodded, pulsing and clenching, frantic now. Beck banged into her again with a roar.

"Fuck, yeah." Seth's eyes darkened. "He's going to fill you up too, angel."

Her reply sounded not like a word, but an imploring warble of desperation.

That turned Beck on even more. "Son of a bitch…"

"Keep fucking her," Seth suggested. "I'll keep telling Heavenly how pretty she looks stuffed full of our cocks…"

That drove Beck up even higher. His restraint began to crumble.

He heaved in lungfuls of air, then began hammering Heavenly, chasing the ultimate pleasure with unabashed fervor, the *bang, bang, bang* of the headboard matching the frenzied rhythm of his heartbeat.

Whenever he sensed Heavenly getting too close to the peak, he tugged on the clamp constricting her clit, deliberately yanking her back to reality with a jolt of pain.

Commanding her arousal was a potent, electrifying high. Beck memorized the sight of her helplessly fighting the ropes as needy cries spilled from her lips.

"*Pleaseee…*" Heavenly sobbed. "I-I…can't take anymore."

Her desperation pushed Beck closer to the edge.

"Be careful what you ask for, angel," Seth warned, laving the tears from her cheeks. "When we give you permission, we're going to take those clamps off. Then you'll really scream."

"Yes. Please. Now!" she sobbed hoarsely. "I need…"

She couldn't even finish her sentence. She gripped him, fluttering and clamping on his cock. Her desperation was a sucker-punch to Beck's restraint. Every nerve ending in his body sizzled. He drew back and stilled, hissing and cursing to regain control.

"Tell me when," Seth murmured, stare glued to Heavenly's damp, flushed face.

With an absent nod, Beck gripped her hips tighter and shoved deep inside her again before pulling back with another growl. He established a brutal rhythm, inflicting maximum sensation on her as he plowed her snug cunt. The friction set his cock on fire. He ignored her throaty pleas and ruthlessly pounded her fiery cunt, filling and stretching her. His balls tightened. His heart drummed against his ribs. The roar of release thundered in his ears.

"You ready to come?" he growled.

"Yes. Oh, god…*yessss!*" she wailed as she rocked, meeting his every driving thrust.

Black spots consumed Beck's vision. He stroked deep inside her, once, twice, then snarled and stilled as the dam of his restraint burst wide open.

"Fuck. Now!" he barked. "Come!"

Like the crack of a thousand single tails, Heavenly's screams sliced the air. She fluttered and clenched, bucking and shuddering through her orgasm, convulsing around him as pleasure consumed them.

As she basked in the throes, Seth removed the clamps, heaping pain on top of her ecstasy.

Heavenly's eyes flew wide. Her cries rolled into high-pitched shrieks of pain. Beck felt her agony all the way to his bones as he gripped her hips harder, manically shuttling in and out of her contracting pussy.

The friction multiplied.

His hips jerked.

Lightning flashed behind his eyes.

Flames seared his spine.

Ecstasy yanked off its chain.

A beastly growl tore from Beck's chest as he spilled every ounce of hot come inside her quivering cunt until he swore he was going to black out.

Sexual haze clouded his vision. He was still fighting to catch his breath when he spied Seth gently laving and slurping at Heavenly's angry nipples. Their girl was panting, perspiring, pumped full of sensation overload, and totally spent. But her glassy, unfocused eyes found his. A sated smile curled the corners of her lips, punctuated by a satisfied moan. Beck's heart swelled.

On her right, Seth eased back, pressed a tender kiss to her forehead, then released her wrists from the ropes. Together, they sandwiched her in their arms and collapsed on the bed.

"Feel better, little girl?" Beck asked softly.

She moaned. "That was…"

"Incredible?" Seth asked.

"Beyond," she whispered.

Seth leaned close to her ear. "I love you."

Beck's chest tightened at the vulnerability his friend didn't even try to hide. That had to be a good sign, right? Seth wasn't shutting down.

"I love you, too," she murmured back, then turned Beck's way. "Both of you."

Beck dropped a kiss on her lips, then gripped Seth's shoulder in silent support. "We've got you, man. Whatever happens next, we're here."

Seth met his gaze. The wild look and half-hidden panic Beck had seen in his eyes earlier was gone, replaced by gratitude.

The PI leaned in and softly kissed Heavenly, sealing their bond in the quiet afterglow. For the moment, they were happy. Whole. Complete.

But life seemed determined to keep throwing them curveballs, and Beck couldn't help but hug Heavenly tighter and wonder if the next blow would be the one to pull them apart.

Chapter Fourteen

Seth's eyes opened at five forty-five, his internal clock as reliable as ever. For a moment, he lay still, savoring the warmth of Heavenly pressed against him and Beck's steady breathing on her other side. Last night had been exactly what he'd needed—intense, consuming, a chance to lose himself completely in pleasure and exert control when life seemed determined to steal his.

They'd pushed Heavenly's boundaries in ways they never had, and she'd responded beautifully. The memory of her gasps, her unbridled surrender, the way she'd trusted them completely, sent heat coursing through him even now. He'd needed to dominate her, stop thinking about the chaos crowding his head—his failure at the old house, the shock of Hudson's existence, the weight of suddenly being responsible for a teenager.

Thank God Beck had been there to keep him grounded and present. Without Beck's steady presence and quiet check-ins with Heavenly, Seth feared he would have pushed her too hard.

This morning, he felt settled enough to face the day ahead.

Carefully, he slipped out of bed, not wanting to wake either of them, and pulled on his workout clothes. Hudson was probably still asleep, but they had an appointment to pump iron at six-thirty, and Seth intended to keep it.

When he padded downstairs to the home gym, however, he found Hudson already there, dressed in basketball shorts and a tank top, stretching near the free weights.

"Morning," Seth said, pleasantly surprised.

"Hey." Hudson straightened, looking more alert than a typical sixteen-year-old at this early hour. "I wasn't sure what we were doing, so I hung out and waited."

"Good call. You work out much?"

"With football and stuff, yeah."

"Nice. You work out much before that?" Seth asked, noting that Hudson looked at home with the equipment.

He nodded. "Couple years now. There's a gym in our apartment complex in Cromwell. I go pretty often. It's good to blow off steam."

"That's about when I started working out, too. Same reason."

In companionable silence, they started with a warm-up, then moved to the weight stations. Seth watched Hudson's form carefully and was impressed. The kid knew what he was doing—proper positioning, controlled movements, good breathing technique.

"You sleep okay?" Seth asked as they worked through their sets.

"Better than the first night. I'm getting used to the place." Hudson adjusted his grip on the bar and glanced at Seth with a half grin. "But if you and Beck are going to tag-team Heavenly, maybe keep it to a dull roar? She's kind of a screamer."

Seth nearly dropped his weights. "Jesus, Hudson."

The kid laughed, clearly enjoying Seth's discomfort. "I'm just saying, maybe invest in some soundproofing or something."

Seth gave him a playful smack upside the head. "Invest in some ear plugs, smart-ass."

Minutes passed while they continued their workout before Seth asked the question weighing on him. "You still cool to stay for a while?"

Hudson froze. "You want me to go?"

"No." That was the last thing Seth wanted Hudson to think. "I just want to check in and see how you're feeling."

Hudson considered the question as he moved to the next exercise. "I needed out of Cromwell. I love my mom, but her life is different now. New husband, new baby—she's got her future mapped out...and I don't really fit into it anymore."

Laura hadn't given Seth the impression that she didn't want him around, but he understood that Hudson's feelings were just that and might not be rooted in reality. "What are you hoping to find here?"

The kid shrugged. "Something different, I guess. Someone who doesn't baby me but actually gives a shit about what I'm doing and where I'm going."

"I'll give you that," Seth said quietly. "If you can handle it."

"I can handle anything," he said with teenage swagger.

That wasn't true. After all, Hudson had come here for a reason. The teenager was high on youth and testosterone. He'd have to mature some to understand that everyone needed support and people to help them through the tough times.

"If you're good with it, I need to tell my mother about you. Maybe after breakfast?"

Hudson's expression tightened. "Will she freak about having a bastard grandson who's almost grown?"

Of course the kid would wonder that. Everyone and every situation around him was new. "She'll be surprised, but she'll be over the moon. Trust me. My mom lives for family."

Hudson nodded, some of the tension leaving his shoulders. "Okay. I'm good with you telling her."

"Thanks." Seth patted the kid on the shoulder.

In companionable silence, they finished their workout and headed toward their separate showers. When Seth emerged from his bathroom upstairs, Heavenly was just waking up, her hair tousled and a sleepy smile on her face.

"Morning, angel," he murmured, dropping a kiss on her forehead.

"Mmm. Good workout?"

"Yeah. Hudson and I did good. It was nice having company. How are you feeling?"

A soft blush colored her cheeks. "Sore in all the right places."

Seth's chest tightened with satisfaction and something deeper—love, possessiveness, gratitude that she trusted them enough to let them take her so far.

"Glad to hear it. Where's Beck?" He glanced at the empty bed.

"His turn to work out. Once he's done and cleaned up, we'll be heading to the hospital. He's got rounds and patients. I'm going to get in some volunteer hours. You heading to the office today?"

"Long enough to catch up with River. Then I've got to get Hudson enrolled in school somewhere."

Heavenly squeezed his hand. "You'll make the right decision. I think he really needs you."

Despite how sudden incorporating Hudson into their life felt, Seth was of the same mind.

He dressed and trekked downstairs to make coffee. Heavenly followed a few minutes later, looking absolutely fresh in pale pink scrubs with her long hair in a fat braid that brushed her spine. She'd made a breakfast casserole that filled the kitchen with the savory scents of eggs, cheese, and bacon.

"You're an angel." Seth sidled up behind her and wrapped his arms around her middle as she poured herself a cup of java.

"Just taking care of my boys." She leaned back against him. "All three of you now."

After heavy footsteps, Hudson appeared at the top of the stairs, hair damp, dressed in jeans and a T-shirt. "Smells good."

"Help yourself," Heavenly said, gesturing to the casserole. "There's plenty."

Seth laughed. "That's the wrong thing to say to a teenage boy. They're like human garbage disposals."

"Hey, still growing here!" Hudson objected.

"So you don't eat everything in sight?" Seth raised a brow.

That made Hudson laugh. "Okay, maybe I do."

As they shared a chuckle, a sweaty Beck thundered up the stairs from his own workout, grabbed coffee, and kissed Heavenly breathless.

"Morning, little girl," he said against her lips. "Seth. Hudson." He nodded to them both. "I need a shower and a few bites, then we're out of here."

"Morning, doctor." She gave him a saucy wink. "Ready when you are."

He gave her ass a playful smack before he headed up for a shower.

Hudson's stare followed all the action. "Him touching her doesn't bother you at all?"

Seth shook his head. "It used to. But now…this works for us. For a lot of reasons. We know our relationship isn't typical and that some people will never get it, but that's on them."

"Sure." But Hudson's voice said he didn't understand, either.

Like a lot of things, it would take time.

Fifteen minutes later, Beck and Heavenly headed to the garage with a wave, leaving Seth and Hudson to tackle the dishes. The kid pitched in without being asked. Seth approved.

After they finished, he pulled out his phone. "Ready to call your Grandma Grace?"

Hudson dried his hands on a dish towel, his nervousness evident. "I guess. What should I call her? Hopefully not grammy. That was my mom's mom."

Good question. Danny was waiting for Anna to get verbal and see what she called his mom, but with Hudson here the question wasn't going to wait. "We'll ask her."

Seth's palms were sweating when he hit the FaceTime button. He wished he could tell his mother that she had a teenage grandson in person, but he couldn't wait to break the news until his next trip back East. Mom deserved to know now. He hoped she took it well. No question she'd accept Hudson. But Seth wasn't holding his breath that she'd be all smiles once she did the math.

His mother's face filled the screen, her smile bright and immediate. "Seth! This is a nice surprise. How are you, sweetheart?"

"I'm okay, Mom. You good?"

"I am. It's quiet here now. Carl's at work, and I was just cleaning up the kitchen and making a grocery list." She frowned. "You look serious. What's going on? Please tell me you're not calling to say you can't come to the wedding."

"No, that isn't why I'm calling. I'll absolutely be there."

"What about Heavenly? She's still coming, I hope. You know I'm dying to meet her."

Yes, Mom hadn't been shy about that. "She is. Beck, too. But…we're hoping to bring a fourth person, if that's okay."

"Oh, is your doctor friend bringing a date?"

"No." Seth took a deep breath. "Mom, you should sit down."

Her smile faltered as she sank into her chair. "Oh, no. What's going on?"

Here goes nothing. "I can't think of an easy way to say this but…I found out yesterday that I have a son. His name is Hudson." Seth blew out a breath and went for broke. "He's…sixteen."

His mother stared at the screen for a long moment, her mouth gaping wide.

"Mom? Did you hear—"

"He's *sixteen?*" she breathed. "That's impossible, Seth. You would have been—"

"Fifteen. Yeah." Seth's throat felt tight, and he resisted the urge to wince. "I know you're shocked."

"Oh, my— I knew you weren't a baby then, but…" She scrubbed a hand down her face. "How did that happen?"

Seth grimaced. "Do you really want me to answer that?"

She scowled. "I meant, didn't you use protection and—"

"Mom, focus."

"But fifteen? Seth…" She huffed. "Where is Hudson now? Who is his mother? What—"

"He's been living in Connecticut with his mom, who was a waitress I met when I was staying with Grandma and Grandpa that summer. Hudson tracked me down. He's here in LA with me now, and he's going to stay for a while."

Again, Grace didn't speak right away. "How did he get to LA? Did you have any idea—"

"Until yesterday, no. I would have told you."

Her eyes filled with tears. "Oh, Seth. A grandson! But we've missed out on so much—his first words, his first steps, his first day at school… I can't— Why didn't you know about him?"

"It's complicated. His mother never told me she was pregnant. She tried to contact me years later, but I was married to Autumn then, and she decided not to interfere."

"And you're sure he's yours?"

Seth slanted a glance at Hudson. "Yeah. There's no question."

"Oh, that poor boy," Grace breathed. "Sixteen years without knowing his father. Is he— How is he handling all this?"

Hudson stood frozen by the sink, looking beyond nervous. No, like he was afraid to be rejected.

"Honestly, he's handling it better than I am. Do you…want to meet your grandson?"

"What kind of question is that? Of course! He's a Cooper."

Well, legally he was a Clarke. Seth intended to change that, but now wasn't the time to get nitty-gritty with his mother. It would just upset her.

"Good. If it's okay with you, I'd like to bring him to the wedding. That way you and the whole family can meet him."

"Oh! That would be fantastic! Don't think I don't still have questions for you, young man. But I can't wait to clap eyes on him."

Seth wasn't shocked in the least. "Are you ready to talk to him? He's right here."

"Can I? Please."

Seth motioned Hudson over and handed him the phone. "Hudson, this is your grandmother, Grace."

His son took the phone with an unsteady nod and slightly shaking hands. "Um, hi."

She gasped, then her face lit up like Christmas morning. "Oh, my goodness. You look exactly like your father when he was your age. And your grandfather, too." Her voice was thick with emotion. "Welcome to the family, sweetheart."

"Thanks," Hudson murmured, slightly red-faced. Seth could see how much his mom's immediate acceptance meant to him.

"Are you settling in all right? Is your father taking good care of you?"

"Yeah, he's… It's good here so far. It's only been a day or so, but…"

They talked for a few more minutes, his mom asking gentle questions about school and interests, Hudson gradually relaxing under her obvious delight in his existence.

When Hudson handed the phone back to Seth, she was wiping tears from her eyes.

"Will you send me a picture of you two?" she all but begged. "I can't wait to show Carl when he gets home. And your brothers— oh, Seth, they're going to be so excited."

"I'll send something later today. And we'll call during family dinner on Sunday so Hudson can talk to everyone else."

"Perfect. Hudson?" she called out, and the teenager stepped back into view. "I can't wait to hug you in person, sweetheart. The whole family is going to love you."

After they ended the call, Hudson stood quietly for a moment, staring at the now-dark phone screen.

"You okay?" Seth asked.

"Yeah." Hudson's voice was carefully casual, but Seth saw the emotion he tried to hide. "She seems really nice."

"She is. And she meant every word she said." Seth stood and grabbed his keys from the counter. "Come on. Get your shoes. We're going to check out some schools, then head to my office so you can see what the PI business is all about."

Hudson nodded and headed for the stairs. "Do I have to pretend to be excited about institutionalized learning?"

"Nope. Just don't be a complete ass to anyone we meet."

"I might be able to manage that." He grinned. "No promises."

Seth rolled his eyes as his son disappeared downstairs. He felt a cautious hope. The call with his mother had gone better than he'd dared to hope.

Of course, he still had to figure out how to tell his mother about his relationship with Beck and Heavenly. That conversation would go far less easily. But that was another problem for another day.

For now, Hudson was here, Mom was thrilled, and they were taking things one step at a time. At the moment, that was the best Seth could hope for.

The sound of teenage laughter drifted up from the game room as Heavenly chopped veggies and mixed dips for this evening's barbecue. Through the sliding glass doors, she watched Beck clean the grill on the patio while Seth arranged chairs around the dining table by the pool.

Today, they would introduce their friends to Hudson. And announce their engagement.

Heavenly was beyond giddy. But to make the event full of strangers easier for the boy, they'd suggested he invite a friend from his new school. Hudson and Casen had been downstairs for the past few hours, their shouts competing with the gun blasts and driving music from their video game.

Hearing Hudson sound happy, even normal, eased Heavenly's heart. Of course having a teenager in the house still felt surreal. All week, Seth had tried to be the perfect father for the teenage son he was still trying to understand. But the kid was settling in better than any of them had dared to hope. The co-ed academy he'd started on Wednesday, with Laura's input and blessing, had seemingly been the right choice—small classes, strong academics, and a football program that had immediately welcomed Hudson's skills as a wide receiver.

Slowly but surely, they were chipping away at that chip on his shoulder.

Casen seemed like a good kid, polite and respectful when he'd arrived earlier, though she could see why he and Hudson had clicked. Both carried themselves with that particular brand of teenage swagger that came from being good at sports and having pubescent girls pant after them. How long before Hudson got wrapped up in some fight or drama?

The doorbell rang, interrupting her thoughts. Heavenly's pulse lurched with anticipation as she rinsed her hands in the sink.

"I'll get it." Seth dashed in from the patio and headed for the front door.

She followed as he tugged it open. Raine, Hammer, and Liam entered, all smiles.

As soon as Raine caught sight of her, the woman squealed and ran, arms wide open. "Oh, my god, I've missed you so much!"

Laughing, Heavenly met her bestie halfway and enfolded her in a happy hug. "Same! I'm so glad you're back."

Between their Paris honeymoon and Hudson's unexpected arrival, she hadn't seen Raine since her wedding two weeks ago. That was the longest they'd been apart in months.

Heavenly scanned her bestie up and down. "You look amazing. Marriage suits you."

"I admit, I'm pretty happy." Raine all but preened. "But you're the one who looks gorg. I swear you get more beautiful every time I see you. If I didn't love you so much, I'd hate you."

Hammer and Liam looked on from the doorway, bro-hugging and fist-bumping Seth before they grinned broadly and greeted Heavenly with warm hugs.

"So…where's this teenage son of yours?" Raine pulled back from Seth's welcoming embrace. "And did you really think the world needed another you?"

He slung an arm around Heavenly's waist and grinned. "Of course. Hudson is my gift to humanity. You're welcome."

Everyone laughed as they wandered into the kitchen. Footsteps thundered up the stairs. Seconds later, Hudson appeared at the top, dressed in board shorts and a T-shirt. "Did I hear my name?"

"Speak of the devil," Seth said with obvious pride, moving to stand beside his son with a clap on the back. "Hudson, I'd like you to meet our best friends. This is Macen Hammerman—call him Hammer—Liam O'Neill, and their wife, Raine."

Hudson stepped forward with easy confidence. "What's up? Nice to meet you."

Raine's eyes went wide as she took in Hudson's face, her gaze darting between father and son. "Wow. You *are* a dead ringer for your dad."

"No kidding," Hammer added, extending his hand to Hudson. "The resemblance is incredible."

"Good to meet you, lad." Liam shook with the kid, then turned back to Seth, his smile sly. "If he's the devil, it's no surprise. He *is* half you, mate."

"Fuck you. Just wait until those twin girls of yours grow up. We'll see how angelic they are since they're half *you*."

The Irishman laughed even harder. "If they're not angels, blame Raine. After all, they're half her, too."

The tsking brunette swatted his shoulder. "Ciara has my sweet disposition, thank you very much. Catronia, the little hellraiser, is all you."

"Try the other way around," Liam drawled.

Heavenly laughed. "Where are those precious babies?"

"With Liam's sisters. They're leaving for Ireland day after tomorrow, so they wanted to spend a little more time with their nieces. But

Meg will be back with Liam's mother when this one is born." Raine slid her hand over her seemingly flat stomach.

Honestly, the woman didn't look as if she'd recently had twins and was already pregnant again.

Seth jumped into the banter. "Hammer's son will undoubtedly be a menace to society."

Hammer shrugged. "The kid has no prayer. After all, Raine will be his mother."

"Hey!" she objected. "You can both do without for the rest of the weekend."

Liam leered at her. "But we know *you* can't, love."

"Besides…" Macen bent to murmur in her ear. "That's not going to happen, precious."

Blushing, Raine stuck out her tongue as Heavenly heard another set of footfalls on the stairs. Moments later, Hudson's friend appeared, dressed for the pool.

"This is Casen," Hudson told the others.

Raine waved. Hammer shook his hand.

Then Liam followed suit. "Are you lads on the football team together?"

"Yeah, I play safety," Casen replied. "Hudson's our new starting receiver. Guy's got serious hands."

Hudson looked embarrassed by the praise. "Or I just got lucky with a few good throws."

"Lucky, my ass," Seth said with a grin. "You earned that starting position."

With a shrug, Hudson changed the subject. "Can we swim now?"

Seth nodded. "Be sure you each grab a towel from the linen closet before you dive in."

"Got it." Hudson took off running, Casen right behind him.

"And don't forget sunscreen!" Heavenly called as the boys darted for the patio.

"We know," Hudson said with exaggerated patience as he slung open the sliding door.

"Come on out," Beck called, closing the lid on the grill.

As the teenagers tossed their towels on the nearest lounge and hastily applied sunscreen, the rest of the men meandered outside, Liam and Hammer greeting Beck with good-natured jibes and smiles.

The second the door closed behind them, Raine whirled on Heavenly, who resumed prepping the food. "Okay, how are you all *really* adjusting to this new development? I'm sure the fact Seth has a sixteen-year-old son was mind-boggling."

Heavenly nodded. "That's an understatement. I mean, he's no monk, but…"

"Right? And going from a threesome to suddenly having a teenager in the house… I can't even imagine the upheaval."

Heavenly pulled cherry tomatoes and chopped celery from the refrigerator, laying them out on the tray with the accompanying dip. "It was awkward at first. Hudson's a good kid, but when he first arrived? He was *so* angry at everything and everyone, especially Seth."

"That's what my brother said. River swore the kid looked just like Seth, but had an attitude so toxic it was almost nuclear."

"Seth is trying so hard to be the father Hudson needs, and it's working…most of the time. But there are moments when he…reverts. I see the attitude again."

"Well, he's a teenage boy. I was twelve when River left home, but I remember the way he acted." Raine rolled her eyes. "He was a shit, always playing pranks on me."

"Hudson is a total teenage boy. Some backtalk and rebellion is expected. But I can see how much pressure Seth's putting on himself to be everything the kid needs."

"That's a lot for anyone, but especially for the man who's already lost a son so tragically."

Heavenly pulled crackers from the pantry and sliced some cheese from the fridge before retrieving another tray. "Exactly, and I keep trying to help out, lighten Seth's load, find ways to make him smile—"

"A good blow job always does the trick." Raine winked, taking over the appetizer plate.

Heavenly rolled her eyes. "I'm being serious."

"I am, too. Don't underestimate the value of a good orgasm to put a smile on your man's face."

"Normally, I'd agree. But everything is more complicated now."

Understanding broke across Raine's face. "Oh, because you and Beck want babies. Is Seth even more reluctant now?"

Heavenly glanced toward the patio and lowered her voice. "I don't know where we stand. The night of your wedding, he came around, and we started…trying. But then he had to go to New York. His mother found the twins in bed with the same girl and—"

"All hell broke loose?"

Heavenly nodded. "Then Hudson turned up, and…we really haven't talked about having kids again."

"Well, you don't get pregnant by talking, girl." Raine sent her a sassy glance.

"I mean, he says he's not where he needs to be mentally. I don't know what to make of that."

Her bestie frowned. "Have you had sex since he met Hudson?"

Heavenly blushed. She hadn't stopped thinking about last Saturday night. She'd seen a whole new side of Seth, and she didn't know what had prompted his uber-Dominant behavior. "Yes."

"Did either of them glove up?"

"No, but they both knew I was at the end of my cycle." Heavenly grabbed the baby carrots and arranged them on the veggie tray, pushing down her disappointment. "In fact, I got my period early this morning. But Seth double-checked that I wasn't fertile before…you know."

"He and Beck fucked you senseless? What about—" Raine stopped abruptly and grabbed her wrist, staring at Heavenly's ring as the diamond caught the kitchen lights. "Wait. Is that what I think it is?"

A smile she couldn't hold back crept across Heavenly's face. "Maybe?"

"Oh, my god!" Raine squealed. "You're engaged? When? How? Tell me everything!"

"The night of your wedding. They proposed together. They didn't plan anything romantic, but somehow it still was." Heavenly's smile turned uncertain. "But don't tell anyone. We want to announce it tonight."

"I'm so thrilled for you. The three of you will be happy. And bonus, I won't be the only girl I know with two husbands." Raine's expression turned serious. "But you're worried Seth's question about your cycle means he's rethinking having babies?"

Heavenly clutched the appetizer tray. "He's not only dealing with Hudson; he's still trying to figure out when and how to tell his mother about our relationship. Plus, I don't think he's fully come to grips with losing his wife and son. I'm worried that Beck and I pushing is too much for him right now."

"You think he'll crack?"

"Maybe. He seems happy, but sometimes…I can tell he's not as okay as he wants us to think. I worry he's just pushing down his feelings to make us happy, and it will ultimately come back to haunt us."

"Speaking from experience? Upheaval and trauma either make you stronger or break you apart entirely. Seth has you and Beck. Keep reminding him he can lean on you two."

"I do, but he seems determined to be our pillar, you know?" Heavenly shook her head. "Enough about my problems. How was Paris? Tell me *everything*."

Raine's face lit up. "It was everything I imagined—and more. We toured Notre Dame and the Louvre, took a boat down the Seine at sunset. Liam took us to this amazing little jazz club in Montmartre, and Hammer surprised us with an incredible dinner at this tiny restaurant. They didn't even have menus, just brought us whatever the chef made that night. The guys let me shop, and I may have gone a little crazy." She grinned before she dissolved into a dreamy sigh. "And the time together, just the three of us—no businesses, no babies, no distractions—was idyllic. Ten out of ten. Highly recommend."

"You deserve every moment to celebrate your love and all you've overcome. How are you feeling this pregnancy? Morning sickness and exhaustion, like last time?"

"Mixed bag. I'm not as tired, but the sickness sometimes lasts most of the day. And I want spicy food constantly." Raine dropped her voice. "Yesterday I put hot sauce on ice cream."

Heavenly tried not to wince. "That's…creative."

"Your face says disgusting. Don't judge." Raine slid a hand over her middle. "Hammer's son is very demanding, just like his father."

"You're barely pregnant. Liam is sure it's a boy?"

"Oh, yeah. His mother even called to congratulate us. She knew before we did."

The O'Neill psychic abilities still surprised Heavenly, but they were too uncanny not to be real.

After a quick knock on the front door, it opened and River appeared in the kitchen. He looked withdrawn. "Ladies."

Raine took one look at her older brother's face and scowled. "What's wrong?"

"The fucking mattress at the rent-by-the-week shithole is almost as bad as Seth's sofa at the office. I might be desperate enough to take Heavenly's suggestion and ask Pike about renting a room at his place. I just hate the thought of living with that asshole."

"You and Pike under the same roof?" Raine shook her head. "That will end in war, especially when he finds out you've been stalking Jasmine like some obsessed—"

"Hey, I figured out where she lives, where she gets her coffee, where she works out, and what her daily schedule is. That doesn't mean I'm stalking her."

"Um…that's exactly what it means, big brother."

"I'm being attentive. Protective, even."

Raine rolled her eyes. "You're being delusional. Taking her virginity doesn't mean you own her."

River ignored her and turned to Heavenly with an imploring stare. "You understand, right?"

Heavenly grimaced. "Actually…it sounds like stalking to me, too. Sorry."

"Of course you're siding with my sister. Jasmine and I have unfinished business, and I'm not letting up until we hash it out."

"Give her some space," Heavenly suggested gently. "She'll come around."

River wasn't having it. "I've given her months. I'm done waiting."

"Translation: you still haven't taken anyone else to bed, so you're getting horny and desperate." Raine's smile was pure saccharine.

"No, I'm annoyed that my little sister won't stop being a shit."

"What are you going to do?" Heavenly asked.

"Right now? Go out to the patio and enjoy myself." River headed for the door.

With the men, who would ostensibly understand him.

"I meant about Jasmine," Heavenly called to his retreating back.

"Oh, I have a whole new strategy." His grin was an implacable mixture of determination and mischief.

Based on that expression, Jasmine didn't stand a chance.

Once he shut the sliding door behind him, Raine shook her head, suppressing a laugh. "It's official. He's insane."

"I think you're right."

The doorbell rang, and Heavenly whirled. "I'll get that."

She hustled to the foyer and found a familiar man—tall, dark-haired, and casually dressed—on her porch. He wore a polite smile on his stern face and held a bottle of wine. He didn't look lethal. She knew better.

"Jericho! Good to see you again," she welcomed. "Come in. I'm glad you could make it."

"Thanks for inviting me." He smiled as he stepped inside and handed her the vino. "After five years in San Bernardino, I'm happy to be back in LA. But most of my friends have either gotten hitched or moved away. So I appreciate being included."

"Of course. Happy to have you! How are you settling in?"

"Can't complain. I like my new place. Was lucky to find it, that's for sure. Nice neighbors." He shrugged. "We'll see."

"Sounds like you made the right decision. Beers and bottled water are in the cooler on the patio, where the guys are, probably swapping grilling techniques."

"Or telling dirty jokes," Raine quipped, appearing beside her. "Good to see you again."

"You, too, Mrs… What's your married name?"

"Hammerman-O'Neill. But just call me Raine."

"So you married Liam, then?"

She grinned. "We chose the name because it's alphabetical. But who I legally married is a secret we'll all take to our graves."

As Jericho raised a brow, Zach appeared on the walkway behind him, his face quietly reserved.

"Zach!" Heavenly moved in to hug him, keeping it brief since he still seemed reluctant to touch his brother's girlfriend. "I'm so glad you could make it. Where's your date?"

"Hannah and I decided to take a step back. After what she endured in her sect, she's not ready for more yet. I respect that."

"Understandable." Heavenly hoped he wasn't hurt. She had no doubt he was lonely. "Tried the pool again?"

"Since I'm still closer to drowning than swimming, no." Then he turned to Jericho. "Hey! I didn't know you'd be here."

"Good to see you, man." Jericho shook his hand. "How've you been?"

"Pretty good. You?"

"Can't complain." Jericho clapped him on the shoulder. "Let's grab a beer."

The two headed out to the patio.

Together, she and Raine finished plating the last of the appetizers and side dishes. As they worked, Heavenly could see the men gathered around the grill, their laughter carrying on the evening breeze. Hudson and Casen splashed around the pool, clearly enjoying themselves.

"Are we waiting on anyone else?" Raine asked.

"No. Ready to join the party?" Heavenly picked up a tray of food.

Raine grabbed another platter of food and paused at the patio door. Heavenly watched Seth laugh at something Hammer said while keeping an eye on Hudson in the pool. He looked relaxed, happy even, surrounded by friends and family.

But tonight they were announcing their engagement and introducing his long-lost son. Soon, Seth would have to devise a strategy for telling his mother about their unconventional relationship. So many life-altering decisions up in the air and out of their hands. How long would Hudson stay with them? What kind of impact would he have on their lives? And, Heavenly wondered, what if she got pregnant?

Would settling all those uncertainties finally heal Seth…or push him over the edge?

Chapter Fifteen

Seth leaned against the patio railing, watching Hudson and Casen cannonball into the pool with the reckless abandon typical of teenagers. Their splashes sent water cascading across the deck, but neither boy seemed to notice or care as they surfaced, laughing and immediately plotting their next stunt.

The late afternoon sun cast the backyard in golden light. Seth took it all in, enjoying both the anticipation and normalcy of the moment. Beck, Hammer, Liam, and River stood nearby, drinks in hand, the easy camaraderie of old friends settling over the group like a comfortable blanket.

At the patio table, Raine and Heavenly set out the food, the women's laughter mixing with the splash and chatter from the pool.

"Ready to eat in five," Beck called out.

"Perfect," Heavenly said back.

"So…" Liam appeared at Seth's elbow, nursing a beer. "How does it feel? Being a father again?"

Seth blew out a breath, his gaze drifting back to Hudson, who was now attempting to dunk Casen. "A shock. Still is, sometimes. I look at him and think, 'Jesus, I have a sixteen-year-old son.'"

"But you're managing?"

"Beck and Heavenly have been incredible. And Mom…" Seth paused, remembering his mother's initial reaction. "She took the news pretty well, all things considered. Though she did point out something I hadn't thought about before."

"What?"

"All the milestones I missed. First steps, first words, first day of school…" Seth's throat tightened. "It's weird, you know? I've been a father twice, and I've missed most of the firsts with them both."

Liam's expression softened with understanding. "That's not your fault, mate. You didn't know."

"True. But it doesn't make missing out any easier."

They stood in comfortable silence for a moment, watching Hudson and Casen attempt increasingly elaborate pool tricks, their whoops and hollers echoing across the water.

"How's he been integrating into the house?" Liam asked.

"Pretty easy so far, actually. The kid loves video games, which gives us something to bond over. He's on the quiet side—well, except when he's snarky—but he seems to be settling in. School's been good for him. Gives him focus and structure. And he's already making friends."

Seth paused, watching his son execute a perfect dive. "We'll have to tackle the bigger stuff soon—driving, dating, going out with friends. But it's only been a week."

"Early days," Liam agreed, then took a swig of his beer. "Speaking of early days...better luck with the conception thing next month."

Seth nearly choked on his drink. "Jesus. Do you have to know *everything?*"

"I don't *try* to know. It just... happens." Liam shrugged apologetically. "For what it's worth, I imagine you're both disappointed and relieved."

Seth couldn't deny that. When Heavenly announced this morning that she'd gotten her period, he'd felt that conflicted mix of emotions. "We'll have more opportunities."

"You will. Hopefully you, Beck, and Heavenly will see some pink or blue booties in your future. But since nothing concrete has happened yet, I can't see that far ahead."

"Right." Seth rubbed the back of his neck. "Actually, while we're on the subject of your... gifts, why didn't you give me a heads-up about Hudson? A little warning would've been nice."

Liam winced. "Sorry about that, mate. My abilities aren't always clear. I knew something significant was coming your way, but I didn't know what or when."

"Fair enough." Seth took another drink, then felt Liam's penetrating stare. "What?"

"Does being a father again make the idea of having another baby easier?"

The question squeezed Seth's heart. He sought out Hudson again, stare solemn. "I'm still trying to figure that out. On one hand,

Hudson's made it to sixteen and nothing horrible has befallen him. That's…encouraging."

"But?"

"I still worry. Look what happened to Tristan." Seth's voice dropped. "That was my fault. What if I somehow put Hudson in danger, too? I'd never forgive myself."

"First, Hudson isn't Tristan," Liam reminded. "And he's not a replacement or a second chance to get it right."

"I know that—"

"Do you? Because I've been watching you with him all evening, and you're not the same man who lost Tristan. That Seth was reckless, obsessed, tunnel-visioned. This Seth?" He gestured Seth's way. "More balanced. You're not chasing ghosts to salvage a dead man's reputation anymore."

Seth felt his chest begin to loosen. "I'm trying to be better, do the right thing."

"Just remember, Hudson isn't your chance to fail again. Maybe he's proof that your luck has changed."

"Or maybe that's the universe telling me to wait on having a baby with Heavenly and Beck," Seth mused. "Part of me wants to hold off a few months—after Hudson's more settled, after Mom's wedding…" He trailed off, then shook his head. "But then what? Beck's birthday is in November. He'll be thirty-seven, and he keeps reminding me that he's not getting any younger."

Liam scoffed. "Isn't it interesting how Hudson showed up right when you committed to starting a family? Maybe the universe isn't dictating your timeline. Maybe it's testing your resolve."

"How do you mean?"

"Oftentimes we get exactly what we need in order to face what we're avoiding. Like Hudson showing up out of the blue."

Seth snorted. "More like fate kicking me in the ass."

"Living in the past robs you of enjoying the future," Liam continued. "You can't stand still, Seth. There are too many people—Beck, Heavenly, Hudson—who rely on you to stay present. And think about the future."

Seth pondered that for a long moment, watching Hudson attempt to teach Casen some complicated pool maneuver. Then he found himself confessing something he hadn't planned to share.

"When I was in New York last week, I went back to the old house I shared with Autumn and Tristan." Seth shrugged. "I figured it was time to truly put the past behind me and finally put the place on the market. But standing in the foyer…the past nearly knocked me out, like you said it would." He met Liam's eyes. "Was the house what you were warning me about?"

Liam paused, looking uncertain. "I don't rightly know. Could be."

"But?"

His Irish friend shrugged. "Keep your head on a swivel, mate. Eyes wide open."

A chill ran down Seth's spine. "What the hell does that mean?"

"Everything's subject to change. I don't know anything concrete, but I can't shake an uneasy feeling. I even consulted my mum about it."

"What did Bryn say?"

"She didn't have any specific insight, but she shares my sense of… disquiet."

Before Seth could press for more details, Liam's attention shifted to the pool, where the boys were attempting to see who could hold their breath underwater the longest. "Keep an eye on Hudson's friend."

"Casen seems like a good kid, but the two of them together…" Seth shook his head. "They're troublemakers. I already overheard Hudson telling him that his girlfriend Brielle is 'hotter than hell.'"

Liam chuckled. "The apple doesn't fall far from the tree. Better make sure Hudson has condoms, or history might repeat itself."

As much as Seth hated to think about it, Liam was right. "I know I'm not going to stop him from being sexually active. That genie is out of the bottle, so the best I can do is keep him stocked."

"Aye. Come on. Let's mingle with the others."

As Zach moved toward the cooler to grab a drink, Seth sidled up to Jericho. River joined the bunch.

"Great party," the FBI agent said, extending his hand. "Thanks for including me."

"Of course." Seth pumped his hand in return. "How are things going? You settling in okay?"

Jericho's face lit up. "Actually, things are going great. I moved in with my old friend Dean."

River froze, staring at Jericho. "You're living with Dean? Dean Gorman?"

"Yeah. We've been friends for years, and we make a good team. So why not?"

"A good team." River's voice went dangerously quiet. "So you've taken my place as his new wingman."

"I..." Jericho looked between River and Seth, clearly confused. "What?"

"It's not his fault," Seth rushed to say, recognizing the dangerous gleam in River's eyes. "Don't get pissed off."

River didn't look happy, but he let it go...for now.

"Burgers are ready, everyone," Beck hollered. "Grab one off the grill, then fill your plates with all the apps and sides."

After most of the guests had dished up, Seth grabbed his own burger.

Beck took a bite of his burger, then swallowed it down. "When do you want to make our announcements?"

Seth glanced around the patio. Most of their friends were talking, drinking, and laughing.

"Now," he decided, looking to Heavenly for confirmation.

Heavenly's face lit up, and she squeezed both their hands. "You're right. Let's do it!"

"Hudson," he called to his son, who was sitting with Casen, guzzling sodas. "Come here for a minute."

Then Seth stood. His angel got to her feet beside him, and Beck flanked her. "Everyone! Can I get your attention? Beck, Heavenly, and I have some announcements."

Conversations quieted as all eyes turned their way.

Seth took a breath, his hand resting on Hudson's shoulder as the teenager stood beside him, looking equal parts nervous and curious.

"First," Seth began, his voice carrying across the patio, "I want to introduce someone important. Most of you have met him already, but you might not know the full story." He squeezed Hudson's shoulder. "This is my son, Hudson."

A few surprised murmurs rippled through the group. Hammer raised his beer in acknowledgment. Liam smiled knowingly.

"I didn't know he existed until last week," Seth continued, his tone matter-of-fact but warm. "His mom never told me she was pregnant. So finding out I had a sixteen-year-old son was...a hell of a shock." He glanced down at Hudson, whose ears had gone red. "But a good one. Hudson's living with us now, and he's part of this family. Our family."

Hudson ducked his head, clearly embarrassed by the attention but trying to hide a small smile.

"Welcome to the chaos, kid," River called out, raising his beer.

The group echoed the sentiment with cheers and applause. Hudson's smile grew a little wider.

Seth waited for the noise to die down, then caught Heavenly's eye. She was beaming at him, her hand already reaching for his. Beck slid his arm around her waist.

"And since we're making announcements," Seth said, his voice softening as he looked at his angel, "there's something else Beck, Heavenly, and I want to share."

He pulled Heavenly close, and Beck mirrored him on her other side. The three of them stood together, a united front.

For months, he, Beck, and Heavenly had been building toward this moment—through heartbreak and healing, through fear and hope, through every obstacle that had nearly torn them apart. Now they were here, and nothing could be sweeter.

"Last weekend, Beck and I asked Heavenly to marry us," Seth began, his voice carrying across the patio as he took her hand and flashed her ring. "She said yes!"

Their guests erupted with cheer. Even Hudson smiled and clapped with the others, looking genuinely pleased.

Beside Seth, Beck kissed their fiancée's temple. "We haven't picked a date yet. But soon. None of us want to wait."

"So…yeah. We're getting married!" Heavenly squealed with delight.

Raine shrieked with excitement and jumped up from her chair, enveloping Heavenly in a fierce hug. "I'm so happy for you! And I didn't tell a soul, I promise."

Heavenly held out her left hand, the diamond catching the last rays of sunlight and sparkling brilliantly. Raine moved in to hug her while the men offered hearty congratulations, back-slapping Seth and Beck.

"Champagne!" Beck laughed, producing bottles from the outdoor bar. "We need champagne!"

As corks popped and glasses were filled—water and soda for Hudson and Casen—Seth felt Heavenly's hand slide into his. When he looked down, he saw her follow suit with Beck. Then she beamed up at him, her eyes bright with unshed tears of joy. Beck flanked her other side, his expression soft with contentment.

"No regrets?" the surgeon asked quietly.

"Not a single one," she whispered, then turned to Seth. "You?"

"None." Their road would never be easy, and there were more than a few bumps they still had to navigate, but the three of them had scaled mountains and crawled over glass to reach this moment. And he'd never been happier. "I love you."

"I love you, too," she whispered.

And as their friends and family raised their glasses in celebration, Seth allowed himself to believe that maybe, just maybe, everything was going to work out exactly as it should.

Chapter Sixteen

Just before midnight, Seth packed up for a last-minute stakeout.

Dressed in an oversized T-shirt and nothing else, Heavenly kissed him goodnight. "Be careful out there."

"I will, angel. Get some sleep."

After he'd gone, Beck hustled Heavenly upstairs and settled her into bed with a heating pad and pain relievers for her menstrual cramps, then eased in beside her. "Better?"

She curled up with a pillow and a soft moan. "I'm sorry things didn't work out this month. I was hoping we'd been successful."

At conceiving? He'd been hoping, too. He was disappointed that she'd started her period, but the doctor in him wasn't surprised. Conception wasn't a given. Most people didn't succeed the first time.

"We have plenty of time, little girl." He tilted her chin up to him and winked. "Besides, they say practice makes perfect."

"That's the fun part." She smiled sleepily.

"With you? Always." He kissed her again, then held her tight.

Within minutes, she was breathing deeply in his arms.

Careful not to wake her, Beck eased out of bed and slipped downstairs. Since he didn't want to leave the party mess for Heavenly to deal with in the morning, especially after she busted her ass preparing all the food, he headed down to finish cleaning up the kitchen.

He was drying the last of the platters when strange sounds drifted up from the floor below. Were Hudson and Casen still playing video games? Casen was spending the night, but they were supposed to be settling in and turning down the volume, damn it.

But when a distinctly feminine moan, followed by masculine grunts, floated up the stairs, Beck froze. The sounds of sex weren't coming from *Call of Duty*.

Jaw tightening, he tossed down the dish towel and glanced up toward his bedroom. The last thing he needed was for the boys' porn viewing to wake Heavenly.

As he headed down the stairs, the sounds grew clearer, louder, and more concerning. Jesus, he really hoped Hudson and Casen weren't downstairs jacking off together to some streaming site. That conversation would be awkward as fuck—and one he'd rather leave for Seth.

When he reached Hudson's door, he gripped the knob and paused, ear pressed to the wood.

"That was amazing," a female sighed breathlessly from inside the room. "When can we do it again?"

Beck froze. That voice wasn't a recording, a porn site, or the TV. She was live.

The boys had a girl in the room.

Fuck.

But it sounded like they already had.

"Anytime you want, gorgeous," Casen replied. "I gotta admit, that was fucking hot."

Hudson's voice followed, thick with satisfaction. "Yeah, way hotter than I thought it would be. No wonder my dad is into this shit."

Beck's stomach dropped to his feet. He cursed under his breath, wishing like hell Seth was here to handle this clusterfuck. Who was this girl? When had she gotten here? And what the hell had these kids been thinking?

Mentally, Beck counted to ten, sucked in a deep breath, and opened the door.

The scene that greeted him was exactly what he'd feared.

In the shadowy room, relieved only by the spill of light from the bathroom, he could make out three figures on Hudson's bed, tangled in his sheets. Sandwiched between two teenage boys was a pretty, petite blonde panting in post-orgasmic satisfaction.

Purposely averting his gaze, Beck cleared his throat. "You three done?"

Hudson jerked away from her, then leapt to his feet in panic. The girl yelped and yanked the sheet around her while hiding her face in Casen's chest beneath.

"Oh, my god! Dude, get out!" Hudson screamed as he grabbed his shorts off the floor and covered himself.

Beck clenched his jaw. "This is *my* house."

Hudson disposed of his condom and yanked on his shorts with angry jerks before he stomped toward Beck. They stood toe-to-toe, fury rolling off the teen. Beck prayed the kid wasn't stupid enough to take a swing at him. He'd hate trying to explain to Seth why he'd KO'd his son.

He caught a flurry of movement in his periphery—Casen and the girl untangling from the sheet. He ignored them, keeping his gaze fixed on the defiance blazing in Hudson's eyes. "You're in a shitload of trouble. But I'll come back to you. What's your name, young lady?" He refused to even glance her way.

"B-Brielle."

"How did you get here?"

"I drove," she whispered, sounding somewhere between embarrassed and terrified.

"After you get dressed, you can drop Casen off at his house on your way home."

Hudson planted himself more firmly in Beck's path. "My friends aren't going anywhere. They're spending the night."

Beck scoffed. "You and Casen can snuggle up and read bedtime stories some other time, but Brielle is *not* staying so you three can have another fuckfest. Not in my house."

Hudson's chin jutted out. "It's half my dad's house, too."

"Your dad would say the exact same thing," Beck shot back.

As Casen led Brielle toward the door—both thankfully dressed—he sent Hudson an apologetic grimace. "It's cool, man. I'll call you tomorrow."

Brielle paused at the threshold, glancing at Beck with wide, worried eyes. "Please don't tell my mom about this."

But before Beck could answer, the pair raced out the door and up the stairs, slamming the front door behind them.

Then…silence. Beck knew it wouldn't last, not while Hudson pinged with anger.

"You're such a fucking hypocrite," the kid snarled. "You and my dad do the exact same thing with Heavenly."

"We're *adults*. You're sixteen, not mature enough for what you just did." Beck's voice turned icy cold. "You think we share her just because the sex is hot? Newsflash, dude. That's not why at all."

"Then why?"

Beck snorted. "The emotional connection. And the fact you even have to ask proves you don't grasp the concept of a real relationship."

"I don't have to listen to you. You're not my dad."

"I'm not." Beck nodded with a calmness he didn't feel. "But I'm as invested in your well-being as any biological child your dad or I will have someday with Heavenly. Like it or not, we're a family now."

Hudson rolled his eyes. "What do you know about family? You ran away from home and married a hooker."

Beck dropped his voice to a dangerous quiet. "You think you're tough, kid?"

"Tougher than you, old man," Hudson sneered.

"You think so? By the time I was your age, I'd already killed someone."

Hudson scowled. "Bullshit?"

"God's truth. You never asked *why* I ran away from home. Let me tell you—"

"Because mommy and daddy didn't give you enough love."

"You're right." Beck sent him a brittle smile. "They didn't. So, when I was your age, I slit my father's throat. And a few months ago, I watched my mother bleed out in front of me. I had the medical skills to save her, but I didn't. I just watched her die because she deserved it."

Hudson's face went white. "You're lying."

A humorless chuckle rumbled the back of Beck's throat as he pulled out his phone and tapped a news article. "This details the day my *family* came to kill me at Liam's lodge. Your dad's tactical knowledge helped save nearly everyone's lives." He scrolled to another page. "And this is about Jericho leading the FBI raid on the compound where my mother and middle brother's followers lived. You met my younger brother, Zach? They murdered his wife and eleven-year-old daughter, too."

Hudson took the phone with shaking hands and scanned the articles. His face turned even paler as his teenage bravado crumbled and reality set in.

Eventually, he swallowed and handed the phone back, not quite meeting Beck's eyes. "Shit."

"Do I finally have your attention?" Beck asked, pocketing his phone.

Hudson nodded, not saying a word.

"Good. Let's talk about what you just did with Brielle and Casen." Beck leaned against the doorframe, studying the teenager. "What the fuck were you thinking?"

Hudson shifted uncomfortably. "Casen asked questions about the three of you after you guys announced your engagement. I told him that you guys were all…together."

"Okay. For your sake, I hope you told him not to blab that to everyone at school."

"Of course I did. I'm not an idiot. You think I want the other kids whispering shit behind my back?"

"Smart. Go on."

"Casen kept talking about it. I could tell he liked the idea. Next thing I know, he called Brielle and asked if she wanted to come over."

"So, she did and then you two…what? Stripped off your clothes and hopped into bed?"

"No," he bit out. "We played video games for a while. Casen started kissing her, and he told her that I thought she was pretty. Then I admitted that watching them was hot. Casen asked Brielle if she wanted me to kiss her. She blushed, but she said yes. So…I kissed her. And…we just went from there."

"So what now?" Beck asked, brow arched. "You going to be the third in their relationship?"

"No… Maybe. I don't know. Since you barged in, we didn't really have a chance to talk about what's next."

"If you three are smart, you'll be one and done. None of you are emotionally mature enough to handle this."

Hudson mulishly pressed his lips together. "Are you going to tell my dad?"

"Yes."

"Why? What's the big deal? He knows I have a sex life."

"Because we don't keep secrets in this family. Your father needs to know what the hell you're up to."

Hudson's face flushed with anger. "You can't—"

"I can, and I will." Beck straightened and pushed away from the doorjamb. "Listen, you may not have had a father before, but now you have two. And if Seth needs backup handling discipline and reminding you that you're still a minor, I'm happy to help."

The teenager opened his mouth to argue, but something—probably Beck's expression—stopped him.

"Good. Now lemme tell you how this is going to work," he continued, his voice deadly calm. "You're going to stay in this room and think about the choices you made tonight, decide if they were worth the consequences. And tomorrow, when Seth wakes up, we're all going to have a nice, long conversation about boundaries and expectations."

"Ugh. Jesus…"

Beck flashed him an acidic smile and moved toward the door. "Oh, and one more thing. If you think I don't have the balls to enforce the rules in this house, you're mistaken. Don't test me."

He left Hudson standing there, mouth agape, and headed upstairs to set the house alarm. Seth was paranoid about security. Tonight, that paranoia would not only keep them safe, but if Hudson tried to sneak out, Beck would know immediately. And there'd be hell to pay.

Once he'd armed the system, he pulled out his phone, sighed, and texted Seth.

> Need to talk when you get a chance. We have a problem.

He stared at the screen for a moment, then added:

> Hudson's fine, but there's something you need to know.

Beck pocketed his phone, headed to the kitchen, and poured himself a whiskey. He didn't expect to hear back from Seth during his stakeout. But as he settled into his chair and lifted the glass to his lips, his phone buzzed with an incoming message.

As Seth read Beck's text, dread settled like a stone in his gut. What the hell had happened with Hudson?

He responded immediately.

My targets haven't shown up yet, and it's getting late. I'm pretty sure they're no-shows, so I'll be home in ten. Anything you want to tell me now?

Beck's reply came quickly.

Better to talk in person.

"Fuck," Seth muttered under his breath, his dread expanding as he quickly broke down his surveillance equipment and packed it away. Whatever Hudson had done, it was bad enough that Beck didn't want to discuss it over text.

During the drive home, Seth's mind raced with possibilities, none of them good. Clearly, Hudson had pulled some shit the minute his back was turned. He'd dealt with BS, sneakiness, and crappy behavior when he'd been a father figure to his younger brothers, so discipline was nothing new. But he hadn't expected to have to open a can of whoop-ass on his son this soon.

Seth pulled into the garage and eased inside the house. He found Beck waiting for him in the foyer with a whiskey in hand and a deep frown creasing his features.

That wasn't a good omen.

"I hurried. What happened?" Seth asked, though he wasn't sure he wanted to know.

Beck didn't sugarcoat it. "I caught Hudson and Casen sharing Casen's girlfriend, Brielle. Walked in on them just after the deed was done. Hudson had to pull out of the girl's ass to have a conversation with me."

Seth closed his eyes, feeling as if he'd been sucker punched. Anger flooded him, followed immediately by a wave of guilt that made his stomach churn. Would Hudson have tried a threesome if he hadn't come here? If he hadn't known that his dad and Beck shared Heavenly?

Probably not.

"Fuck."

"Casen and Brielle left. Hudson's in his room, probably shitting his pants because I refused to keep his antics to myself. He's not expecting you until tomorrow, but…" Beck shrugged. "My philosophy is, when you need to come down like a ton of bricks, there's no time like the present."

Seth ran a hand through his hair. "Yeah. Thanks for breaking that shit up."

"You're welcome." Beck drained his glass and turned toward the stairs.

"Wait." Seth stopped him. "Come with me? I think we should do this together."

Beck paused, one foot on the bottom step. "Because?"

"As far as I'm concerned, if Hudson's staying here, we're all going to be responsible for him. I don't want him getting the idea that all he has to do to get away with shit is wait for me to leave the house."

Beck nodded. "I didn't want to step on your toes, but you're right. We have to deal with Hudson as a cohesive unit. If Heavenly wasn't in pain and already asleep, I'd suggest she come, too."

"I'll loop her in tomorrow," Seth decided. "For now, we need to deal with my son."

Beck fell in beside him as they headed down to Hudson's room. Seth knocked once, then opened the door without waiting for permission. Hudson sat on his bed in sweats and a T-shirt, phone in hand. He looked up with the expression of a kid who'd been caught with his hand in the cookie jar.

"We need to talk." Seth stepped into the room, Beck close behind.

Hudson set his phone aside. "What's the big fucking deal? So I had sex. It's hardly the first time. I don't need you two on my dick."

"After the shit you pulled tonight, you're lucky you still have a dick," Beck said dryly.

Seth nodded. "As long as you're legally a child and you're living under my roof, I'll do whatever I need to keep you safe and on the straight and narrow. Beck and I have some questions, and you're going to answer them. Honestly."

Hudson glanced between them, clearly weighing his options. Finally, he sighed. "Whatever."

"Was this your first threesome?" Beck asked without preamble.

"Holy shit. You said questions, not an interrogation. Don't I get any privacy around here?" Hudson protested.

"You're sixteen," Beck said flatly. "Living in our house. Privacy is earned."

Hudson glared at both of them. "This is bullshit."

"Answer his question," Seth snapped.

Hudson's cheeks flushed, but he lifted his chin. "Yeah. It was. Okay?"

"It needs to be the last time for a long while. First time having anal sex?" Seth continued.

"No."

Jesus. How sexually active had Hudson been? And for how long? Was there anything else he hadn't tried?

"How old were you when you first had sex?"

"Fourteen. But I got my first blow job the year before."

Seth felt his stomach clench. Hudson had been getting blow jobs at thirteen, younger even than Seth himself. *Where the hell was his guidance? His supervision?*

Seth raked a hand through his hair. His son's answer wasn't shocking…but a potential problem. They fucking didn't need consequences. "Since you said you have sex regularly, do you always carry condoms with you?"

"Always. Yeah."

At least the kid was being safe. That was something, but that didn't make Hudson's behavior okay.

Seth studied his son's face, seeing echoes of his own teenage recklessness staring back at him. "What you did tonight was incredibly stupid. You're sixteen. You don't have the emotional maturity to handle sharing someone, especially not someone else's girlfriend."

"Beck already gave me this lecture—"

"And now you're getting it from me," Seth cut him off. "Your choices tonight showed poor judgment, disrespect for Brielle's relationship with Casen, and a complete lack of understanding about the possible repercussions of your actions."

Beck stepped forward. "Sharing a woman isn't a game. It's complicated, emotionally demanding, and requires a level of maturity you don't possess."

"You and Seth do it—"

"We're *adults*," Seth said sharply.

"Beck gave me that part of the lecture."

"Then I'll give you the rest. We've both been through hell and back, learned how to communicate, how to handle jealousy and insecurity and all the other shit that comes with a relationship like ours. We know how to listen, compromise, and put each other first. What we have with Heavenly is a lifelong commitment based on love. You're a kid who thinks a three-way is just for shits and giggles. You're not prepared for the difficulties of keeping a relationship like ours together."

"He's right," Beck added. "And trust me, kid. You have a lot to learn before you're ready for *anything* serious with another person, much less two."

Hudson shifted uncomfortably. "I'm not looking for forever with Casen and Brielle."

"Good. You're grounded for the next two weeks. No video games, no TV, no movies, no going out with friends. You can have your phone for school and football, in case there's an emergency. You'll hand it over as soon as you get home, and you'll get it back before you go to school the next morning. You can swim laps, work out, read, or help around the house. That's it."

"That's bullshit!" Hudson exploded, jumping to his feet. "You can't just—"

"I can. If you don't like it, I'll put you on a plane back to Connecticut—after I tell your mother what happened tonight."

After the ultimatum left his mouth, Seth felt a moment of pure panic. Letting Hudson feel the consequences of his actions was the right thing to do, but…what if the kid called his bluff? What if he actually chose to leave?

That possibility wrecked Seth.

He'd found his son a week ago. They were just starting to build a relationship. And now he might lose Hudson? The kid clearly needed structure, needed a father figure who would hold him accountable. If Hudson went back to Connecticut...

God, please don't let him choose to leave.

Hudson paled, his bravado crumbling. "What if I stay?"

Relief flooded Seth. The kid would only ask that if he wanted to remain.

"I won't tell your mother about this incident unless you give me a reason to. And once you turn eighteen, I can't control what you do. But for the next eighteen months, you either follow our rules or you go back to your mom and Ted. Those are your two choices."

Hudson fell quiet, his gaze darting between Seth and Beck. Finally, he nodded. "All right. Fine. Just...don't send me back there. This school is better. I like my new friends. And I…" He swallowed hard. "Living with you three is better."

Seth had to work to keep the relief off his face. He wanted to be Hudson's father, wanted to help shape him into a good man.

That realization hit him with unexpected force.

"Good choice," Seth said simply. "But understand this: in the future, Casen is welcome to come over, but if he's here, Brielle better not be. And any girls you date will meet the family before you're allowed to take them out. Your curfew is midnight. And if you get anyone pregnant, there will be hell to pay."

Hudson scowled. "You got Mom pregnant at fifteen. Pot, meet kettle."

Those words hit hard, but Seth didn't flinch. "How did not having a father your first sixteen years work out for you, Hudson? You want to repeat that pattern? Want your kid to grow up not knowing his dad? Thinking he's unwanted?"

Hudson's face crumpled. "No. It sucked. I wouldn't want that for my kid. And I'm not ready to be a father."

"That's exactly my point. You need to consider the consequences before you act. Think about what *could* happen, not just what feels good in the moment."

Hudson nodded miserably. "Okay."

"We'll get through this, okay?" Seth clapped a hand on his son's shoulder, squeezing gently. "I'll see you for tomorrow morning's workout. Goodnight, son."

"'Night," the kid muttered.

The moment Seth closed the door behind them with a sigh and headed upstairs, the tension left his shoulders. "Thanks for helping."

Beck clapped him on the back. "You handled that really well, Daddy."

Seth snorted, but there was warmth in his chest at the words. "Apparently I'm Daddy whether I'm ready for it or not."

"You got this," Beck insisted.

With Beck and Heavenly's help? "Yeah."

As he reached their bedroom, Seth felt something shift inside him. Tonight had been a wake-up call—not just about Hudson, but about himself. He'd almost lost his son before he'd really had a chance to be his father. He knew what it felt like to lose a child forever. Tristan's death had nearly destroyed him. This would have been different, sure. Hudson would still be alive, but it would have been another failure as a father.

Thank fuck Hudson had chosen to stay. Chosen them and this family they were building. If Seth could be the father his son needed, despite all the risks and potential for heartbreak…then maybe he could handle being a father to the children he and Beck would have with Heavenly.

Maybe.

Chapter Seventeen

In the quiet hush of the Airbus, Seth glanced down at Hudson sleeping in the seat beside him. His son had been out cold for the better part of an hour, his head propped awkwardly against the headrest as they cruised somewhere over Colorado. The kid had been dragging ass since the four-thirty wake-up call for their seven a.m. flight, grumbling about missing both sleep and his upcoming football game. Now, with sleep smoothing his perpetual teenage scowl, Hudson looked younger than his sixteen years.

Behind them, Seth heard the low murmur of Beck's and Heavenly's voices. He'd sat them together so they could steal a few hours together before his family forced them to pretend they were merely friends.

Fuck. He was asking a lot of the people he loved. His guilt for this subterfuge wouldn't let up, and the ways this trip could go sideways felt endless.

Unfortunately, the situation he'd wedged Beck and Heavenly into wasn't the only thing Seth felt bad about. Hudson's reckless threesome with Casen and Brielle ten days ago was proof that his influence on the kid wasn't all positive.

He glanced at Hudson again. Since that night, he'd been trying to connect with his son beyond laying down rules and delivering consequences. Hudson needed to know he mattered. Belonged. That he was family—and always would be.

Beck seemed to understand, bless him… The morning after Hudson's impulsive ménage, the surgeon had joined Seth's usual morning workout with Hudson. At first, the mood in the gym had been tense. Talk had been stilted. Gradually, begrudging monosyllables had become conversation. Then banter, followed more recently by jokes and laughter. What had started as father-son bonding time had evolved into something richer—two father figures working with their son, forging something stronger.

That developing connection had been evident last weekend when

Hudson had played in his very first football game for his new high school. Hudson had scored the game-winning touchdown, and his eyes had lit up when he'd noticed Seth, Beck, and Heavenly in the stands cheering wildly. At the kid's answering grin, Seth's heart had melted.

After the game, Hudson wheedled and groused that he needed to celebrate the win with his teammates. Seth reminded him that he was grounded, but rather than taking him home, they had stopped at a burger joint so the four of them could enjoy a victory dinner together.

"Congrats!" Seth toasted his son with a milkshake. "When you scored, I wanted to run out onto the field and high-five you."

Hudson clinked with his fizzy soda. "Yeah?"

Beck nodded, swallowing a bite of his burger. "Same. You're damn good."

"He's right. I enjoyed watching you play." Heavenly smiled, dipping a fry in ketchup.

"So…you're proud of me?"

Hudson's question felt like a kick in the gut. If his son wasn't sure how he felt, he needed to make it clear. "Damn right I am."

Hudson's answering grin had felt like progress.

What hadn't? Taking the teenage boy shopping the next day for a suit to wear to Mom's wedding.

"Shopping?" Hudson reared back. "I'd rather shave an angry lion's ass with a rusty razor."

Seth had tried not to laugh as he'd shoved his son into a dressing room. Despite the kid's sighing and grumbling, they'd outfitted him for the wedding and the cooler weather ahead.

Getting Hudson a haircut hadn't been much easier. He'd labeled the salon where Seth had his hair cut "bougie." But…by the time the stylist had finished, Hudson was checking himself out in every passing mirror, all grins.

"That wasn't so bad, was it?" Seth had asked on their way home.

"Getting out of the house for a while didn't suck."

Not exactly a five-star review, but they'd checked everything off their to-do list.

As the memories melted away, Seth glanced between the airplane seats at Beck and Heavenly behind him. The surgeon's hand covered hers on the armrest, their heads bent close in quiet conversation. She smiled softly at something Beck said.

Watching them, Seth's heart swelled.

Some part of him wanted to fuck this whole charade. He wasn't a little boy, and he'd chosen the people he intended to spend his life with. His family needed to accept that.

But he couldn't rob his mom of her well-deserved wedded bliss.

But after the wedding… Seth wasn't sure exactly when or how, but he wasn't going home without telling her the truth.

Behind him, Beck laughed. Seth glanced back at them again, his gaze lingering on the tender intimacy.

He'd never had any doubts that Heavenly would be an amazing mom. But in the past ten days, Beck had proven he'd be a firm yet fair father. That should have allayed some of his fears of fatherhood. But whenever he pictured the three of them with an infant? He couldn't fucking breathe.

How could he be afraid of getting Heavenly pregnant when the idea turned him on so much?

Seth didn't have an answer. Even more baffling, despite being conflicted, he'd enthusiastically joined Beck in taking Heavenly unprotected every night since her period had ended. And he loved every minute of it.

Would he regret that if she missed her next period?

Suddenly, the speakers in the cabin crackled. "Ladies and gentlemen, we're beginning our descent into LaGuardia Airport. Please return your seats to their upright position and…"

Beside Seth, Hudson stirred, blinking groggily as he straightened in his seat. "We there yet?"

"In about fifteen minutes. Good nap?"

"Yeah. I was fucking tired."

Seth felt that down to his bones, but they still had an eventful evening ahead of them. Hell, an eventful weekend.

Besides showing off Heavenly to his family and announcing their engagement while also introducing Hudson and Beck to everyone, he'd be meeting Laura and her new husband to finalize Hudson's custody arrangement.

He was definitely going to need extra coffee. And his wits.

"You know you'll have to watch your mouth in front of Grandma Grace," he told his son.

Hudson gave a typical teenage roll of his eyes. "I figured." Then he peered out the window at the sprawling cityscape below. "Holy shit, this place is massive."

Seth followed his gaze, feeling mixed emotions tighten his chest. He loved the city, but returning always brought back a mixed bag of memories. "You've never been to New York before?"

"No. Mom always said it was too expensive and too dangerous."

"Only if you don't know where to go and how to act. We'll visit a lot, and I'll show you."

A surprising hint of a smile played at Hudson's lips. "Cool."

Finally, the plane touched down with a gentle bump. Seth's anxiety ratcheted up. He just had to keep everyone happy and his secrets intact until after the wedding.

As they taxied to the gate, Seth turned in his seat to catch Beck's eye. "You two good back there?"

"Great," Beck replied, but Seth caught the tension in his posture. Heavenly looked nervous, worrying her bottom lip between her teeth.

"Hey," Seth said softly. "Stop worrying. Everyone will love you."

"I hope so," she whispered. "I just… I want to make a good impression."

"Be yourself and you will."

When the plane rolled to a stop, Hudson gathered his backpack. "So what can I expect? Will your family give me the third degree?"

"First of all, they're *your* family, too. Grandma Grace will want to know everything about you. Fair warning: besides being very Catholic and traditional, she's not exactly subtle."

"Got it."

"She means well. And your uncles Jack and Connor… Well, don't take advice from them—on anything."

"Why not?"

"Because they're twenty-two, impulsive, and they'll try to drag you into shit you'll get grounded for. You've been warned. Make good choices."

They made their way off the plane and through the jetway, Hudson sticking close to Seth's side as they navigated the crowded airport. The kid looked wide-eyed, taking in everything—the controlled chaos of travelers, the cacophony of announcements, the sheer scale of it all.

"Baggage claim is this way." Seth guided the others.

As they walked, he found himself falling into step beside Beck while Heavenly and Hudson chatted about a funny T-shirt in a passing sundry shop. This was probably the last chance they'd have to talk freely until they were all home.

"You good?" Seth asked quietly.

Beck's expression was carefully neutral. "I'll do my best not to screw this up for you."

"I know, and I'm sorry to put you through this shit. It's temporary. I promise."

"Heavenly and I will hold you to that." Beck's voice was low, meant only for Seth's ears. "I'm not a good liar, and I'm nervous as hell about pretending she means nothing to me."

"Four days," Seth vowed.

"Four days," Beck seconded. "I don't know if I can keep up the farce for longer than that."

"I won't ask you to. After the wedding, you'll never have to pretend again." Seth looked forward to that day.

They reached baggage claim and found their carousel, joining the crowd of waiting passengers. Hudson stood next to the conveyor belt, absently watching the luggage go by.

Their bags finally appeared. Together, they made their way toward ground transportation, a surprisingly cool breeze whipping in the air. A few minutes later, they were settled in a black SUV, Hudson claiming the passenger's seat so he could gawk at the city.

"First time in New York?" their driver asked, catching Hudson's wide-eyed expression.

"Yeah," the kid replied. "It's something…"

The driver, a middle-aged man, laughed. "We're barely out of the parking lot. You ain't seen nothing yet, kid."

Since the driver already had Grace's address in Westchester County, Seth settled back to watch the familiar landmarks—and the traffic—slide by.

Sandwiched between him and Beck, Heavenly took in the sights with wide eyes, clearly fascinated by her first glimpse of New York. On her other side, Beck held her hand, alternately squeezing and thumbing her knuckles while Hudson kept up a steady stream of questions about everything he saw.

"It's so bright and noisy here. How did you ever sleep when you were a kid?" Hudson asked.

"I didn't grow up in the city. We lived in the suburbs. It's quieter there."

"But you grew up in New York?"

"Born and raised." Seth watched a group of kids about Hudson's age navigate the sidewalk with casual confidence. "Never really thought about leaving until I met Heavenly."

"Do you miss living here?"

"I miss my family. But California is home now."

Hudson nodded thoughtfully, then went back to staring out the window. Seth wondered if or when his son would consider LA his home.

As they left the city behind and headed north, Seth felt his anxiety shifting into a different gear. Soon they'd be pulling into his mother's driveway—and everything would change.

"Almost there," he said, as much to himself as to the others.

Hudson straightened in his seat, suddenly looking younger and more uncertain. "What if they don't like me?"

"Impossible. They'll love you," Seth said firmly. "You're a Cooper. That's all that matters to them."

"But what if—"

"Hudson, I know this is scary. But they're going to be so excited to meet you that you'll probably get sick of the attention."

That earned him a small smile. "Promise?"

"Promise."

As they turned into the quiet neighborhood where Seth had grown up, he dragged in a deep breath. The charade had to start now. The three of them had a plan. Seth would control the narrative and handle all family interactions, managing what information got shared and when.

"Heavenly?" He bobbed his chin in the direction of her engagement ring.

Her face fell. Beck's expression tightened. But she slipped the diamond off her finger and slowly handed it to Seth. He almost hated himself as he pocketed the ring and met her big blue eyes. "I'm sorry."

She shook her head. "It's fine. I knew this was coming."

"You'll have it back soon."

But they both knew that when she slipped it back on, his whole family would think she was merely engaged to him.

That reality brought down the mood in the car, except for Hudson who was too busy watching the suburbs fly past the windows.

Finally, the SUV slowed and turned into the familiar driveway of Seth's childhood home—a white colonial with black shutters. It looked exactly like it had when he'd left here a few weeks back. The carefully maintained flower beds now sported mums instead of the colorful petunias. But the place had the same sense of warmth and permanence that had shaped his understanding of family and home.

"This is it," Seth said, his voice coming out rougher than he'd intended.

The driver began unloading their bags from the back. Seth jumped out and caught movement behind the front windows—his family no doubt watching their arrival with the same mixture of excitement and anxiety he was feeling.

Hudson climbed out next, looking up at the house with curious eyes. Heavenly followed, smoothing her clothes and hair nervously. Beck emerged last, his expression settling into the carefully neutral mask he'd wear for the next four days.

Seth shouldered his bag, looking up at the house where he'd learned what it meant to be part of a family. Where he'd been taught that love was worth fighting for, even when it scared you.

Especially when it scared you.

"Ready?" he asked, looking at the three people who had become his world.

Heavenly straightened her shoulders. Beck nodded grimly.

Hudson took a deep breath and stepped closer to Seth's side. "Ready."

Seth started up the front walk, his heart hammering against his ribs. Before they even reached the front door, it flung open.

Cue the circus…

Seth barely had time to shoulder his duffel before the front door burst open.

"Seth!" His mom rushed out the front door, her face lit with pure joy. She threw her arms around him, squeezing tight enough to crack ribs before pulling back to study him. "Oh, honey, I'm so glad you're all here."

His mother's gaze darted between Heavenly and Hudson, her expression shifting from delighted to stunned. As she zeroed in on Hudson with wide eyes, she pressed a hand to her heart.

"Oh, my goodness." Her voice was barely a whisper. "You look exactly like Seth when he was your age."

Hudson shifted like he wasn't sure what to make of his new grandmother's attention, but she was already moving, pulling the teenager into a fierce hug, her voice cracking with emotion. "Welcome to the family, sweetheart. I'm so happy to meet you."

Seth looked on, his throat tightening. His mom held Hudson as if he'd always belonged. Slowly, his son embraced her in return.

When they broke apart, she smiled brightly, then turned to Heavenly with open arms. "And you must be Heavenly. You're even more beautiful than Seth's photo."

His girl returned the hug with a careful smile, and Seth understood. Not only was his mom a stranger, but Heavenly hadn't had a maternal figure in her life in damn near a decade. And if there was one thing his mom exuded, it was maternal energy.

"It's wonderful to meet you, Mrs. Cooper," Heavenly said. "Thank you for having us."

"Call me Grace, please. Besides, I'll be Mrs. Mahoney in a few days." His mother beamed, then turned to Beck with a welcoming expression and pulled him into a hug with a laugh. "I'm a hugger. And you must be Dr. Beckman. Any friend of Seth's is welcome here. I'm glad you could join us."

Surprise flickered across Beck's face. He hadn't expected warmth, much less immediate acceptance. Because he'd grown up with a family who rejected outsiders? Or because he was well aware that if Grace Cooper knew the truth, she wouldn't be quite so welcoming?

Before Seth confessed all, he hoped Beck saw that the Coopers had big hearts, especially his mom. Because if they were all going to be family someday, Beck had to like them, too. If not…he could see some really awkward Thanksgiving dinners in their future.

"Mom, let them breathe," Matt called from the doorway, where the rest of the clan had gathered, jostling each other and grinning. "You're going to suffocate them before they even get inside."

"Let them in already." Danny laughed behind Matt. "Maggie wants to meet everyone."

"And you don't?" his wife called from the doorway.

Shaking her head, his mom gestured toward the porch. "Let's go inside. Don't let Danny fool you. The whole clan has been dying to meet you."

Seth sucked in a bracing breath and took Heavenly's hand. Beck and Hudson fell in behind them as his mom led them inside.

He prayed this ruse went off without a hitch…or they were fucked.

They pressed in through the gauntlet of Coopers hovering around the doorway—hugs, kisses on the cheeks, backslaps, and good-natured ribbing before he'd even stepped in the foyer.

Inside, the house smelled like his childhood—his mom's signature vanilla candles mixed with whatever she was cooking. He led Heavenly from the entryway into the large family room, Beck and Hudson trailing.

Within moments, they were surrounded by the controlled chaos of the Cooper family. Heavenly was already holding Anna and nodding at Maggie before they'd even been introduced. Everyone else stared at Hudson, whispering about the strength of the Cooper genes. Since he and his brothers all looked a lot alike? Yeah.

His son sent him a WTF side-eye, like he was completely overwhelmed. Same with Beck, who looked on with an expression that asked *is this normal?*

Seth tried not to laugh as Matt and Danny returned moments later with their luggage, setting the bags by the door.

He began introductions next. "Everyone, meet Heavenly, Hudson, and Beck." He gestured first to his mother's fiancé. "This is Carl."

The strapping fifty-something man with the well-trimmed beard stepped forward with a firm handshake and a welcoming smile. "Nice to meet you all."

"Congratulations on your upcoming wedding," Heavenly murmured.

Carl wrapped his arm around Grace's waist and winked. "I'm the lucky one. Naturally, I had to marry her before she came to her senses."

Everyone laughed as Seth turned to his brothers. "This is Matt. And Danny." After they offered handshakes and hugs with typical Cooper warmth, he slid a hand to his sister-in-law's shoulder. "Danny's wife, Maggie. And Heavenly, you already met their adorable daughter, Anna." He tickled the baby girl's chin, earning a gurgle. "And the twins, but you already know those knuckleheads."

"I do," Beck drawled. "Troublemakers through and through."

"Aww, you're just being nice," Jack returned to more laughter as they shared fist bumps and bro hugs.

"Or honest," Heavenly quipped, pretending to roll her eyes before she hugged them both fondly.

"How's Zach?" Connor asked. "Haven't talked to him in a while."

"He's doing well," Beck replied. "Still adjusting to his new life, but he's finding his footing."

"Good to hear. Tell him we're going to come visit him again for spring break." Connor winked.

"You mean threaten," Jack returned. "We put him through the wringer last summer. But he learned a thing or two."

Beck snorted. "Yeah, about keggers and hookups, whether he was ready or not."

"Valuable life skills, my friend," Jack protested.

Everyone laughed, then Seth turned to Hudson. "This is the terrible twosome, Jack and Connor."

"The college boys, right?" Hudson said with obvious excitement.

"That's us." Connor grinned. "If you want, we'll show you around campus while you're here."

Hudson perked up. "Yeah? That would be cool!"

Seth winced and made a mental note to have a serious conversation with the twins about appropriate influences on his sixteen-year-old son. "And that's everyone... Or is Gene coming?"

His mom shook her head. "He couldn't make it tonight. Work called. You know how it is."

"Oh, I do." Seth turned to Beck and Heavenly. "I've told you about Gene, my dad's former partner. Friend of the family."

Beck nodded. "I remember."

Heavenly's eyes softened. She knew Gene had saved his life at sixteen. "I'm looking forward to meeting him."

"You will." Seth turned to see Maggie shaking hands with Hudson, remarking on how tall he was for his age.

When Anna started fussing, his sister-in-law plucked the girl from Heavenly's arms. "I'll take her. She's hungry. Be right back."

"She's adorable," Heavenly called to Maggie as she headed for the kitchen.

She grinned over her shoulder. "Thanks. Danny and I think so, too."

With the introductions concluded, the family room buzzed with energy as everyone settled in their seats, voices overlapping in the familiar symphony of Cooper family dynamics. His mom exclaimed at least twice more how much Hudson resembled Seth.

Hudson handled all the attention with surprising poise. His mom had claimed the spot on the couch beside the boy, frequently ruffling his hair. On Hudson's other side, Heavenly fielded questions with her natural sweetness, and Seth could see his mother was already impressed.

Beck sat across the room, deep in conversation with Danny and Carl, playing his role of platonic friend to perfection.

Relief wedged between Seth's ribs as he watched Beck fit in. His easy confidence, sharp intelligence, and genuine warmth would win over everyone in time.

But time was the one thing they didn't have much of. He had four days to integrate the people he loved most into his family…or he'd risk splitting up the Cooper clan forever.

Beside him, Matt whistled. "Damn, you lucky bastard. Heavenly's not just gorgeous, she's sweet as hell. Are you sure she doesn't have a sister? A cousin? A bestie?"

"Sorry, she's an only child. No cousins that I know of. And her bestie is taken." He slanted his brother a glance. "I've never known you to be hard up. You slipping?"

"Bite my ass. I'm *busy*. In case you haven't read the reports I've sent you, the PI business out here is hopping."

"Oh, I know. And I've cashed the checks. You're killing it."

"Damn straight."

They high-fived.

As Matt drifted toward Beck and Danny, Seth sidled close to Heavenly and addressed Hudson. "You doing okay?"

The kid nodded, clearly doing his best to keep up. "Yeah. Just…not used to this much family. Especially one this loud."

"It was a whole lot louder when we were kids," Seth assured him. "But yeah, it's a lot. You'll get used to it."

"I like Grandma Grace," Hudson said quietly. "She's nice. Kind of reminds me of my grammy."

"Good. This family will always be here for you, son. They already love you."

Hudson nodded, still taking it all in. And he probably would be for days.

When his mom excused herself to the kitchen to finish dinner, Heavenly jumped up to help her.

"Oh, sweetheart, that's kind of you, but I'm almost done," his mom insisted. "You had such an early flight. Relax."

As his mother bustled away, Seth bent to whisper in Heavenly's ear. "Congratulations. You've already won her over."

Worry creased Heavenly's brow as her voice dropped to a whisper. "For the moment. But what happens…later?"

When Seth spilled the truth? Yeah, he was wondering that, too. He knew he was playing a dangerous-as-fuck game that might leave all the Coopers stunned and divided.

"One day at a time, angel." Seth bent and kissed her cheek. "The future will be what it's going to be. We just have to let it unfold."

She nodded…but she clearly wasn't any more comfortable with the uncertainty than he was.

After a few minutes of chatter, his mom called everyone to dinner. Seth helped Heavenly to her feet, his hand lingering at the small of her back as they made their way to the dining room. Beck and Hudson fell in beside them as they settled around the long wooden table set for twelve, candles flickering between food that smelled like heaven.

Seth helped Heavenly into her chair, hyperaware that his family watched every gesture. Beck slid in beside her, maintaining a proper distance and a platonic smile.

So far, so good. Everyone seemed to be buying the cover.

That didn't make him any less nervous.

As everyone filled their plates, his mom sent Beck an apologetic smile. "I'm sorry we haven't had a chance to talk yet, Dr. Beckman."

"Please, just Beck. And no apology necessary."

"So…are you married?"

Seth tensed. Jesus, his mom wasn't even being subtle, and if she invited Celeste Hagaman over for dessert in some attempt to play matchmaker, he was going to lose his shit.

Thankfully, Beck handled the question smoothly. "Divorced, though my ex-wife Gloria is still a good friend. I'm happy for her and her new husband."

Seth caught Hudson's barely suppressed snort of laughter and sent the kid a warning glare. Yeah, his mom didn't need to know that Gloria was Vegas's most notorious madame. *Talk about a conversation killer…*

"Oh, I'm sorry it didn't work out. But remaining friends… That's very mature of you both," his mom said. "What about the rest of your family?"

Beck glanced at Seth, who gave a subtle nod. They'd discussed this; Beck would stick as close to the truth as possible.

"I was raised in a religious sect called Messiah City. You may have heard about it on the news this past spring," Beck said. "I escaped when I was about Hudson's age."

"Oh, my goodness. I *have* heard about it. You were raised…there?"

The table fell silent, all conversation stopping as Beck nodded. "Unfortunately. But I was lucky to get out young. Some of the others, particularly the girls… What you heard on the news is merely a fraction of the horrible truth. And when the FBI finally moved against them at Big Bear—"

"That's why you were there?" his mom asked with a gasp. "When you called to tell me you were all right?"

"Yeah, we were all there, even Heavenly." Seth didn't dare tell his mom they'd nearly died. She wouldn't take it well, even now. "It was…a terrible day."

"My youngest brother Zach helped the FBI take down the compound. Other than him, I don't have any other family," Beck finished quietly.

The silence stretched for a moment before Grace's expression softened with compassion. "Well, as far as I'm concerned, you're an honorary Cooper now."

The rest of the family echoed the sentiment.

Seth exhaled in relief. That explanation could have been all kinds of messy, but Beck had handled it deftly, downplaying the violent massacre. What his mother had heard? That Beck was basically an orphan who needed mommying.

Repressing a smile, he sent Beck a glance that said *well done.*

Beck raised a brow. *I've got a trick or two up my sleeve.*

"Well, Mom," Matt said with a grin, "looks like you finally got your wish. You always wanted one of your sons to be a doctor."

The table erupted in laughter, and Grace swatted at Matt playfully, then turned back to Beck. "Do you live close to Seth?"

Beck tensed, then deferred to him with a look.

Seth cleared his throat. "Actually, Heavenly and I moved in with Beck a few months back. LA is really expensive, and Beck has a huge house… Since she's still in nursing school, and I'd just started the business out West, it made sense."

He hoped the explanation didn't sound as clumsy as it felt. The twins' knowing smirks made him want to slap them upside the head. Thankfully, no one else seemed to notice.

"Oh." His mother frowned, her maternal concern evident. "Is Cooper Investigations West all right?"

"Great, actually," Seth assured her. "But it was still new when we first moved in with Beck. Besides, he has a fabulous pool. When he asked if we wanted to move in, there was no reason not to say yes."

"Beck's house is sick. Nice neighborhood. And it has everything, especially super sturdy chaise lounges in the backyard," Jack told their mom with deliberate innocence.

Seth shot him a warning glare. The little shit's eyes just danced with mischief.

Heavenly smoothed over the awkward exchange, bless her. "Beck's house is centrally located, so it's a short commute to the hospital where Beck works and I volunteer. And Seth's office isn't far at all."

Grace still looked a bit confused but smiled politely. "That sounds lovely."

"It's great," Seth assured, then changed the subject before their facade got derailed.

After dinner, Mom brought out dessert—her famous apple pie.

Unfortunately, that signaled the moment Seth had been dreading all evening.

Dragging in a deep breath, he stood, taking Heavenly's hand and bringing her to her feet. The room fell silent, all eyes turning to them with expectant faces.

Except Beck's. He stared down at his untouched dessert, white-knuckling a cup of coffee, jaw clenched.

Guilt threatened to crush Seth. This would slice Beck in two. Seth knew that. Heavenly, too.

Even though Beck had agreed to this charade, even though it was temporary, Seth hated it on every level.

Beck lifted his gaze to Seth and gave him an almost imperceptible nod.

Get it over with.

Fuck. He should have rehearsed what he was going to say.

"I have an announcement to make." Seth swallowed hard, then forced a smile as he reached into his pocket. He pulled out the engagement ring and slipped it on Heavenly's finger, letting the diamond catch the light. "I asked Heavenly to marry me…and she said yes. We're engaged."

After a split second of silence, his mother gasped. The rest of the room stood, exploding in a chorus of applause and congratulations in a typically loud Cooper family celebration.

Seth turned to Heavenly. Her smile looked as fake as his felt, but he kissed her, squeezing her shoulder in a silent promise. He'd make this up to both of them.

The tear sliding down Heavenly's cheek threatened to gut Seth. He wiped it away as she risked a glance at Beck, who still sat in his chair, looking even more frozen.

Oblivious to the undercurrent, his mom looked beside herself with excitement. "I'm so happy for you two! Oh, my goodness. You said you were thinking about proposing, but…when did this happen?"

"A few weeks ago." Seth wrapped an arm around Heavenly's waist and let her hide her face in his chest.

He could feel her pain. Feel Beck's. Guilt ripped through him. Maintaining this fucking facade was hell. The next four days were going to be *long*.

When could they cut this evening short and head to their hotel in the city?

"Have you chosen a wedding date?" his mom pressed.

"Not yet," Heavenly said softly. "Everything's up in the air with my school schedule, but I'll graduate next May."

"You're smart to wait. School is important. Have you decided if you're getting married in LA or here in New York?"

"Probably LA." Seth saved her from answering. "I know you'd love us to do it here, but we got together out West. And hey, it's a good excuse to get you all out to Cali."

Mom turned to Heavenly with bright eyes. "Have you picked out a dress yet?"

"I haven't even started looking. I haven't done any planning at all," Heavenly admitted. "It's a little overwhelming."

"Oh, I'd love to help you!" his mom offered eagerly. "I mean, if that wouldn't be stepping on your toes."

"I'll help, too," Maggie added, full of smiles, bouncing a gurgling Anna on her lap.

Heavenly looked teary. Everyone probably assumed his fiancée was overjoyed. But she felt tense against him, and he knew she hated every one of the lies coming out of their mouths.

"That's lovely," she murmured noncommittally. "Thank you."

Plastic smile in place, Seth navigated the barrage of wedding talk, but his attention drifted back to Beck. He'd gone completely silent, mechanically sipping his coffee while ignoring his dessert.

The fucking guilt was eating Seth alive. What had seemed like a simple plan—a few white lies to get through the weekend—felt destructive, like he was slowly poisoning the people he planned to love, honor, and protect.

While the adults discussed wedding plans, the twins drew Hudson into a conversation about football and school. They were bonding too well. That made Seth nervous as fuck.

Finally, the torment of dessert was over. Everyone pitched in to clean up before meandering back to the family room. Maggie settled with baby Anna, feeding her a bottle before rocking her to sleep.

Seth watched Heavenly stare at the baby with a yearning that made his chest buckle. She hadn't been half so animated talking about their wedding… Had his mom noticed?

With a smile, Maggie placed the sleepy girl in Heavenly's arms. His mom caught the glow on her face and sent him a look with one directive: *Get busy making me more grandbabies.*

Seth tried to smile, but Heavenly's expression both blinded and crushed him. There was no question that she ached to be a mother. It wasn't merely a want; it was necessary for her soul.

Beck stared at her and the baby with such raw devotion… Jesus, if anyone else saw that expression…game over.

Worse, Seth felt like he was running in place, still scared shitless, no matter how hard he'd tried to embrace the future.

Finally, he cleared his throat sharply. Beck snapped his head around, quickly looking away, jaw clenching.

Seth's chest burned. Fuck, they'd only been with his family for a handful of hours, and already this subterfuge was threatening to tear them up. How would they keep their feelings under wraps until Sunday afternoon?

Finally, Danny and Maggie left with the baby, and the twins headed out to a party. Matt wasn't far behind, kissing his mom's cheek as she hid her yawn behind her hand. Then he was out the door.

Seth was grateful the evening was winding down.

He wrapped his mom in a hug, hoping she'd forgive him…eventually. "You look tired, Mom. Go to bed."

"I was so excited about your arrival today that I barely slept last night."

He smiled. "We didn't sleep much, either. Early flight and all."

"Of course. I just need to finish readying your rooms upstairs."

Seth tried not to grimace. "Since it's Heavenly's first time in the city, we're going to spend a few nights in a hotel, make it a little romantic getaway while I show her some sights before we get too busy with wedding festivities. I booked us a room where Beck's staying. That way, he won't be alone between his speech and other medical conference duties."

Grace's expression deflated slightly. "Oh. I was hoping you'd stay here so we could spend more time together."

"You're going to be busy with wedding stuff. But come Friday, we will."

"Friday? Isn't Heavenly flying home with Hudson and Beck on Sunday?"

"Yeah. But you'll have me until Tuesday. Like I said when I made the reservations, I need to finish getting the house ready to put on the market. And it gives me more time to spend with you. That still okay?"

"Of course!" his mom assured. Then she hesitated. "Could Hudson stay here? I'd love some one-on-one time with my grandson." She turned to him. "You could sleep in your dad's old room."

"Can I? I'll totally dig up his embarrassing high school secrets." He grinned.

Seth cringed theatrically. "Don't try to blackmail me later, kid."

"Can't promise that," Hudson shot back.

When his mom laughed, Seth rounded up Beck and Heavenly. After saying their goodnights to Carl and making sure Hudson had everything he needed, they wandered toward the door.

"Thank you for a lovely dinner," Heavenly murmured, hugging his mom.

"Everything was delicious," Beck added politely. "I appreciate the hospitality."

"You're both welcome. I'm so happy you could come. How about we all meet for brunch tomorrow morning?" His mother suggested a family favorite place not far from the house.

Seth didn't see a way around it. Besides, he wanted to share some of his favorite childhood haunts with Beck and Heavenly. "Sounds good. Ten?"

"Perfect." His mother clapped.

Beck started to protest. "You all go ahead. I should register for my conference. I speak at two."

Maybe their charade would be safer if he spent less time with Heavenly around his family, but Seth was determined that Beck be accepted as part of their unit, not some peripheral friend. "Come with us, man. We'll make sure you get there in plenty of time."

A look passed between them. Seth knew he was asking a lot.

Finally, Beck sighed. "All right."

When their Uber arrived, Seth gathered their bags and led Beck and Heavenly out the door. As they climbed into the car and pulled away, Seth caught one last glimpse of the house—warm light spilling from the windows, his mom still waving from the porch.

He slammed back against the Uber's leather seat with a curse. If tonight was any indication, the next four days were going to be far more difficult than he'd imagined.

Chapter Eighteen

Relieved that his performance was over—at least for now—Beck scrubbed a hand over his face with a frustrated sigh.

Pretending Heavenly was merely a friend had been way fucking harder than he'd anticipated. He'd known Seth announcing his engagement to her would sting. But he hadn't expected it to fucking eviscerate him.

Hours later, a low-key anger was still grinding his gut.

He didn't want to blame Seth. But this fucked-up situation wasn't Heavenly's fault. Or really Grace's. But he feared it would get worse before it got better. And that pissed him off even more.

Seth stared straight ahead, silent and unblinking, as if he carried the weight of the world on his shoulders.

What's your goddamn problem? At least you get to touch our girl.

As if she sensed his tension, Heavenly cleared her throat. "Your family is amazing, Seth. Really warm and welcoming."

"Yeah. Your mom is way warmer than the she-devil who gave birth to me. Then again, Esther set the bar really low," Beck quipped.

Seth flinched. "I'm sorry. Mom means well. She basically adopted you. It's a good sign."

Yeah, that had shocked Beck.

Before this trip, he'd been prepared to dislike Grace Cooper. She was religious. She talked about high-handed morals while closing herself off from people who didn't believe what she did. But now that he'd met her…he couldn't hate her. Grace wasn't trying to be narrow; she just didn't know another way.

"It is. And despite their mischief, even the twins were sweet." Heavenly was trying to find any silver lining.

Now that he could, Beck dropped a hand to her thigh. "They mostly behaved."

"For once," Seth said dryly. "Hudson will be safe with Mom, but we need to keep an eye on him when Jack and Connor are around."

"Likely so, but they made Hudson feel welcomed. Except for football, I've never seen him light up the way he did around your family."

"Yeah." Seth sighed heavily. "Which makes the bullshit we're pulling on them even worse."

Heavenly took Seth's hand. "What choice do we have?"

"To make sure Mom gets married in peace? None. But that doesn't make it right." Pain etched his face as he glanced between the two of them. "I'm so fucking sorry. I never should have asked you to lie."

Emotion clogged Beck's throat. For months, he'd assumed Seth was too much of a pussy to come clean with Grace about their unorthodox relationship. But after meeting her and the rest of the Cooper clan—experiencing the love and warmth they shared—Beck understood Seth's dilemma.

"You're in a really hard spot. But I have to be honest... Announcing our engagement while Beck sat there pretending he wasn't a part of us..." Heavenly's voice cracked. "I hated every second of it."

"Me, too. I felt like I was ripping out his damn heart."

Beck couldn't lie. "You were."

Tears gathered in Heavenly's eyes. "I'm sorry."

"I'm the one who needs to apologize," Seth groaned. "And I'm so fucking sorry—both of you. I swear, after this wedding I will never again ask either of you to deny your feelings around my family."

"Good, because I don't know how much longer I can pretend to be okay while you two play the happy couple. It fucking gutted me."

Seth clapped Beck's shoulder. "I know. After Sunday, I promise...if Mom doesn't approve of our relationship, that's her problem. It's our fucking lives. My peace, future, and happiness are with you two. That won't change."

"I don't want you at odds with your family..." Heavenly bit her lip. "But I needed to hear that."

Beck nodded, so grateful they were all on the same page. "Thanks."

A long sigh told him that wasn't the end of Seth's issues. "But we have to be more careful. When Heavenly held Anna, I saw the way you looked at her. If anyone else had noticed..."

"Fuck. It's probably a good thing I'll be tied up with this medical conference tomorrow and most of Friday. I'll have my poker face in place by the time the rehearsal dinner rolls around."

"Thanks." Seth nodded. "I know I'm asking a lot and—"

"How about we quit talking about your family and enjoy our first night in New York?" Beck suggested. "We have a gorgeous suite and the whole night alone. I vote we stop talking and start fucking."

Heavenly gasped, sending a wide-eyed glance at their driver, who wasn't looking…but was clearly listening.

Seth's smirk turned filthy. "I'm…up for that. Angel?"

His little girl just blushed.

The Uber stopped in front of the hotel. The French château architecture rose majestically into the clear night sky, commanding the corner with quiet elegance. When Heavenly gaped, Beck felt a surge of satisfaction. Ornate balconies jutted from tall windows, and the building's classic lines spoke of old-world luxury and refinement. Her expression told him that she loved it on sight.

Heavenly blinked at him. "Your conference is *here?* This is where we're staying?"

Beck nodded, unable to suppress his grin. "For the next two nights."

He was thrilled he could spoil her during her first trip to the city. Unfortunately, the timing couldn't be worse. She should be fertile this weekend…and they had to pretend to be just friends.

"I'll do what I can to make sleeping at Mom's on Friday night bearable," Seth promised as they climbed out of the car.

Beck's stomach tightened at the reminder. Seth and Heavenly would likely share a bed at Grace's house. He'd be relegated to some guest room, probably near Hudson. And the thought of being alone, of knowing Seth and Heavenly were together while she was primed for pregnancy… It would be torture.

He didn't care if she and Seth had sex and she got knocked up. Hell, he'd be overjoyed to start their family. But the idea that he wouldn't even be in the room when their child was conceived was killing him.

"Saturday night will be better," Seth promised, as if reading his thoughts. "After the wedding, Mom and Carl are staying in a honeymoon suite somewhere in the city. So, except for Hudson, we'll have the house to ourselves."

Beck's tension eased. One less night of pretending. One more opportunity to indulge in Heavenly's ripe body.

While the bellboy gathered their bags, Beck led Seth and Heavenly through the hotel's entrance into the lobby. As he approached the front desk to check in, he couldn't miss her sharp intake of breath.

"Oh, my god," she whispered. "It's beautiful."

Beck smiled as she spun in a slow circle, taking in the soaring ceiling with its elaborate moldings, the gleaming marble floors, and the crystal chandeliers that cast warm light over the opulence. Fresh flowers arranged in towering displays perfumed the air, while elegant seating areas invited guests to linger in luxury.

Her delight made him damn glad this suite was part of his compensation for speaking. This weekend was about Grace Cooper's wedding, but Beck was happy he could give Heavenly an experience she'd never forget.

Once he'd checked in and received their keycards, they entered the crowded elevator, punching the button for the twentieth floor. The ride up was silent. Tension hummed between them, increasingly taut as others slowly exited.

Until they were finally alone.

Beck's heart raced. His blood churned as he sent a sidelong glance at Heavenly. On her other side, Seth slanted her a dark, hungry stare that said he intended to swallow her whole.

He stalked in Heavenly's direction until her back pressed against the wall. He tilted her chin up to meet his stare. "I've been dying for you all evening, angel. I need you naked."

Beck closed in, his hand finding the small of her back…and trailing down her pretty pert ass. "Same, little girl. For the next twelve hours, I intend to keep you in bed and stuffed full of cock, coming so hard you forget your own name."

"What he said." Seth covered Heavenly's mouth in a kiss that had her melting between them.

Beck trailed his lips up her throat, gratified when she whimpered sweetly. When Seth finally broke the kiss, Beck claimed her lips next, tasting both her softness and her desperation.

By the time the elevator dinged and the doors parted, they were all breathing hard.

Together, they piled out, both men holding Heavenly's hands, and made their way down the hall. At the end, Beck slid the keycard in the slot and pushed open the door, gesturing for Heavenly to enter first.

She stepped inside and went completely still, her eyes flaring wide as her hand flew to her mouth.

The suite stretched before them in understated elegance—rich fabrics, gleaming surfaces, and well-appointed luxuries. A living area flowed into a dining space, while floor-to-ceiling windows promised spectacular views.

"Wow," Heavenly breathed as she explored every room, exclaiming over the marble bathroom, the walk-in closet, and the fully stocked bar.

When she finally made it to the windows, she frowned. "It's dark. I see some city lights in the distance, but…"

"Central Park is right below us. But in the morning, you'll love this view." Seth sidled up to her, palming her hip. "Trust me."

The bellboy arrived with their luggage. Beck tipped the guy generously for being speedy, then hustled him out the door.

The moment they were alone again, Beck turned to them, brow raised. "Come here so I can strip you naked, little girl."

Heavenly blushed as she sauntered in his direction with a sway of her hips that had a knot of lust stuck in his throat and his cock beyond eager. He looked just past her to Seth, who wore a crooked grin as he followed Heavenly with blazing eyes.

Beck was determined to come inside their fertile girl as many times as possible this weekend. He fucking hoped Seth was prepared to do the same.

Either way, he refused to waste another minute.

Beck prowled toward Heavenly, his gaze locked on her lush curves and golden curls glowing beneath the dim light of the chandelier. When he hugged her to his chest possessively, Seth moved in behind her, cupping her shoulders and inhaling the enticing female scent clinging to her skin.

Hidden away in their private oasis, away from his family and all the other distractions, Seth looked past the suite's plush carpets and silk drapes. He tuned out the hum of New York's traffic filtering through the windows.

All he saw was her.

All he wanted was her.

All he craved was her—spread wide and under him.

The glint in Beck's dark eyes matched the desire burning in Seth's veins.

He dragged in a deep breath and focused on drowning Heavenly in pleasure.

Sandwiched between their hard bodies, Heavenly's breath hitched. Seth spun her to face him. Her blue eyes clung to him, soft with trust. Her sweet submission drove him wild.

He cupped her face, brushing his thumb across her downy cheek while Beck pressed against her back, dragging his lips up her neck and whispering something apparently filthy in her ear that made her close her eyes and shudder.

Seth took advantage, capturing her mouth in a bruising kiss, plunging his tongue in deep and claiming her with a possessive growl.

With a breathy moan, Heavenly dug her fingers into his shoulders and pressed her pebbled nipples against his chest.

He lost himself in the heat of her kiss, tugging at the hem of her shirt while Beck reached around her middle and unbuttoned her pants. Heavenly melted between them while they tore at her clothes and guided her to the bedroom, leaving a trail of cotton and silk whispering across the floor.

"I've been waiting all night to touch you, little girl." Beck nipped her lobe, his voice rough with need. "To sink balls deep inside you."

Seth tore from her lips, breathing hard. "You and me both."

"I'm all yours, Sirs," Heavenly murmured, eyes downcast.

Beck fit a finger under her chin and turned her head in his direction. "You going to be a good girl and let me fuck your pretty pussy, aren't you?"

She nodded wildly, and he swooped down, crushing her lips beneath his and swallowing her soft, needy whimper.

Her total surrender to Beck's indecent demand stoked Seth's need even higher. He skimmed his lips down her throat, savoring her pulse fluttering under his tongue.

"We're going to keep you busy tonight," Seth growled in her ear, his smile wolfish. "*Very* busy."

Then he bent and latched his mouth over her warm breast, lips skating over her skin before he dragged her nipple between his greedy lips and onto his tongue, pulling her in deep. Heavenly tossed her head back and tangled her fingers in his hair with a gasp.

Music to his ears.

Beck watched as Seth worked over her glistening peaks, alternating between them, biting gently and savoring every little gasp. Beck groaned, his hands impatient as he roamed across her skin.

Reluctantly, Seth lifted his head and spun her to face the other man. "Take a taste of our girl."

"I need more than a taste." Feverishly, Beck swooped down and latched on to her other nipple.

Heavenly gasped, one dainty hand digging into Beck's shoulder. With the other, she gripped Seth's arm in silent pleading.

He grinned. If she was looking for mercy tonight, she was about to find out neither of them had any.

Beck devoured her breasts, moving from one to the other, sucking and nipping so thoroughly that she began trembling. Seth watched, easing from them just long enough to rummage through his bag. When he returned, he tossed a tube of lube on the edge of the bed and tore at the button of his fly.

Beck lifted his head, his gaze flicking over the item. A furrow settled between his brows.

Yeah, the good doctor had questions. He'd been relentlessly trying to get Heavenly pregnant for weeks. Hell, they both had, taking turns spilling inside her unprotected pussy over and over. But Seth had a method to his madness—one he'd share with Beck soon.

For now, Seth shot him a look that promised everything was just fine. Jaw clenched, the doctor slowly resumed tormenting Heavenly's nipples, which now looked swollen and temptingly rosy.

With a grin, Seth skated his fingers down Heavenly's warm, silky skin—a tease that made her shiver. "Do you like Beck feasting on your tits? That feel good, angel?"

"Yes…" she hissed, fisting the surgeon's dark hair.

Seth dropped his hand between her legs, dipping his fingers between her swollen folds. She was hot, slick, and absolutely drenched. Her clit was hard as a diamond as he began circling her sensitive nub. In seconds, her breaths grew shallow and her eyes fluttered shut with a moan.

"You're so fucking wet for us, angel," Seth murmured, using his free hand to brush her blonde hair aside and lave his way up her neck, savoring her soft shiver and gasp. "The things we're going to do to you tonight…"

"Please. D-don't torture me like last time," she mewled.

Beck released her nipple and arched a brow. "You didn't like us edging you?"

"No." She clung to Beck's biceps as she ground herself against Seth's hand.

"You sure? You came incredibly hard…" Seth smirked, still stroking her clit in slow, merciless circles. "Maybe you need a reminder."

"No!" she begged. "Please don't…"

"Don't worry, little girl. We're not going to edge you." Beck flashed her an absolutely obscene grin. "At least not tonight."

"We have a different torture planned," Seth murmured in her ear, low and dark.

Her eyes went wide, her voice breathy. "Tell me…"

Beck raised a stern brow at her. "You making demands?"

She dropped her gaze submissively. "No. Please. I just… Will you tell me?"

"We're going to spend all night dragging orgasms from your sweet little cunt—one after the other—until you think you can't come anymore," Beck growled, releasing her long enough to yank the elegant duvet off the bed. "Then we'll make you come again."

He lifted a gasping Heavenly off her feet and spread her across the mattress before he started shucking his clothes. Seth followed suit, unbuttoning his shirt as Heavenly rolled to her stomach and stared with hot eyes.

Seth raised a brow while he released his zipper with a hiss. "Enjoying the show, angel?"

When his cock burst free, he kicked off everything below his waist and fisted his throbbing length.

Heavenly gawked and blushed. "I am."

"If you're ready to do something besides stare, little girl…" Beck fisted his hard cock and approached the side of the bed, his voice rough and commanding. "Open your mouth, stick out that pretty tongue, and suck me."

"Yes, Sir." She clambered to her knees, blue eyes sparkling, and parted her lips.

At the sight, desire crashed through Seth's system. He moaned, low and needy, as he watched Beck cup her nape and align his crest to her swollen lips.

"That's it." Beck's breath hitched as he entered her mouth. "Suck me deep."

Lashes fluttering to her cheeks, Heavenly complied, opening wider as the surgeon loomed over her and drove nearly every inch into her silky, wet heat.

Beck ignored her stuttering breaths, gripped her hair in his fist, and shuttled past her lips in a sharp, relentless rhythm. Seth pumped his length in his palm, his stare glued to the sight of Beck fucking their girl's mouth. Jesus, he could practically feel the sensual slide of her tongue gliding up his own shaft.

"Wrap your fingers around him," Seth murmured hotly in her ear. "Stroke him while you suck him."

She did, wrapping her slender hand around Beck's cock. The surgeon sucked in a hiss, tossed back his head, and began rocking his hips.

"Harder," Seth insisted. "Grip him harder and squeeze. Now stroke him at the same time."

She did. Beck's breathing roughened. He hurled an unintelligible curse.

Seth just smiled, not at all surprised Beck couldn't speak. Whenever Heavenly wrapped her mouth around his cock, stringing words together was somewhere between grueling and impossible.

With urgent fingers, Seth tucked her hair behind her ear for a better view. "Yes. Just like that. Now draw him all the way out. Good. Suck on the head. Good girl. Hmm. Suck it hard."

Beck's stare zipped his way, eyes narrowing. "Shit. Stop 'helping.'"

"Why? You're obviously enjoying it." Seth chuckled as he stroked Heavenly's crown. "That's pretty, angel. Use your other hand to rake your fingernails over his balls. Gently. Slowly." When she hesitated, he encouraged, "I promise he'll love it."

Heavenly peered up at the surgeon, eyes watchful as Seth guided her other hand between Beck's legs. "Do it, angel."

Tentatively, she scraped her nails across his sac.

Beck's whole body went taut. "Goddamn it!"

Seth ignored him and heaped more praise on Heavenly. "That's a good girl. Perfect."

"Too perfect. You motherfucker," Beck snarled.

That made Seth smile as he pressed his palm to the back of her head. "Keep sucking. He might be growling, but he doesn't want you to stop. Do you, man?"

"No," Beck bit out as he shuttled his way into her mouth, fisting her hair tighter. "Fuck no."

"See? He'd love it even more if you flicked the tip of your tongue against the underside of his crest."

"Oh, fuck," Beck groaned as Heavenly complied. Then the surgeon snarled at him. "Shut. Up."

"No chance in hell," Seth countered with a smirk before lowering his voice. "Now suck him to the back of your throat and swallow."

Moments later, she did, a kitten-soft whimper reverberating in the air.

"Fuck!" Beck tightened his grip in her hair and took full control, guiding her sinful mouth up and down his shaft with ever-demanding thrusts.

The sight of Heavenly's lips stretching impossibly wider around Beck's glistening cock was a visual torment that clawed at Seth's patience and restraint.

"Yes…" Seth murmured with a low rumble of approval. "That's it."

"Jesus, little girl," Beck bit out roughly. "You're killing me."

Heavenly lifted her lashes and peered up at him. The love and sweet submission shining there called to Seth on a primitive level.

He couldn't resist touching her for another second.

With a groan, he climbed onto the bed behind her and skimmed her warm skin while trailing kisses down her spine. She shivered. He basked in her response as he retraced his way up to pepper kisses along her shoulder and lave his way up her neck.

"You look so fucking beautiful worshipping his cock," he whispered before he nipped her lobe.

"She fucking does," Beck growled as he fucked her mouth all the way to the back of her throat.

Based on the desperate tone of his grunts and the way he clenched his jaw, Seth knew the surgeon's restraint was unraveling. He smiled.

"Fuck!" Beck snarled as he yanked free from Heavenly's lips.

Panting wildly, he slammed his eyes shut and clamped down on the base of his cock, staving off the pending orgasm.

"Not going to finish?" Seth rolled to his feet and rounded the bed to face Heavenly.

"Not in her mouth. She's mid-cycle, man. She's ripe." Beck scowled his way.

Seth nodded, but he'd known Heavenly was likely ovulating.

For now, he cupped her chin and dragged his thumb across her swollen lips, losing himself in her smoky blue eyes. "Ready to suck my cock, angel?"

"Yes, Sir," she whispered as she leaned in, parting her lips.

As she closed her eyes with a moan, he watched raptly. His breath froze as she swiped her pink tongue over his weeping crest. Streaks of lightning splintered up his spine.

She hadn't even sucked him inside her wicked mouth yet, and Seth was already climbing out of his skin. Heavenly and her innate ability to decimate his resolve was nothing new, but he was determined to hang on.

"Open wide," he commanded in a raspy groan.

Heavenly complied, wrapping her plump lips around his dripping crest and pulling him deep. Sparks flashed behind his eyes as he fisted her hair with a growl and launched into a bone-rattling rhythm, plundering and fucking her throat.

"Everything you did to me?" Beck climbed onto the bed next to Heavenly. "Do the same to him, little girl."

"Now who's a prick?" Seth rasped between clenched teeth as she wrapped her slender hand around the base of his dick with firm fingers and started stroking.

"Paybacks are a bitch." Beck smirked. "Let's see how long you last when I make her come and she starts screaming over your cock."

Beck's threat, coupled with Heavenly's swirling tongue, burned Seth's brain and scorched his resolve.

That didn't stop Heavenly. She stroked him harder, sucking him impossibly deep as she whimpered the neediest little sound. He tried to brace, but it was useless. Her moan vibrated up his shaft and rolled through his balls. It threatened his goddamn restraint.

Seth clenched his jaw, his growled curse cut short as Heavenly swallowed, compressing his crest in her hot, velvety vise. His heart lurched. He stopped breathing. His eyes rolled to the back of his head. Jesus… When had she gotten so good at that?

Probably when you told her exactly how to dismantle Beck, dumbass.

Each tormenting stroke up his cock sent desire scalding through him, shoving him closer to the brink of insanity.

Desperately, Seth peeled his stare off her lips bobbing up and down his glistening shaft and watched Beck tweak her nipples.

"Spread your knees," the good doctor demanded in her ear.

With a greedy mewl, she did, never altering the rhythm of her mouth on Seth's cock. He swore he was about to lose his goddamn mind.

Beck bent behind Heavenly, his dark gaze devouring her bare body.

The sight of them—his partners, his future—sent heat blasting through Seth's veins.

When the surgeon lowered his mouth to her waiting pussy, Heavenly jolted with a muffled cry. The sound vibrated down Seth's cock. He hissed, scalding need threatening to burn away his teetering restraint.

Beck lapped at Heavenly with obvious hunger, worshipping their woman. She went wild between them—moaning, whimpering, and grinding against Beck's tongue while she worked feverishly up and down Seth's shaft. The dual sensations of her hot mouth and her desperate mewls pushed Seth even closer to the edge of his control.

He gripped her hair tight in his fingers. "If you keep making those sounds, I'm gonna lose it, angel."

She didn't let up one bit. Instead, she urged him on. With sawing breaths and clenched teeth, he drove deeper and faster into her mouth, keeping time with the demand pounding his system.

As the mounting friction threatened to bend his spine with pleasure, he watched Beck lift his head from her cunt just long enough to grope for the lube and squeeze a dollop onto his finger.

"Ass in the air, little girl," Beck demanded in a low-voiced growl.

She complied, sticking her backside up obediently. He ringed her back opening with his slick finger, then thrust inside. Heavenly squealed and bucked, breathing hard and shuddering as she moaned even louder around Seth's cock.

Sweat dripped. Seth's vision blurred. *Jesus…* "I'm two fucking seconds from losing it."

In response, she quickened her stroke and bathed him with her tongue like a woman possessed.

"Do it," Beck said with a grin before he dove back between her thighs.

Seth watched him—finger pumping, mouth relentless on her clit. Heavenly whimpered desperately around his cock.

Then Beck added a second finger to her ass, stretching her, preparing her. Her whole body shook, her mouth growing even more frantic. Seth struggled to hold on as she began to unravel so beautifully right in front of him.

"Fuck, yes," Beck ground out while working her with ruthless precision. "Come, little girl."

She tensed, breath held, the moment suspended... Seth's heart roared between his ears as he ground his teeth against his violent urge to come.

Heavenly screamed, her wail muffled by her mouthful of his cock. Then she convulsed in ecstasy.

Seth looked on helplessly. The vibrations, the sight of her in pleasure, the knowledge that Beck had pushed her over crashed through him.

"Fuck. Fuck. Fuck!" he roared, unable to hold back as he gritted his teeth, gripped her tighter, and spilled down her throat in a thunderous release that seemed to last half of forever.

When the blindsiding rapture finally subsided, Seth withdrew slowly, panting. Dizzy. Bowled over. His knees threatened to give out. He braced himself with one hand. With the other, he cupped Heavenly's chin and pressed his forehead to hers. Her face was flushed, eyes glazed with a plea for his approval.

Christ, she'd never looked more beautiful.

"That was amazing. I love you, angel," he rasped, his voice raw with emotion.

"I love you," she whispered, then glanced over her shoulder at Beck. "I love you, too."

"Come here." Beck hauled her on top of him. "I'll show you how much I love you."

Heavenly barely had time to blink in question before he grabbed her hips and pushed her down onto his straining cock with a possessive growl. He arched up, shoving even deeper inside her pussy. She gasped out, gripping the sheets in her delicate fists. The sight of Beck's desperate need and her willing surrender fueled Seth all over again. He always wanted pleasure. But he craved permanence and future. Family.

One he hoped they'd be starting tonight.

While Heavenly rocked on top of Beck, the surgeon clutched her hips and fucked her relentlessly. "You watching or fucking?"

"Fucking." Seth fisted his cock and roughly stroked it. The sight of

Beck swiping his thumb across her clit as he jackhammered into her made him hard and eager again.

"Hurry," Beck snapped. "Neither of us are going to last."

Cursing, Seth grabbed the lube and climbed behind her, coating himself thoroughly. Beck seized the moment and pulled free with a grimace, giving Seth the opportunity to press into her ass and tunnel deep. His eyes rolled back at the tight grip and exquisite pleasure.

Quickly, they found their rhythm, Seth withdrawing while Beck thrust deep, then reversing. Heavenly unraveled between them with sensual cries that bounced off the luxurious walls of their suite and rang in his ears. The scent of sex, the slick slide of their bodies, her desperate pleas for release all combined into something beyond mere orgasm. This was communion. Connection. Coming home.

"Please," Heavenly begged, her voice breaking. "I need to come."

"Fuck," Beck panted. "I can't...hold on."

"Same." Seth was shocked to feel his control shattering again.

Raw hunger consumed every cell in his body. The feel of her gripping him was both euphoric and blistering. Demand coiled tighter and tighter. His muscles grew taut as blood thundered in his ears. He fucking trembled with both restraint and need.

But seconds later, his restraint crumbled. Need won out. And the cataclysm of release crashed fast and hard, utterly shattering.

"Come, angel. Now!" he demanded.

With a scream that likely echoed across the entire floor of the hotel, she did. Beck growled a curse and followed, pressing himself deep inside her pussy as he let go. Seth hurtled over, too, as if his previous orgasm had never happened.

Together, they collapsed onto the bed in a tangle of trembling limbs, harsh breaths, and pounding hearts. Seth held Heavenly from behind while Beck pressed himself against her front, both of them still buried inside her, as if unwilling to separate. As if none of them wanted this moment to end.

But it wasn't long before passion stirred again. Moments bled into hours as their bodies entwined again and again in relentless need. Seth reveled as Beck filled her cunt with single-minded determination over and over, his hunger desperate while Seth took her ass, worshipping her with every touch.

By the time dawn crept under the blackout curtains, they were exhausted, sated, and irrevocably bound on what felt like a whole deeper level. That truth was burned into his gut. His psyche. His heart.

With a little whimper, Heavenly finally slipped from bed and crept gingerly to the shower. When the sound of running water hissed through the suite, Beck moved to follow.

Seth did his best to shelve his lazy satisfaction and stepped in front of the surgeon. "Have fun last night?"

Beck's jaw tightened, and Seth saw the question forming. He'd anticipated it. Beck wanted to know why Seth hadn't once taken her pussy.

"Obviously, but—"

"I know what you're thinking," Seth cut in, meeting Beck's stare. "I'm not backing out of having a family. But I've had two sons, and I've got my hands full with Hudson. Plus…I owe you for dealing with my family's bullshit this weekend. The shot at her this month? It's all yours. If she gets pregnant, I'll be a proud daddy, too. Promise."

Beck's throat worked. Emotion flickered across his face—surprise, gratitude, something deeper.

"Seriously?"

Seth nodded. "Yep. Absolutely."

"And Friday night?" Beck asked quietly. "When you'll be alone with her at your mom's house?"

Seth shrugged, a wry smile tugging his lips. "Her mouth, her ass, or just a snuggle—I'm good for any of those. I'm sure my mom would prefer the last option, but whatever makes Heavenly happy."

Beck chuckled, and Seth felt the last of the tension between them ease. This weekend would be a minefield with his family, but the night the three of them had just spent together? Worth every second of torture over the coming days. They'd crossed a line together, made an unspoken promise about their future.

And as Seth clapped Beck's shoulder, they headed to the suite's giant shower to join Heavenly. In that moment, Seth had never been more certain of anything in his life.

Chapter Nineteen

At ten a.m., Seth dragged ass as he ushered an exhausted Heavenly into Batter Up, the diner the Cooper clan had been frequenting for thirty years. Beck slowly brought up the rear. Despite being wrung out, their smiles were all replete with satisfaction. Seth hoped like hell his mother didn't notice.

As Seth ducked inside, he scanned the place. It looked exactly the way it had when he'd been a kid. Same baseball-themed motif, same red vinyl booths, same black-and-white checkered floor. The smells of bacon grease and coffee had permeated the walls decades ago, adding to the cafe's dubious charm. The waitresses called most everyone "hon" and knew the orders of their regular patrons by heart. And everyone who came here loved it.

He had so many memories of this place. Usually, the familiarity and nostalgia made him happy.

Today, anxiety gnawed at him. He had to start softening his mom's attitude or coming clean with her would go over like a turd in a punchbowl.

"This is adorable!" Heavenly exclaimed as she sized up the diner.

"Wait until you try their pancakes. They're legendary," Seth quipped, though he was more focused on what he was going to say than on food.

Across the restaurant, he spotted Mom, Carl, and Hudson already waiting for them at one of the big tables.

"There they are," his mother called, waving them over with a bright smile.

Hudson jumped up, grinning as they approached. "Hey! How was your night in the fancy hotel?"

Seth pulled his son into a hug, surprised by how much he'd missed the kid, how attached he'd grown in a few short weeks. "Good. How was your night with Grandma Grace?"

"Awesome. I slept in your old room and found your high school yearbooks."

"Find anything embarrassing enough to blackmail me with?"

"I'm still deciding," Hudson shot back with a grin that was pure Cooper mischief. "But dude, your hair was seriously questionable. And that wrestling team photo was a lot…"

"Thanks," Seth said dryly.

Beck ruffled Hudson's hair as he passed. "Other than snooping, did you stay out of trouble?"

"Where's the fun in that?" Hudson laughed.

"He was very well-behaved," Mom insisted as she stood. "And he called Laura last night. They had a long chat."

Hudson nodded. "Yeah. It was good."

Seth was glad to hear that. On top of everything else, Laura's concern was something he didn't need now.

Carl stood as they reached the table, giving Beck a friendly pat on the shoulder before shaking Seth's hand. "Morning, you three. Everyone sleep well?"

"Like a rock," Beck replied as Mom hugged Heavenly. "The sheets at that hotel have some serious thread count."

"Everything was super comfortable." Seth kissed his mother's cheek before rounding the table and sliding across the bench to sit strategically beside her.

With all the wedding craziness, he wouldn't have much time to talk one-on-one with her. He could practically feel the time ticking away before he had to walk her down the aisle and fly home again. Bending her ear while he could was critical.

Heavenly slid in after him, her thigh brushing his as she laid her hand over his and spoke to his son. "I'm surprised I could hear the traffic twenty floors up."

Hudson took the chair across from her, beside Beck. "Really?"

She nodded. "It was crazy."

His mom just laughed. "There's a reason people call it the city that never sleeps, dear."

"I had to see it to understand." Heavenly flashed a self-deprecating grin before changing the subject. "How are you feeling with the wedding two days away?"

"Nervous but excited," his mom admitted. "I'm so afraid I've forgotten something important, but Carl just tells me to relax."

"Everything's going to be perfect." Her groom sent her a reassuring smile across the table.

As he, Beck, and Heavenly began comparing life in New York and California with Hudson hanging on their every word, Seth saw his opening. Time to start laying the groundwork.

"You seem happy this morning," Seth said quietly as the waitress brought their coffee and paused to take their order.

After her departure, his mom smiled and stirred more cream into her cup. "I am, though I feel a bit run ragged trying to take care of all the last-minute details." She glanced at Carl, her expression softening. "But I'm marrying a good man. I never thought I'd get another chance at this kind of happiness."

"You deserve it."

"Thank you, honey." She squeezed his hand. "I'm so happy for you and Heavenly. Having you two here—and announcing your engagement—makes everything even better. And Beck seems like a wonderful friend. I'm glad he came, too. He fits right in with the family."

Seth overheard Beck describe the last medical conference he'd attended with his usual sarcasm. They all laughed, and Heavenly poked gentle fun at him. But the tightness at the corners of his eyes told Seth just how much effort it cost him to keep that smile in place.

"I thought he would." Seth leaned in close to his mom and dropped his voice. "Speaking of family, how are things with Jack and Connor lately?"

Her smile faltered slightly, her fingers tightening around her coffee mug. "Better. Not...normal, but better."

"That's progress." And at least she wasn't hostile anymore. Struggling, he'd expected. She even sounded a bit resigned. Maybe that meant she was trying to accept their choices?

"I suppose. I'm still trying to understand why they share women that way. The glimpse I saw… It was so shocking. I still can't wrap my head around it."

Seth's throat went dry. How could he explain the completeness, the rightness of what he shared with Beck and Heavenly when he couldn't admit yet that their relationship even existed?

"Have you talked to them any more?"

"A little. They've been respectful about my boundaries—no bringing women to the house, no flaunting one in public. And I've tried not to be intrusive." She sighed, her voice dropping. "I love them, but I don't know how to accept this part of their lives."

"Are you hoping they'll grow out of it?"

Her silence was answer enough.

"Mom…" Seth chose his next words carefully, as if he was defusing a bomb. "I've talked to them. This isn't a phase. They're not experimenting or rebelling. This is who they are, the way they've chosen to express love."

"But—"

"I know you don't approve, but if you want them in your life, you're going to have to make peace with their choices."

His mom's eyes filled with tears. "You said the same thing last time we talked, and you made good points. I'm not trying to be old-fashioned. I've been praying about it, thinking about it..."

"And?"

"Logically, I know you're right. They're still the same kind, funny, protective boys I raised." She rubbed her forehead. "It's just…their desires go against everything I was taught about relationships, about what's right."

"What if you stopped focusing on their sex life and just considered who they are as people? On the fact they're your sons?"

His mom blinked. "I'm sure I should, but…how?"

"Easy. When you talk to them or spend time with them, just be their mother. Their romantic choices aren't the sum of who they are, just like Carl's job doesn't define who he is."

"I know you're right."

But that didn't mean she wasn't struggling.

"Why do you need to understand Jack and Connor's sex life to love them?"

"I don't, but—"

"There's no buts. You need to love them for who they are, not who you want them to be."

She stared into her coffee cup for a long moment. When she looked up, her eyes were bright with unshed tears. "When did you get so wise?"

Seth's chest tightened. If she only knew… "You raised us to think for ourselves, and sometimes those choices are going to be different from what you'd pick."

"You're right. I just…" His mom glanced around the table, making sure the others were still absorbed in their own conversation. "What about marriage? Children? How will that work with their… arrangement?"

"That's for them to figure out, Mom. Right now, you only need to focus on you, your wedding, and being happy. One day at a time."

"You're right again." She squeezed his hand. "Thank you for listening. I know it's not easy, having your mother struggle with your brothers' choices."

Seth squeezed back, hoping desperately that she'd remember this conversation when the time for his own admission came. "I love you, Mom. Just like I love Jack and Connor. I want this family to stay together. Whatever it takes. How about we talk again after the wedding?"

"Could we?" She actually looked hopeful.

"Let's plan on it." He kissed her cheek, hoping the breakthrough they all needed was just around the corner.

The waitress appeared with their food, breaking the moment. As plates of eggs, bacon, and toast were distributed around the table, the conversation shifted to lighter topics—picking up tuxedos, last-minute details for the rehearsal dinner, seating arrangements that would keep certain relatives from killing each other.

Seth half listened to the chatter about flowers and photographers, his mind churning.

"So what's the plan for today?" Carl asked as they finished eating.

"Beck needs to get back to the city for his conference presentation," Seth supplied. "Heavenly will go with him to take some photos of him in action for hospital administrators and social media. While they're busy, I'm meeting Tony for a beer so we can catch up. Then we're hoping to take in a show tonight. But we'll see you for breakfast tomorrow?"

"Perfect." His mom smiled.

As they gathered their things and headed for the door, Seth's phone buzzed with a text from their Uber driver. "Our ride's here."

His mom hugged each of them goodbye, smiling and holding on to Heavenly for a few extra moments. "I'm so glad you're here, sweetheart. This weekend means the world to me."

Seth caught his mother's eye over Heavenly's head, seeing the love and acceptance there. The irony cut deep. Mom had embraced Heavenly completely as Seth's fiancée. If she knew Heavenly belonged to Beck every bit as much, what would she say?

At ten past two, Seth stepped into the hotel's swanky bar, striding across the marble floor. As he searched for Tony Marconi's familiar face, he took in the refined elegance around him that screamed old New York money. Rich crown moldings and pale walls gleamed under soft lighting. Crystal decanters lined mirrored shelves behind an ornate bar. Leather banquettes in deep emerald green provided intimate seating, whispering of discreet conversations and billion-dollar deals.

Since Seth didn't see his former partner yet, he settled into a corner booth with his back to the wall. Here, he could watch the entrance—a must since being back in the city tended to make him edgy, like he had eyes on him.

When a server stopped to welcome him, he ordered a beer and settled back to wait, studying the faces around him.

As soon as his beer arrived, he lifted the bottle to his lips. His cell phone chimed with a message, so he swallowed, tapped the screen, and read the text from the Realtor his mother had recommended. She could meet him at his former house at four-thirty. Good.

For weeks, Seth had pondered listing the place "as is" so he'd never have to step foot inside again. After his panic attack a few weeks ago, he'd been reluctant to return. But if they were going to have a baby, they needed a new house—which meant getting top dollar for this one. He'd get a list of repairs from the agent that would maximize the sale price, grab whatever he couldn't bring himself to throw away, then close that chapter of his life for good.

The plan was logical. That didn't mean it wouldn't be hell.

For now, he compartmentalized that chore and glanced at his watch. Beck and Heavenly would be in the ballroom by now, the surgeon launching his speech while their girl snapped pictures, determined to capture the moment like a proud fiancée.

"Hey. There you are, Cooper."

Seth looked up to find Tony approaching. For a moment, the years fell away. His former partner looked more weathered around the edges—hell, he did, too—but the guy's cocky grin was the same.

"Hey, Marconi." Seth stood and gave him a back-slapping bro hug, then gestured for him to sit. "Glad you could make time today."

"Me, too." Tony sank onto the green leather bench, flagged down the server, and ordered a club soda. "It's good to see you, man, especially since we didn't get much time to talk last month. How's life been?"

"Crazy." Seth took another pull from his beer. "Since I saw you last, I found out I have another son…who's sixteen."

Tony's eyes bulged. "No shit? God, you were a teenager."

He nodded. "When I came home from New York last month, the kid was at my house with my girlfriend—well, fiancée now—waiting for me. Hudson—that's his name—is now living with us. We've been getting to know each other."

"Wait. What? Not only do you have a son, you proposed to your girlfriend? Congratulations, man! Obviously she said yes. What's her name?"

Seth couldn't help but smile as he whipped out his phone to show his pal a picture. "Heavenly. She's a nursing student from Wisconsin.

And she's every bit as sweet as she sounds. Smart as hell, too. Works harder than anyone I know."

He didn't mention Beck. Besides Tony knowing some of the cops his mom still talked to, he was a practicing Catholic. Chances were high gossip could get passed on. Or Tony wouldn't understand.

His former partner raised a brow. "Damn, she's gorgeous. How did you meet a girl from Wisconsin in LA?"

"She moved out there for family." Seth opted for the simple version. "And we met through mutual friends. She's incredible. I never thought I'd find someone like her."

Tony grinned. "You're clearly in love."

"Yep, I'm totally gone," Seth admitted without embarrassment.

"When's the big day?"

Seth shrugged, hedging. "We're still deciding. There's no rush, and she's in her last year of nursing school."

When the server set down Tony's club soda, he thanked her before sending Seth a wry grin. "Your life sounds anything but boring."

"You got that right. What about you and Megan? You still planning to make an honest woman of her come spring?"

Tony's face lit up. "Yep. We found a venue, and she's got a dress on order. We're working on the rest. We found a house in Queens—nothing fancy, but it's got a yard and good schools for when we have kids."

"That's great, man. I'm really happy for you."

His former partner raised his glass. "Here's to finding the right women and some happiness before life kills us."

They clinked glasses, and Seth couldn't help but wonder... "You ever think about leaving the force?"

"Every damn day." Tony's smile faded. "Especially lately."

Seth leaned in and dropped his voice. "Last time I saw you, you mentioned that things at the precinct had gone south."

Tony scanned the nearly empty bar, his shoulders tense as he checked for unfriendly ears. "Like I said after the nine-eleven memorial ceremony, things have changed, gotten more political. It feels... corrupt."

"Fucking shame," Seth murmured.

"And getting worse every day."

"We've always known there are a few dirty cops at the station who—"

"This is bigger. Darker."

His dad would be rolling over in his grave, Seth thought sourly. "What do you mean?"

Tony glanced around the bar again, this time even more cautiously. "Good cases are getting tossed. I'm talking slam-dunks, especially drug dealers having their charges dismissed over bullshit technicalities. But it's not like the place has gone soft. Some dealers are getting skewered with felony charges for what should be minor possession. It's shady."

Seth frowned. "That could be shitty lawyers or overworked assistant DAs."

"I thought that, too. At first. But witnesses started disappearing." Tony's knuckles were white around his glass. "Key informants started turning up dead, execution style. Their deaths were ruled suicides. Makes no fucking sense. And it's not just informants. Cops, too. Good cops who asked the right questions got transferred or demoted. Or dead."

His gut tightened. "Someone's offing cops?"

"You remember Patrick Kowalski? Narcotics detective, worked Vice for a while?"

Seth nodded. "Younger guy. Sharp."

"Yep. Patrick came to me about three weeks ago. Said he had something huge that would blow up half the precinct. Next morning, his body turned up in an alley a few blocks from the station with three bullets in his chest." Tony drained his club soda. "The detective in charge of the case called it a robbery gone wrong, but I'm not buying it. Street thieves want shit to sell, not bodies to hide. Bad for business. Patrick's wallet was still in his pocket, cash and all."

That sounded sus as hell…like his dad's death being ruled a drug deal gone wrong. Different people and different situations, but corruption always left behind the same stench.

"Yeah, that sounds fishy as fuck."

"Exactly. Maybe I could believe it was random, but not right after

Patrick said he'd uncovered something big. I've been a cop too long to believe in coincidences like that."

Seth, too. A chill went up his spine. "Be careful."

"I am." But Tony's hand shook slightly, belying his words. "I've done some digging but—"

"Unless it's your case, you should stop. Have you discussed this with the higher-ups?"

"Of course. But nothing changed—except that I feel like I'm being watched now. Followed. Maybe that sounds paranoid but…"

Tony had always been too level-headed for that. Besides, Seth felt the prickle of unseen eyes now, too. Unease crept up his spine as he scanned the bar again. He didn't see anyone obviously watching them, but that just meant that whoever observed them was damn good. "And you have no idea who's pulling the strings?"

"None. That's what scares me." Tony's voice dropped to barely above a whisper. "Whoever this is, they've got friends in high places and the kind of power that buys silence."

The only person with that much power was the chief. The guy was a prick. He'd always been unpopular around the precinct. Even Gene hated him.

Shit. "Be careful, man. Different scenario, but if you're right, I'm living proof that—"

"Anyone can get to you or the ones you love at any time. I know." Tony's stare darted to the entrance again. "My gut's telling me there's danger everywhere and I should keep my head down. Stop asking questions." He met Seth's stare, looking rattled. "Like I said before, it's a good thing you got out when you did. We didn't talk much about it when we were partners, but I knew the rumors about your dad being dirty were bullshit. Everyone did. Michael was one of the good guys—solid, a damn good detective, and as honest as they come."

"Thanks. That means a lot."

"I know it wasn't easy to stop digging when you did. You and your dad were tight. But I'm starting to think you're right and that I should take a page from your book."

Tony didn't know that Seth hadn't stopped digging—that he'd hunted down Silas, spent four days torturing the murderer before executing him. That the page from his "book" had been one of the bloodiest chapters of his life. God willing, he never would.

"It would be safer," Seth pointed out.

"Probably." Suddenly, Marconi forced a bright smile and stood. "I should check on Megan and get back to work. But hey, text me your address and we'll send you a wedding invitation, okay? Maybe you and Heavenly can make it back for the ceremony."

"I'll see if we can work it out." By the time he had to RSVP for the event, the fact that he shared Heavenly with Beck would be out in the open.

Smiling, he stood and clasped Tony's hand, before pulling him in for another slap on the back. "Take care of yourself, man. Seriously."

"You too, Cooper. And hey, tell your mom congrats on her wedding." Tony nodded. "See you around."

"See you." Seth tipped his chin and watched Tony—shoulders tense and head on a swivel—hurry out of the bar.

With a frown, Seth glanced at his phone. Their conversation had wrapped up earlier than expected, and now he was alone with his churning thoughts and a growing sense of apprehension.

Same shit, different day. But the systematic rot of corruption Tony had described made Seth doubly glad he'd given up his badge.

After finishing his beer, he paid the check and strolled out of the bar. Beck's speech would likely run another hour, but after Tony's revelations, Seth felt the urge to look in on Heavenly, make sure she was safe.

He crossed the opulent lobby toward the elevators, rounded the corner—and stopped dead.

There, Heavenly stood, looking wide-eyed and just a bit afraid at the massive, tattooed figure looming over her, pressing her against a wall.

Chapter Twenty

Instantly, Seth recognized the man. Not only did he wear a flashy tailored suit that probably cost ten grand, his dark hair, icy eyes, and ruthlessly carved profile belonged on the big screen. He wielded power like a man meant to reign over boardrooms—but the thin scar running from his left temple to his jaw, his ink, and his thick Russian accent betrayed him as something far more dangerous.

Nikolai Volkov, Bratva boss. The deadliest man Seth had ever called friend—and one he'd never expected to see again, hovering over a terrified Heavenly.

"Nikolai!" Seth raced toward Heavenly and tucked her behind his body protectively. "What the fuck are you doing? You don't talk to her."

Instantly, the Russian's four brutish bodyguards closed in. Seth didn't back down. With a grin, Nikolai waved them away. "Seth Cooper, my friend. Why so hostile?"

Seth eyed the still-hovering bodyguards before turning his glare back on Nik. Christ, if the wrong people saw Heavenly with the Russian… "Whatever reason you're here, she's not part of it. You want to talk? You find *me*. You don't approach her. She knows nothing. She's off-limits."

Nikolai stepped back and raised his hands in a gesture of mock innocence. "I did not think you want me to interrupt meeting with cop friend. A thousand apologies."

That was who'd been watching him and Tony? Why? Nikolai didn't surface in upscale places teeming with polite society without a fucking good reason.

"Heavenly, go upstairs. Text Beck that you'll be in the room and to meet you there as soon as he's done. Do it now."

She frowned, her gaze ping-ponging between him and Nikolai. "Seth, what's—"

"Don't argue, angel. Let me know the second you're safely inside the room. Don't open the door for anyone except me or Beck. No maids, no room service, no one. Do you understand?"

"O-Okay." She looked shaken, but she nodded and pulled out her phone.

Seth watched her text Beck with trembling fingers before he guided her to the elevator. "Don't forget to tell me when you're safe. If I haven't heard from you in two minutes, I'm coming after you."

"I will."

He pressed a kiss to her forehead and watched her disappear behind the closing doors. Once the car shot up, he turned back to Nikolai, his posture still tense. "We shouldn't talk here."

"You are right." Nikolai adjusted his cuff links. "I have arranged small meeting room on third floor. Very private."

Seth's phone buzzed. Heavenly's text confirmed she was safely in the room, alone. Relief flooded him. Now he could focus on the man who'd helped him track down his family's killer eight years ago.

He pinned his glare on Nikolai. "Lead the way. While you do, tell me what the fuck you were doing approaching her?"

"Very beautiful woman, this angel of yours. Pretty diamond on finger. When is wedding?"

"You don't need to know about her, Nik." But he probably already did.

"She looks too sweet for pervert like you." Nikolai's eyes glittered with amusement. "But appearances deceive, no? Who knew that Seth Cooper likes to share his woman? Especially with important surgeon."

Seth's blood froze. Nikolai could only know about Beck if he'd been watching them. And he wouldn't do that without cause. "What the fuck is going on?"

"Relax. I merely talked to your angel."

"About what? I know your usual method of talking, Nik," Seth whispered tersely. "With a well-charged battery and jumper cables."

The big Russian laughed and led him to a stairwell clearly used by employees, bodyguards flanking them. "I would never talk to her like that. I only tell her to have you contact me so your detective friend would not ask, shall we say, uncomfortable questions."

That gave Seth pause. "Fine. What's up?"

"Still straight to business. I like that about you." Nikolai ascended the stairs without breaking stride. Hell, without sounding even slightly winded. And he looked immaculate doing it.

The Russian didn't say anything more until they emerged from the stairwell and strode to the end of the hall. Only after the bodyguards swept the small but ornate meeting room and Nikolai closed the door behind them did he begin. "Done more digging into past since you *talked* to Silas?"

Nik's reminder that he and Seth shared the same brutal "language" was subtle, but irrefutable.

Seth clenched his jaw. "No. After that *conversation* I told you I was done. That hasn't changed in the last eight years."

Nikolai sent him a sharp nod. "And your woman. She knows of... *chat* with Silas?"

"She knows what she needs to know. Leave it—and her—alone."

Nikolai nodded—a silent agreement not to come near Heavenly again. "Since you spoke to Silas, the organization he worked for has grown bigger. Stronger. Too powerful to be allowed."

Seth's jaw tightened. He'd always known that Silas had worked for someone else. The thug had had a rap sheet miles long without any connection to Seth, much less his wife and son. The hit had been too well-coordinated and complex for a lone wolf. But after four days of brutally interrogating Silas, the bastard had never broken and never said who had put him up to the murders or why. So Seth had been forced to choose—continue hunting the criminals who'd offed his wife, son, and father...or walk away and protect what remained of his family. The thought of losing his mother and four younger brothers had been too horrific to continue.

"How much bigger?" Seth asked grimly.

"Big enough to take over. Their leader is Specter. He is like ghost. When my men think we have him cornered, he disappears."

The implications made Seth's blood run cold. "You think Specter also hired Silas?"

Nikolai shrugged, but his expression darkened. "Gut tells me yes.

The methods, the precision, way they vanish when cornered... It feels familiar. That happened to you, too, yes?"

"Yes." But Seth hadn't expected that in the eight years he'd spent building a new life, the criminal organization could be growing stronger. And he should have. "Fuck."

"Could be different group, but how many ghosts in city are this good at hiding?"

"Tell me what you know."

Nikolai narrowed his eyes. "Remember who you are speaking to, my friend."

"Yeah, I know...I know. You don't take orders, you give them." Seth swallowed his frustration. "You came to me, Nik. If you want help, I need information."

"Specter's organization threatens distribution channels. They are drying up. Turf is shrinking, squeezing out organization. Italians and Chinese, too. They have high-level of protection and—"

"You've never played well with others, but you're cooperating with rival families?" If Nikolai was comparing notes with the other mob bosses in the city, Specter's revenue and power must be huge.

"Desperate times..." Nikolai dropped his voice. "I tried cooperating with detective, provide information to take Specter down, but he was silenced."

Seth froze. "Kowalski?"

The Russian scowled, but nodded. "Tell me what you know."

He couldn't give Tony's name to the mobster, or his former partner might wind up dead, too. Nikolai would likely suspect, but Seth refused to confirm. "I heard he was gunned down in an alley recently. Supposedly a robbery gone wrong."

Nikolai scoffed. "I was not born yesterday. Neither were you. It was easy to keep alliance alive—until I told detective that a cop was protecting Specter. He agreed to investigate. Then he called to say he had update. After that...I read obituary."

Holy shit. "When did you last hear from him?"

"Morning he died."

Fuck. His exchange with Tony earlier replayed in his head.

Things have changed, gotten more political. Corrupt. And getting worse every day.

We've always known there are a few dirty cops at the station who—

This is bigger. Darker.

If everything Tony and Nikolai had said was true, that probably meant that whoever had offed his father, whoever had set the bomb for Autumn and Tristan…

Had been a cop.

Someone who'd worked with his father. Someone who might even have shaken Seth's hand at the funeral. Someone still walking around with a badge, still trusted, still protected by the system.

Seth froze, then shoved down his reaction. He shouldn't tip off Nikolai. "What else do you know about Specter's organization?"

He shrugged. "Not enough."

Nik wasn't in a good spot, but Seth couldn't get involved. "I get you, but I left this shit behind. I'm only here for a few days, then I'm flying back to LA."

"You owe me."

That pissed Seth off. "I don't. You gave me one name eight years ago. I paid my debt to you—many times over. You wanted people gone, and I made that happen. We're even."

"It is not so simple. I heard when you arrived yesterday. In September, too." Nikolai's smile was cold. "If I am aware of such things, do you not think they are, too? Be careful, my friend. You have as much to lose as you did eight years ago, no?"

The warning slammed through Seth. He thought of Heavenly upstairs, possibly carrying their child. Of Beck, who'd become as much of a brother as his other siblings. Of Hudson, the son he was just learning to love.

Nikolai was right—he had everything to lose now.

"Jesus." He raked a hand through his hair.

He'd suspected someone could still be watching him, but Nikolai confirming that? And if Seth's suspicions were right, if it *was* a cop, the dirty son of a bitch could be getting the information about his comings and goings from anywhere. From anyone.

"This is not a me-problem. If you hear something, you call," Nikolai demanded.

As much as Seth hated to, he nodded. "If I hear anything concrete, yeah."

"Good. Tell your nervous friend Tony to be careful. People watch him."

Seth's guts seized. It had been one thing for Tony to suspect that, but another altogether for Nikolai to know it. "He's aware."

Nikolai nodded, his expression sober. "Enjoy your mother's wedding, but keep head down. They *are* watching you."

With that ominous warning, Nikolai turned and left the room, his bodyguards surrounding him.

Seth let out the breath he'd been unconsciously holding before he hauled ass to the nearest bank of elevators, frantically stabbing the Up button with his finger. He needed to lay eyes on Heavenly—ASAP. "Come on!"

Finally, the car arrived, blessedly empty. He sprinted in, trying not to climb out of his skin.

When he reached their floor, he heard voices from inside their suite.

"...Big, scary Russian guy stopped me in the lobby. Expensive suit. Lots of tattoos. His eyes were dead." Heavenly's voice trembled. "He knew my name, Beck. He knew Seth. And Seth knew him."

"Who was he?" Beck demanded.

"I-I don't know, but when Seth showed up, he looked ready to kill the guy."

Cursing under his breath, Seth used his key card and opened the door. They both looked up when he entered, Beck pacing while Heavenly sat on the edge of the sofa, her face pale.

Beck's eyes locked on him before the door had even shut. "Who the fuck cornered Heavenly in the lobby and what did he want?"

Seth glanced at Heavenly, silently assuring himself that she was merely rattled before he faced Beck. "Someone I used to know. I told him in the politest way possible to back the fuck off."

"There's more to that story, and you're going to give it to me." Beck's voice was dangerously low. "Heavenly is my fiancée and my responsibility, too. Start talking."

"The less you know, the safer you both are."

Beck growled, lunging into Seth's personal space. "If you think I'm just going to let it slide that some motherfucking Russian mobster—and don't tell me he isn't—not only approached our woman in the lobby, but also knew her fucking *name,* you're out of your goddamn mind!"

Seth ran a hand through his hair. "Nikolai Volkov is an old friend who helped me track down Silas eight years ago. We haven't spoken since."

"Are you fucking kidding me?" Beck bellowed. "You're snooping around the dangerous shit that got Autumn and Tristan killed?"

"No!" Seth barked. "It's not my fault he showed up. I sure as fuck didn't invite him."

"Then how did he know you were here? And how the fuck does he know Heavenly's name?"

"We're on his turf. It's his job to know."

"I don't give a flying fuck about his *job,*" Beck bit out. "I want to know *how* the motherfucker has so much information about her. Did he shove a tracker up your ass eight years ago?"

"Don't be ridiculous." Seth scowled. "He wanted information. I made it crystal clear that I didn't have any. Honestly, I don't expect to hear from him again."

"You better be right," Beck warned, pulling Heavenly protectively into his arms. "If your past gets her hurt—if it gets our baby hurt—I will end you myself."

Though Beck's threat made Seth's blood boil, the mention of their potential child had his chest tightening. "I would never let anything happen to either of you. You should know that."

"You can't control this."

"I can, by not getting involved again. I made it clear that I'm out. What the fuck else do you want me to do? I can't change the past."

"Just don't fucking drag it into our future. If you start that shit, we're done."

The realization that a cop had probably murdered his loved ones made Seth seethe. Made him crave revenge. But… "I've already lost too fucking many people. Do you really think I'm reckless enough to risk you and Heavenly? To risk Hudson, too?"

Beck hesitated, then grimaced and rubbed at the back of his neck. "Fuck. Point taken. I'm just worried."

"I know. And I'm glad you want to protect her. I can't be with her every minute, so it's good she's got you watching out for her, too."

Beck relaxed slightly but kept his arms around Heavenly. "What did he want to know?"

"If I had any information about the organization Silas probably worked for. Apparently, it's grown since I killed him, and now they're infringing on Nikolai's territory. But I didn't have anything to give him. So that was that."

Relief skipped over Beck's face. "Make sure it stays that way."

Seth intended to, but…the organization knew he was in town. They were watching. Despite his best efforts to leave the past behind, the worry that history would repeat itself in the worst possible way buzzed through his brain.

Seth shoved down rising apprehension. As much as their spying pissed him off, he couldn't fall back into old patterns. He'd made his choice to move on.

Life and love, he silently pledged.

"I'll do everything I can." He cradled Heavenly's crown.

"Are you two good now?" Heavenly asked. "I hate it when you fight."

Seth caught Beck's gaze. When the doctor nodded, Seth smiled her way. "We're done. I'm sorry Nikolai scared you. He should never have approached you. I'll die before I let anyone hurt you."

Heavenly sat cross-legged on the hotel suite's sofa, accepting the paper plate Beck handed her before he distributed napkins. The pizza box from the takeout place around the corner sat open on the coffee table, grease already seeping through the cardboard, the scent of pepperoni and Italian spices filling the room. She grabbed a slice and bit in, the cheese still hot enough to burn the roof of her mouth.

Seth finally stopped pacing near the window long enough to snag two slices, though he remained standing, eating mechanically while staring out at the city skyline.

The last two hours had crossed from tense to unsettled. He had apologized for his encounter with Nikolai, but Beck was still furious. Heavenly saw both sides. Yes, she'd been shaken, but Seth had been ambushed by the big Russian. That wasn't his fault.

He'd also sworn he wasn't getting involved in the past again. Heavenly believed he meant that—in the moment. But she was less convinced he'd be able to refuse if his past came for him again.

Even now, hours later, Seth was still on edge, his usual easy confidence replaced by something coiled. Watchful. Dangerous.

"Hey, um…" Seth reached for another slice of pizza. "I have a meeting with a Realtor at four-thirty. To sell my house."

The one he'd shared with his late wife and son. Heavenly's stomach tightened. Seth had already been through a lot today. That would only heap more trauma on his shoulders.

"I shouldn't be long." He didn't quite meet their eyes. "Stay here and…enjoy the room."

She caught his subtext immediately: make love, try to conceive, stay in this safe cocoon while he faced his demons alone.

She met Beck's stare across the room and saw instant agreement.

Absolutely not.

"We're coming with you," Heavenly insisted, shoving her plate onto the table and rising to her feet.

Seth's lips tightened. "Angel, you don't have to—"

"I *want* to." She crossed the room to him, cupping his hard shoulder with a gentle hand. "After what you went through the last time you were there, we're not letting you do this alone."

Beck approached, nodding. "We're not. So stop that bullshit now."

Seth's throat worked, seeming to struggle against emotion. "Thank you."

He always tried to protect them, insisting he was strong and capable enough to handle anything without help. The relief on his face now told her he was glad he didn't have to face this tragic remnant of his past alone.

They finished eating, the weight of their earlier argument and the upcoming meeting stifling their usual banter. When Heavenly began cleaning up, Beck took the empty box from her and discarded it before pulling her against his side.

"This afternoon is going to be rough on him," he murmured against her hair.

"That's why I insisted on going." For the men she loved, she would walk through fire.

Beck kissed her nose. "And that's one reason we love you."

Forty-five minutes later, they climbed into an Uber, the silence so thick it felt choking. Heavenly sat between her men, holding both their hands as the city passed, a blur through the windows. Seth's shoulders were tense, his mouth a flat line as he gripped her almost too tightly. She gave him a supportive squeeze and refused to pull away.

As they drove toward the suburbs, skyscrapers gave way to strip malls. The trees here were more plentiful, their branches creating tunnels of green overhead.

The driver stopped at a red light. Without the forward motion, the strain in the car somehow felt even more uncomfortably tight. Heavenly wished she could think of something to say to break it and make Seth smile.

Suddenly, Beck pointed out the window. "Hey, Seth. Look."

He glanced over. "Yeah?"

"There's a White Castle. Want to stop?"

Seth scowled. "Why? We just ate."

"You could have a quickie in the men's room and…reminisce." Beck's grin turned both teasing and wicked. "Maybe reenact your first time with Mary Jo Bartkowicz."

Seth rolled his eyes, then burst out laughing—a genuine ripple of mirth that lightened the weight on her chest. Beck joined in, and within seconds, all three of them were shaking with it.

"You're both disgusting." Heavenly tsked. "That poor girl. It must have been horrible."

"Hey! She left with a smile on her face." Seth glared indignantly, but she caught the grin curling up his lips.

"More likely, *you* did. Nothing that happens in a bathroom stall is sexy." Heavenly shook her head. "Besides, you were only fourteen."

"So? I was precocious."

"And lasted...what, all of ten seconds? You were just a horndog," Beck corrected.

"Says the man who lost his virginity to a—"

"Shut it! We're not talking about Gloria," Beck cut in.

Thanks to the levity, Seth's grip on Heavenly's hand had loosened, his breathing smoothed out. The joke had done its job. By the time the Uber pulled up in front of a modest ranch-style house with cream siding and hunter green shutters, Seth looked...not calm exactly, but steadier.

Seth climbed out, then extended his hand to her. She took it and eased from the back seat as his gaze swept the empty driveway before lifting to the house.

His mood turned somber again as he pulled the keys from his pocket. "Guess...the Realtor's not here yet."

Heavenly hoped he didn't have to wait long. He hadn't even walked inside yet, but she already feared he was holding himself together by a thread. No surprise. This place held wonderful, terrible memories.

She pressed close, doing her best to provide silent comfort as he unlocked the front door. Once he pushed it open, he glanced down at her, lips curled up woodenly in an attempt to convince her that he was okay. But she knew him too well.

With a sweep of his hand, he gestured her and Beck inside. His fake smile gave way to something grim and stoic that twisted her heart.

God, this was killing him.

Stomach knotting, Heavenly stepped into the house.

One glance, her chest threatened to buckle.

Afternoon light streamed through the windows, illuminating a living room that felt frozen in time. Haunted. Like it was ready for the return of the family that would never step foot inside again. A sectional butted against one soft beige wall, its cushions still plump, as if ready for someone to sit down at any moment. Built-in bookcases flanked a brick fireplace. Family photos lined one wall, their subjects captured in a long-gone moment of normalcy.

This house had once been his *home,* where the people he'd loved had once lived, watched TV, and slept. Where they'd made breakfast and argued about whose turn it was to take out the trash. Where a baby had cried at two a.m. and exhausted parents had soothed him.

Where they'd planned for a future that had never come.

And now, they were all dead…except Seth. He stood here in the present, tormented by his past and rattled by the unwritten future.

Framed photos on the wall of the adjacent hallway drew Heavenly's attention. She shuffled to them slowly, her gaze catching the first image of an impossibly young Seth on his wedding day. He stood beside an even younger brunette with soft doe eyes, wearing a lacy white dress. Autumn. They smiled, looking like barely more than kids, convinced that love alone was enough.

Something in Autumn's posture looked not only submissive but fragile. Seth hadn't spoken much about their marriage, but the woman had been almost dependent on him. Had that played a role in their strain?

The next picture ripped the breath from Heavenly's lungs. Autumn in a hospital bed, exhausted but glowing, cradling a tiny newborn against her chest. Seth leaned over them, pressing a kiss to the baby's downy head like a proud father. The look on his face—raw vulnerability mixed with the unguarded joy of a man who believed his world was complete.

Heavenly's throat closed up. Her vision blurred. She blinked against the tears, but they came spilling down.

The Seth in that photo had been convinced their tomorrows were guaranteed. That he'd watch his son grow to a man, that he'd grow old with his wife.

She turned to study Seth. This version of him was wary and haunted. He was afraid to believe in the future.

And she understood precisely why now—not in a purely academic way, like, of course losing his family had been catastrophic. As she stood amid the rubble of his former life, understanding came with all the subtlety of a punch to the gut.

She swallowed back tears and pressed on.

Hanging to the left was a professional portrait of the three Coopers, maybe two months after Tristan's birth. They all wore white shirts and khakis, smiling against the soft-focus background. They looked like any young family—tired, happy, and convinced they had all the time in the world.

Instead, that world had crashed down less than thirty days later.

Heavenly bit her lip to hold in a sob, but it was no use. Her chest buckled. She pressed her hand to her mouth, trying to breathe.

But the sadness pressed in from every direction, threatening to crush her.

In the living room, she saw neatly arranged baskets of toys—wooden blocks, plastic keys, a stuffed giraffe. A pristine bassinet crouched beside the couch, its white eyelet fabric yellowing with years gone by.

She imagined Seth coming home after a long shift, tie loosened, scooping up his cooing son from his bouncy seat and inhaling his milky-sweet scent. She pictured it so clearly, the vision hurt. Autumn had probably smiled from the kitchen before they'd shared dinner, bath time, then a lullaby. The boring, precious rhythms of family life.

And then, on Christmas Eve, some faceless monster had ripped it all away. Destroyed Seth's family in a single explosion. Made sure that he came home to find—

Heavenly couldn't finish the thought.

She tried to brace herself on the nearby doorjamb. But her knees weakened. Her stomach turned. Her realization felt like a stab in the heart.

How had Seth survived such horrific tragedy? How had he kept breathing and living and pushing ahead when everything he'd known and loved had been cruelly incinerated in the blink of an eye?

Movement in her periphery pulled her back to the present. She turned to find Beck staring at the bassinet, his expression carved with fury and brutal restraint—as if his will alone was keeping something damaged and violent inside him from breaking loose.

Heavenly grabbed his hand. Squeezed. His trembled as he gripped hers in return, his jaw working.

Their eyes met—hers blurry with tears, his taut with glossy restraint. In that moment, they understood without exchanging a single word: *We're asking him to risk everything again. To put his heart on the line and trust that his future wouldn't be ripped away a second time.*

The magnitude of what they'd demanded of him was staggering.

"I'll show you the rest," Seth murmured behind them, his voice rough and raw.

She turned. He looked as if he was made of glass—like one whisper, one sympathetic touch might shatter him into infinite, irreparable pieces. She ached to go to him, wrap her arms around him, and promise him everything would be all right. But she couldn't guarantee that. No one could.

For weeks, she and Beck had given lip service to the idea that tragedy could strike at any moment. But Seth alone had not only known that; he'd lived it.

Shame that she hadn't listened, hadn't really understood, engulfed her.

Beck wrapped a steadying arm around her waist. She leaned into him gratefully as they followed a rigid Seth down the hall in heavy silence.

They entered the master bedroom. The decor was basic—navy comforter, white shutters, and matching nightstands. Surprisingly dust-free surfaces and knickknacks combined with a closet full of clothes. It felt like a place where people still lived. Like Autumn might call out from the kitchen. Like Tristan might fuss from his nursery. As if they'd all return at any moment and resume their lives.

But they wouldn't, not ever again.

Seth had carried that knowledge, adrift and alone, for nearly nine terrible years. And looking around her now, Heavenly wondered how he could possibly be ready to start over and create a new family. He swore he was...but was that wishful thinking? Or more kind lies than actual truth?

Seth stood in the doorway, shoulders rigid, breathing too controlled. He stared at the bed like it was a monster that might roar to life and swallow him whole.

She found Beck's hand and gripped it tightly, fighting back fresh tears.

"Seth?" she finally whispered, aching to offer her love and support.

He didn't reply, didn't move. His carefully blank expression said he was trying desperately not to feel, as if giving into the past he'd never fully grieved would destroy him.

Woodenly, he turned the corner and made his way down another hall.

On the left, they encountered a guest room that held a daybed, a few stacked boxes, and not much else. Dust motes floated in afternoon light.

After a grunt, Seth turned away and led them deeper into the house. He stopped before a door on the right and wrapped his hand around the knob, dragging in a shuddering breath. Then he opened the door.

Tristan's nursery.

The room was perfectly preserved, another horrific snapshot of life interrupted. A shape sorter sat neatly on a shelf with pristine board books, which had obviously seen little use in Tristan's tragically short life. A plush elephant slumped against the wall. A padded rocking chair sat forgotten by the window, and Heavenly could picture Seth here, cradling the son he'd never hold again.

And in the center of it all, the empty crib. Cold, almost barren, except for the mobile of felt stars and moons suspended motionless above the mattress, as if waiting to soothe a baby who would never sleep there again.

The sight was a punch to Heavenly's chest. Her knees threatened to buckle again. A sob stuck in her throat as her vision swam.

Beside her, Beck swallowed hard and gripped the doorframe for support. "Jesus, Seth. How did you survive this?"

Seth didn't answer. She wasn't sure he could. Instead, his throat bobbed once—hard—as if he'd swallowed a scream while he stood frozen in the doorway. His face was a mask of anguish as he stared at the crib like he was watching his son die all over again.

Heavenly's heart threatened to shatter as she bent and picked up a criminally pristine teddy bear. Tristan had never teethed on it, never roughhoused with it. He'd barely had time to cuddle with it.

She squeezed the plushy toy, its cheerful smile shattering something inside her.

Heavenly couldn't hold back anymore. She sobbed. Ugly, gasping tears that tore from somewhere deep in her chest. For Seth, who'd lost everything. For Autumn, who'd perished with her baby. For Tristan, who'd never truly known life.

For the horrific tragedy of it all.

Strong arms wrapped around her from behind. Even surrounded by all the visceral reminders of his loss, Seth pulled her back against his solid chest and held her tight. He buried his face in her hair and comforted *her*, even though he must be bleeding inside.

He finally faced Beck, his voice sounding absolutely wrecked. "I had a lot of dark days. Hell, years. The holidays are still hard. And I'm really not...good on Christmas Eve. I lost everything that day. But now...look what I've gained."

His words made her cry harder. Because yes, he had them now. But that didn't erase the pain. Nothing would.

"God, I'm sorry. So...fucking sorry." Beck sounded closer, his voice thick with emotion. "I've been riding you. Pushing you to get over it, move on, start a family. Like it was something simple. Like grief was a switch you could just flip and—" His voice broke. "I didn't get it. Not really. Until now."

"You don't need to apologize." Seth turned her in his arms, then wiped away her tears with a gentle swipe and a shuddering breath. "You've been patient, and I've been slow. I know I have. Struggling to catch up emotionally—to *want* what you want. A family. A future. But I'm there now. I swear I am."

Heavenly pressed her face against his chest, breathing him in. Beck moved closer, and suddenly they were all wrapped around each other, surrounded by Tristan's sweet, terrible nursery—three people silently vowing to love and support each other.

At least as long as life allowed.

After a profound silence, Seth pulled back. His eyes were red rimmed but dry, like he'd run out of tears years ago.

"Come on." His voice low but surprisingly steady. "Let's finish this."

They moved through the rest of the house in weighted silence—the bathroom with the yellow duck still sitting on the tub's edge, the hall closet with its stack of photo albums, the kitchen that hadn't been used in years.

"What are you going to do with everything?" Her voice came out smaller than she'd intended.

Seth surveyed the place with a too-practiced shrug. "Take a few things. I'll sell the furniture with the house. The rest…I'll leave to the new occupants to either donate or toss."

Because he couldn't be here anymore, couldn't endure this again.

"We'll help," Beck insisted.

"Whatever you need," she echoed, her chest aching.

"Thank you." Seth's smile was ghost-thin as he disappeared into the basement.

He returned with flattened moving boxes and packing tape. For a moment, he just stood there, staring at the house before he let out a ragged sigh. Then they began the grim work of dismantling the remnants of Seth's old life.

In the awful silence, Seth pulled the framed photos from the walls, his hands shaking slightly as he wrapped them in butcher paper. From his home office, he gathered documents: the marriage certificate with slightly yellowed edges, Tristan's birth certificate with tiny blue footprints stamped at the bottom, along with a taped lock of downy baby hair. Then finally death certificates that made everything horrifically real.

They trekked back to the nursery next, grabbing the teddy bear, the baby blanket from the back of the rocker, and a soft blue onesie that read BABY'S HOMECOMING that nearly annihilated her newly forced composure.

After that, they filed back to the master bedroom like they were on a death march. Seth plucked Autumn's wedding ring from the jewelry box on her bathroom counter, then his own band, wrapped in tissue paper, from his dresser.

"I don't need these anymore," he said softly, turning the rings between his fingers. "But I can't throw them away."

"You shouldn't," Heavenly said, her throat tight. "It's part of your history."

He merely nodded, as if it took too much energy to say more.

As Seth finished, Heavenly and Beck remained mute, silently supportive shadows following him from room to room in case Seth needed them.

When they finally returned to the living room, Heavenly settled onto the sofa, her eyes aching, her chest hollow. Had Seth felt like this for months? For years?

The guys taped the last of the boxes shut, and the doorbell chimed through the house.

Seth's shoulders straightened, his jaw setting. "The Realtor."

Beck and Heavenly stood as Seth led a professional-looking woman in her fifties through the house. Her kind eyes took in the empty walls where photos had hung, the gaps on shelves where keepsakes had been removed.

When their voices faded down the hall, Beck pulled Heavenly into his arms.

"I can barely stand being here," she whispered brokenly against his chest. "How has he lived with this?"

"I don't know, but I worry he's lived with it more than dealt with it." Beck stroked her back in slow, soothing circles. "It's like he got his revenge, then mentally locked the past all away and tried to carry on as if the pain didn't exist. But he can't heal what he won't face."

"I know. I've lost people." Heavenly still mourned her dad, still remembered sharply that day her mother ran out. She even lamented the loss of her childhood home. "But never like this. Never everyone at once." She tilted her head back to look at Beck. "How did he survive those first days? The first weeks? How did he even *want* to keep living?"

"I don't know." Beck's eyes were dark with pain. "But we're going to make damn sure he never has to face anything alone again."

"I should have been more understanding." Heavenly's gut twisted with guilt. "When I pushed him about starting a family—"

"Stop." Beck pressed a gentle finger against her lips. "I pushed harder than you did. We both fucked up. Now we know. And we'll do better."

Footsteps signaled the end of the tour. They drifted back toward the kitchen, where the Realtor handed Seth a handwritten list.

"Just minor repairs," she was saying in a smooth, practiced tone. "Touch-up paint in the master bedroom, that loose railing on the back deck, the dripping faucet in the hall bath. Nothing major."

Seth nodded mechanically and skimmed the listing agreement. The pen shook once in his hand before he forced it still and scrawled his signature across the page.

"Excellent." The Realtor smiled. "I'll have the sign up by Monday. This is a wonderful neighborhood, and the house is in great condition. I don't anticipate any trouble finding a buyer."

"Good." Seth's voice was flat. Empty.

After she left, he sagged against the kitchen counter and exhaled like he'd been holding his breath for hours. "Thank fucking god that's over."

Heavenly agreed. The house was haunted—but not by ghosts. It was suffocating under the weight of memories and loss and all the futures that would never be. She hoped desperately that a new family would buy it. Young parents with a baby or toddler who would fill these rooms with noise and mess and *life*. Who would chase away the shadows and let this place finally rest.

Seth checked his phone. "Uber's five minutes out. We can head back to the city. Grab dinner. Maybe catch a show."

"Whatever you're up for, man," Beck said.

They returned to the living room and sat close together on the couch, not speaking. There was nothing left to say. But their bodies said everything—Beck's hand resting on Heavenly's knee, her fingers woven through Seth's, the way they leaned into each other like trees whose roots had tangled together underground.

When the notification pinged, Beck rose and collected the boxes of keepsakes while Seth pulled out his keys one final time.

He stood in the doorway for a long moment, staring back into the house. At his past. At the life he'd built…and lost.

Heavenly slipped to his side and wrapped her arm around his waist. *I'm here.*

Beck adjusted the boxes and gripped Seth's shoulder. *We both are.*

Seth's jaw clenched. His eyes shone too bright in the fading light.

Moving together, the three of them crossed the threshold.

Seth pulled in a deep breath, drew the door shut, and turned the lock.

For the last time.

As they walked toward the waiting Uber, Seth gripped Heavenly's hand like a lifeline. Beck fell into step on his other side, holding the boxes of memories in his arms.

None of them looked back.

Chapter Twenty One

Seth dragged a hand down his face and stared out the Uber window, watching the city blur past. The ride back to their Manhattan hotel gave him time to process.

He'd sworn he was braced for touring the house he'd shared with Autumn, where Tristan had spent his few precious months on earth.

He'd been dead fucking wrong.

Walking through that house had been haunting. Wrenching. It had taken every ounce of his control not to break down.

By some miracle, he'd kept his shit together.

And when he'd finally closed the door behind him for the last time, he had exhaled. Let out his pent-up grief.

The most tragic chapter of his life was almost closed. Yeah, he had to call Carl, who had kindly offered a construction crew from his company to handle the house repairs. After that, other than signing the escrow papers, he'd never have to deal with that house again.

But Seth wasn't bullshitting himself. Despite the years, the counseling, the praying, and him doggedly doing everything he could to move on?

He still wasn't healed.

There. He'd admitted it. No matter how much he fucking hated it, he was still paralyzed by his past.

Maybe admitting it was the first step to healing?

He doubted it would be that simple.

When they reached the hotel, Beck suggested they clean up and head to dinner. The last goddamn thing Seth felt like doing was pretending to be jovial, but this was their last night in the city together. And hiding in the suite wouldn't fix anything.

So Seth strapped on his fake-as-fuck smile and went through the motions.

Dinner at a steakhouse. A Broadway revival. Cannoli and espresso at a late-night bakery Heavenly declared the best thing she'd ever tasted. Then a long walk back to the hotel, city lights blurring around them, Heavenly tucked safely between him and Beck.

Being with the people he loved helped. It distracted the grieving beast inside him. His smile came easier. His jokes felt more natural.

But he recognized now that he was limping along. Surviving.

He had no idea how to actually heal.

Seth was exhausted—mentally and physically—by the time they made it back to their room. After all the danger and upheaval today, his body gave out. He fell asleep almost immediately, Heavenly sandwiched between him and Beck.

The following morning, he woke feeling…if not lighter, at least bolstered so he could handle everything on the agenda today.

As Heavenly stirred, he began kissing her awake. Beck roused in more ways than one and joined in. Their lovemaking was slow and unhurried in the early dawn light, waking as the city did. Seth lost himself in Heavenly's silken mouth, his cock muffling her cries as he watched her shatter between them while Beck spilled inside their girl unprotected.

Afterward, they showered, dressed, and grabbed coffee in the hotel restaurant before heading to the house to have breakfast with Mom, Carl, and Hudson.

As usual, she went all out, even making her world-famous waffles before they all climbed into Carl's Mercedes SUV to start their afternoon of errands. Seth and Beck sat in back with Heavenly between them, Hudson in the third-row seat, and his mom rode shotgun next to Carl, with her color-coded wedding binder in her lap.

Carl headed into the city, driving with the patience of a man who'd figured out that wedding planning required surrender to forces beyond his control.

Mom flipped through her notes frenetically. "On our way back home, we'll pick up the tuxes. Then I'll gather up everything that needs to be packed for tomorrow—the guest book, the cake knife, the card box—"

"Don't worry, Mom. We'll get it all done," Seth promised from the back seat in a reassuring voice.

"I know. I'm just nervous. What if I forget something?"

"With all the lists you've made?" In the rearview mirror, Carl looked like he was suppressing a grin. "I don't think that's possible. If I had known getting married was going to put you in a tizzy, I'm not sure I would have asked."

She sent a saucy grin his way. "Too late. I just can't believe the wedding is tomorrow!"

Carl reached over and squeezed her hand. "Stop stressing. This is supposed to be a happy occasion. You got this."

"I know. You're right," she whispered, gripping his hand in return. "And you've been such a rock. Thank you."

The depth and certainty of their love was palpable.

It seemed almost surreal yet somehow natural that tomorrow, his mom would clutch his elbow and fight back happy tears as he walked her down the aisle to pledge herself—before God, their combined families, and close friends—to this man she loved.

Openly.

Freely.

Without a whisper of fear, judgment, or condemnation.

Jealousy pricked Seth. But when he glanced at Heavenly and Beck, his envy cooled. Regardless of what anyone else thought, their love was equally deep and certain. And in time, they'd show the world.

That day couldn't come soon enough.

It took roughly an hour to finish the final tux fitting and leave with their penguin suits in tow. As they strolled to the parking lot, Seth caught Heavenly gazing at Beck. It was just a glance, long enough for something soft and warm to pass between them before Heavenly lowered her chin and darted back inside the SUV.

Seth's breath caught.

They were doing their best. But those looks—those small, stolen moments—were both hard to resist and impossible to misinterpret. A combination of anxiety and tenderness rushed him. Thankfully, his mother was too absorbed to notice.

But he was beyond ready to be honest about their feelings.

The end of this weekend couldn't come fast enough.

"Oh, the traffic is horrible. The girls and I have mani-pedis at two, and we're going to be late." His mom scowled.

"Don't worry, you'll get there in time," Carl vowed.

As promised, he pulled into the driveway as Danny, Maggie, and baby Anna arrived. Inside the house, his mom raced around, quickly placing the items needed for tonight's rehearsal dinner on the dining room table before she, Heavenly, and Maggie rushed out for the salon, leaving baby Anna behind with the guys.

After they'd gone, Seth and Beck packed the items into a large duffel bag for tomorrow's wedding and reception, with some help from Hudson. Carl supervised, checking each item off her list with methodical precision.

"Grace is incredibly organized." Beck blinked as he tucked decorative sachets filled with bird seed into a smaller box.

"She's always been like a female drill sergeant. Raising five boys, you have to be." Seth chuckled as he wrapped the cake knife in bubble wrap. "Besides, she's been planning this wedding for months. So yeah…she's organized."

While they finished securing the last few items, Carl excused himself, stepped into the kitchen, and pulled out his phone. As he confirmed delivery times with the caterer and florist, his voice carried a note of quiet pride.

Another pang of envy pierced Seth. This man got to express his love for the woman he wanted to spend the rest of his life with in the way he yearned to. Right now…Seth couldn't. And he knew all the reasons why, but keeping their love on the down-low like his dirty little secret was really beginning to chafe.

Beck eased in beside Seth, his face full of concern. "You're frowning. Everything all right?"

Seth paused with a shrug. "I just wish…"

"Me, too. It's not easy."

That gouged Seth with even more guilt. He could imagine the shoe being on the other foot—and having to act like the third wheel would hurt like hell. "Not much longer. I promise."

"I know." Beck nodded.

"How are you going to tell Grandma?" Hudson whispered.

Seth shot him a look. His son asked a valid question…he just didn't have an answer. "Carefully."

"Way to dodge the question." Beck sent him a sober stare. "I know it won't be easy. And you'll be risking a lot."

"Pretty much everything." Seth let out a sigh. "But I have to. It's… past time."

Beck clapped him on the back. "We're in this together."

"Thanks."

They fell silent when Carl entered the room again. It wasn't long before they had everything packed up and ready to be loaded into the car for tomorrow.

The women returned from the salon not long after that, freshly manicured and glowing, not to mention slightly tipsy, their laughter carrying through the house.

"Thank you," his mom said, inspecting the guys' work. "Everything looks great."

"You're welcome," Seth murmured as she hugged each of them, even Beck. He held his mother a moment longer than necessary, breathing in the familiar scent of her perfume, trying to memorize this moment.

Next time he saw her, everything would change.

"Well…that's all I've got on my list. I guess we just need to get ready." She smiled before pressing a kiss to Seth's cheek and easing from his hug. "The rehearsal begins at five-thirty."

Seth nodded and held out his hand to Heavenly, who came running and put her hand in his. "We'll meet you at the church."

They said a quick goodbye to Hudson and dashed back to the city, scrambled into their clothes, and Ubered to the venue. They arrived in the softly candlelit sanctuary as Carl, Mom, and Hudson did.

Father Heasley greeted them at the entrance, his weathered face creasing into a warm smile as he shook Carl's hand, then bowed respectfully his mother's way. Seth introduced Hudson, Beck, and Heavenly, then he shook the priest's hand himself, finding solace in the man's familiar, reassuring grip.

"The rest of the family should be here shortly," Mom assured.

As if on cue, the church doors opened and Seth's brothers filed in. First, Danny and Maggie, who carried Anna in a frilly dress on her hip. Matt followed, with Connor and Jack bringing up the rear.

As greetings ensued, Carl's children entered the church.

Blake, the older, was tall and broad-shouldered, like his dad. He also possessed Carl's easy smile and steady demeanor as he shook Seth's hand with a genuinely warm greeting. There was something protective and proud in the way he stood near his father—a son watching his dad step into new happiness.

Catherine—who asked everyone to call her Cat—was a surprisingly poised nineteen-year-old college student. She had striking dark hair and her father's blue eyes. When she hugged his mom, her smile was warm and genuine, as if she embraced her new family with open arms.

"It's nice to meet you." Cat smiled.

"I'm so happy to finally meet you," his mother whispered. "Aren't you lovely?"

Cat blushed. Then his mother's attention was quickly diverted by a question from the chapel's wedding coordinator. Of course, Mom had the answer.

Situation handled, she hugged Blake next, talking rapidly about how wonderful it was to finally have everyone together. Carl stood beside his children, beaming with love and pride.

Minutes later, the rehearsal began. The wedding coordinator walked them through the processional, explaining positions and timing. Seth stood at the back of the church with his mom on his arm, waiting for their cue.

"Thank you, for doing this," she whispered, her hand trembling slightly where it rested on his elbow. "For being here. For giving me away. I'm guessing it's not easy—"

Seth swallowed down his emotions. "You don't need to thank me, Mom. I'm happy for you, and I wouldn't have missed this for the world."

Her eyes turned misty. "It feels so strange to be a bride again. Your grandfather walked me down the aisle when I married your father. And now you're doing it for me. It feels...different, but still right." She sniffled. "Listen to me, blathering on."

Seth's throat and chest tightened. His dad had loved her completely. Together, they'd built a life and filled it with five boys, chaos, and laughter. Michael Cooper never would have wanted his wife to spend a decade and a half alone.

He smiled at his mother. "You're not. You're a beautiful bride."

She gave him a watery laugh. "I'm a nervous one, too."

"The boys and I are happy for you. And Dad would want you to be happy, too."

Mom choked on a sob and dabbed at her eyes. "Don't make me cry. I'll ruin my makeup."

Finally, Father Heasley gestured them to walk down the aisle, then again for good measure. She relaxed a bit with each step, growing steadier with each beat. By the third run-through, she was confident and practically glowing.

But then Seth noticed that Jack and Connor had positioned themselves out of their mom's line of sight…and right next to Cat. They sent Carl's daughter heated glances in tandem, in what appeared to be a well-practiced seduction. The girl seemed startled, like she wasn't sure how to handle identical twins—and her soon-to-be stepbrothers—piling on the flirtation.

Seth grimaced. Goddamnit. He was going to have to shut this shit down.

While Father Heasley gave Mom and Carl some last-minute instructions, Seth grabbed both twins by their collars and dragged them into an adjacent hallway.

"Ow—hey!" Jack protested.

Seth smacked them both upside the head with just enough force to convey his annoyance. "What the hell? Are you two trying to ruin this wedding? Or incapable of thinking about anything but sex for more than two minutes?"

"What do you mean?" Jack asked.

"Don't play stupid. Stop staring at Cat like you want to tumble her into bed between you."

"We're just being friendly," Connor said, all innocence.

"Stop bullshitting me. I know exactly what you're doing. I've seen you two in action."

"What? We're just welcoming her into the family and all," Jack insisted.

"Not with your dicks, you're not," Seth bit out. "Back off, horndogs. This is Mom's *wedding rehearsal,* and Cat is about to become your stepsister."

Jack grinned unrepentantly. "We know. But she's hot, and we're not related by blood."

Seth struggled not to punch him in the mouth. "You will *not* cause drama by trying to tag-team Carl's daughter or I will beat you black and blue. Do you understand or do I need to speak in smaller syllables for you to get it through your thick skulls?"

Connor had the decency to look sheepish. Jack was less moved, based on his I-don't-give-a-fuck shrug. "We haven't actually touched her. Hell, we've barely even talked to her."

"Keep it that way. And keep it in your pants."

"Oh, so you've kept it in your pants since you brought Beck and Heavenly here for Mom's wedding?"

"No, but I also haven't whipped it out near Mom. So unless you want to piss off Carl and start their marriage off on a really shitty note, treat her the way you'd treat Anna."

"Like a baby?" Connor rolled his eyes, then grumbled. "Fine."

Seth turned his glare to Jack. "Did you hear me?"

"Hard to miss, *Dad*. Whatever."

"Not whatever. Just remember, you won't get much pussy in the future if you're missing all your fucking teeth."

"Oh, don't let Mom hear you say that in a church," Jack drawled.

"Can it, smart-ass. Get back to the gathering. And *behave*."

He left the grousing twins in the hallway and returned to the sanctuary. When he looked up, he spotted Hudson coming toward him, wearing neatly pressed khakis and a collared shirt…with a knowing smirk.

"I can guess what Jack and Connor are thinking."

Jesus, who else had seen? "They didn't try very hard to hide it."

"If they thought they were being subtle—"

Seth scoffed. "You're assuming they were thinking at all."

Hudson flashed a half smile that quickly faded. "Um… Do you think sharing women is hereditary or something? I mean, there's you and the twins…and I didn't hate the night with Casen and Brielle."

His son's keen awareness gave Seth pause. Not much got past the kid.

He glanced around to make sure no one was in earshot. "It's a fair question given…everything, but I don't think there's a 'prefers ménage' gene, son. When I was your age, sharing a woman never even occurred to me. I was much older before I tried, but you have both experiences. You'll need to think that through, preferably when you're older."

"Too late. I'm already thinking. It's cool that Jack and Connor want to be…happy like you, Beck, and Heavenly."

Seth scoffed. "If that's what they were doing, I might support them. But there's a big damn difference between the twins looking to get laid and my relationship with Beck and Heavenly."

"So you're saying their 'emotions' don't reach above their waist?" Hudson snickered.

"Clearly. But sex is way better when you care about the person—"

"Or people." Hudson raised a brow.

Seth hated to concede this point to a sixteen-year-old, but he couldn't be a hypocrite. "Yeah."

"Did you…ever care about my mom?"

Of course the kid wanted to know, and Seth was surprised he hadn't asked sooner. Seth had grown up, knowing his parents had been mad about each other. Poor Hudson must have wondered for most of his life if everyone considered him a mistake.

"At the time, I had a huge crush on your mom. I really wanted her to like me, and I was more than a little heartbroken when she abruptly quit her job and I didn't hear from her again. Now I know why, but…"

Hudson nodded. "She'd talk about you sometimes, you know. Not your name or anything, but every so often when I bugged the shit out of her, she'd say you were tall and handsome and funny. That I looked just like you. Then she'd clam up. But…I think she had feelings at the time, too."

"Water under the bridge now. I'm just sorry you and I lost so many years. If I'd had any idea—"

"I know." Hudson smiled at him. "It would have been cool, but… yeah."

"Don't blame your mother. She was young and scared."

"I know. I can't imagine… If someone told me I'd have a baby in the next year or two, I'd flip out."

He clapped his son on the shoulder. "Exactly. She did the best she could. That's all any of us can do."

Hudson nodded.

After yesterday's crushing reminder of Tristan's loss, he was so fucking grateful that he had this moment with Hudson. That their bond seemed to grow more each day. And maybe it was all the turmoil, the change, the future coming at him fast, but he found himself blinking back tears.

"I'm glad you're here now." Seth clapped him on the back as they strode to the parking lot.

"Me, too. Even if this family is a little crazy."

Seth laughed. "They are, but they mean well. And Grandma loves you already."

The kid's smile widened. "I know. She's actually pretty cool."

"She is. And speaking of moms, yours is meeting us in the morning, before the wedding. At ten."

"Yeah, I know. At that diner off the turnpike. She's bringing Ted and the baby."

Completing the official paperwork naming him Hudson's father would give him some assurance and rights. Then, after an upcoming court appearance and a couple of minutes with a notary…Hudson would be his son legally. "I'm really glad you came to find me. And you chose to stay with me. Honestly."

Hudson kicked at a rock, like the emotion was a bit too heavy to face head-on. "Me, too."

The others joined them outside, organizing rides to the country club for the rehearsal dinner. Mom still glowed as she talked animatedly with Carl. Beck and Heavenly stood with Seth's brothers, maintaining careful distance—practiced, deliberate, and completely unnatural for people who loved each other as much as they did.

Seth watched them, the weight of this pressure-cooker situation pressing in on him.

A couple more days and nights. His mother deserved a wedding day full of joy, without his romantic drama overshadowing it.

But after that? He wasn't wasting another damn moment pretending to be something he wasn't.

Even if he hadn't pinpointed when or how to tell his mother, he looked forward to stopping this awful pretense. His announcement might turn everything nuclear, but whatever happened, he would face it with Beck and Heavenly—strong, united, and together.

Beck sighed as he stepped out of the car and into the cool October evening. He was so fucking ready for this weekend to be over.

He couldn't bash tonight's rehearsal dinner at Carl's country club. The food had been good, the wine decent. Everyone had been polite, pleasant even. But the whole time, Beck had felt eyes on him. The glances had lingered a beat too long, constant silent questions that grated on his nerves. *Who is this guy? Why is he here?*

He'd kept his answers vague when anyone asked. Smiled. Made small talk. Played the part of Seth's friend from LA who just happened to be here on business.

Lies. All lies.

The whole thing had left him on edge, second-guessing every word, every gesture. Had he stood too close to Heavenly at any point tonight? Had his gaze lingered on her a fraction too long? Did the fact that he was desperate to touch her show on his face? In his eyes?

The constant vigilance was exhausting.

And don't even get him started on Seth's weird mood.

Thirty-six more hours. He could handle thirty-six more hours before he and Heavenly flew Hudson back to LA. Then he could take a breath. Then he could touch Heavenly without blowing up Seth's world.

As Beck followed Carl and Seth, who held Heavenly's hand, to the front door, she turned. Their eyes caught before her stare slid away quickly. Still, Beck saw the strain on her face. She held herself a little too carefully.

Yeah, she was tired of pretending, too.

Grace bustled past him, Hudson in tow, and unlocked the door. Warmth spilled out onto the traditional portico, already decorated for fall. Inside, the family room glowed with soft lamplight.

In the foyer, Heavenly shrugged out of her coat, and Beck clenched his fists. Under normal circumstances, he'd help her. Slide the fabric off her shoulders, let his lips brush her nape, maybe lean in to whisper something inappropriate.

But Grace was right there, hanging her own coat in the closet, chattering about whether she'd remembered to pack the emergency sewing kit. So Beck just stood back, keeping a careful two feet of distance between himself and the woman he loved. And hated every second of it.

Carl stepped up beside Grace, resting a hand on the small of her back. "Sweetheart, you've checked that list three times today. I promise you, it's in the trunk."

"I know, I know." Grace laughed with breathless excitement. "I just keep thinking I've forgotten something."

"You haven't," Carl assured in the kind of low, steady voice that could talk someone down from a ledge. "Come sit before you fall down."

They moved into the family room. Seth guided Heavenly to the sofa, settling beside her with the ease of someone who had every right to be there. Beck took the armchair across from them—as close as he dared, but far enough to appear respectful, removed.

Keeping appearances was grating on his goddamn nerves.

Grace perched on the edge of the loveseat, still buzzing. "I can't believe the wedding is tomorrow. After all the planning—"

"All *your* planning," Carl corrected, easing down beside her. "I just showed up when you told me to."

"That's not true." But she smiled, some of her manic energy softening into something warmer. "You helped."

"By nodding and agreeing with everything you said. That's helping, right?"

Seth chuckled. "Yep, and I'm sure Mom appreciates it."

"I do, and by the sounds of it you'll make a 'helpful' groom, too."

Grace laughed before she settled her gaze on Heavenly with growing affection. "You're going to be such a beautiful bride."

She would, but the fact that Beck couldn't agree without raising brows made him grit his teeth. He was going to be her groom, too. He wanted to shout that from the rooftops.

He couldn't even whisper it.

Heavenly's smile settled somewhere between genuine and awkward. "Thank you. But tomorrow is *your* day, and everything you've planned is gorgeous."

Grace waved her way, but her expression said she was flattered. "I just hope it all comes together."

"It will," Carl insisted. "If we've forgotten something, we'll tackle it tomorrow. Tonight, you relax, enjoy the company—and your last night of being a single woman."

Grace laughed again. "I can't help it. I'm excited. And nervous."

"We know." Seth's voice was warm, affectionate. "But you got this. You always do."

"I did my best." Grace said, then turned her attention to Beck with that same open, welcoming expression she'd worn all weekend. "I know you're recently divorced, Beck. Romance may not be on your radar, but I hope you find someone someday who makes you as happy as Carl makes me."

"Thank you. I'm sure I will." Beck tried to keep the sarcasm from his voice.

Hudson, currently sprawled in the remaining chair, phone in hand and thumbs flying, glanced up and caught Beck's eye. He flashed an ironic grin—there and gone—before resuming whatever he was engrossed in.

Thank god no one had seen that and the kid kept his mouth shut.

The conversation drifted after that—Seth's childhood, the brothers' antics, high school pranks. Beck mostly listened. Watched. Laughed where appropriate. This wasn't his family. Not yet. Maybe not ever, depending on how Grace reacted when Seth finally told her the truth.

Half an hour later, Carl stood and held out his hand to Grace. "Time for bed, sweetheart. Big day tomorrow."

Grace hesitated, then took his hand, letting him pull her to her feet. "You're right. I should sleep. Don't want to look tired for our pictures."

Seth stood as well. "Sleep good. We'll see you in the morning."

"Bright and early," Grace agreed, smiling. "Good night, everyone."

They exchanged goodnights, hugs, the kind of easy affection that came with family. Beck nodded politely, hanging back, before Grace and Carl headed upstairs.

Seth glanced at Hudson. "Time for bed."

"Yeah?" Hudson pocketed his phone, then offered a wry smile. "And what about you?"

"None of your fucking business. Now go to your room."

Hudson dropped his voice. "Yeah, yeah. But a little advice: don't let her scream like she does at home. She'll wake the whole damn house."

Heavenly's cheeks turned bright red. Beck stifled a laugh as Seth *whapped* the kid upside the head, ruffling his hair. "Thanks for the safety tip. When we get home, I'll get you some earplugs. Now off to bed."

With a one-fingered wave, Hudson darted upstairs and disappeared into his room.

After Seth killed the lights in the family room and ensured the house was secure, Beck followed him and Heavenly up. At the top, they crowded together in the hall. The house was quiet now, just the faint creak of floorboards down the hall as Carl and Grace got ready for bed.

A long pause fell between them. Beck looked at Heavenly. Then at Seth. His chest tightened.

He ached to reach for her. Pull her close. Feel her warmth against him. At least fucking kiss her goodnight.

But he couldn't. Not here. Not now.

"Well…good night," he murmured, his eyes saying everything he couldn't. *I hate this. I miss you. I want you.*

Heavenly squeezed his hand for just a second, her fingers warm and reassuring, before she reluctantly released it. Then she mouthed a silent *Soon.*

Seth nodded, his gaze steady, promising. *Last time. Never again.*

Beck held onto that promise as he turned and ducked into his room across the hall. He closed the goddamn door, the silence pressing thick and stifling around him, and sighed.

Keeping his friendly good-doctor mask on all day had been exhausting. But he'd played his role—Seth's buddy who'd tagged along for the eventful weekend. And he'd played it well. But now that he was alone, he let everything drop.

God, he was fucking exhausted.

He pulled off his tie, tossed it onto the chair by the window, and started on the buttons of his shirt. His fingers moved automatically, but his mind drifted back to their trek to the house where Seth lived with his first family.

He'd known the facts about Seth's loss—wife and infant son murdered. Horrific. Tragic. The kind of thing that destroyed people. Beck had felt sadness, empathy even. He thought he'd understood—until he'd seen Seth moving through the house, face so tightly locked down as he'd stared at the remnants of his past... That had driven home the devastation in a way nothing else—especially facts—could express.

In that instant, Beck had finally understood. Time wasn't the sole barometer of grief. Sure, their deaths had been nearly nine years ago. To him, that had sounded like a long time to mourn. But he'd seen Seth's face yesterday and suddenly understood the horror and guilt his friend still carried. Maybe he always would. And honestly, Beck couldn't blame him.

In fact, he worried his friend wasn't half as healed as he'd claimed.

Another problem for another day.

Feeling restless and cooped up, Beck paced to the window, then back to the bed. The room was comfortable—understated wallpaper, a quilt that looked handmade, the kind of guest room that said *you're welcome here* without being overly fussy. But it felt too quiet. Too peaceful for his unsettled mood.

Still, he had nowhere to go and nothing to do, so he climbed into bed with a curse and tried to close his eyes. They bounced open again seconds later. He stared at the ceiling fan as it turned lazy circles overhead, too wound up and too mired in how wrong all this felt.

Across the hall, Heavenly was curled up with Seth. Beck could picture them—her tucked against Seth's chest, his arm wrapped around her as they fit together like two pieces of a puzzle. He wasn't jealous. Seth loved her, and Beck didn't begrudge him a damn thing. But he should fucking be there, too. That bed wasn't complete without all three of them. Hell, Heavenly slept better when she was between them. For that matter, so did he.

He was tempted to throw caution to the wind and sneak into their room. If he was quiet, he'd get away with it. Grace and Carl were at the other far end of the hall. As long as he and Seth didn't make Heavenly scream, no one would hear…probably.

But *probably* wasn't good enough. Not the night before Grace's wedding. Not when one wrong move could blow all their carefully constructed facades to hell.

Hating every minute of this, Beck jerked the covers and turned over, staring out the damn window at the quaint suburban street with a huff.

The fact that he couldn't hear anything from across the hall—no murmurs, no creaking of bedsprings, no soft laughter—only made his mood more surly. They were holding back for him; he knew that. And he felt guilty as hell.

Beck tried to drift off, but sleep required stillness. His body refused to cooperate. He shifted onto his back. Then his other side. The pillow was too flat. The blanket too warm. Every position felt wrong because the bed itself was too big, too empty.

He checked his phone. Quarter 'til one.

Fuck.

He set the phone back on the nightstand and closed his eyes, forcing himself to breathe slowly. In through the nose, out through the mouth while counting back from one hundred.

It didn't work.

His mind kept circling back to the same place: Heavenly, just across the hall. So close and yet completely out of reach. He rolled over again, punched the pillow into a different shape, and glared at the ceiling.

Time dragged. He watched the rotations of the ceiling fan. Listened to the house settle around him—the creak of old wood, the hum of the refrigerator downstairs, the faint whistle of wind against the windows.

Nothing helped.

He grabbed his phone again. Quarter after one.

Damn it.

Suddenly, his phone flashed in the darkness. An incoming text. From Seth.

She can't sleep.

Beck hesitated. Was Seth asking what he thought?

Cursing, he launched himself out of bed and eased his door open. A quick scan told him the dimly lit hallway was empty. The house was silent. No light seeped under the door from Grace and Carl's room.

Still, did Seth really want to risk it?

Cooper cracked the door, wearing nothing but a pair of sweatpants. He whispered across the dark hall, "She needs you."

It would be so easy to hustle into their room and cuddle Heavenly. Hell, he ached to. But… "It's risky."

Seth hesitated, then nodded. "I know. Just for a few minutes, until she falls asleep."

He nodded sharply, pulse revving, as he darted across the hall in three strides, bare feet silent on the hardwood. Seth pulled the door open just wide enough for Beck to slip through, then closed it behind him with a soft *click* that sounded impossibly loud in the quiet house.

The second Beck stepped inside, he sought Heavenly. She sat against the headboard, knees drawn up, her hair a messy halo around her face, her soft face illuminated by the moonlight filtering through the curtains. Instantly, her stare latched onto him with an intensity that bordered on desperate.

When their gazes fused, relief and joy transformed her expression like a sunrise breaking through storm clouds. Heart kicking up, Beck crossed to her without a word, arms outstretched.

She launched herself against his chest. He kissed her forehead. He wanted to kiss more…but he held back. She needed sleep, not sex.

Still, she clung to him, looping her arms around his neck with a whimper, face tilted up to his. How the fuck was he supposed to resist that, especially after days of needing her like oxygen?

"I've missed you," she murmured against his lips.

"I've missed you, too, little girl." He captured her mouth and kissed her deeply, slowly, drinking her in like he'd die without her.

Seth sidled up behind her, hands on her hips as he dropped a kiss to her shoulder.

They were whole, complete. Beck felt like he could breathe.

Together, they fell to the bed in a heap. He and Seth folded Heavenly between them like she was something precious. Because she was.

Three adults in a queen-size bed felt somewhere between ridiculous and impossible. It was a bit like cramming into a clown car—and he didn't care. They made it work.

They always made it work.

Beck pressed his lips to hers again in a slow, tender kiss that had nothing to do with sex and everything to do with need.

Heavenly exhaled. "I'm sorry. I couldn't be without you anymore."

"I couldn't sleep either," Beck murmured against her mouth. "Close your eyes."

"We've got you, angel," Seth promised, his hand sliding over her hip to rest on Beck's arm, anchoring them all together.

Gradually, they shifted until Seth ended up on his back with Heavenly tucked against his side, her head on his chest. Beck pressed against her back, one arm draped over both of them, his face buried in her hair.

It was cramped. The mattress wasn't wide enough, and Beck didn't dare move or he'd probably fall off the bed, ass first. But none of that mattered. *This* was what he'd been missing. The warmth of her body against his. The steady rhythm of Seth's breathing. The way Heavenly's hand found his and held on tight.

"Better?" Seth whispered.

"So much," Heavenly breathed.

"Perfect." Beck tightened his hold, feeling something in his chest unclench for the first time all night.

Seth lifted his head and stared at Beck. "Is it? Really? I feel like a sardine."

"Thank fuck you don't smell like one," Beck quipped back.

Heavenly covered her mouth to muffle her giggle. Beck pressed his face into her neck, stifling his outright chortle. And Seth pressed his lips into a thin line, as if that could keep his bark of a laugh from escaping.

They lay tangled together in the dark, in the postage-stamp bed that was uncomfortable as hell. And for the first time since they'd arrived in New York, Beck finally felt like things were right.

He and Seth stayed like that, wrapped around her, both whispering soft reassurances until her breathing evened out and her body went slack with sleep.

Beck felt the exact moment she let go—the way her grip on his hand loosened, the small sigh that escaped her lips. He pressed one more kiss to her hair, careful not to disturb her.

Seth shifted slightly, adjusting his position so Heavenly was cradled more securely between them. His eyes met Beck's over her shoulder in the dim light.

For a while, neither of them spoke. Just lay there, listening to her breathe, feeling the rise and fall of her chest.

Then Seth's voice came, barely a whisper. "I couldn't sleep either, so I've been thinking, trying to decide when and how to tell my mother. About us. About this."

Beck's entire body went still. His pulse kicked up, but he kept his breathing steady, his gaze locked on Seth's.

The air seemed to leave the room—and his body—in a rush. "And?"

"I need to look her in the eye and tell her. I respect her too much to call her from the other side of the country. You know that."

He'd said that before, and Beck had always thought it was a BS excuse…until he'd met Grace. "Yeah."

Seth's eyes held his in the darkness. "So I've decided to tell her Monday."

Beck's breath caught. Monday. Two days away. After months of pretending. After days of subterfuge under Grace's roof. The lies would be over. Hopefully the torment, too.

He wanted that more than anything for Seth. For Heavenly. For their collective future. But now that he'd met Seth's mom and saw how close this family truly was, he hesitated. "You're sure?"

"It's past time," Seth whispered. "I need to ask Carl if he's talked to

Mom since my visit last month and if she's relented any. I'll take any help I can get."

Grace softening her stance? Beck hadn't seen that. "He hasn't volunteered anything?"

Seth shook his head. "I haven't been able to get him alone for even a moment. But tomorrow, I'm hoping to get a few private moments with him before the ceremony. Once I've gotten the scoop, I'll pull my brothers aside one by one, get their read on things. I need to know if I can count on their support when the shit hits the fan."

When, not *if*. Clearly, Seth was under no illusions about how this would go.

"You said they didn't seem shocked by the idea when you talked to them last month." That gave Beck *some* hope Seth would have allies.

"They weren't. I think they'll be on our side. Then…I'll start looking for the best way to approach Mom." Seth's jaw tightened. "I have to do it gently."

Beck's chest constricted. He'd waited months for Seth to commit to telling his family the truth. Now that the moment was here, the magnitude of what the big guy was undertaking hit him hard.

"Not to be an asshole, but what gentle way is there to say, 'Hey, Mom, I'm in a committed threesome'?"

Seth winced. "Three seconds, and you found the flaw in my plan. There isn't a gentle way to say it. But I have to try."

"You don't have to do it alone. I can stay," Beck offered quietly. "If you want to tell your mom on Sunday before we fly out, I'll stand by your side. Help you explain. Answer her questions."

"No." Seth's answer was swift and firm. "My family. My problem."

"And it's our future. Seth—"

"You want to help, I know. I appreciate it. But—"

"A stronger, more united front might be more persuasive. If Grace *sees* how much we love Heavenly, how happy she is and how much she needs us both—"

"Mom will feel ambushed. She'll get defensive." Seth's gaze dropped to Heavenly sleeping between them, his fingers brushing a curl back from her face. "And in case Mom loses her temper and says something…cruel, I don't want Heavenly anywhere she might hear.

She would die if Mom thought less of her." His voice roughened. "I won't put our girl through that."

Beck hated it, but he couldn't disagree. Protecting Heavenly came first.

"Besides, I have to consider Hudson," Seth added. "If this turns ugly, I don't want him overhearing that. He's been through enough upheaval. Better to get him on a plane, back to his routine, before I detonate my mother's world."

Not to mention your own.

But the quiet conviction in Seth's voice was unshakable. He'd decided, thought it through from every angle. By every standard Beck could see, Seth was prepared to face the consequences.

"All right. But if you change your mind—"

"I won't." Seth's expression showed nothing but steely determination. "Thanks, but my mind's made up."

But Beck also saw the flicker of fear Seth was trying so hard to hide. This was going to cost him. Maybe everything. And he felt a little guilty that he'd pushed to make this happen on his timetable, not Seth's.

They fell silent then, the weight of the coming storm settled over him like a heavy blanket—and it wasn't even his mother.

He tightened his hold on Heavenly. Whatever happened Monday, Beck vowed to stand beside him and pick up the radioactive pieces if Grace Cooper's reaction turned nuclear.

A handful of minutes passed in contemplative silence. He pressed close to Heavenly's warmth and breathed her in.

Beck knew he should go, slip back across the hall while the house was silent and everyone still slept. Every minute he stayed increased the risk of someone waking up—Grace padding down the hall early with pre-wedding excitement or Carl fetching a glass of water.

But Beck couldn't make himself move just yet.

Heavenly slept against him, her breathing deep and even. Leaving meant crawling back into that cold, empty guest bed, lying there alone, staring at the ceiling for hours, and counting down until he could see her again. Not that he could touch her.

Beck jackknifed up. "I should go."

Seth shook his head in the darkness. "Stay. Just a little longer."

"You sure?"

"No one will be up for a few hours." Seth's hand rested on Heavenly's hip, his thumb moving in slow circles. "And if she wakes up and you're gone, she might not settle again."

The big guy had a point. Guilty relief flooded Beck's chest. "True. I'll stay for a few minutes."

He settled deeper into the mattress, careful not to jostle Heavenly.

But a few minutes stretched to ten. Then fifteen.

Her sleep-soft body against his, the steady rhythm of Seth's breathing, the quiet darkness wrapping around them like a cocoon—it all felt like home. It conspired to pull him under.

His eyes grew heavy. He'd just rest them for a moment...

Beck's last conscious thought was that he needed to get up. Cross the hall. Get back to his own bed.

His body had other ideas.

Beck didn't know how much time had passed when he jolted awake. He was still tangled up with Heavenly, her back pressed against his chest, his arm draped over her waist. He opened his eyes and scanned the dark room. Seth lay against her, his breathing deep and steady.

Beck's heart hammered against his ribs. Shit. What fucking time was it?

His gaze snapped to the clock on the nightstand. 5:07 a.m.

Son of a bitch.

He hadn't meant to fall asleep. He meant to slip back to his room hours ago, not spend the entire night in Seth's bed like some kind of idiot courting an avoidable disaster.

Wincing, he pressed a kiss to Heavenly's forehead—soft, lingering, trying to memorize the feel of her skin against his lips. Then he started extracting himself from her warmth.

On the far side of the bed, Seth stirred and opened his eyes.

"Sorry," Beck mouthed. "I'll go."

"Tonight," Seth whispered. "Mom and Carl will be gone."

Beck grinned. "Then we'll have our little girl all to ourselves."

Seth's mouth curled up. "Exactly."

Looking forward to that, Beck eased out of bed, his insistent cock pressing against his sweatpants. Hours wrapped around Heavenly without being able to do a damn thing about it had left him aching and frustrated.

He wasn't angry at Seth. He understood why it was necessary now. He was beyond ready to stop sleeping in separate rooms like they had something to be ashamed of.

Tiptoeing across the floor, Beck reached the door. He raked a hand through his mussed hair, trying to look less like a man who'd just spent the night in someone else's bed. Then, hand on the knob, he took a breath and listened.

Nothing. The house was still. Silent.

Relief washed over him. They'd managed to spend the night together without getting caught.

Slowly, he turned the knob and eased the door open just enough to slip through, then stepped into the hallway.

Off to his left, he heard a soft *click* and whipped his head around.

At the end of the hall, Carl stood, wearing pajama pants and a T-shirt, his salt-and-pepper hair slightly mussed, as the door closed behind him.

Chapter Twenty Two

Their stares met. Beck's entire body went rigid. Dread slammed into Beck's chest like a freight train.

He'd fucked this up. Seth had specifically asked for one thing: no drama on his mother's wedding day. And here Beck was, about to deliver it in spades before the sun had even risen.

Carl approached on silent feet, his brow lifted. "Everything okay?"

Beck scrambled for a reply, something logical. Anything believable that would explain why he was standing in the hallway outside Seth and Heavenly's door at five in the morning, looking like he'd just rolled out of their bed.

Heavenly had a headache. I was checking on her.

No. Why would he look sleep mussed if he'd been seeing to her medical needs? Besides, Seth could have found her a fucking aspirin.

Seth was sick. He needed a doctor.

Nope. The minute he rolled out in his tux to walk his mom down the aisle, Carl would see right through that BS.

I couldn't sleep. Went for a walk. Got turned around in the house.

Even worse. The house was hardly a maze.

They were busted. Completely, utterly busted.

Fuck.

Seth appeared in the doorway of his bedroom—wearing only sweatpants— and saved Beck from gaping like a fish on shore. His gaze swept to Carl and back to Beck. Understanding flashed across his face.

Seth moved to stand beside Beck, shoulder-to-shoulder, his gaze locking on Carl's. "This isn't how I wanted to do this, but…we should talk. About me and Heavenly. And...Beck."

Beck's heart stopped.

Holy shit. Seth was doing this *now,* the morning of the wedding? Before anyone had even had coffee?

What terrible fucking timing. If Carl lost it, raised his voice, woke

Grace—this would blow up in Seth's face and destroy everything. The wedding. Grace's happiness. The fragile lie they'd been so carefully trying to preserve.

Beck had no one to blame but himself. If he'd left when he was supposed to and hadn't fallen asleep, none of this would be happening. Guilt twisted in his gut.

Yes, he wanted the truth out in the open, but not like this. Not on Grace's wedding day. Not in a hallway at barely five in the morning with disaster looming.

Beck braced for Carl's face to flash red with fury. For his booming voice to rise and wake the entire house. For the inevitable destruction of peace.

Seth didn't flinch. His jaw was set, his shoulders squared. He looked determined to plow ahead no matter what happened next. Beck stood beside him in solidarity and hoped to hell this wasn't about to become a complete shit show.

"I'm listening," Carl said finally. "Something you want to tell me?"

Seth kept his voice barely above a whisper. "Beck and I are friends…who are both in love with Heavenly. We're partners in her care."

Carl's brow crept higher. "Meaning?"

Seth's jaw clenched. "Meaning we…share her. Beck and I aren't romantically involved with each other. We just happen to love the same woman and realized we're all happier together."

Beck's heart hammered against his ribs as Carl listened, arms folded. His gaze moved between them, studying their faces. His expression was terrifyingly impossible to read. Silence stretched on, every second seeming to last an eternity.

Suddenly, Carl's mouth curved into a soft smirk. "Tell me something I didn't figure out days ago."

Beck's breath caught. He and Seth exchanged a startled glance. *What the fuck?*

He'd been so careful. Maintained his distance. Played the role of Seth's friend perfectly. Heavenly had done the same—barely a word between them beyond a few stolen whispers about how hard the façade had been to maintain.

Despite all that, Carl had seen straight through them.

"What gave us away?" Beck asked, his voice rough.

Carl's expression turned knowing. "The way you and Heavenly looked at each other when you thought no one was watching. And Seth..." He glanced at his soon-to-be stepson. "That speech you gave your mother at Batter Up? You were too invested to just be talking about the twins. You sounded like you spoke from experience."

Carl didn't yell. He didn't judge. He just quietly accepted them.

Cautious relief spread through Beck. Another glance at Seth said he felt the same.

"Does Mom suspect?" he finally asked.

Carl shook his head. "That woman has been so busy with wedding planning that Bigfoot could stroll through her living room and she wouldn't notice." His tone turned serious. "But after this weekend, if you don't get honest with her…she will."

The message was clear. They were on the clock.

"Duly noted," Seth said carefully. "I won't apologize."

Carl nodded. "You shouldn't. Your love life is none of my business. If Heavenly and Beck make you happy, as far as I'm concerned, that's all that matters."

But his opinion wasn't the one that mattered. Grace's was. At least Carl wasn't going to be a roadblock.

"If you knew," Beck said slowly, "why didn't you say something?"

"Didn't want to start drama before the wedding," Carl replied easily.

"Same reason we didn't," Seth offered. "She deserves to focus on her own wedding without worrying about us. I had Beck come because I wanted Mom to meet him before I sprang the truth on her. It would have been worse trying to convince her to accept a stranger."

"You're right. So…which of you two is engaged to Heavenly? Or was that a lie for your mother's benefit?"

"No," Beck put in so Seth wouldn't feel so put on the spot. "We're both engaged to her, and we're looking for ways to cement our bond—legally, spiritually. Whatever we can manage."

"Exactly." Seth nodded. "Obviously, we'll never be married in the Church, and I know that will be tough for Mom to take. But that's our reality, and I'm okay with it." His voice was steady, resolute. "I've done the big church wedding once. I don't need that again because I know in my heart that what we have is real. Mom is going to have to be okay with that. One of us will marry Heavenly legally, but we haven't decided who yet."

Carl looked thoughtful. "Sounds like you three have thought this through."

"Carefully," Seth assured. "And…we're trying to have a baby."

Carl's eyes widened with surprise. "You ready for that?"

Seth's jaw tightened, but his gaze didn't waver. "It's been a struggle at times. I won't lie. But I'm determined to embrace the future. This is the way forward." He paused. "I hope my mom and my brothers can accept that—and the children we plan to have."

Beck stood silent beside him, relieved to hear Seth laying his feelings bare without bullshit or reservation.

Seth outlined the rest of his plan—talking to his brothers during the reception, then sitting down with Grace on Monday.

"Have you had a chance to talk to her since my visit last month? Has she softened any after the twins' situation?"

Carl hesitated. "Some, just enough for me to realize the wedding has consumed most of her waking thoughts. She's barely thinking about Jack and Connor now. But once the distraction is over, she'll start thinking about them again."

Seth nodded like that was a fact. "Thank you for trying."

"Sorry I couldn't do more, but you know when that woman gets focused…"

"She's singularly fixated, yes." A smile tugged at Seth's lips.

"Once you tell her, she'll need time. But she'll come around." Carl clapped Seth's shoulder, a tinge of a smile curling his lips. "Even Grace Cooper—soon-to-be-Mahoney—won't be able to deny you're building a life based on love—especially when the babies come. Your mother has been dying for more grandchildren."

Seth smiled. "Yep. She hasn't been shy about that."

"Not even a little. So if she's not okay with this threesome right now…well, a bundle of joy just might solve everything."

Beck had to grin. "Trust me. We're working on that. Judiciously."

Carl winked. "I'm sure you are."

Beck turned to Seth, and they fist-bumped. Relief was all over the big PI's face.

Grace's acceptance wasn't guaranteed, but having Carl on their side... That was more than they'd had ten minutes ago.

"Thanks for listening," Seth said solemnly. "And not judging."

"Anytime. And if you're going to...make more inroads toward that baby this morning, keep it down, huh? I'm getting married to a beautiful woman today."

Then Carl started down the stairs, heading for the coffeemaker. As soon as he disappeared around the corner, Beck let out a pent-up breath. Beside him, Seth did the same.

"Holy shit," Beck muttered. "That...went better than expected. At least you'll have an ally." Since Seth intended to face Grace without him or Heavenly by his side.

He understood the woman, but her beliefs couldn't be the reason Seth became estranged from his family. He hoped like fuck she loved her son more than she hated the life he'd chosen.

"Thank fuck." Seth slumped against the wall.

Behind Seth, Heavenly cracked the door to Seth's room wrapped in a towel, water droplets beaded on her shoulders. Her gaze darted between them, concern creasing her brow. "What's going on? I heard voices."

Seth crossed to her and cupped her face, his voice quiet and steady. "Carl knows. About us."

She gasped. "Oh, no. How did he find out?"

Beck winced. "He caught me leaving your room. But...he's okay with it. In fact, I think everything is going to be all right."

And for the first time since they'd arrived in New York, he actually believed that might be possible. At least he hoped so. Carl was in their corner. But after Seth confessed all, would that be enough?

Seth sat alone in Grace's kitchen, cradling a cup of coffee between his hands. Upstairs, he could hear the house coming to life—water running through the pipes, footsteps creaking across floorboards. But for now, he had a few minutes of quiet.

He needed them.

His early morning conversation with Carl had gone better than expected. Hell, better than he'd dared hope. Carl was in their corner, and that was huge. Now he just had to get through today—talk to his brothers during the reception, feel them out, and pray they were as open-minded as he hoped they'd be.

But first, he had another potentially awkward situation to navigate.

In a couple of hours, he'd be meeting Hudson's mother at a diner off I-95. They'd go over the custody arrangement one last time, sign the papers, then head to a nearby bank to get everything notarized. His attorney in California had worked with Laura's in Connecticut to hammer out the details. Primary custody to Seth, generous visitation for Laura—two weeks in the summer, every other Christmas, and at least part of every spring break. Hudson had agreed, and both he and Laura thought this arrangement was for the best.

Barring any unforeseen difficulties, he'd officially be Hudson's father by noon. Meeting Laura on his mother's wedding day wasn't ideal timing. He'd be racing to get back in time, but it was the only day that had worked for everyone's schedules.

With one potential snag: he was bringing Beck and Heavenly with him.

Seth refused to be less than honest with Laura. He was done pretending. Done acting like he was ashamed of the people he intended to spend his life with. Laura deserved to know who would be part of Hudson's life, helping him raise the kid, going forward. If Laura had a problem, they'd deal with it. But he wasn't going into this arrangement with secrets hanging over his head.

Besides, withholding the truth had landed them here. He hadn't been honest about his age that summer. She'd never told him she was pregnant. So now had to be different.

Seth took another sip of coffee, letting its warmth settle in his chest.

Beck entered the kitchen and made a beeline for the coffeemaker, pouring himself a generous cup before dropping into the chair across from Seth.

He took a long sip, then exhaled with satisfaction. "How you feeling?"

"Better now that I'm caffeinating." Seth lifted his mug in salute. "It's going to be a long day." He leaned closer, dropping his voice to a whisper. "And hopefully a long night alone with Heavenly."

Beck smirked. "Amen."

They sat in comfortable silence, the kitchen warming as morning light filtered through the windows. Somewhere upstairs, a door closed. The pipes groaned as someone turned on a shower. A hairdryer hummed.

"So...you ready to see Laura this morning?" Beck studied him over the rim of his mug.

Seth shrugged, rolling his shoulders to ease the tension knotting there. "As ready as I'll ever be. I hope she won't change her mind about shared custody once I tell her about the three of us. I've really gotten attached to Hudson."

Beck smiled. "I've gotten attached to the little shit, too."

That made Seth laugh. "I know. I've seen it. He's a teenager, so it's a given he's going to test his limits, but with affection and boundaries, he's coming around."

"Not as much pushback. And definitely a lot less snark," Beck agreed, lowering his cup. "He can be a handful, but he's got a good heart. It really shows when he's not trying to act all tough. Especially around your mom."

Seth nodded. "Exactly. She already loves him unconditionally. He needs more of that."

"Yep." Beck peered at him with curiosity. "It's been…what, seventeen years since you saw Laura?"

"It has. We've talked on the phone a few times since Hudson moved in with us, but I haven't actually seen her since I was fifteen." Seth grimaced. "So I'm expecting this reunion to be awkward as hell."

Beck tilted his head. "Were you serious about her back then?"

"I thought I was. Hell, I thought I was in love." Seth gave a self-deprecating laugh. "But I was fifteen. I didn't know what the fuck love was. And now that I do? I realize it was just a crush."

Beck's lips curved into a sly grin. "So teenage Seth was clueless? Shocking."

"And you weren't?" Seth's mouth twitched despite himself. "At fifteen, you were still masturbating in the shower. You had no idea what a naked girl even looked like."

"Bite my ass. Besides, I learned fast, thanks to Gloria."

Together they laughed, but the levity faded. Seth's expression turned serious. "All joking aside, I hate that I lost all those years with Hudson."

"C'mon. What kind of father would you have been at fifteen?"

Seth shrugged, conceding the point. "Shitty. I couldn't have been the father he needed as a teenager. I was just a kid myself. I would have tried, but..."

"Probably why Laura left. What about later, after you were grown and married?"

"Honestly? I'm not sure I would have been much better. Hudson would've created a mountain of friction between me and Autumn. She wouldn't have handled Laura's presence in my life well."

Beck leaned forward slightly. "Because she would have been jealous? You hadn't touched Laura in years."

"That wouldn't have mattered," Seth said without hesitation. "Autumn never felt comfortable around my family. Mom didn't like her much, so adding an ex and a kid into the mix?" He shook his head. "That would've been a disaster."

"Grace seems to like most everyone. What did she have against Autumn?"

"She thought Autumn was too needy, too clingy. Lacked independence. That was true, but..."

"Even then your inner Dom wanted to care for and protect her."

"Exactly. And anything that took my focus from Autumn scared her. She hated my job, so she would have viewed Laura as a threat and Hudson as competition for my attention." Seth shrugged. "After she and Tristan died...I wouldn't have been capable of even being present for Hudson, much less giving him what he needed. To find Silas, I went dark. Worked for Nikolai. I disappeared for almost a year. Hudson would've been…eight? Nine? Too young to understand why his dad abandoned him. So even though Hudson's childhood was rough and I hate that he was damn near grown before we met…it was probably for the best."

Beck studied him, clearly turning that over in his head. "Things happen for a reason."

Seth met his eyes and nodded slowly. "Even when those reasons suck."

The sound of footsteps on the stairs drew their attention. Then Heavenly appeared in the doorway, flashing them both a warm smile as she headed for the coffeemaker. "Morning."

Hudson trailed behind her, dressed and ready but still half-awake as he poured a glass of orange juice. "Hey."

"Morning, you two," Seth greeted.

Beck grinned. "Everyone sleep okay?"

Heavenly shot him a reproving glance that went straight over Hudson's head. "Kinda. Hard to sleep, you know?"

Seth looked at his son, chest swelling with pride. "This morning is a big deal for us, buddy."

"Yeah." Hudson shrugged like he was playing it cool, but there was a flicker of excitement in his eyes. "And it'll be good to see Mom, too."

"I'm sure she's looking forward to it," Seth replied.

Carl and his mom swept into the kitchen next. She was already dressed, her energy buzzing as she made a beeline for the coffee pot and poured herself a cup. "Good morning, everyone."

"Morning," Seth said, leading the chorus that Beck, Heavenly, and Hudson joined.

Carl tipped his head and saluted him with a nod and a knowing grin.

"Ready to be a bride today?" Seth asked. His mom's excitement was endearing.

"As I'll ever be."

"You are, and you haven't forgotten anything." Carl kissed her softly.

She sent her groom a sheepish smile. "You're right." Then she turned to Seth. "So you'll be back from meeting Laura by two?"

"Should be," Seth assured her. "Still plenty of time."

"The wedding is at five, and there's still so much to do."

"Like what?"

"Hair and makeup starts at three. And I still need to pack our bag for the honeymoon suite tonight, plus—"

"Grace." Carl cupped her shoulder, his tone warm but firm. "We'll get it all done. Everything is going to be fine."

She exhaled, visibly steadying herself. "You're right. Of course you're right." She looked back at Seth. "Call if you're going to be late, okay?"

"We'll be there way before five," Beck said easily. "I'll make sure."

His mom smiled, then squeezed his shoulder. "Thank you. When Seth was a teenager, I didn't think he could tell time, since he almost always stayed out past his curfew."

"That was on purpose, Mom," Seth quipped.

Everyone laughed.

"I'll take your tux to the church," Carl offered. "One less thing to worry about."

"Perfect," Seth said. "I appreciate it."

Mom crossed the room to Hudson, who leaned against the kitchen counter. She set down her coffee, expression softening as she wrapped him in a tight hug. "It's not just my big day, but yours, too, sweetheart. I'm so excited! Next time I see you, you'll officially be a Cooper."

Despite being sixteen, Hudson towered over her as he returned the hug, gently patting her back without a trace of teenage snark. "I'm excited, too, Grandma."

Seth pinged with pride as he watched their exchange. By his side, Heavenly looked a bit wistful.

Moments later, his mom released Hudson, her eyes glassy as she cupped his cheek. "We'll have a special toast just for you tonight at the reception."

"Really?" The teen grinned.

"Yep. Grab your coat and shoes. We need to leave soon."

"On it," Hudson replied before he raced out the kitchen.

"He's such a good boy, Seth," his mom cooed, gaze trailing after him.

"Like father, like son." Seth winked.

"Oh, please. You were a handful at his age." She swatted his shoulder playfully before suddenly turning somber. "I know it was only because you'd taken on so many adult responsibilities."

"I'd do it all again in a heartbeat." Seth captured her hand and gave it a squeeze. "Someone had to keep my bratty brothers in line."

"You did an excellent job," she announced before bending and planting a quick kiss on the top of Seth's head. "And you turned into an amazing man."

Seth stilled. Would she still think that come Monday, once he'd spilled the truth?

"Come on, my beautiful bride-to-be. Let's go pack that suitcase for tonight." Carl slipped his arm around his mom's waist and guided her upstairs. "See you at the church."

"Goodbye." Grace blew them all air kisses.

"See you then," Heavenly promised.

Seth stood, draining the last of his coffee and setting the mug in the dishwasher. Beck and Heavenly followed suit before Heavenly moved to his side, slipping her hand into his. "Ready? Do you have the paperwork?"

"I do. We should get going." Seth tried not to let his nerves show.

What if Laura was so appalled by his life choices that she refused to sign the paperwork?

Chapter Twenty Three

Fuck, he had to stop borrowing trouble. He'd cross that bridge when he was pushed off it.

Hudson returned, shoes on as he shrugged into his coat. Everyone else grabbed theirs, too, then they piled into his mom's SUV as the morning sun climbed in the painfully blue sky.

Seth slid into the driver's seat. Beck took shotgun while Heavenly and Hudson settled into the back. Once the engine turned over, Seth headed toward the highway, excitement and trepidation warring inside him.

If everything went as planned, Hudson would legally be his son within hours. If not…

He shoved the thought down and pressed the accelerator.

The ninety-minute drive felt interminable. Beck tried to lighten the mood, and Heavenly chimed in with bright observations about the scenery, but the forced cheer only underscored the tension thrumming through the car. Hudson stared out the window, lost in his own thoughts. Seth kept his eyes forward, his mind cycling through a thousand what-ifs.

As if sensing his anxiety, Beck squeezed his shoulder. "You got this."

Seth wanted to believe that…but the final decision wasn't up to him.

By the time they pulled into the diner's parking lot, Seth's nerves were a tight knot of tension in his gut.

He pushed the door open and ushered Heavenly in before him. Beck followed like a silent sentry watching his back.

Inside, the smell of coffee and bacon greeted them. Seth scanned the small crowd. There, at the big table at the back, Laura stood, looking tense and tremulous. She tried hard to keep herself together, but the second she spotted Hudson, her face crumpled.

She rushed forward, tears spilling down her cheeks as she pulled him into a fierce hug. "Oh, Hudson… I've missed you so much. You've gotten taller in the last month."

Hudson hesitated for just a beat. Then he wrapped his arms around her. "I've missed you, too, Mom. Don't cry."

Seth's chest tightened. Clearly, this separation had been hard on Laura. And maybe harder on Hudson than he'd thought.

When they finally broke apart, Ted rose, cradling a baby girl with Laura's eyes and Ted's chin against his chest.

Then Seth shifted his gaze to Laura, and for a moment, the world seemed to tilt. His past collided with his present, beginning to form a future he was desperately trying to shape.

Laura offered him a hesitant smile, her voice soft. "Wow. You look almost the same. Just…more grown up."

Seth approached slowly, his own smile tentative. "You, too."

Her hair had darkened, her hips had rounded, but her face—those eyes—they were achingly familiar.

For a split second, he was transported back to that summer, to the restaurant where they'd worked together, huddled in the dark after closing, driven to take shelter during a nasty storm. Now, here they were, seventeen years later, deciding the fate of the son Seth hadn't known he fathered until a short month ago.

Laura closed the distance between them with an awkward little laugh and pulled him into a hug. Seth froze for a heartbeat, surprised, but then he returned it. They'd been friends before they'd been anything else, and that friendship had always been easy. This felt like an unexpected icebreaker. He hoped it was a good sign for what came next.

"Good to see you," he murmured.

"You, too." When they stepped back, Laura gestured to the man beside her. "Seth, this is my husband, Ted. And our daughter, Emma."

Ted nodded, his expression stoic as he stuck out his hand. "Good to meet you."

"Same," Seth said as they shook.

Hudson gave Ted a quick wave, then leaned toward the baby, his face softening. "Hey, little Emma girl."

She smiled. Then he made exaggerated faces at the infant that had her giggling and kicking her little feet.

Hudson's grin widened. For just a moment, the kid looked like he'd missed his baby sister. Seth hoped like hell he was doing the right thing for his son. But Hudson wanted to be with him—had hopped on a plane as a fucking minor without telling anyone to find the father he'd never met. Since then, he'd insisted in every way possible that he didn't want to go back to Connecticut.

Seth could make that happen.

If he didn't fuck up this reunion.

In the ensuing silence, Laura's gaze drifted to Heavenly and Beck, who stood near Seth. Her brow furrowed slightly, curiosity flickering across her face. She probably wasn't surprised that he'd brought his fiancée to their custody discussion. After all, from Laura's perspective, Heavenly would be helping him raise Hudson.

But she was probably very confused about why he'd brought another man to this meeting.

Seth resisted the urge to scrub a nervous hand down his face and fastened on a smile as he gestured toward his angel. "Laura, you've spoken on the phone to my fiancée, Heavenly."

She stepped forward, hand extended. "It's nice to finally meet you."

"You, too." Laura shook it, her smile polite.

But her attention strayed to Beck, the predictable question all over her face.

Seth cleared his throat, nerves jangling. "And this is Dr. Beckman. Beck to his friends."

Recognition crossed her face, and Seth saw the moment she relaxed, as if she thought she had the proper context to understand why Beck had come along. "The doctor you share a house with. Nice to meet you."

Beck nodded, his expression locked down as he shook Laura's hand, then Ted's. "Good to meet you both."

But Seth saw a muscle tick in Beck's jaw. He hated being the third wheel, and he'd been shoved into that role too much these past few days—a situation Seth needed to change.

Starting this morning.

Another silence fell. The moment stretched on, everyone standing in the middle of the diner, not quite sure what to do next while other patrons gave them curious side-eyes. Finally, Ted gestured to the big table in the corner. "Should we sit?"

"Yeah." Seth forced a smile, grateful for the redirect.

Fuck, this was awkward.

They all shuffled to the back. Laura slid into the seat next to the high chair after she strapped in a happily babbling Emma. Ted took the seat on the other side of the baby, at the foot of the table. Hudson hesitated, then sat on Laura's right. Immediately, she reached over and squeezed his hand with a strained smile, her eyes glassy.

Seth took the chair at the head of the table, gesturing Heavenly to his right. Beck flanked her, sitting directly across from Laura and the baby. As everyone focused on their menus, the tension around the table continued in a silent hum.

The waitress appeared carrying a tray of water glasses and a carafe of coffee, her cheerful greeting temporarily filling the stilted silence.

Once she was gone, Laura turned to Hudson. "Is LA still as cool as you told me when we talked last week?"

"Yeah." The teen nodded.

"That's good. Tell me more about your school."

"Mom, it's a school. But the people are okay."

"So you've made new friends?"

"A few, mostly through the football team."

"Now that you're the new wide receiver, I'll bet lots of girls are interested in you." Laura grinned.

Seth and Beck shared a knowing glance. He prayed the kid didn't say anything about his sexual exploits with Casen and Brielle.

"A few." His smirk was cocky, but he didn't stray into dangerous territory.

"Of course." Laura grinned, then sobered. "What about your grades? You still working hard?"

"Yes, Mom."

"He really is," Beck seconded. "Especially since we all hound him about his homework every night."

Hudson rolled his eyes, but nodded his mom's way. "They really do."

Heavenly smiled with affection. "We check in with him every day. Not just about his homework, but also how he's doing. If there's anything on his mind."

Laura smiled back. "Thank you."

"They care a lot, Mom," Hudson confirmed. "Everything's good, I swear. I have my own room. Plus they have an awesome pool in the backyard."

Laura studied him as she dragged in a deep breath. "It sounds like you really like it there."

"I do."

"And…you want to stay in LA?"

"Yeah. Absolutely." Hudson nodded solemnly. "I'm happy there. I have rules, structure, consequences… I don't love that part, but…they all listen to me."

Laura frowned. "I listened to you, honey. Always."

"I know. I just mean...it's different. I don't know how to explain it. I just...I feel like I belong there."

Laura pressed her hand to her mouth, tears pooling in her eyes. Clearly, she was struggling to let go, and Seth didn't know how to soothe her. If the shoe were on the other foot, he'd be upset, too.

Ted grabbed his wife's hand and squeezed. "This might be exactly what he needs, sweetheart."

Laura wiped away the tear as she sent Hudson a smile full of forced cheer. "I just want you to be happy. That's all I've ever wanted."

"I promise, Hudson's happiness and wellbeing are my top priorities. Actually, *all* of ours," Seth assured.

"Exactly. And I *am* happy, Mom," Hudson vowed. "Really, truly."

Laura absorbed his words, her chest rising and falling as she tried to hold herself together. "Well…then I won't stand in the way of you living with your father."

"Thanks," Hudson murmured. "I know this isn't easy on you."

"No," she replied with a watery scoff. "It's not. And if you ever change your mind—"

"You'll be the first to know," the teen promised.

Laura gave him a shaky nod, then looked away, as if she needed a moment to process the fact her son was no longer just hers. A thick silence settled over the table.

Heavenly darted an anxious glance at Seth, then turned to Laura and cleared her throat. "So…tell me about you. What do you and Ted do for work?"

Laura's expression said she was grateful for the reprieve as Ted plucked a plushy bunny from the diaper bag for baby Emma. "I'm a loan officer at a bank, and Ted took over his father's plumbing business a few years ago. Hudson mentioned you're in nursing school."

"I am. I'll graduate in the spring. I already have a job lined up at one of the hospitals where Beck practices."

"That's wonderful." Laura smiled before glancing at the good doctor. "Seth said you're a surgeon?"

Beck nodded. "Vascular, yes."

Laura grimaced self-consciously. "I…um, Googled you when Hudson said he was living in your house. I wasn't trying to invade your privacy, but…"

Beck smirked. "You wanted to make sure I wasn't a pervert."

Seth bit back a knowing grin. Beck *was* a pervert, though strictly with consenting adults. But Laura didn't need to know those details.

"Something like that…" She blushed. "I have to say, your accomplishments are really impressive."

Beck sent her a polite smile. "I love what I do."

"I'm sure you're very busy and it's hard for you to get away."

Laura was fishing subtly to determine why Beck was here.

"It is, but I spoke at a medical conference in the city on Thursday, so I just extended my stay to attend Grace's wedding."

"What a happy coincidence." Laura smiled, clearly still unsure why Seth had brought him along.

She'd understand soon enough.

The thought made his stomach knot.

The server returned then, notepad in hand. They all ordered quickly—bacon, eggs, pancakes, and juice. After she left, a brief lull fell over the table. Emma babbled into the sudden lull as she reached for her toes, not caring about the adult drama around her.

Seth blew out a nervous breath. Time was ticking. Before they left this table, he had to tell Laura the truth—and hope she didn't insist on taking Hudson back to Connecticut with her.

But how the hell did he broach this topic? Blurting out that he shared his fiancée with the doctor who had become his best friend would be fucking awkward. Possibilities had been circling his brain for hours, but everything just sounded…wrong.

Laura cut into the silence by clearing her throat and addressing Heavenly with a hesitant smile. "So, have you and Seth set a wedding date yet?"

His angel's smile froze. She lifted her gaze to him. Seth knew that look. She was handing him the opening Laura had inadvertently created for him to drop this flaming truth bomb.

"We're working on a date. It's, um…complicated," he finally said.

Laura's brow furrowed. "In what way?"

Here goes nothing...

"The truth is, Heavenly isn't just my fiancée. She's also Beck's. We both are going to marry her. Together. At the same time."

The table went silent. Laura blinked, her expression frozen somewhere between confusion and disbelief. Ted's hand stilled on Emma's high chair tray.

God, he was already fucking this up.

Seth groped for a better explanation, but Laura was already responding.

"I-I don't…I'm not sure I understand what you're telling me." Laura looked at Beck, then Heavenly, then back at Seth. "You're…both with her? At the same time?"

"Yes." Seth exhaled through his nerves. "We came today to be completely honest and transparent. So here's the truth: Beck and I are both in love with Heavenly. He and I aren't together…romantically. We, um—"

"At all," Beck cut in firmly.

Seth nodded. "We're just in love with the same woman, and we're planning to spend the rest of our lives with her."

Laura stared at him, her face cycling through shock and confusion.

"And you all live together." It wasn't a question. "Hudson said you did, but I thought… I assumed it was because LA is so expensive—"

"It's not about finances," Seth admitted. "It never was."

"How long has this been going on?" Laura's voice had an edge now, protective instinct kicking in.

"Since March," Seth answered. "Hudson has known since day one."

Laura reared back, her face full of shock. Then her stare skipped to their son, taking in his total lack of surprise. Her expression changed to something that said she wasn't taking this well.

Seth feared this revelation was going down like the Titanic.

Fuck, fuck, fuck.

"You told a sixteen-year-old boy that you three are sleeping together?"

"We didn't have to," Seth said wryly. "He figured it out on his own. But yes, we've been completely open with him from the start." He held her gaze. "I didn't want to keep secrets, Laura. Not from him, and not from you."

She looked stricken, her gaze dropping to the table. Seth could see her mind racing—her teenage son living with three adults in an arrangement she'd never imagined and probably didn't condone.

He waited, heart pounding, giving her space to think or ask more questions. He just hoped she wasn't already judging him—and deciding that his love life made him an unfit parent.

Hudson surprised him by jumping in. "Mom, it's no big deal. Think of it this way: most kids have two parents. In LA, I've got three. It's not weird—at least not to me. So, please…don't freak out."

Seth held his breath as he watched Laura's face, gauging her reaction.

"Not weird?" she challenged, sounding slightly incredulous.

"Yeah." Hudson nodded. "It's not like they're fucking in front of me."

Seth exploded—at the same time Laura did. "Hudson!"

Their stares met. He sent her a look that was something between a grimace and grin. After a tense moment, she grinned back.

That broke some of the tension.

"Clearly, we're both parents," Seth drawled.

"It would seem."

Laura's expression shifted. The rigid tension in her shoulders eased. Hudson hadn't conveyed his point the way Seth would have chosen...but maybe his son had known how to reach Laura in a way he couldn't.

Finally, Laura turned back to Hudson. "If it's not weird, what *is* it like?"

"Honestly? Balanced. Heavenly is kind of...the beauty to their beasts, you know? She keeps the place homey. Plus, she's a really good cook. Dad is supportive but firm. And if I screw up, Beck is a straight-up hard-ass."

Seth bit back a grin. Clearly, Hudson had been paying attention.

Laura blinked, her thoughts obviously racing. Finally, she glanced at her husband, as if seeking his input.

Ted shrugged.

The silence stretched on. Uncomfortable. Heavy. Seth's pulse kicked up again. Despite his son's assurances, she could still decide that he wasn't fit to finish raising Hudson.

"Honey..." Ted said into the silence, surprising Seth. "Hudson is almost an adult. You didn't raise him to be naïve." He glanced at the teen, then back at Laura. "This situation might not seem ideal...but he's clearly okay with it. Hell, he seems like he's thriving. If it's not hurting him, then why does it matter if Seth sleeps with the same woman Beck does?"

Laura blinked, absorbing the question. Then her gaze drifted back to Hudson, and she really looked at him, as if she was seeing someone she didn't fully recognize. "Not only have you gotten taller, but you've also matured."

Hudson ducked his head slightly, a little embarrassed but also pleased. "He's a good dad."

Seth's pride swelled. He'd barely had a month to make an impact on the kid. To hear Hudson say that out loud was both a relief and an affirmation he'd treasure.

He held his breath and watched Laura's expression shift again. Shock gave way to something softer. Acceptance?

Seth leaned forward slightly, wanting to stress his final point. "Look, I know our relationship is unconventional, but the three of us together actually benefits Hudson. Like he pointed out, he has three parental figures looking out for him, not just two. We can keep a closer eye on him. There's always an adult around." He allowed himself a wry smile. "Besides, both Beck and I were rowdy teenagers, so we know exactly what to look for—and how to nip any bullshit in the bud."

Laura's gaze flicked to Beck, who nodded once, his serious expression its own confirmation.

She closed her eyes. Seconds passed, feeling like half an eternity. Seth's heart continued hammering. *Everything* rode on whether she could accept the life he'd built.

Finally, Laura opened her eyes and exhaled slowly. "Of all the things I thought you'd say today, this wasn't what I expected."

"I'm sure that's an understatement," Seth drawled.

"And then some. But I trust my son. If Hudson is okay with it…" She blew out a breath. "Then…I guess I am, too."

Relief crashed over Seth like a wave. *Holy shit.* She'd actually said *yes.*

He knew accepting his news hadn't been easy for Laura. But she'd still trusted him enough to do it.

Maybe his mother would take the news better than he expected when he sat her down on Monday.

Laura turned to Hudson, her expression soft but serious. "But I need you to make me another promise. If you're ever not okay with this—if anything makes you uncomfortable or if you change your mind—you tell me. Immediately."

Hudson nodded without hesitation. "I will. But that's not gonna happen." His voice was steady, confident. "Once I got used to the idea, it just felt…normal."

Laura exhaled, her shoulders sagging slightly as the last of the fight drained out of her. Ted reached over and squeezed her shoulder—a quiet reminder that she wasn't losing Hudson. He was just growing up. Making his own choices. And she was supporting him.

Seth gripped Heavenly's hand under the table. She glanced at him, her eyes full of warmth and understanding. Beside her, Beck caught his gaze and sent him an affirming nod.

They'd done it. Together.

The food arrived, and Hudson immediately dug in like a typical teenage boy, eating everything that wasn't nailed down.

Beck and Heavenly kept the conversation moving, asking Ted about his plumbing business and Laura about Emma's sleep patterns. Surprisingly, Ted warmed up, jumping in to smooth the lingering tension while bouncing a happy Emma on his knee.

Seth caught Laura watching him again—studying him like she was still taking his measure. He met her gaze steadily, projecting every ounce of confidence and stability he could muster. *I've got this. I've got him.*

She seemed to believe it. Or at least, she clearly wanted to.

Laura picked at her eggs, barely eating. Seth understood. His own appetite had vanished somewhere between the relief and the dread still churning in his gut. They'd cleared one hurdle—Laura's acceptance—but more loomed on the horizon. Tonight, he'd talk to his brothers. On Monday, his mom.

That conversation was going to be a hell of a lot harder.

"Seth?" Laura's voice pulled him back to the moment. "Have you… I mean, I know it's a bit early, but have you decided where you're spending Christmas? Any chance you'll be visiting your mom? So I can see Hudson?"

He hadn't thought about the holidays yet. Seth had been afraid to. Everything depended on his mom's reaction.

He glanced at Heavenly, then Beck, brow raised.

Heavenly spoke first. "Since I don't have any family left, if you want to spend the holidays in New York, that's fine."

Beck shrugged. "If I don't see Gloria this year for the holidays, we'll survive."

God, he owed them both big.

"I'll talk to my mom and let you know," Seth assured.

She'd say yes…if she was still speaking to him.

"If you could work that out, that would be…great," Laura rushed to say. "I've never spent a Christmas without my baby and—"

"I'm not a baby, Mom," Hudson said between a bite of pancakes and his last swallow of juice.

Her face softened, and she looked like she was fighting tears. "You'll always be my baby."

Hudson grimaced, but Seth was pretty sure he was secretly pleased to know his mom still cared so much.

The waitress returned to clear their plates, and Seth handed her his credit card before anyone else could argue. "I've got it."

Ted nodded his thanks. As soon as the waitress came with the receipt, Seth signed. Then they all stood, gathering coats and bags. Emma fussed, and Hudson distracted her with a silly face as they headed for the door.

When he stepped out into the cool mid-morning air, Seth exhaled slowly. The hard part was over. The rest was mere paperwork.

And once those were signed, he'd be able to breathe.

At least until Monday.

Everyone jumped in their respective cars and headed for the bank a few blocks away. Since Laura worked for a different branch of this same bank, she'd been able to arrange a notary to meet them.

As Seth backed out of the diner's parking lot, Beck turned to him and blew out a breath. "Good job. That went better than I expected."

"Thank fuck," Seth muttered. "For a minute there, I thought she was going to change her mind."

"Nah," Hudson put in from the back seat. "Mom just needed a minute to get used to you three. She'll be fine."

Shockingly, it seemed as if the kid was right.

Once they arrived and piled out, the bank manager led them to a small conference room—private, quiet, with a polished table and enough chairs for everyone. Emma squealed, turning a few heads. The notary, already waiting, smiled at the baby girl.

Seth pulled out the final documents his lawyer had conferred with Laura's to draw up and spread them across the table. The notary looked them over, asked a few questions, then thrust them in Laura's direction.

With unsteady hands, she glanced over the documents as if she hadn't read them at least a hundred times, as Seth had. Finally, she picked up the pen. Slow. A bit hesitant.

Then she gave a shaky nod and, with tears slipping down her cheeks, signed her name on the custody agreement everywhere Seth's attorney had planted a tape flag.

Behind her, Ted stood, one hand on her shoulder in quiet support, Emma nestled in his other arm.

Seth slid into the chair beside her once she was done. Heart hammering, he dragged in a bracing breath as he took the pen and scrawled his name across every necessary line.

Once he was finished, he set the pen down, the small clatter seeming like an explosion of sound in the otherwise quiet room.

It felt monumental. Final. Because it was. Hudson was legally, officially his son.

Beck stepped forward and signed as witness, his expression calm and steady. Then the notary stamped each form with a decisive thud, the sound echoing in the small room.

They were done. Fifteen minutes and a few strokes of a pen later, and his life had changed completely. As terrified as he'd been to have another baby since Beck and Heavenly had been pushing to start a family, he couldn't imagine life without Hudson now.

Would it be like that, so seemingly natural and inevitable, if the three of them had a child?

Seth didn't have the answer, but he exhaled, the weight he'd been carrying for weeks finally lifting.

At least for now.

Heavenly squeezed his hand, her smile soft and proud. "I'm happy for you. For us."

"Thanks, angel." He kissed her temple. "Me, too."

Beck clapped him on the back, grinning. "Congratulations, man."

Seth turned to Hudson, his throat tight. Their eyes met. God, staring at the kid really was like looking back in time.

A moment passed between them, a deep sense of connection that both soothed and scared the shit out of him. But he pulled his son into a firm, almost desperate hug. "Son."

"Dad." Hudson's voice cracked, barely a whisper.

At the sound of his son's obvious emotion, Seth nearly broke. He held on a moment longer, blinking hard, then pulled back with a smile.

It was done. And now, no one could take Hudson away.

The soft murmur of voices and the faint scent of lilies filled the church. Seth stood in the vestibule with his mother, watching her fidget with her bouquet. She looked beautiful in her ivory lace dress, her hair swept up in soft curls, and the delicate veil framing her face. She was glowing, radiant in a way he hadn't seen in years.

"You look beautiful, Mom." He sent her a soft smile.

Her eyes misted immediately. "Seth… Don't make me cry before we even start down the aisle."

He reached for her hand. "I'm happy for you. After everything you've been through, raising five boys alone, you deserve nothing but joy."

She squeezed his hand, her voice trembling. "I never thought I'd get married again. I loved your father with all my heart, and after he died, I couldn't imagine ever wanting to. But I met Carl and…" She trailed off, shaking her head with a small, disbelieving laugh. "He stole my heart."

"He seems like a good man. Solid. Kind." Then Seth sent his mother a teasing stare. "But if he ever hurts you, I promise no one will ever find his body."

"Seth Michael Cooper!" She swatted his arm playfully. Then her expression turned tender. "I'm so grateful for you. You've always been my rock. Even as a boy, you stepped in to help raise your brothers. I don't say it enough, but I'm so proud of you, of the man you've become."

Seth's throat tightened. He wanted to hold onto this moment, to freeze it before he turned her world upside down on Monday. Before he shattered her image of him.

But for now, he could give her this.

"I love you, Mom."

"I love you, too."

The organ music swelled, signaling their cue. Seth offered her his arm, and she took it, fingers trembling as she steadied herself with a deep breath.

"Ready?" he whispered.

"Yes," she replied without hesitation.

Seth squeezed her hand before they stepped into the sanctuary.

The small crowd rose. As he and his mom began walking down the aisle, he felt a tiny tremor ripple through her. Her hand tightened on his arm. Her chin quivered.

"Breathe," he whispered. "You got this."

With a nod, she drew in a bracing breath and steadied herself, smile firmly in place.

Seth saw familiar faces occupying the pews, people he'd known for years. His mom's friends from church, neighbors, and Dad's former beat partner, Gene, had all come to see her tie the knot, wearing warm, nostalgic smiles.

Halfway down the aisle, Seth glanced to his left. Beck, Heavenly, and Hudson—who cleaned up nicely in his dark suit—stood. Next to his son, Connor and Jack stood beside Matt. Danny and Maggie, who held a wiggling Anna on her hip, rounded out the row.

On the groom's side, Carl's kids, Blake and Cat, were near the front. What Seth presumed were Carl's friends and co-workers smiled just behind them.

As Seth and his mom approached the front of the church, his gaze locked with Heavenly's. She watched him, her blue eyes soft and shining. For a moment, the world narrowed to just the two of them. His chest tightened with a swell of emotion so powerful it nearly staggered him.

Beside her, Beck sent him a ghost of a smile and a barely perceptible nod, silently conveying the same sentiment.

Soon, this will be us.

He wanted that—more than life itself. He wanted to stand at the altar beside Beck as Heavenly glided toward them in white. He wanted her between them as they each spoke vows from the heart. He wanted the certainty, the permanence, the forever love they'd built together.

And he wanted to make it official in every way he could.

At the front of the church, Father Heasley stood, hands folded, watching Seth and his mom approach with a calm, steady smile. At the altar, Carl waited, wearing his crisp, dark tux, gaze fixed on his bride as if she was the only person in his whole world.

When they reached Carl, he stepped forward, hand outstretched. Seth lifted his mom's hand from his arm and placed her fingers in the palm of the man who would soon vow to love, honor, and cherish her.

"Be happy, Mom," he whispered softly in her ear.

She nodded, tears spilling, as she gazed up at Carl with complete devotion and joy.

Seth stepped back and turned, then eased into the pew beside Heavenly. He leaned in, skimming a glance over each of his brothers' faces, at the love and pride etched there.

Father Heasley began the ceremony, his warm voice filling the sanctuary with familiar words about love, commitment, God's blessings, and second chances. Mom and Carl stood facing each other, hands clasped, eyes brimming with love and hope for their future.

Seth watched his mother. She'd held their family together after his father's death, shouldered responsibility without complaint. She'd been the rock everyone leaned on. Now, standing there with Carl, she looked lighter.

Because, starting today, she would no longer be alone.

They spoke vows, the quiet weight of their promises solemn but clear. His mom's voice cracked through tears, but didn't break. Carl's voice was strong and sure, his love for her unmistakable in every word.

Then they exchanged rings, looking into each other's eyes with certainty as the bands slipped into place.

When Father Heasley finally pronounced them husband and wife, the church erupted in cheers and applause as Carl pulled his new wife into a tender, lingering kiss.

As he watched them, relief and reassurance settled with a warm glow in Seth's chest.

Finally, his mom was happy. Settled. Safe.

"Ladies and gentlemen," Father Heasley announced with a broad smile, "I present to you Mr. and Mrs. Carl Mahoney."

As the newlyweds turned, the applause grew louder. Both grinning wildly, they clasped hands and began walking back down the aisle together.

With his heart overflowing, Seth grinned and clapped as the couple passed. Then he glanced at Heavenly and Beck.

Very soon. We've waited long enough.

Chapter Twenty Four

With Heavenly on his arm and Beck at his side, Seth entered the hotel's sophisticated ballroom, smile firmly in place. Hudson followed, gaze swiveling as he took in the floral centerpieces and linen-draped tables under warm amber lights. The low hum of music and conversation already filled the room, and along the back wall sat an elegant tiered cake topped with delicate sugar flowers and swirled icing. Guests grabbed drinks from the bar, seemingly all smiles as the small band set up behind a glossy wooden dance floor.

"This is beautiful," Heavenly murmured.

Seth nodded. "If there's one thing my mom is good at, it's throwing a party."

"She looks really happy," Beck commented.

"She is." Despite everything else going on in Seth's life, that fact gave him solace.

Unfortunately, in less than forty-eight hours, he was going to ruin that.

But tonight was all hers.

As they circulated around the room, they exchanged pleasantries with Grace's church friends and neighbors, who congratulated him and Heavenly on their engagement and remarked about his handsome son. Hudson all but blushed at the attention. Heavenly smiled graciously, handling it all with her signature warmth. Beck stayed quietly supportive at Seth's side.

Across the room, he spotted an old friend standing near the bar, nursing a whiskey and chatting with one of Carl's crew.

With a grin, he tugged his crew in the man's direction. "Come on. There's someone I want you to meet."

When they reached the corner, the man looked up and broke into a wide grin. "Seth!"

"Hey, Gene." Seth extended his hand.

Instead of accepting, the man pulled him in for a strong hug, clapping him on the back. "Good to see you, kid. You clean up nice."

"So do you. Damn, man. It's been a while. I'm so glad you're here."

"I wouldn't have missed it for the world," Gene assured. "Your mom is one in a million. I've done my best to watch over her through the years, like your dad would have wanted me to. I'm really happy she found love again."

"Me, too." Seth turned. "This is Gene Hammond, my dad's best friend and former partner on the force. He's been there for the Coopers through thick and thin for twenty years."

The man had even saved Seth's life when he was sixteen and hell-bent on ending it all by slamming his car into a concrete barrier at a hundred miles an hour. But Seth kept that to himself.

"And this," he went on, "is my fiancée, Heavenly."

Gene's eyes lit up as he smiled and gently took her hand. "I'm glad to finally meet you. Seth, you're a lucky man."

"Thank you," she said warmly. "It's nice to meet you. I've heard a lot about you."

"All good, I hope." Gene winked before eyeing Hudson up and down with a wide grin. "And this must be your son, Seth. If I didn't know better, I'd think I was looking at you at sixteen. There's no denying who your father is."

Hudson laughed. "I get that a lot."

"And this is my good friend, Dr. Beckman."

Gene shook Beck's hand, his grip firm. "Doctor, huh? Good man to have around."

"I try."

"You doing okay out in LA?" Gene asked Seth with the familiar assessing-cop expression he always wore.

"Great," Seth replied. "PI work is keeping me super busy."

"Good to hear." Gene nodded. "No plans to move back, I take it? It would make your mom happy but…"

"I know." Seth shook his head. "But no."

Seth considered asking him about the corruption at the precinct. But his mom's wedding wasn't the time or the place for that, and he'd sworn he was done digging into the past.

Gene's expression softened. He reached out and squeezed Seth's shoulder. "Your old man would be proud of you, kid. You know that, right?"

Seth swallowed hard. "Thanks, Gene."

They exchanged a few more pleasantries before Gene excused himself to grab another drink. Seth watched him go, feeling the familiar ache of his father's absence settle deep in his chest.

"I've smiled so much, I think my face is going to fall off. Can I grab a soda?" Hudson asked, eyeing the bar.

"Sure." Seth ruffled his hair. "Go enjoy yourself."

Moments later, the band struck up a flourish, and the room quieted as the emcee's voice boomed over the speakers. "Ladies and gentlemen, please welcome Mr. and Mrs. Carl Mahoney!"

The double doors opened, and Carl swept Mom in on his arm. The crowd erupted in applause and cheers. Happiness and love buzzed through the room as her new husband guided her to the middle of the room, his hand firmly clasped in hers.

Seth clapped along with everyone else, watching his mother bask in the moment. After sixteen years alone, she deserved every second of this.

"I'm going to run to the ladies' room," Heavenly whispered near Seth's ear. "Be right back."

Seth nodded, brushing a quick kiss against her cheek.

As she slipped away, he turned to Beck. "While she's gone, I'm going to grab the twins—before they get too shit-faced to have a coherent conversation."

Beck's brow lifted slightly, then he nodded. "Your son has glued himself to their side. Want me to keep him occupied?"

"Please. Jack and Connor are *not* the role models he needs." Seth sighed.

"No shit." Beck moved smoothly toward Hudson, who hovered near the twins at the bar, and steered him toward the cake table with some comment about checking out the dessert options.

Seth shot him a grateful look before trekking toward Jack and Connor. Both were swigging beers and scanning the room, no doubt looking for any eligible ladies under forty.

"Having fun?" Seth asked, brow raised.

"The free beer is helping mask the scent of Icy Hot and Depends. What's not to love?" Jack quipped with a sardonic smirk.

Seth glanced across the room to where Cat stood near her brother Blake, laughing at something he'd said. She looked happy, relaxed. "Thanks for not eye-fucking Cat today. I know she's one of the few girls here who might interest you."

"You mean one of the few females here who isn't old enough to be our mom," Jack drawled.

"So you're proud of our restraint?" Connor asked.

"No. I'm expressing my shock that miracles actually exist." Seth snorted.

"We're just in a giving mood. You're welcome." Jack grinned.

Connor chuckled and downed another swallow of his beer.

"Aren't you adorable?" Seth stepped closer. This was his moment. Now or never. He lowered his voice. "Look, I'm giving you a heads-up. On Monday, I'm sitting Mom down and telling her the truth. I'm telling her that Heavenly, Beck, and I are getting married."

Both twins stilled, their expressions shifting from amused to alert.

Jack recovered first, his smirk returning. "Wow. You're really doing it? That's brave. Stupid, but brave."

That's likely how the twins saw it…and they might be right.

"Yeah. But necessary."

"If you say so…" Connor didn't look convinced.

"Don't worry," Jack said, his tone dripping with mock sympathy. "You'll always be our brother, even after Mom disowns you. We'll come visit you in LA."

Seth shot him a reproving glare, but Jack had inadvertently voiced his true fear, that after he confessed, his mom would never speak to him again.

On the other hand, he couldn't build his future on half-truths and lies.

"Shut the fuck up," he muttered.

Connor shifted, his tone turning serious. "You sure about this?"

"Yeah. And just so we're clear—this is not a green light for you two to jump on some girl right under Mom's nose. Got it? This is me saying that if you're ever serious about sharing a wife someday, I'm paving the way. You're welcome."

Jack raised his beer in a mock toast. "Our hero. Probably not going to happen, but..."

"We appreciate the sentiment," Connor finished.

Seth studied them for a long moment. "You can't randomly fuck your way through life, boys."

"Says you." Jack's smirk softened slightly. "Good luck, bro. Seriously."

"You're gonna need it," Connor added, his tone more sympathetic than mocking.

Seth knew they understood precisely what was at stake, even if they weren't taking the situation seriously.

"Thanks," Seth said quietly.

"We'll be rooting for you—from a safe distance of course." Jack winked.

Seth shook his head, biting back a grin despite the weight pressing on his chest. "Asshole."

"Always," Jack said cheerfully.

Blowing out a breath, Seth made his way back to Beck and Heavenly, who stood near the dance floor. As he approached, Heavenly caught his eye, her expression silently questioning.

"How'd it go?" Beck asked quietly.

Seth rolled his eyes. "About as expected. Jack's still a smart-ass who doesn't appreciate the fact that I'm taking a risk that will help them when they finally grow the fuck up. But they're in my corner—as long as it's from a safe distance."

Beck snorted. "Sounds about right. Hopefully they'll lie low for a while."

Seth lifted his glass in a mock toast. "We can only hope."

"You pulling Matt aside next?" Heavenly asked.

"Yeah. Before dinner." Seth glanced across the room to where Matt stood with Danny, Maggie, and little Anna.

Beck nodded. "You got this. We'll hold down the fort."

Seth took a breath, steeling himself, then caught Matt's eye across the room and tilted his head toward the terrace. Matt's brow furrowed slightly, but he nodded and excused himself.

Seth's throat tightened. Out of all his brothers, he was closest to Matt. They'd been through hell together after their father died—Seth stepping up to help raise the younger boys, Matt right there beside him, shouldering the weight.

Together, they stepped outside, into the cool evening air. The terrace overlooked a small courtyard, decorated with strings of white lights that cast a soft glow. Through the windows behind them, Seth could see the reception in full swing—guests mingling, laughter rising and falling.

Matt leaned over the railing, elbows braced on the ornate metal. "What's up?"

Seth exhaled, rubbing the back of his neck. He'd rehearsed it in his head a dozen times, but now that the moment had come, the speech stuck in his throat. "I need to tell you something. About Heavenly and me. And…Beck."

"You mean the fact that you and Beck are both with her?" Matt said calmly.

Seth froze. "You knew?"

Matt's mouth quirked up into a wry smile. "C'mon. I'm a PI. Of course I figured it out. It's my job to look for clues."

"Shit. What gave us away?"

He shrugged. "Nothing overt. Just…the way you three are when you're together. You're comfortable. You speak each other's languages. You move like a unit. The chemistry between Beck and Heavenly is the same kind of chemistry you have with her. It wasn't hard to put together."

Seth stared at him. "If you knew, why didn't you say something?"

Matt shrugged again. "Figured if you wanted to talk about it, you'd bring it up."

Seth exhaled roughly, filled with something between relief and concern. "Damn."

"Who else knows?" Matt asked.

"Jack and Connor caught us together in the backyard one night last summer."

Matt's laughed. "Jesus. So when Mom asked you to talk to them last month about their lifestyle…"

"Peak irony," Seth admitted dryly. "Then, this morning…Carl caught Beck sneaking across the hall, back to his room. Surprisingly, he's okay with it, though. I'm hoping that'll make a difference when I break the news to Mom on Monday."

"You know she's going to lose her fucking mind."

"Yep," Seth said quietly. "But I can't keep lying to her. And we can't keep pretending. It's not fair to Beck."

Matt nodded slowly. "I get it. And for what it's worth, you're doing the right thing. It won't be easy, but you deserve to live your life the way you want, without hiding."

"You really feel that way? You're not weirded out or disappointed?"

Matt studied him for a long moment, his expression serious. "Seth, I don't care what your love life looks like. You're my brother, and I love you no matter what." He paused, then his mouth curved into a wry smile. "But I do want to know what kind of flowers you want on your grave."

Seth huffed out a laugh despite himself, the tension breaking slightly. "Asshole."

"I am." Matt nodded with a grin. "But I've always got your back."

"Thanks, man," Seth said, his voice rough.

Matt's support meant the world to him.

"Think Danny has any inkling?" Seth asked.

"I doubt it. If he'd figured it out, he would have said something to me."

Seth nodded, his chest loosening slightly. "True that."

"You telling him next?"

"I've got to."

Matt tensed. "Yeah. But Maggie—"

"I know. She can't find out before Mom. I've got a plan."

"Thanks for trusting me enough to come clean," Matt said. "I miss having you around, but now that I've met Beck and Heavenly…you're where you belong."

"I miss you, too, bro."

Just then, the emcee's voice rang out over the speakers. "Ladies and gentlemen, dinner is now being served. Please find your seats."

Matt straightened, gesturing toward the doors. "Guess that's our cue."

Seth nodded and glanced back through windows, watching as waiters began moving through the room with plates, before they headed back inside together.

He collected Heavenly from where she stood with Beck near the dance floor. Together, they retrieved Hudson, who had taken up with the twins again. They made their way to the family table. Heavenly sat between him and Beck—a deliberate choice, meant to unconsciously prepare others to accept them as a trio. Hudson sat on his other side, a little put out that his dad and Beck the hard-ass had hauled him away from hearing some likely inappropriate frat-party story.

Appetizers appeared. Casual expression locked in place, Seth pushed stuffed mushrooms around his plate.

Across from him, Jack and Connor wolfed theirs down, then announced that they were heading back to the bar.

"Not without me." Matt followed, leaving them alone with Danny, Maggie, and Anna.

As the server cleared his plate, Beck leaned over Heavenly and whispered, "What's wrong? Seems like everything has gone well so far."

"Yeah, but one more conversation to go." He glanced Danny's way. "And he's the wild card."

Beck frowned. "Think he'll push back?"

Seth shrugged. Danny by himself? Probably not. But he and Maggie were a package deal. Her opinions mattered to him…and she was a lot like his mom.

Beck grimaced.

"You'll find the right words," Heavenly murmured softly, squeezing his hand.

Seth's heart swelled. The people he loved wanted to help; he could see that plainly. But this was his job alone. No way around that.

"I hope you're right." He pressed a kiss to her cheek. "I just need an opening."

And fast. If Danny rejected Seth and the future he had planned… Mom might never come around.

His younger brother was the lynchpin.

As the waiters cleared the last of the appetizers, Danny stood and excused himself, heading toward the restrooms.

Beck raised a brow at him. Heavenly gestured to Seth with a little nod.

He waited exactly thirty seconds, then rose. "I'll be back."

"You got this," Beck insisted.

"Good luck," Heavenly whispered.

Seth crossed the room, then turned down the narrow hallway. He'd barely reached the bathroom when Danny pushed the door open and reared back in surprise.

"Going in?"

"No." Seth shook his head, then dragged in a deep breath. "Can we talk for a minute?"

Danny's brow furrowed. "Sure. What's up?"

Seth scanned the hallway. Other than the muffled sounds of the reception drifting in, it was empty and quiet. But the clock was ticking.

"I need you to hear me out before you say anything, okay?"

Danny's expression turned cautious. "Okay..."

"There's no easy way to put this." Seth took another deep breath. "Straight up? Beck and I share Heavenly. We're all planning to get married next year. I'm telling Mom on Monday."

Danny stared at him in silence for long, excruciating moments. Then he rubbed the back of his neck, clearly processing. "You're serious?"

"As a heart attack," Seth said firmly.

Danny's gaze dropped to the floor. "I mean… On the one hand, I'm shocked. You were married to Autumn and—wait. Did you share her with someone, too?"

"No." Autumn could barely handle one man, much less two. Beck would have completely overwhelmed his late wife.

"I didn't think so, but after that conversation we had last month after Mom caught the twins fucking Gia in her family room… I kind of wondered. You were more supportive of Jack and Connor wanting to share than I thought you'd be. I never imagined you'd actually want that kind of situation permanently, but..." He looked back up. "I caught some looks between Beck and Heavenly, looks you saw and didn't seem to mind. So, on the other hand, I'm not super surprised."

"And how do you feel about that?" Seth's voice was tight.

Danny was quiet for another beat, clearly turning it over. "Not my life. I'm just worried... I mean, does being with them make you happy?"

"Honestly? Happier than I've ever been. Happier than I thought I could ever be after...everything."

Danny nodded slowly. "What you three do as consenting adults is none of my business. But I'm not gonna lie. It's outside the box. People will point, stare, and talk shit."

"They already do." Seth shrugged. "We're used to being judged. We just don't care what strangers think."

"But you *do* care what the people you love think."

"Exactly."

"I don't have a problem with it. And if knowing you have backup to watch your woman and your kids gives you peace...I don't blame you."

Seth blinked. He'd never consciously thought about it like that, but yeah. That was at least part of the appeal. Mitigating the risks of losing the people he loved again. The comfort of knowing he wasn't alone in protecting the ones who mattered most to him.

"I appreciate that. But we both know it's not that simple. You have Maggie to think about, and her opinion matters to you. As it should."

"Yep, and that's my only hesitation." Danny nodded slowly. "She's probably going to be a little weird about it at first. But she already adores Heavenly. So far, she seems to like Beck. And she thinks you're the best. She would never want you estranged from the family because of who you love. She'll come around. I'll help her. But...it may take time."

"Thank you. A little time and understanding is all we need to show everyone we're good together. Really solid. The three of us are hoping to come back for Christmas—as a committed unit, not the lie we've been peddling for Mom's benefit." Seth held his brother's gaze. "To make that happen, Maggie needs to accept us. If she doesn't, Mom might follow suit, thinking she has an ally."

"You're right. But if all us boys are on your side—I'm assuming the others know?" At Seth's nod, Danny went on. "Mom can't fight all of us. She won't."

Seth hoped like hell Danny was right. "That was my assumption, too. But I need you to keep this from Maggie for a few days. I can't risk her telling Mom before I've had the chance to sit her down and explain."

"I don't love keeping things from my wife, but for you?" Danny sent him a reassuring nod. "I'll keep this to myself until you tell me otherwise."

Relief crashed over Seth, so strong he damn near felt faint. He'd done it—gotten all the men in his family on his side. That was more than half the battle.

Time would tell if he won the goddamn war.

Seth stepped forward and clapped Danny on the shoulder, his grip firm. "Thank you. Really."

Danny scoffed as he pulled Seth into a real hug—tight and meaningful. "You disappeared once. When you went dark for that year, it almost destroyed us all, especially Mom. The Cooper clan isn't the same without you."

Seth's throat tightened. "It almost destroyed me, too."

"I don't pretend to understand what happened then. I never asked—"

"Don't." He was better off not knowing.

Danny pulled back, meeting his stare with a tight smile. "I figured. Look, Mom can't *not* welcome you, Beck, and Heavenly back for Christmas. Since Dad died, you've been the glue that's held us together, man. So if I have to fight to keep it that way, I will."

Seth swallowed past the lump in his throat and smiled. "I appreciate that more than you know. Your support and help mean everything."

"You got it." Danny clapped his shoulder. "Always."

Together, they headed back toward the reception. Half the weight Seth had been carrying around finally lifted. Every single person he needed was in his corner now—Matt, the twins, Carl, and now Danny.

Together, he hoped they could collectively bring his mother around.

But only time would tell.

He grinned as he returned to the table with a nod that made Beck and Heavenly smile from ear to ear.

By the time the waitstaff cleared the main course and people began filtering onto the dance floor, Seth noticed a shift. His brothers—all of them—had started gravitating toward Beck. He'd caught Jack and Connor handing Beck a beer earlier as they all laughed about something. Matt had pulled him into a conversation about sports, joking with him like they'd known each other for years. Even Danny had spent a few minutes talking with Beck near the bar, their body language easy and relaxed.

Their behavior was subtle, but deliberate. They were signaling acceptance without making it obvious. Seth was grateful for it—more than he could put into words.

The music suddenly stopped and the emcee's voice crackled over the speakers. "And now, the bride's son, Seth Cooper, would like to say a few words."

Seth stood, grabbing his glass and tapping it lightly with a fork. The room quieted, all eyes turning toward him. He cleared his throat, his gaze settling on his mother.

"Mom," he began, his voice steady. "I could stand here and tell everyone how you held this family together after Dad died. How you worked two jobs, kept food on the table, and somehow still managed to make sure we all felt loved. But honestly, if I did that, we'd be here all night."

Soft laughter rippled through the crowd. Mom's eyes were already glassy.

"The truth is, you raised five boys—and let's be honest, that's a miracle in itself." More laughter. "There were moments I wasn't sure we'd all make it to adulthood in one piece. But you were patient, strong, and determined. And you never gave up on us, even when we probably deserved it."

She pressed her fingers to her lips, tears spilling over.

Seth's tone softened. "You've spent sixteen years taking care of everyone else. And now, finally, you have someone who's vowed to take care of you." He turned to Carl. "Carl, you're a good man. And I'm proud to officially welcome you—and Cat and Blake—into this family. Family is everything. It's what we lean on when things get hard. It's what keeps us grounded. And I know that with you by her side, Mom's going to have the life she deserves."

He raised his glass. "To Carl and Grace. May your marriage be filled with love, laughter, and a whole lot of patience—because trust me, you're going to need it with this crew."

The room erupted in applause and laughter. His mom stood and crossed to him, pulling him into a tight hug. "Thank you, sweetheart."

Seth held her close, his chest tight. *Please remember this on Monday,* he thought. *Please remember how much I love you.*

When they pulled apart, Carl stepped forward and gave Seth a hearty hug. "Thank you."

Seth nodded and handed the microphone to his mom.

Before he could step away, Blake approached and extended his hand. "I guess that makes us brothers now. You already got a bunch. I hope you don't mind one more."

Seth shook it firmly. "I'm happy for another one. And a sister. Never had one of those…"

"I can't believe I have five more brothers now. I'm definitely outnumbered." Cat grinned, wrapping him in a brief hug. "That was a great speech. "

"Thanks." Seth nodded her way.

Suddenly, his mom raised a hand, drawing the room's attention back to her. "Before we go any further, I have one more announcement to make. Seth, don't sit down." She motioned for Hudson to join them. His son's eyes widened, but he shuffled forward, looking both embarrassed and curious.

Mom beamed as she pulled Hudson close. "I'd like to introduce my grandson, Hudson Cooper. We didn't know about this handsome young man for too many years, but now that we do, he's officially Seth's son—as of this morning."

The room erupted in applause and cheers. Hudson's face flushed as he grinned.

Mom continued, her voice warm. "And I'm beyond thrilled to have Hudson as a part of this family. Welcome!"

She raised her glass in toast. The crowd followed.

More applause. Hudson ducked his head, clearly rattled but pleased. Seth reached over and squeezed his son's shoulder, pride swelling in his chest.

His mom kissed Hudson's cheek, then turned back to the crowd. "Thank you all for being here to celebrate with us. Now let's dance!"

The band struck up again, and people began moving back toward the dance floor. Mom was all smiles—completely unaware of the storm brewing.

Chapter Twenty Five

When the reception ended, Seth helped Heavenly into the passenger seat of Grace's SUV. Beck and Hudson climbed in the back.

As Seth pulled from the parking lot, warmth still bloomed in Heavenly's chest from watching Grace and Carl pledge their vows, the way they'd looked at each other—like the rest of the world had fallen away. The soft glow of happiness that had lined their faces reminded her of everything she wanted. Everything she and her men were so close to having.

If Grace accepted them.

Letting out a shaky sigh, she glanced down at the engagement ring on her finger. One day soon, she, Beck, and Seth would recite their vows and live their happily ever after without hiding. Without pretending.

Maybe then she'd forget the sight of Beck sitting white-knuckled and frozen at Grace's dinner table, forced to listen while Seth announced his engagement to her.

From that moment on, everything about this visit had stripped Beck of what made him *him*. No control. No dominance. He couldn't claim her. He couldn't even touch her, except like a casual friend. He had to be careful when he spoke to her. Even when he so much as looked at her.

Since then, she'd seen Beck bleed in silence while maintaining his carefully constructed mask. This subterfuge was killing him inside. And she hurt for him.

Seth wasn't doing much better.

God, spending Thursday afternoon in that house he'd once called home, surrounded by the ghosts of his murdered family, she'd sobbed her heart out. Beck had been overwhelmed, too. But Seth had nearly broken in front of them.

Heavenly couldn't stand it anymore. Her men were hurting.

Deeply. She needed to heal them—and she only had one thing she could possibly give them tonight.

Herself.

Finally, at one a.m., they pulled up in front of the Cooper house. Relief flooded Heavenly as Seth killed the engine. Since Carl and Grace were spending their wedding night at a hotel in the city, they had the house to themselves.

Beck could stop pretending. Seth could exhale.

And she could finally give them both what they needed.

They climbed out of the SUV. Hudson grabbed a box of leftover cake Grace had insisted they take home while Seth collected the gifts that hadn't fit in Carl's car.

Beck moved to the back, reaching for a box at the same moment Heavenly did. His hand closed over hers. Too tight. Then gone.

She glanced up and caught the rigid set of his jaw, the tension vibrating through him like a wire pulled taut. He wasn't impatient. He was restrained—but the kind that frayed at the edges.

Heavenly let her fingers trail up his arm as she withdrew, slow and deliberate. Her silent way of telling him she saw him. She felt him. And soon, she could give him what he'd been denied.

Beck snapped his stare her way, dark and hungry, before he turned sharply and headed for the house.

Seth moved with his usual efficiency, gathering the last of the bags, but Heavenly knew him too well. His calm came from bracing, not peace. He was holding himself together by a thread.

It was going to snap. Beck's composure, too. She could feel it.

Inside, Seth locked the doors and set the alarm. They deposited everything in the mudroom, then climbed the stairs together. Each step made Heavenly's pulse accelerate. Anticipation coiled in her chest.

Soon…

Down the hall, Hudson paused at his bedroom door. "Night, guys."

"Hey, Hudson Cooper," Seth called softly.

"Yeah?"

"Sleep tight, son."

A slow smile tugged at Hudson's lips—pride and belonging wrapped in two words. "You too...Dad."

"See you in the morning, kid," Beck added, his voice rougher than usual.

"Today was a big day. Get some good sleep," Heavenly murmured.

Hudson grunted in reply and nodded, then disappeared into his room. His door clicked shut.

An electric silence followed. The air between the three of them crackled.

They were finally alone.

Now she could begin making them whole again.

All of them.

Beck rolled his shoulders and flexed his hands like he was itching to touch her now that he was finally allowed to. "Inside."

Heavenly swayed into the bedroom. Beck followed, hovering behind her as she removed her jewelry—earrings, necklace, engagement ring—and set them on the dresser. Seth entered behind them and closed the door.

They were alone.

Before she could turn around, Beck slid a thick arm around her waist and spun her to face him. Her heart skittered as he devoured her with a dark, desperate stare. The distant, polite mask he'd worn for Seth's family shattered, replaced by a fierce, consuming gaze.

The palpable urgency rolling off his body practically singed her skin.

Heavenly didn't wait for Beck to take the lead. She twisted from his arms, stepped to the center of the room, and slowly, deliberately, sank to her knees at his feet, head bowed.

The air left Beck's lungs in a harsh breath. "Heavenly—"

She lifted her chin and peered up at him with beseeching eyes, letting him see the total surrender she offered. Freely. Intentionally.

"Little girl, you don't have to—"

"I want to." Her voice was steady. Sure. "I need to…*Sir.*"

She saw the moment he realized she wasn't just giving her body, but offering to refill what days of denial had taken from him—to restore the control he desperately needed.

Beck's eyes flashed dangerously, his chest heaved, but instead of the harsh command she expected, his expression softened. He lifted his hand and cupped her face, his thumb brushing across her cheekbone. "I know what you're doing. You're giving yourself to me, to take what I need."

"Yes, Sir," she murmured.

For a long moment, he stared. Heavenly began to squirm as he slid his trembling thumb against her bottom lip. Had she misread him?

Seth moved closer, eating her up with his stare before he settled his hand on her crown, his fingers threading through her hair—gentle where Beck was demanding, tender where Beck was raw.

"You're beautiful like this, angel." His voice sounded thick with emotion. "Giving him what he needs."

She looked up at Seth, saw the understanding in his eyes. He knew what Beck had endured. And he was giving this moment to Beck without hesitation.

"I will, Sir."

Seth caressed her one last time, then stepped back, leaning against the dresser—present and supportive, but ceding control.

Then Beck's eyes darkened, something fierce and hungry burning through the tenderness. He glanced at Seth briefly—a silent question, maybe even a challenge—before his gaze snapped back to her.

"You know what you're offering me." Not a question. A statement.

"Yes, Sir."

"And you know I'm going to take it." His voice dropped, dangerous and dark.

Her breath caught. "Please."

Something shifted in his expression—the last of his softness hardening into an utterly dominant hunger. He curled an impatient finger under her chin and forced her stare to meet the demand in his.

"Be very sure, little girl," he warned, his thumb pressing against her pulse. "Because I'm starving, and I'm not going to be gentle about reclaiming what's mine."

Her breath caught.

Her heart raced.

Heat flooded her pussy, quivering with the same desperation etched on his face.

"I'm sure," she whispered.

"I'm going to make you beg for me, little girl. I'm going to use your sinful little body until you're sobbing and pleading. And if you're good, I might let you come. But not when you want to. Not when you're ready. Not even when you're hanging on by the tiniest thread." His grip tightened fractionally. "You'll come when *I* decide to let you. Not before."

Her nipples beaded.

Her womb cramped.

Desire thickened her voice. "I understand, Sir."

Beck's eyes flared. "You think you do. Stand."

It wasn't a request.

Heavenly's stomach whirled with excitement as she kept her eyes locked on his and complied.

"Strip," Beck ordered, brushing his lips over hers before curling his hand around her throat in pure possession. Then he reluctantly released her. "Slowly. I want to watch you reveal every inch."

She trembled with anticipation as she clasped the zipper of her dress and dragged it down, letting the sound fill the sexually charged silence. Then she lowered the silk, inch by deliberately measured inch, until it whispered down her legs and pooled at her feet.

Until she stood before him in nothing but delicate lace.

Heat blazed from Beck's eyes, searing her skin as he raked a greedy stare down her body. "Now the rest."

Seth exhaled hot against her neck as she unhooked her bra. When it fell away, he stepped in beside Beck. She slowly slid her thong down her legs and stepped out of it.

Both men groaned in unison—low masculine sounds suffused with hunger and need. Their hot stares of appreciation were like live touches, pumping liquid fire through her veins.

"Oh, little girl." Beck trailed his fingers over her breast before brushing a teasing thumb across her nipple. When she gasped, he flashed her a dirty smile. "There she is."

He bent to her, skimming his lips up her neck until he found her thrumming pulse. "God, I've missed the taste of your skin. Missed the sounds you make when I touch you…"

Then he dragged his tongue over the spot and rolled her nipple between his thumb and fingers, twisting, tugging, torquing.

She quivered under his touch. Her knees threatened to buckle.

"Missed seeing you naked and waiting for me to command you."

She moaned at the raw emotion in his confession. "I've missed you, too. So much it hurts. Every night without your hands on me, your body against mine—"

"Yes…" Beck gripped her hips and rolled his forward, pressing his stiff length against her pussy.

She shuddered at the contact. "Beck!"

"That's 'Sir' to you. And as much as I've missed watching you come apart for me, if you can't behave, I won't see that tonight, either."

"You can't do that," she whined, purposely provoking him. "It's been too long. I need you to make me come, Sir."

"You don't make demands, little girl. That will cost you. On the bed. On your back. Now."

Heart drumming against her ribs, Heavenly scrambled onto the mattress, suppressing a smile. She stretched out on her back and arched to him, thrusting her breasts up. The cool evening air bit into the sensitive tips as she slowly spread her legs.

"Christ," Seth muttered, his hands already working his belt. "Look at her…"

Beck growled a barely human sound as he rushed to strip off his clothes.

Beside him, Seth shucked off his shirt, then stepped impatiently out of his pants.

As always, the sight of her men and their sculpted, inked bodies made her sigh. Seth's broad chest and the trail of hair leading down to his thick, veined cock. And Beck's carved muscles, flexing and bunching while his hard length pointed toward the ceiling, dripping with need.

The sight of them, naked and ready, made her whole body quiver.

Anticipation spiked, her breaths turning rough, as Beck climbed onto the bed, settling himself between her feet.

"Spread your legs wider," he commanded, stare raking her. "That pretty pussy is mine, and I want to see every inch of it."

Heavenly bit her lip to hold in her excitement as she obeyed, dragging her heels apart and exposing herself completely.

"Fuck," he breathed, his black gaze devouring her. "Look at you. Already so wet."

"And begging for cock." Seth sounded almost censuring as he approached, staring at her with eyes full of fire.

Heavenly lost herself in the heat of Seth's stare as he plucked at her nipples—rolling, pinching, sending sharp pleasure-pain straight to her clit. Beck's warm breath ghosted hot over her inner thigh, so close.

She whimpered, her hips shifting involuntarily. Seeking in silent plea.

"Stay still." Beck clamped his hands around her thighs.

She froze, panting.

"Now put your arms above your head," Beck growled. "Wrists together."

Slowly, heart thudding, she stretched them above the pillow.

She wanted this, ached for it with every cell in her body. But as she obeyed, a switch flipped in her brain, screaming that she was now under Beck's control—a slave to whatever sensations he decided to heap on her, a victim of whatever torment he used to unravel her.

"Look at you all spread out for me," Beck moaned before he climbed on top of her, his big body pinning her. He captured her wrists in one big hand and shoved them against the mattress, his face hovering a few scant inches above hers as he arched a brow in warning. "If you move your hands—if you even flex your pinky—I'll stop everything. I'll pull out of your quivering little cunt and leave you aching all night. Is that clear?"

Seth rounded the bed, then settled on the mattress beside her before wrapping a big hand around her throat. "He means it, angel. And I'll help him."

They would do it; she knew that from experience.

"Yes, Sirs."

"Remember that." Beck lifted his hand from her wrists and shifted his hips, pressing the thick head of his cock against her entrance with a hiss.

That first touch—hot, hard, insistent—had her sucking in a gasp.

"Tell me what you want, little girl."

"You, Sir. Inside me."

He pushed forward slightly, letting her feel only his thick crest. When Heavenly's pussy fluttered and clasped and her hips jerked up involuntarily, he pulled back with a growl. "Can you follow directions?"

"Yes, Sir," she breathlessly assured.

"And who makes the rules?"

"You do, Sir."

"That's right. Don't forget it," he cautioned, holding her prisoner with a hungry stare. "Now beg me. Make me believe you want… No, make me believe you *need* my cock."

Heavenly swallowed back a mewl. "Please, Sir. Please. I need you inside me. Need you to fill me."

"Do you? I'm not convinced." Beck smirked, pushing another inch inside her before he stopped again. "If you want more, you'll have to do better. Tell me how my cock feels."

"I-It…" She groaned in frustration as he withdrew again. "It feels good. Too good. You're so thick and hard and…" She gasped as he flexed and backed away again. "No. Please… I need all of you."

"Such pretty begging, angel," Seth praised as he resumed tormenting her nipples and glanced Beck's way. "Pretty enough to give her what she wants?"

"Not a chance in hell. I don't think she understands who's in control yet." The surgeon flashed a filthy smile. "But she will."

Seth softly chuckled as he pulled and pinched. "We won't rest until she does."

Their burning stares and relentless teasing had her fighting the urge to twist and arch. She'd beg more if they demanded it. Whatever they needed to put her out of her misery, she'd do it.

With agonizing slowness, Beck pressed forward, filling and stretching her as he drove deeper in her fluttering pussy. An exquisite burn had her gasping—legs spreading, hips lifting—as pleasure assailed her.

"Yes. Yes…" she begged in a shuddering exhalation, eyes sliding shut, as he worked in another blistering inch.

"Eyes on me," he snarled. "I want to watch you take every inch. Watch the pain and pleasure ripple over your face as I wreck your snug little pussy. Watch those pretty blue eyes dilate just before you shatter all over my cock."

Heavenly lifted her heavy lids and locked stares with Beck. Her heart leapt. His eyes were nearly black, and the slow smile that tugged his lips did absolutely nothing to comfort her.

He was going to wreck her tonight, and he was going to love every minute of it.

She would, too, knowing that she was giving him exactly what he needed.

That knowledge unlocked something inside her—deep and primal and femininely fundamental. They'd taught her to embrace her submission—to crave it, to sink into it, to revel in it.

But this was different. Clearer. Her submission wasn't something she did strictly for her own peace. Tonight, it was her gift to them.

And watching Beck take it—watching him reclaim himself through her body—filled her with something fiercer than mere pleasure.

"That's it," he hissed. "Good girl. Don't look away. No matter what I do, you keep your eyes on me. Understood?"

"Yes." She nodded, a desperate bob of her head. "Yes, Sir."

He withdrew nearly all the way in a molasses stroke that had her mewling and aching. Before she could recover, before she could even find the words to plead again, he thrust deep.

Hard.

To the hilt.

Heavenly bowed her back and screamed.

Fire razed through her veins. Tingles skittered. Need pooled hot between her legs.

She gave herself over completely.

"Take all of him. Let him use you," Seth urged, squeezing her nipples. "God, you look so damn beautiful."

"And she feels so tight." Beck settled into a powerful juggernaut of a rhythm. Deep. Banging. Unrelenting.

Beck's feral tone blended with Seth's growled praise, spilling over her like sandpaper and silk.

"Hmm. You're squeezing my cock," Beck huffed as he drilled her again. "Clamping down on me like you don't want to let me go."

"I don't," she cried out with a beseeching stare.

"He's fucking you so good. Isn't he, angel?" Seth taunted. "I know you like that."

"Yes," she groaned as Beck dragged his wide crest over the sensitive bundle of nerves inside her. "I feel him everywhere. Stretching me. Filling me."

"I'm claiming you, little girl," Beck roared. "And I'm taking what's mine."

Jaw clenched, his thrusts turned faster, rougher, more demanding.

Seth's fingers on her nipples were unrelenting—rolling, pinching, plucking—his breath hot on her neck as he watched Beck pound into her.

"She's aching to please you, man," Seth murmured. "She's giving you everything. Heart. Mind. Body. And she's surrendering all her sweet, sweet power."

As if his words flipped some internal switch inside Beck, his rhythm turned punishing. Teeth bared, he strained, grunting with every surge inside her, hips bunching, back arching, as if being inside her wasn't just pleasure, but biological imperative. He growled her name over and over.

And he kept proving how completely he owned her body and commanded her pleasure.

The fiery friction sent her reeling. Her head spun. Her breaths caught. Her orgasm tightened and coiled between her legs, building and swelling to something far beyond her control. She keened out, sharp cries that left her throat raw. And still, she didn't stop.

"Don't." Beck's fingers tightened around her wrists. "You don't have my permission to come. You haven't earned it."

"Please," she wailed, fighting the relentlessly rising pleasure. "Please…"

With a growl, he gripped her thighs, shoving them up and wider, changing the angle so his cock dragged across her G-spot with devastating precision.

"Look at this pretty, greedy cunt," he moaned low and dirty as he stared down where their bodies joined. "Taking me so deep. Dripping all over my cock. You love this, don't you, little girl? Love being used rough and hard."

"Yes," she sobbed, the pressure building higher, harder. "I-I love it. I love you."

"I love you, too." His voice softened for just a moment before hardening again. "Which is why we're going to make you scream. Seth, wreck her clit. Let's see how long she can hold out."

"Fuck, yeah," Seth said with an unholy chuckle as he lowered his fingers between her legs and strummed her swollen nub with firm, steady pressure.

Heavenly cried out, jerking beneath the onslaught of sensations pinging off every nerve. "No. No, please… I can't—"

"You can, and you will," Beck thundered, eyes boring into hers. "You will *not* come until I give you permission. Do you understand?"

"Yes, Sir," she gasped, tears streaming down her temples as she fought against the massive orgasm threatening to steamroll her.

Beck didn't seem to care. He drove on, crashing into her over and over, while Seth's fingers worked her clit with perfect precision—circling, pressing, torturing the swollen bud until she could barely form words.

Their mastery over her was the most crushing, excruciating, and exquisite torture she'd ever known.

"Please," she begged, voice cracking with desperation. "Please, Sir. I need to come. I can't—I can't hold it—"

"Not yet," Beck growled, jaw clenched as sweat dripped from his brow. "Show me how badly you want to come all over my cock. Beg me, little girl."

Seth's fingers never stopped their ruthless circles on her clit, dragging her closer and closer to the edge Beck wouldn't let her fall over.

"Please, Beck! Sir. Please!" The words tumbled out in a panicked rush as sensations climbed, blood pooled, her heart roared. Orgasm went from desirable to inevitable. "I'm trying…to. Hold back…but—Oh, god. I-I…can't stop—it. P-please…"

Her whole body was trembling, her muscles quivering and quaking as she tried to stave off her release. But the orgasm was bearing down on her, demanding and undeniable, as her keening cries filled the room.

Lights flashed behind her eyes, but she kept her stare on Beck, her expression vowing that she was his.

He plowed into her, breaths sawing, headboard banging against the wall as he yelled, "Come, little girl. Come all over my cock!"

His demand filled her head, spread to her heart. And on command, she shattered, screaming as the orgasm detonated through her—violent, devastating, all-consuming. Her body convulsed, back arching off the bed, inner walls clamping down on Beck's driving cock as her pulsing contractions seemed to go on forever.

Hips jerking, Beck cried out as his own release tore through him and he flooded her with everything he had.

"Take it," he choked out. "Every fucking drop."

He ground deep, his cock twitching and pulsing as he finished emptying himself against her unprotected womb.

Seth's fingers gentled on her clit, now lightly circling her sensitive nub, easing her through the aftershocks.

As she slowly floated back down to earth, Heavenly lay boneless, sated and gasping. Beck stared down at her, his eyes soft now, filled with satisfaction. With awe. With love.

"Jesus, little girl. What the hell did you just do to me?" he whispered, brushing sweat-dampened hair from her face before gliding a tender kiss across her lips.

A tear slid down her temple as she cupped his cheek. "I hope I gave you what you needed."

"God, did you ever." His voice cracked as he buried his face against her neck.

They laid together for several silent minutes before Beck carefully eased from her pussy and collapsed beside her, pulling her to his chest. Their hearts hammered in sync as their breathing slowly leveled out.

Heavenly could practically feel the peace flowing through his veins. Her heart swelled with a satisfaction she'd never experienced.

She'd done it. She'd restored what these past few days had stolen from Beck. She'd given him back the dominance he needed to feel whole again.

But as Seth's gentle hand stroked her hair, as she felt his quietly loud presence crowding beside her, Heavenly blinked up at him.

She wasn't done with her men yet. Seth needed her, and she needed to feel him as deep as possible.

"Do you want me to start a shower for you two?" Seth rose from the bed and reached for his pants.

"Not yet." She planted a kiss on Beck's cheek before whispering in his ear, "I need to connect with Seth, too. Bring him back to us."

Beck darted a glance at Seth. Surely he saw how tightly strung Seth was?

"Do it," Beck murmured for her ears only.

With a lingering smile, she scrambled off the bed, pussy throbbing and thighs slick with Beck's come, and sank to her knees. "Sir?"

Seth froze, a confused furrow forming between his brows. "What are you—"

"You hurt, too. I saw and felt it at the house."

His face slightly crumpled but he slammed a mask of control in place so fast it made her chest ache.

"No. I won't let you hide your feelings from me…from us. Not anymore."

"Angel—"

"I *see* you, Seth. I see your pain. I didn't understand before, and I'll forever hate that I gave you an ultimatum. I know now the emotional price you've paid. It was undeniable when we walked through that house on Thursday."

"Heavenly…" He tucked a stray curl behind her ear. "Angel, you don't have to—"

"I need to. And I think you need me. Please." She gripped his thighs, feeling the tension coiled in his muscles. "I understand now how scared you've been to start another family. Beck does, too. And now we get why. But you're not alone this time. We'll make sure you never are again. When bad memories resurface and try to drag you under, lean on us. We'll carry you. You don't need to be afraid anymore. We're right here beside you. We always will be."

Something fierce and desperate flashed across his face. His hands trembled as they cupped her cheeks, tilting her face up to his. "Angel… I wish it was that simple. What you're asking is…"

"Incredibly difficult. And terrifying, I know. I do." Heavenly tightened her grip on him and willed him to understand. "I'm asking you to choose us. To choose love and family and future. If we're blessed with a baby, all three of us will love and protect him or her forever."

Seth stared at her, jaw clenched, his shaking fingers wiped away tears she hadn't realized were falling. He swallowed as if he was struggling to put the barrage of his emotions into words.

"Please…" she sobbed. "Our family won't be complete without you."

"She's right," Beck whispered.

"Please believe in us, in our future," she begged as she rose slowly to her feet, kissing her way up his body. "Please try."

Seth froze. His nostrils flared. His breaths turned rough.

And his control suddenly snapped.

He pulled her against his body and crushed his mouth over hers in a ruthless kiss that tasted of desperation, hope, and a need so potent it nearly drowned her. His lips claimed her. His tongue swept deep, devouring her as if she were his last meal as he hauled her against his rigid cock with a groan.

Yes. God, yes.

Suddenly, he tore his lips from hers, then scowled Beck's way. "I was giving this month to you."

"I know, and I appreciate it. But the three of us, this future we're creating…it's more important than whatever you think you need to atone for."

"Seth?" Heavenly held her breath. "Please."

At her soft plea, Seth spun back to her, his eyes blazing with something wild, untamed, and breathtakingly intense.

"On the bed. On your back. I want to see your face while I take you and make you shatter for me."

Heart soaring and body trembling with relief and renewed arousal, she climbed onto the bed before rolling onto her back. She let her thighs fall open, let him see Beck's release still coating her folds—glistening and provoking.

"Claim me, Sir," she begged.

"Breed her," Beck commanded so softly she wasn't sure Seth had heard him.

At least not until Seth clenched his jaw and climbed onto the mattress, settling between her thighs. His eyes were locked on her slick pussy. His thick length was still hard, still weeping. For several seconds, he simply knelt, stroked his cock, and stared.

His chest heaved with each ragged breath, and sweat began beading on his brow.

Then he sucked in a shaky breath and aligned his slippery, wide crest to her opening.

But instead of pushing inside, Seth paused. His hand stilled, trembling around his shaft before darting an unreadable glance between her and Beck.

Heavenly held her breath.

Her heart stuttered.

Please don't pull away. Please.

She felt his fingers slightly tremble as he splayed his hand over her stomach and dragged his gaze to hers. The vulnerability, fear, and hope swirling in his eyes crashed over her in waves, stealing her breath. "Are you sure, angel? Are you absolutely positive?"

"I've never been more sure of anything in my life." She smiled, her voice quivering as she placed her hand over his, still pressed to her womb. "I love you, Seth."

Without a word, Beck eased onto the bed next to her and placed his hand on top of hers.

Seth swallowed tightly and nodded, then eased his hand from the bottom of the pile.

She and Beck lifted theirs together, both watching Seth intently.

"Fuck…" he groaned, pressing forward with devastating tenderness as he slowly stretched and filled her, inch by careful inch.

Still sore and swollen from Beck's savage use, Heavenly gasped as she struggled to accept Seth. The burn was gentler this time, but not less intense.

As if aware, Seth continued entering her even slower, keenly watching her face for any sign of discomfort.

Where Beck took, Seth worshipped.

Where Beck commanded, Seth coaxed.

Where Beck ravaged, Seth dismantled…piece by piece.

When he was fully seated inside her, they both exhaled a shaky breath, gazes tangled.

"Fuck, I can feel Beck's come inside you…marking you, mixing with your slick juices," Seth murmured gruffly.

"She needs yours, too," the surgeon whispered, cupping Heavenly's breasts and thumbing her nipples.

A spark flashed in Seth's eyes as he began to stroke in and out of her pussy, slowly. Deeply. Heavenly gasped as he filled her, arching beneath him. Each thrust was purposeful, controlled, designed to make her feel every inch of him.

"That's it," Beck encouraged. "Make love to her. Show her how precious she is to you. How much you want her. And if you happen to knock her up…"

Heavenly felt Seth's cock jerk inside her. Felt his grip tighten on her hips.

"I want to," he choked out. "God help me, I do. My head is a fucking tangle, but I want you pregnant. Want to watch you grow round with our baby. I want our family."

His desperate declaration echoed through Heavenly's body. Her heart answered with love while tears of relief and joy filled her eyes.

"Then breed her," Beck growled to Seth as he filled her again. "Breed her like you mean it."

A single-minded desire tightened Seth's face, narrowed his eyes. He stilled.

"Seth…" Heavenly called out to him, that one syllable a plea wrenched from deep inside her.

"I'm going to fill you so full. Going to fucking get you pregnant," Seth snarled as he completely withdrew before slamming back inside her with devastating force.

Heavenly screamed as he began pounding into her with wild, desperate intensity—his control obliterated, his defenses crumbling, his fear spiraling into primal, unstoppable need.

"Yes! Yes!" she wailed, tossing her head from side to side as he consumed her.

Beck leaned in and engulfed one of her nipples in his mouth, nipping at her before lashing it with his tongue.

Fire licked up her spine. Dissolving under her need, Heavenly dragged her hand down her side, trying to slide it between her legs to stroke her throbbing clit.

Beck lifted from her nipple with a low growl and snagged her wrist in his fist. "Did we give you permission to touch yourself, little girl?"

"No," she whined.

"No, *Sir*," Beck corrected.

Exerting his renewed dominance, he clasped her other wrist, then dragged her arms over her head. Pressing her hands to the mattress, he flashed her a dirty smile, then glanced up at Seth.

"Look at your angel, all bound and helpless. Totally at your mercy."

Seth raked a blazing stare up her body, stopping, eyes narrowed, on Beck's restraining fist around her wrists. A low growl rolled from deep inside Seth's chest as his hips jerked. Then he clenched his jaw and slammed into her again. Harder. Faster. Stealing her breath and what little was left of her sanity.

"You like that, don't you, little girl?" Beck taunted. "Like being helpless. Like us holding you down and taking what we want. Giving you pleasure. Giving you pain. Marking you with our seed."

"Yes," she panted, feeling her self-control slip away under the onslaught of Seth's softly insistent demand.

While Beck worked over her already stinging nipples, Seth began rubbing at her clit.

She sucked in a gasp as a cascade of sensations deluged her.

"Fucking gorgeous," Beck murmured across her nipple before he dipped his head and latched his mouth over the sensitive bud.

Tugging and nipping, he sucked first one breast then the other. His teeth followed, sinking tenderly into her vulnerable flesh. Heavenly cried out at the sweet sting of pain before he laved it away with the slow drag of his tongue.

Lost in the sweet friction of Seth's relentless cock against the contrast of Beck's demanding mouth, she moaned in rising bliss. She keened even louder as Seth stepped up the torment of his fingers on her clit.

Orgasm grew, pooled and swelled so fast, so overwhelmingly huge, she struggled to hold back.

She trembled and tensed, her arms and legs tingling before going numb. Stars flickered behind her eyes. Liquid fire followed, thundering through her veins. It coalesced behind her clit, threatening to undo her completely.

"P-please," she panted, lifting her hips off the bed, pussy gripping Seth's shuttling cock. "I-I…can't hold—"

"Yes, angel," he growled. "Fuck! Now. Come while I fill you."

At his command, her orgasm detonated—bigger, deeper, soul-robbing, equally devastating.

Heavenly screamed his name as she clamped and quivered around his shaft with violent pulses that wracked her body and filled her with a raw satisfaction that left her blinking and stunned.

"Fuck!" Seth roared, slamming deep one final time and grinding deep inside her. His cock jerked and swelled seconds before she felt him flood her in a hot rush. "Take it, angel. Yes. Fuck. Fuck, yes! Take *everything*."

His broken plea shattered Heavenly's heart and pieced it back together all at once.

Then Seth collapsed over her, burying his face in her neck as they both gasped for air.

In the next instant, Beck kissed her forehead as he released her hands and draped her arms around Seth's back. With a watery smile, she hugged him tight as, together, they quaked and jerked with aftershocks.

Beck stretched out against Heavenly's side and stroked his fingers through her hair. She felt their combined releases pooling inside her. She was fertile this weekend. They all knew it.

Tonight felt momentous—at least in her heart. Time would tell if the same held true for her womb…

Long minutes later, Seth gently eased from inside her and rolled to her other side. Beck grabbed a pillow and slid it under her, elevating her hips before he settled in alongside her again.

Finally, Seth looked at her, his stare direct, almost hopeful as he placed his hand on her belly. Heavenly smiled as more tears gathered, then she threaded her fingers through his. Without a word, Beck cupped his hand around theirs.

They stayed like that—connected to one another—for long, silent minutes, the moment aching yet complete.

And Heavenly knew with bone-deep certainty that they were finally whole. No matter what happened with Grace Cooper, the three of them had each other. And they always would.

Lying there between them—filled with their love and their seed, their hands protectively draped over her womb—Heavenly smiled. She'd accomplished what she set out to do; she'd healed them. And she'd brought herself more joy than she could ever have imagined.

Chapter Twenty Six

Seth woke to the soft glow of sunlight filtering through the window of his childhood bedroom. For a moment, he was disoriented—caught between the past and present, between the boy who'd once slept here and the man he'd become.

Warm curves cuddled against him. He turned his head to find Heavenly, asleep between him and Beck, her face peaceful and unguarded in the early morning light. He smiled at the sight of Beck pressed against her other side, one arm draped protectively around her waist, his breathing deep and even.

Last night had been perfect.

Seth savored the memories of their passion before they'd collapsed—completely sated, spent, and exhausted. Something like peace infused him—welcome after days of pretending, of careful distance and half-truths. This quiet moment felt like oxygen. Tomorrow, he'd tell his mother the truth, then nothing else would get in his way.

Fears aside, Seth refused to let it. He'd embrace the future with both arms and—

His and Beck's phones simultaneously buzzed on the nightstand.

Seth plucked his up while Beck groped for his, both careful not to disturb Heavenly. He squinted at the screen and found a text from Liam to them both.

Then he read the message, his grip tightening on his phone with every word.

> Congratulations, Daddies! Heavenly conceived last night. Mum and I both saw it. Well deserved.

Seth's heart stopped. An icy rush surged through his chest—joy and terror colliding so hard he couldn't breathe for a second.

Heavenly conceived.

She's pregnant.

A baby.

That reality threatened to close his throat. His vision blurred. Frantically, he blinked to clear it, then glanced over at Beck.

The surgeon stared at his screen, his expression gaping. A long second later, the corners of his lips turned up in a slow, unfiltered grin before he gave Seth a fist bump and mouthed two words that summed up the situation.

Holy shit.

Even as his chest tightened, Seth flashed him an answering smile.

Beck had stepped into the future, already seeing diapers, first steps, late-night feedings, and everything that came with fatherhood.

While Seth…he knew he stood trapped between past and present, unable to let go of what he'd lost long enough to embrace what he was gaining. Instead, the fucking fear had returned to choke him with the reminder that happiness was fragile and safety an illusion.

Where was all the certainty he'd felt last night? Gone, as if it had never existed.

But he didn't say that. He couldn't. Instead, he did his best to lock down his hesitation and only show joy.

Their phones buzzed with another message from Liam:

Want to know the biological father? The baby's gender? I know...

Beck shifted, careful not to wake Heavenly, and whispered, "Do we?"

Seth shook his head. Even the thought of knowing made him break out in a cold sweat. "I don't need to know. This baby is ours—doesn't matter what the sex is or whose biology it carries."

"Agreed." Beck nodded, grin widening. "I'll let him know."

The surgeon quickly tapped out:

No thanks. We like surprises.

A second later, Liam's response came through:

Seth's fingers shook as he set his phone down and turned toward Beck. They exchanged a long, silent stare—steady, grounded, resolute. He wondered if the snarky surgeon could read his thoughts? His worries?

Beck shifted his gaze to Heavenly, still asleep between them, and his voice dropped even lower. "We should wake her. She should know."

She would be incredibly excited.

Seth nodded. "Absolutely, before Mom and Carl come back."

Which would be soon.

Beck nodded, then nudged her soft shoulder while Seth brushed a strand of hair from her cheek.

"Angel," Seth murmured. "Wake up. We've got news."

Heavenly stirred, her lashes fluttering as she blinked at them, groggy and confused. When she saw their serious expressions, her brows furrowed. Her gaze sharpened.

She sat up, whispering, "What's wrong?"

Beck shook his head, smile filled with joy. "Nothing, little girl. In fact, everything is perfect."

Seth's throat tightened. "Liam just texted us, angel. According to him, you conceived last night. You're pregnant."

The words hung in the air.

Heavenly blinked. Her lips parted, but no sound came out. Tears welled up in her big eyes and spilled over.

"I'm..." Her voice cracked as her hand instinctively dropped to her stomach. "I'm pregnant? Really?"

"Really." Beck's voice came out rough. "We did it. We're going to have a family."

She looked between them, searching their faces. "You're sure?"

"Liam and Bryn both saw it." Seth nodded. "It's real. How do you feel?"

A sob broke from her chest—half laugh, half cry. She pressed both hands to her stomach as tears streamed down her face. "Oh, my..." Her voice trembled. "It's real."

"It is, little girl." Beck's smile widened as he pulled her close and kissed her tears away.

He hugged them close, love filling his aching chest. But fear coiled around it, so tight it threatened to smother his breath and strangle his joy. "You're going to be a mom."

Which meant he was going to be a father again—and not to a teenager like Hudson, but to a fragile newborn who would depend on him for everything.

I can't lose this again.

Seth closed his eyes and made a silent promise. He would not let history repeat itself. He would be vigilant as hell and protect them. Ready or not, he would leave the past behind, and embrace the future...whole, complete—exactly like Beck was doing now.

Heavenly's tears dripped onto his shoulder. Beck's hand gripped his arm.

Seth buried his face in Heavenly's hair, breathing her in. Beck's forehead pressed against his shoulder.

This was his family. His future.

And he'd protect it with everything he had—no matter what.

Heavenly sniffled again. Tenderly, Beck dried her tears. Seth watched, wishing he could lose himself in the moment with them. He gave them what he could while his thoughts raced, caressing her crown and kissing her forehead.

Then he pulled away, breaking the moment.

Fuck, he needed space, needed to breathe. No time to linger or wallow or reverse-engineer how to jettison his fears enough to fully embrace his future. Mom and Carl would be home soon to prep for their post-wedding brunch—friends, family, and out-of-town guests gathering for one final celebratory moment before saying goodbye. Later this afternoon, he'd take Beck, Heavenly, and Hudson back to the airport for their flight to LA.

Then tomorrow…he'd sit his mom down and come clean. The weight of that responsibility pressed down on him—not panic, but something heavier. Unavoidable. With a baby on the way, telling her about the three of them wasn't optional.

Whatever he felt, whatever the fucking tangle in his head…it had to wait.

With a last, lingering kiss on the bow of Heavenly's mouth, Beck slipped out of bed and grabbed his clothes. "As much as I hate to break up this party and what could be a really promising morning, I'll head across the hall and start getting ready. After all, we have to keep up appearances."

Beck's expression was tight, resentful.

Seth didn't blame him. "Last day."

"Thank fuck." The surgeon slid a lingering smile Heavenly's way before he left, closing the door behind him.

If not for his mom's convictions about right and wrong, the three of them would probably pass a lazy Sunday in bed, laughing, talking, and making love as they celebrated their pending future.

Instead, they had to resume their roles and hide their love. They had to pretend they didn't know about the child growing in Heavenly's womb. Seth knew Beck and their girl hated that. He hated it for them, too.

Heavenly grabbed Seth's hand. She must have read something in his expression because her voice was searching and soft. "Now that Beck's gone, tell me how you really feel. Are you happy?"

"Yeah, angel. I'm happy. Of course I'm happy." He cupped her cheek. "I won't lie and say I'm not scared shitless. I am, and I don't know if that feeling will ever go away."

She sent him a sympathetic smile and wrapped her fingers around his still against her cheek. "I know. But whatever happens—the baby, the move, all of it—we'll handle it. Together."

Seth wanted to believe her more than anything.

"It's going to be okay," she assured. "You don't have to carry the weight alone. The three of us will move heaven and earth to keep our child safe."

He nodded. "I know you're right. We won't let anything happen to him or her."

"Ever," she reassured, kissing him long and deep.

Seth groaned before sinking a fist in her hair and taking control of her mouth. The need to be inside her clawed at him. Unfortunately, he couldn't invite Beck back to his room, and making love to Heavenly again would be like playing Russian roulette with the clock.

Reluctantly, he broke the kiss with a heavy sigh and pressed his forehead to hers, breathing hard. "If we don't stop now, I won't."

Heavenly traced a finger down his bare chest. "I wouldn't object to more time in bed with you…but I guess we need to get ready."

"Yeah." Seth backed away and watched her sigh as she padded to her suitcase.

She rummaged through her clothes. "Is the brunch a casual thing, or do I need to dress up?"

"Definitely casual. It's just family and a few close friends."

"Oh, good." She plucked up a burgundy cotton V-neck, a black cardigan, and a pair of distressed jeans, along with a clean bra and panties, then laid them across the bed. Then she turned and scanned the dresser, a scowl slowly forming as she turned to him. "Have you seen my ring?"

"No."

"Did you move it? I put it here last night with the rest of my jewelry. But—"

"Don't panic." But she was. He heard it in her voice. "It can't have gone far."

Seth scanned the top of the dresser. Earrings, check. Necklace, right where she left it. Engagement ring? Gone.

"Huh…" How the hell had that happened?

"Where did it go?" Her voice pitched higher, edging toward panic.

Seth pulled her against his side. "Easy, angel. It's got to be here. Maybe it fell last night when I bumped the dresser on my way to the bathroom."

"I don't remember you doing that."

Seth chuckled. "You wouldn't. You and Beck were…busy."

"Oh." Her cheeks turned pink.

"Oh." He smiled, tapping her nose. "Why don't you jump in the shower? I'll look for it."

"I'll help."

Seth shook his head, almost grateful to have something to focus on besides his low-level panic over this baby and the white-hot terror of coming clean with his mother.

"You have to start getting ready or we'll run out of time. Trust me, angel. I'll find your ring. It didn't grow legs, and I'm a detective. This won't be a hard case to crack. Go."

Heavenly wasn't thrilled, but she nodded and made her way to the bathroom down the hall. A moment later, he heard the door close behind her and water rushing through the pipes as she turned on the shower.

In the blessed quiet, Seth devoted himself to the task, opening the blinds to let in more light. Then he gripped the edge of the dresser and scanned the area with a scowl. Nothing.

Maybe the ring had fallen under it? Behind it?

Careful not to scuff his mom's hardwoods, he carefully lifted it away from the wall and crouched, peering into the sliver of space he'd created between the back of the dresser and the wall.

And he found Heavenly's ring—pristine and sparkling in the morning light. But it hadn't fallen to the floor, and it wasn't alone.

Instead, the ring had snagged on the edge of dusty, yellowing paper, which looked as if someone had affixed it to the back of the dresser.

"What the hell?" he murmured as he retrieved the ring and placed the shimmering diamond on top of the dresser.

Then he leaned in to study the mysterious piece of paper he'd never noticed. Hell, never even seen.

It wasn't a page, but an envelope. It had been duct-taped to the back of the dresser.

Why?

Had someone deliberately hidden it?

That was Seth's guess.

His pulse kicked up as he picked at the tape. It lifted slowly, so brittle with age it mostly flaked away. Coupled with the yellowing envelope, Seth had to wonder… How long had this been affixed to the back of his dresser? Years? A decade? More?

And who would have put this here? One of his brothers? Someone else?

How had he not seen it?

Seth hadn't lived here since he was eighteen, so why would anyone bother hiding something in *his* room after he'd gone?

Questions with no good answers swirled in Seth's head as he leaned closer still and wiped away a thick layer of dust.

He caught sight of faint writing on the front of the envelope.

And he'd recognize that handwriting anywhere.

The air froze in his lungs. His heart chugged. His blood ran cold.

Seth knew without a shred of doubt who had hidden the note on the back of his dresser.

His father.

Chapter Twenty Seven

Afraid to move—to breathe—Seth stared at his father's stark handwriting on the envelope.

For a moment, he considered shoving the dresser back and pretending he'd never seen it. He had a future to worry about—Heavenly, the baby, Hudson, Beck.

He couldn't fucking let the past drag him back now.

But how could he ignore this? If his dad had written him a note, hidden it in his room—where no one else would find it—there was a damn good reason.

Seth didn't see how he could just turn his back on that.

And he had to be fast, before Heavenly finished her shower.

"Fuck." He peeled away at the duct tape, the adhesive crackling and threatening to disintegrate under his fingertips.

Finally, he pulled the envelope free with shaking hands and turned it over, studying the faded ink on the front.

SETH.

His name written in his father's careful block letters.

Nothing else.

He sat still. Stunned. Praying that the content inside was something innocuous, like a letter of fatherly advice his dad had written during a reflective moment. Or encouragement about handling responsibility as he grew into a man. Seth hoped like hell that he could read the page, fold it back up, and tuck it away with a bittersweet smile.

He had a sinking feeling it wouldn't be that simple.

Seth's heart pounded as he crossed to his side of the bed. His legs felt unsteady, so he sank onto the mattress and angled his body to block the view of anyone who might burst into the room. If worse came to worst, he'd shove this into the nightstand drawer.

He exhaled, trying to steady himself, as he slid his thumb under the flap and lifted it.

Inside, he found a single sheet of folded paper, along with a business card to a climate-controlled storage unit a couple of miles from the house. On the back of the card, his father had left a gate code and a unit number. In the bottom of the envelope, he found the kind of small key used for padlocks.

Seth's stomach dropped. This wasn't sentimental. This was the past coming back.

This was dangerous.

Dread coiled as Seth unfolded the letter. The date at the top of the page was exactly one week before his father died.

He scrubbed a hand down his face, dragged in a ragged breath, and read on.

Seth,

If you're reading this, I'm sorry. I've failed. I'm equally sorry to leave this on your shoulders, but I don't have any other choice.

There's real danger. I'm afraid for you, your mother, and your brothers. I've been looking into things—corruption, bad people doing unspeakable things—and I think they're onto me. I don't know how much time I have. Maybe I'm being paranoid. I hope I'm overreacting. But if I'm not, and something happens to me, I need you to understand why.

I don't trust the people in charge to investigate this properly. They're part of the problem. So I'm leaving this for you, because you're smart. Because I know you'll be cautious, and you should be. And because, when you're old enough, I know you'll know what to do.

I'm not asking you to finish what I started or to seek vengeance. I don't want you to put yourself in danger. But I need you to know this threat exists. Pretending it doesn't could get people killed—your mother, you, and your brothers—all the people I love who don't deserve to be collateral damage in this corrupt war.

I prayed I'd never have to write this. Prayed you'd never have to read it. But if you are, I couldn't stop the threat and keep everyone safe. I hope somehow you will understand why I couldn't stay silent.

Be careful, son. These criminals are dangerous and not above murder.

I love you. I'm proud of you. And I'm always with you. But most of all, I'm sorry.

—Dad

Seth's throat closed. His eyes burned. He blinked hard, forcing himself to focus.

How terrified had his dad been when he'd written the letter? How worried had he been to put all his faith in his teenage son?

Seth stared at the note, reading it again. His dad hadn't come right out and stated there was evidence in the storage unit. He didn't need to. But why else would he send Seth a key and the security codes?

Something was hidden there. Something his father had died protecting.

Something vitally important that had been sitting untouched for sixteen years.

He zipped his stare to the closet—to the box that held his father's notes. The same box Seth had combed through a million times trying to figure out why his father had been killed.

What if…he'd never solved his dad's murder because he'd been missing vital clues? What if those clues were in that storage unit?

Seth stared at the letter in one hand, the card and key in the other.

He was at a fucking crossroads.

He didn't feel triumph or excitement. He didn't even feel determination.

Instead, a cold, sinking certainty settled into his bones.

Clearly, his father had known he'd been in danger sixteen years ago. What he couldn't have known was that this threat would show up to exact its vengeance on Autumn and Tristan eight horrible years later.

He thought about Tony's skittishness at the bar when he'd talked about the precinct. *Things have changed, gotten more political. It feels... corrupt.*

He thought about Nikolai's cryptic comment minutes later. *I heard the minute you arrived in town. If I am aware of such things, do you not think they are, too?*

Whatever his father had discovered, it sounded as if the threat was ongoing. And according to Nik, bigger and stronger than ever.

Seth froze. His body motionless. Dangerously controlled.

But his mind raced.

Once, he'd had everything—a wife, a son, a future. Then they'd been ripped away in a single fucking night.

And now he had Heavenly. Hudson. Beck. A baby on the way.

He'd be a lying motherfucker if he said he wasn't terrified of losing them the same way because he knew damn well that digging got people killed. Worse, the danger never came for him. It preyed on the people he loved.

For now, Seth had to shelve this discovery. They had to maintain their careful façade during this brunch—pretend Beck wasn't a part of his relationship with Heavenly—and not let news about the baby slip. Adding a murder investigation on top of that was too much.

And if his mom found out he'd discovered a warning from his dad, she wouldn't stand still. She would do *something* and put herself at risk. A chill slid up his spine. Seth was eternally grateful his mom had never found that envelope. If she had, she likely wouldn't be here, like his dad.

Still, Seth knew he couldn't keep this to himself indefinitely. Eventually, he had to come clean with Beck and Heavenly. A secret like this would tear them apart.

But she didn't need this level of anxiety now. It could be bad for the baby, and he didn't want to risk them.

So he needed to tell Beck. At some point. If he could get the good doctor alone before he took them to the airport... Of course, Beck would be livid. Seth would have to convince him, swear that he wouldn't go recklessly chasing the truth again.

Hudson didn't need to know. The kid had enough on his plate, and Seth refused to drag a sixteen-year-old into shit this dangerous.

Which told Seth how threatened his dad must have felt if he'd been compelled to leave evidence with his teenage son.

Fuck.

Seth let out a shaky breath. Logic told him to walk away. His allegiance was to the future, not the past. He owed the family he was committing to now his protection. He didn't owe answers to a cold case that had been shoved in a dusty storage unit over a decade ago.

But...whatever his father had stashed could not only explain his loved ones' deaths, but possibly end the danger for good. The investigation he and his father had tried to dissect had torn their family apart twice. The cost of all he'd lost had haunted him for years.

Could he simply ignore the chance to finally get the answers he ached for?

Wouldn't that negate everything his father had died for? Everything Autumn and Tristan had died for?

But he owed his new and growing family as much as he owed the ones who'd died on his watch.

Fuck. Seth raked a hand through his hair. He didn't know what to do.

Suddenly, the shower shut off. Pipes groaned. Heavenly would be back any second.

Cursing, Seth shoved the letter and key into the envelope, his heart hammering.

He had to plan...and he was out of goddamn time.

Downstairs, Seth heard the front door open and close, followed by the murmur of voices—his mother's light laugh, Carl's deeper rumble.

They were back—and he was holding a piece of paper that could blow up his entire life.

Seth's hands shook as he shoved the letter into the drawer of his nightstand and closed it, but he pushed too hard. The drawer jammed in its track.

With a curse, Seth yanked on the handle. At his brute force, the lamp on top rattled. He grimaced.

Fuck. He had to calm down, get himself together.

He sucked in a breath, then let it out as he scanned the room for anything else out of place. *Shit.* The dresser was still askew.

Seth leapt to his feet and ate up the distance across the floor, lifting the heavy dresser back until it nestled against the wall.

When he finished, his palms were sweating. His heart hammered so hard he could feel it in his throat.

No one could see him like this, or everyone would know something was wrong. They would ask questions, and Seth didn't have any answers.

For now, he rolled his shoulders and forced his expression into something neutral before yanking open the bedroom door.

At the top of the landing, Seth paused to listen. Mom and Carl were moving through the house, their voices clearer. He could hear the rustle of bags, the clink of dishes as he descended the stairs, his jaw already aching from clenching it.

Showtime.

He just had to get through this morning without anyone—especially his mother—suspecting something was wrong. After all, the secret his dad had left behind had been sitting in that storage unit for sixteen years. A few hours wasn't going to change anything.

When he reached the kitchen, his mom looked up from the coffeepot, her face bright. "Seth! Good morning, sweetheart. How are you? You look…sleepy."

"I'm fine," he lied, crossing the room to kiss her cheek before he took two grocery bags from his stepfather's arms. "Let me help with that."

"Thanks." Carl nodded as he placed a box of pastries on the counter with a wry smile. "We picked up a few extra things on the way back from the hotel this morning."

That didn't surprise Seth. "Of course you did."

Grace Cooper took hostessing seriously. She refused to let her guests go hungry.

His mom tsked at them both as Seth started unpacking the bags—bagels, cream cheese, another fruit tray, croissants. He kept his hands busy, his movements controlled. Casual. Like his father's final message wasn't burning a hole in the nightstand two floors above them.

"Where's everyone else?" Grace frowned.

"Beck is in his room, getting ready. Heavenly's finishing up in the bathroom. She'll be down to help soon. Hudson is—"

"Still sleeping, I'll bet." She rolled her eyes. "He's a teenage boy, after all."

"Exactly. I'll wake him when I go back upstairs."

Grace grinned as she pulled out serving platters. "Perfect. Guests should start arriving around nine-thirty. We're expecting people to come and go until noon or so. Beck, Heavenly, and Hudson's flight leaves a little after four, right?"

"Yeah, I should have plenty of time to get them there afterward." Seth watched his mom arrange bagels on a plate like it was the most important task in the world.

And to her, it was. She had no goddamn idea that sixteen years of silence had just shattered in her oldest son's bedroom.

His mom and Carl moved around the kitchen together, working in silent harmony as she spread out food while Carl ferried champagne flutes for mimosas from the dining room.

Suddenly, she sighed and whirled to Carl. "We forgot more orange juice."

Carl set the crystal down, turned to his new wife, and took her hands. "It's fine. If we need more, we'll get more."

That should be the least of his mom's worries today. "I'll go later if you need."

"Thank you." She smiled brightly. "I hate to trouble you but—"

"It's no trouble, Mom." He pressed another kiss to her cheek, willing his voice to remain steady. "The mini-mart is just down the road."

"You're right." She let out a steadying breath. "I shouldn't be nervous. Everything will be fine."

"Exactly what I've been saying," Carl poked before he sent Seth a sideways glance. "It's like she actually listened to me for once."

Seth forced out a hollow laugh and did his best to tease back. "Don't get used to it."

After his mother huffed and threatened to snap a dishtowel at her husband, they went back to preparing for brunch. Seth was grateful that it kept them occupied…and prevented them from questioning why his behavior was off.

His shoulders loosened a fraction. Maybe he'd managed to bury his disquiet enough that no one noticed.

Mom wiped her hands on a towel with a little scowl. "If you two are done giving me a hard time, I think we're in good shape. I just need an extra hand or two whenever Beck or Heavenly come down."

"They won't be long," Seth promised, already heading for the stairs. "I'm going up to get ready."

He took them two at a time, eager for a few minutes alone to center himself. Just that brief exchange had proven that shoving aside the turmoil in his head wouldn't be easy. And the fact that the people he lived with were flying home today—leaving him to tell his mother the gaping secret about his love life while not telling her what his father had left him?

Seth's gut twisted. Could this get any more unnerving?

When he reached the second floor, he pushed open the door to his bedroom and shut it behind him with a ragged exhalation.

Heavenly was waiting, wrapped in a robe, damp curls tousled around her face. She took him in with a frown. "You look…off. Are you all right?"

"Fine." The word came out sharper than he'd intended. Instantly, guilt twisted through him, and he gentled his voice. "Just…hate that you're going home without me. I'll miss you."

It wasn't the whole truth. But the lie would protect her.

Heavenly softened against him, cuddling close. "I'll miss you, too. But it's only two days."

She was right, but with everything bashing around his brain pan… "That's two days too many." Even if it was true, he had to stop bleeding worry and start distracting her. "But…guess what I found?"

When he tipped his chin toward the dresser, Heavenly whipped around. Relief washed over her face when she spotted her engagement ring. "Thank goodness!"

Seth crossed the room and plucked up the ring. "As I suspected, it fell when I bumped into this hunk of wood last night."

He clasped her hand and slid the ring back onto her finger, then pulled her close, wrapping his arms around her. He needed this, needed to feel her, solid and warm and safe against him.

She melted against him again, her arms circling his waist. "Are you sure you're okay?"

He did his best not to wince as he pressed a kiss to the top of her head, breathing in the scent of her shampoo. "Just...a lot on my mind."

"I know. This weekend was a lot—the wedding, telling your mom about us, and now the baby…"

"Especially the baby."

The weight of all his secrets sat heavy in his chest when she tilted her head up, studying his face. "It's going to be okay, Seth. Really. It has to be."

Odds were, she was right. Problem was, he didn't like that the chance of violence, loss, and heartbreak wasn't zero. But that wasn't her fault.

He kissed her softly, letting himself bask in her for a long moment. Then he pulled back and forced a smile. "You're right. And as much as I'd love to hold you—and do other pleasurable things to you—brunch is starting soon. Mom could use some help when you're ready."

"I'd love that, too, but…" She cast a meaningful glance toward Beck's closed door across the hall. "We can't. But when you get home on Tuesday…"

She trailed a finger down his chest and sent him a tempting smile.

He grabbed her wrist, his throat tight. "I'll drown you in orgasms."

Her smile slanted to something more alluring. "Please do."

He kissed her one more time, inhaling her in a desperate moment.

Then he stepped back. "Unfortunately, I have to wake Hudson and hop in the shower, or we won't be ready in time."

Seth didn't wait for her reply, just grabbed his clean clothes and ducked into the hallway, heading for the shower.

He locked the door behind him, turned on the faucet, and stood staring at his reflection in the mirror as he brushed his teeth.

The envelope was sitting in his nightstand like a ticking time bomb. His father's handwriting. His dire warning. And the evidence to solve his murder?

Every minute that ticked by without Seth actually knowing, was killing him.

There's real danger. I'm afraid for you, your mother, and your brothers.

Seth spit out his toothpaste and stashed his toothbrush before he braced his hands on the basin, his knuckles going white.

Fuck, he shouldn't dig.

But if the evidence in that storage unit could end the suspicion and uncertainty around his dad's death—once and for all…

What if it got everyone killed?

Cursing, Seth stepped into the shower, letting the hot water beat down on his shoulders as he reached for the soap, going on autopilot while his thoughts churned.

Maybe there was nothing left in the storage unit. Sixteen years was a long time. For the evidence to still be there, his dad would've had to have prepaid all this time. Who the hell did that, especially someone who had five kids and lived on a cop's salary?

Seth sighed. Maybe he was stressing about nothing. Maybe he was too late and everything his dad died for had been tossed out for non-payment or featured on an episode of *Storage Wars.*

But he had a sinking feeling it was still there. Still waiting for him.

He braced his hands against the shower stall and let the water beat on his shoulders.

His father had suspected he was going to die. Known he was knee-deep in something dangerous enough to warrant hiding evidence instead of trusting his own department.

Seth clenched his fists and resisted the urge to punch the wall. He really shouldn't dig into this cesspool of a case again. Not after it had already cost him Autumn and Tristan. Not when Heavenly was carrying his child.

But his father had hidden his evidence and trusted him—and only him—to find it for a reason.

How could he just ignore that?

Chapter TwentyEight

Beck leaned against the doorway between the kitchen and dining room, coffee mug in hand, watching the organized chaos unfold.

"Carl, could you grab that folding table from the garage?" Grace called from the kitchen, her voice bright. "The one against the back wall?"

"On it." Carl set down his coffee mug and headed for the garage, side-stepping a cluster of Grace's neighbors who were visiting in the kitchen.

Beck followed suit and trailed him, lifting one end of the table. "Figured you could use a hand."

"Appreciate it." Carl grabbed the other end.

Together, they navigated the narrow doorway back into the house and into the dining room. Despite the fact the formal table was groaning under platters of bagels, pastries, and fruit, Grace had apparently decided to set out more food.

"Where are we supposed to put this?" Beck asked.

Carl grimaced as they maneuvered around a pair of mismatched chairs someone had dragged in from god-knew-where. "By the window, I guess."

Beck eyed the available floor space with a raised brow. "That won't be tricky."

Carl sighed. "She's been planning this for weeks. I've learned not to question the vision."

Beck bit back a grin. "Smart man."

They set the table up, and Carl clapped him on the shoulder, the gesture both welcoming and accepting, before heading back toward the kitchen.

Beck rolled his shoulders and let his gaze sweep the room.

The house was already filling up—neighbors, church friends, a few people Beck vaguely remembered meeting at the reception last night.

The air smelled like fresh coffee, cinnamon, and the flowers leftover from the wedding.

Grace moved through the space with ease, filled by warmth and the low hum of conversation. She was clearly in her element, stopping to hug arrivals and direct them toward the food.

Sunlight poured through the windows, catching on champagne flutes lined up for mimosas. It should've felt perfect—relaxed, warm, the morning after a wedding well done.

And it did. Mostly.

Except…

Beck's gaze drifted across the room and snagged on Seth. His chest tightened.

Seth handed Hudson a stack of napkins, murmuring something that made the kid nod and head toward the dining room. On the surface, everything looked fine. Seth smiled when someone thanked him for moving a chair. He laughed when Carl made a joke about the mimosas being stronger than the coffee. He played the helpful son. Polite. Relaxed.

Beck couldn't put his finger on why…but he wasn't buying the act.

He glimpsed a tightness around Seth's eyes he hadn't seen yesterday. He seemed distracted. Guarded. Something that didn't belong at a family brunch. He went through the motions with an empty smile in place.

But Beck swore Seth's mind was somewhere else entirely.

Most people wouldn't notice. A glance around the room confirmed that everyone else seemed oblivious. Beck wanted to believe he was overreacting…but he knew Seth too well to believe that.

"Coffee?"

Beck turned to find Heavenly at his elbow, holding the carafe and smiling up at him. She looked happy, almost giddy. And seemingly unaware of whatever storm was brewing inside Seth's head.

"Yeah, thanks." He held out his mug, watching as she poured. "You doing okay?"

She sent him a secretive smile. "Great. One of the best days ever, don't you think?"

God, he ached to take her in his arms and kiss her.

Monday. After Seth finally told his mother the truth, they'd never have to pretend again.

But until then, he had to suck it up and behave like a pal.

He sent her a strictly polite nod, but added a touch of warmth to his voice. "Amen."

As if she remembered their act, Heavenly blanked her expression and spun away to offer coffee to more of Grace's guests.

Seth stared at them with an unreadable expression that had the wheels in Beck's brain turning faster.

The pregnancy.

That had to be what was freaking Seth out. He'd seemed fine most of the weekend.

Until this morning.

After Liam's text, Seth had sworn that, despite his fear, he wanted this baby. But maybe the reality was proving too much. After all, fatherhood wasn't abstract anymore. Heavenly was pregnant. They were having a baby by summer.

Or maybe Seth was concerned about Hudson's response to their growing family. After all, the kid had already run away from his mom's because of a newborn. Was Seth worried it would happen again? Surely he knew they'd work together to make damn sure the teenager felt valued and accepted.

"Fresh coffee is ready," Grace called from the kitchen. "Carl, can you bring the spare pot?"

"On it." Her new husband headed back toward the kitchen.

Time dragged. Beck kept watch. Grace and Carl's friends came and went. Seth seemed absorbed by mundane tasks. He carried more folding chairs inside. Hudson trailed behind him like a shadow, mirroring his father's movements.

The doorbell rang.

"I'll get it," Grace said, wiping her hands on a towel as she hurried toward the front door.

When she pulled it open, Cat and Blake stood on the porch, all smiles, the morning sun lit behind them.

Grace welcomed them inside.

Cat pulled her new stepmother into a warm hug. "There's the bride! How are you feeling?"

"Wonderful." Grace squeezed her back. "I'm so glad you could stop by before your flights."

"Wouldn't miss it." Blake kissed Grace's cheek, then turned to his father. "Hey, Dad. Did you save any coffee for us?"

"Pot's fresh." Carl gestured toward the kitchen. "Help yourselves."

"And eat up!" Grace insisted. "They don't feed you anything on those planes anymore."

"You're right." Blake grimaced. "And it's a *long* flight back to Tokyo."

"I'm only going to Indiana, but I'm still eating everything I can before our Uber comes. Nothing is worse than airport food." Cat reached for a plate.

Blake poured himself a mug and grabbed a pastry, then settled against the counter near Seth. "Morning. Hell of a wedding. You gave a good speech."

"Thanks." Seth's expression warmed slightly. "Sorry you have to leave so soon."

"Me, too. But reality calls, you know?" Blake took a bite. "I'm just glad I was able to get some time off work. Seeing Dad this happy, and getting to meet you, your mom, and your brothers makes the long flights worth it."

"It was great meeting you and Cat as well," Seth said automatically.

Blake nodded. Their conversation stalled, as if Seth suddenly lacked the patience for social skills. Then he excused himself and grabbed more coffee.

Whatever plagued Seth's thoughts wasn't letting up.

Cat drifted over to where Heavenly was arranging fruit on a platter, the two of them chatting quietly. Grace hovered nearby, smiling happily when the doorbell rang again.

Grace opened the portal to reveal a familiar man with graying hair and sharp eyes that cataloged the scene in a single sweep. He stepped inside with the easy confidence of someone who'd been here a hundred times before.

"Gene!" Grace's face lit up.

"Morning, newlyweds." Gene Hammond's voice was gravelly and warm. And when he hugged Grace, it was brief but genuine.

"Glad you're here," Carl said, shaking Gene's hand.

"Me, too." Gene's gaze swept the room, landing on Seth with a grin. "There's the troublemaker."

Seth looked up, and for the first time all morning, something like a real smile crossed his face as he strode toward the man and offered his hand. "I was hoping you'd choose brunch over fishing."

"Only for the Cooper clan. Besides, I wouldn't miss one of your mom's spreads." Gene smiled, shaking Seth's hand with a fatherly grip on his shoulder.

As more friends and neighbors arrived, the living and dining rooms filled with the hum of voices and laughter, layering over the clink of glasses and the rustle of plates.

Grace's phone rang shrilly on the counter. She glanced at the screen, frowned, and answered. "Danny? Is everything okay?"

Beck watched her expression shift—concern replaced by relief.

"Oh, no. Poor baby." Grace pressed a hand to her chest. "No, no, don't even think about it. You stay home with Anna. She needs you more... Yes, of course. Give her a kiss from Grandma... Okay. Love you, too."

She hung up and sighed. "Anna's sick. Danny and Maggie aren't coming."

"Oh, I hope she's okay," Heavenly said with concern.

Grace waved a hand. "I'm sure she will be. You know how babies are. They get sick all the time until they build up their little immune systems. But they said to say their goodbyes to you, and they hope they'll see you soon."

"Give them all a hug from me," Heavenly murmured as Seth slipped past her, slinging an arm around her waist and pressing a kiss to her cheek on his way to the table with a platter of muffins.

His mother frowned. "Have you heard from the twins? They should be here by now."

"No." Seth quickly set the muffins down and pulled out his phone. "I'll call them."

"Thank you. Those two..."

Beck couldn't miss the annoyance in Grace's tone. He sidled closer and exchanged a glance with Seth as he dialed. "Twenty bucks says they're too hungover."

Seth snorted. "As drunk as they were last night? I'm not taking that bet."

Then he stepped into a quiet hallway. Beck couldn't hear the conversation, but saw the exact moment Seth's jaw tightened.

Moments later, he returned with a scowl. "Yep. They're hungover, and they're not coming. When the fuck are they going to grow up?"

"When they're dead plus ten days?" Beck quipped.

"You're being optimistic." Seth crossed the room to Grace. "They're…not well. Sorry, Mom."

Grace closed her eyes briefly, shaking her head. "You mean they drank too much and now their heads are pounding?"

"They were all apologies and said they'll see you later." Seth's tone was dry. "I tried texting back…but they stopped answering."

Grace's mouth pressed into a thin line. "I'm going to throttle them."

Clearly, she wasn't happy. Beck suspected she was still pissed off that Jack and Connor liked to share girls. That didn't bode well for Seth's conversation with his mom tomorrow.

And he was probably feeling that, too.

Fuck.

Seth pocketed his phone and turned back toward the dining room when Matt walked through the door.

Immediately, he pulled Grace into a hug with a smile. "How's married life treating you?"

"It's been less than twenty-four hours, but so far? Wonderful." Grace beamed up at him. "I'm so glad you're here. Danny is home with a sick baby, and don't get me started on the twins."

"Hungover as fuck?"

"Language!" Grace snapped, then sighed. "But yes."

"Called it."

"Me, too." Carl smirked, moving in and shaking Matt's hand.

"Some things never change…" Seth's brother grabbed a coffee and made his way through the crowd, stopping to greet Gene with a hearty handshake and a few words Beck couldn't hear from across the room.

He turned back to Seth. They exchanged bro hugs and a few words. Matt said something that made Seth smile, but the happiness didn't quite reach his eyes.

Heavenly approached next. Matt hugged her briefly before he strolled in Beck's direction and shook his hand, the gesture welcoming. "Morning. How're you holding up?"

"Fine. You?"

"Just 'fine'?" Matt raised a golden brow.

Beck glanced Heavenly's way, then shrugged. "You know."

"Yeah." Matt looked back toward his mom as he grabbed a pastry off a nearby platter, voice dropping low. "She'll come around."

"For your brother's sake, I hope so."

"Give it time. No other trouble in paradise?"

Beck frowned. What was Seth's brother getting at? "Why would there be?"

"Well..." Matt's gaze drifted back toward Seth, who was rearranging chairs that didn't need rearranging. Matt's brow furrowed slightly. "Something's up with Seth. Any ideas?"

"Not entirely," Beck replied, purposely vague. If Seth was struggling with the fact that Heavenly was pregnant, it wasn't his place to spill the news. "But it's bugging the shit out of me. When this is over, he and I will be having a long talk."

"Good plan." Matt studied Seth for another moment. "Don't let him fester. When he stews, he usually—"

"Pulls inward and stops talking? Yeah, I know."

The look Matt shot him was both wry and full of respect. "Clearly, you do."

"Not my first rodeo with your brother. I'll get him sorted out."

Matt hesitated. "He's lucky to have you. I know you two aren't, like...together, but after all the shit he's been through, I'm glad he's surrounded by people who love him."

Beck couldn't help but smile. "When Seth and I first met Heavenly, we fucking hated each other. But the bastard has grown on me."

Matt laughed. "I'm glad. If no one else has said it yet, welcome to the family."

That actually choked Beck up. "Thanks. I like you a hell of a lot more than Jack and Connor."

"God, I hope so. They're fucking morons."

"They are." Beck lifted his coffee mug.

Matt did the same as they clinked and shared a grin. "Hope to see you at Thanksgiving or Christmas, man."

"If...things don't work out"— Beck cast a glance at Grace—"you're always welcome in LA."

"I just might take you up on that. The twins did say the girls are pretty out there..." Matt shook his hand. "I should probably go mingle. If I don't see you before you head to the airport, it was good to meet you."

"You, too."

With that, Matt crossed the room and approached Gene, ready smile on his face.

Beck stayed where he was, coffee in hand, focused on Seth, still circling the thinning crowd like a man trying to outrun his own thoughts.

As the guests began making their way to the door, hugging Grace and thanking her for the lovely brunch, Beck helped clear a few plates. The room had gone from packed to manageable. The energy loosened. Conversations grew quieter as the house emptied out.

Blake's phone chimed. He pulled it out and glanced at the screen, then turned to his sister. "Uber's five minutes out. Ready?"

"Yep." Cat turned to her dad and Grace. "Sorry we have to leave so soon."

"It's all right, sweetheart. We know you two have to get back," Carl assured, setting down his mug before hugging his daughter tightly.

"We're just so happy you came for the wedding," Grace said, smile warm but tinged with sadness.

"Me, too." Cat's eyes were glassy.

Blake pulled his father into a tight hug. "I'm thrilled to see you happy, Dad. You deserve it."

"Thanks." Carl's voice was rougher than usual. He quickly cleared his throat. "Let me walk you two out."

Grace wrapped her arms around Cat, hugging her a beat longer than necessary.

Seth clasped Heavenly's hand before striding over to the group. He gave Cat a sisterly pat on the shoulder, then Heavenly gave the girl a warm hug. He shook Blake's hand before Heavenly did the same. After more goodbyes from Matt, Gene, and Hudson, Carl escorted his son and daughter out the door.

"Have a safe flight," Grace called after them. "Text when you land!"

"I will," Cat promised, waving over her shoulder.

"It will be a while, but I will when I get there," Blake quipped.

Everyone laughed. Then the door closed behind them.

The house began settling back into its hum of conversation and clinking dishes. Fewer voices, less movement. Beck exhaled, glancing around. Just family now. And Gene, who was clearly an honorary Cooper.

Grace moved through the room with a fresh pitcher, topping off glasses. "Who else wants a mimosa besides me? We've got plenty of champagne left."

"I'll take one," Matt said, holding out his glass.

"Me, too." Gene lifted a flute.

Grace poured with a smile, the tension from earlier—the twins bailing, Danny's absence—seeming to melt away. She looked lighter now, more at ease. Especially when Carl wrapped an arm around her waist and pressed a kiss to her cheek.

The social obligation part of the brunch was over. Beck hoped that whatever had been eating at Seth all morning would ease now that hosting duties were largely over. But when Beck looked at him across the room, Seth didn't look any more relaxed.

Grace poured another mimosa and frowned. "Seth, honey. We're running low on orange juice. Would you mind running to the mini-mart? Just in case more people come by after the late mass."

"Sure." Seth all but ran for the stairs. "Just need to grab my wallet."

"Thanks," Grace called after him. "My car keys are on the hook."

Beck started and frowned. *What the fuck is wrong with you?* But he couldn't ask. Seth had already taken the stairs two at a time and disappeared from sight.

Seth bolted up to his childhood bedroom, grateful for a few minutes of peace.

The brunch had been fucking exhausting. Smiling. Pretending everything was fine when all he could think about was his father's unexpected letter. He'd felt Beck's assessing stare on him, like he knew something was off. Matt had noticed, too. Seth had caught the look his brother shot him, a subtle scrutiny that said he was filing away questions to ask later.

Seth had stayed busy, doing any and everything he could think of to keep from standing still long enough for someone to interrogate him.

But finally, he had a reason to escape. And maybe…a chance to do something about this fucking weight crushing his chest.

He pushed open his bedroom door and strode straight for his wallet. After tucking it into his back pocket, he reached out again, his hand hovering over the knob on the drawer.

With a curse, he yanked it open. The yellowing envelope sat where he'd left it, his father's handwriting stark against the aged paper.

Seth's throat tightened. But he didn't stop to second-guess. He pulled out the storage facility's business card and the small key his dad had left. He turned them over in his palm. This place was barely two miles away. A handful of minutes out of his way.

He could swing by, take a quick look, and be back before anyone even noticed.

His chest constricted. He could…but he'd sworn he wouldn't dig into the past anymore. When he did, violent shit happened.

But what if this was his only chance?

Tomorrow, he'd sit his mother down and tell her the truth about Beck and Heavenly. If that conversation went sideways—and there was a real possibility it would—she might tell him to leave immediately.

And if he went back to Cali without seeing whatever his father had left behind, the not-knowing would haunt him forever. After sixteen years of wondering who'd killed his dad and why, of living with Autumn's and Tristan's losses—he might finally have a solid lead. Some fucking answers.

Could he really walk away from that?

Without conscious thought, Seth shoved the key and card into his pocket. Then he tucked the envelope back into the drawer, burying it beneath an old paperback, and slid it shut.

Three minutes. Low risk. In and out.

He exhaled hard. If he got on the road and something felt off, he didn't have to go. He was merely...keeping his options open.

As he loped down the stairs, he scanned the room. Grace sipping her mimosa and laughing at something Carl said. Heavenly stood near the kitchen, listening to their conversation and grinning. Beck stood near the window, coffee in hand, talking to Matt. And Hudson sat sprawled out on the couch, absorbed in his phone.

No one was paying a goddamn bit of attention to him.

Seth's gaze landed on Gene near the hallway—and an idea hit him. He couldn't tell Beck yet what he'd found, not without a lot of arguments and explanations he didn't have time for. But Gene would understand. He knew this case inside and out. He'd grasp the implications instantly. And on the off chance something went sideways, Gene would be able to get Seth reinforcements faster than anyone.

He moved quickly, catching Gene's elbow and steering him into the empty hallway. "Got a second?"

"Absolutely," Gene assured. "In fact, I wanted a minute to talk to you."

Seth frowned. "Everything okay?"

"I'm fine. But I ran into Tony on Friday. He's a good guy, and you two were tight back in the day. He told me you'd met up for beers the other day."

"Yeah, he came to our hotel. Why?"

Gene leaned closer. "Did he...seem okay to you? I only know him in passing, so maybe I'm off base. But he seems...off. Jumpy. Something. I don't know. He practically bit off the record clerk's head the other day, which isn't like him. And I'm not the only one who's noticed. I've heard whispers..." He held up his hands. "If it's personal, I don't want to pry. I just worried that Kowalski's death messed him up."

"Tony took it hard. You know anything about that?"

"Not much. I didn't know Kowalski well. The new guys aren't that interested in rubbing elbows with us old-timers." Gene shrugged wryly. "But Kowalski's death shocked everyone. And I gotta be honest, that situation doesn't feel right. There's some weird shit going on at the station. It's pissing me off."

"Tony said the same thing." Seth frowned. "And you don't know anything?"

"Not much." Gene winced, looking a bit ashamed.

"You're a sergeant. Surely, you can do something to stop—"

"I don't know who I can trust, kid." Gene's lips flattened to a thin line. "Over the years, people who ask too many questions wind up dead...like Kowalski. I should have dug more, but after your dad, I just...put my head down, hoping I'd live another day and eventually avenge Michael. But I never figured out what happened. Now, I'm retiring in six months."

And Gene didn't want to make waves. Seth understood. He'd made the same choice after losing Autumn and Tristan.

"I get it."

"That I'm a coward? Yeah." Gene looked contrite as hell. "Michael was a good man. I owed him more."

Seth patted Gene's shoulder. "He wouldn't have wanted you to die, too."

"I keep telling myself that. The truth is, whoever is orchestrating this shit? It's got to be someone way above my pay grade."

"The chief?" Seth asked, gut twisting with dread for his friend.

"That's my best guess. Greedy fucking prick," Gene spat. "I'd love to blow the lid off this mess. Once, a few years after your dad's death, I thought I'd found some evidence...but it got buried immediately, covered up so tight a crowbar couldn't pry it free. Then I got demoted out of the blue. I knew it was a warning. That's one reason I tried so hard to keep you from pursuing your dad's case. I didn't know they'd come after your family and—"

"I might have the evidence." Seth glanced over his shoulder. Still no eyes on them.

Gene froze, then he leaned in, a smile spreading across his face. "What do you mean?"

"This morning, I found something. Some stash dad left for me a week before he died. It might be evidence, proof of what happened to him."

Gene's expression shifted—shock, then something sharper. "What? Here?"

"No. He hid a note in my room. I found it taped to the back of my dresser this morning." Seth's jaw tightened. "He left me a unit number and a key to the storage unit down the street." He rattled off the name of the facility.

Gene's eyes widened. "Jesus. Just like that? That's…that's shocking. After all these years..."

"I'm as blown away as you are." Seth kept his voice barely above a whisper. "Since Mom is sending me on an errand, I'm going to swing by and check out this place."

"Now?"

"It's gotta be now or never. Do me a favor? Keep my mom occupied." He sent Gene a grim expression. "And if I'm not back in thirty minutes, come look for me, okay?"

"Wait!" Gene gripped Seth's arm. "You shouldn't go alone. What if the place is being watched? It could be dangerous. Let me come with you."

"I need you to stay." Seth glanced back toward the family room. No one had moved. "If I take you with me, people will notice. Someone will ask why. I won't be long. I just need to get in, see what's there, and get out. Quick and quiet."

Gene's jaw worked. He didn't like it—that much was obvious. "It's risky, kid."

"It shouldn't be. Even if someone watched that facility in the past, who would still be doing it after sixteen years? They would either have cleaned the place out by now or given up. Hell, I'm half expecting it to be empty. But I have to see for myself."

Gene stared at him for a long moment, concern written across his face. Finally, he exhaled hard. "Thirty minutes. Not a second more, or I'm coming after you."

"Deal."

"And Seth?" Gene's expression was grim. "Don't worry about anything here. I'll take care of everyone."

Seth nodded, something loosening in his chest. Gene had his back. Always had. Just like he'd had Dad's.

"Thanks. It means a lot."

Gene squeezed his shoulder with a nod, then stepped back.

Then, before he caved in to second thoughts, Seth turned, grabbed his mom's keys, and darted for the door.

Before he could make a clean break, he heard footsteps stomping behind him.

"Hey!" Matt all but growled. "Hold up."

Cursing under his breath, Seth worked to get his expression under control before he turned.

Matt shut the front door behind them and gestured toward the driveway. "I'm heading out. Walk with me?"

Seth's stomach tightened. Normally, he'd think Matt wanted to talk shop, but his brother's face said otherwise.

"Sure." He tried to sound casual.

Together, they moved down the steps, stopping beside his mother's SUV.

Matt leaned against the vehicle, arms crossed. "What's going on? You're off today."

"I'm fine."

"Don't give me that bullshit." Matt's tone was patient but firm. "This is me you're talking to. You've been wound tight all morning. I noticed. Beck noticed. What's bothering you?"

Seth looked away, his jaw working. He could keep lying, but he was already keeping too much from Matt. His brother ran his East Coast office; the arrangement only worked because they trusted each other.

And Seth knew that if he didn't tread carefully, he'd fuck that up.

On the other hand, he didn't want to spill this to Matt, get his hopes up, if it turned out to be a big, fat nothing.

"All right. Just between us? Heavenly is pregnant." Seth managed a smile. "We just found out this morning."

Instantly, a grin split Matt's face. He clapped Seth on the shoulder. "Holy shit. That's incredible, man. How do you feel?"

Seth swallowed, joy and terror warring in his chest. "Excited… mostly, but I won't lie. I'm scared shitless, too."

"Of course you are." Matt squeezed his shoulder. "But you've done this before."

"Not in a long time."

"Doesn't matter. You're a great dad," Matt pointed out.

Seth's voice dropped. "Am I? The last time..."

"I know." Matt's expression sobered. "But you're doing amazing with Hudson. And this time is different. You've got Beck. You've got Heavenly, who is definitely not Autumn, thank fuck. And you're not doing this alone."

Matt was right—all the way around. And those were precisely the points Heavenly and Beck had made last night.

Unfortunately, that still didn't stop the fear.

"That's what I keep telling myself. It's just… I wasn't sure I'd ever be in the position to be a father again. Hudson shocked the hell out of me, and I'm damn glad now for my teenage stupidity. He's a good kid. But a baby?" He rubbed at the back of his suddenly stiff neck. "I didn't think I'd ever go down that path again."

"I get it. I'd be gun-shy, too. But you're strong, bro. You got this."

The confidence and empathy in Matt's expression nearly undid him. "Thanks."

"Do you know whose baby it is?" Matt asked.

"No, and we don't care," Seth said firmly. "So I'm hoping it doesn't matter to anyone else."

"It doesn't to me." Matt's tone was absolute. "If you claim that kid as yours, as far as I'm concerned, he or she is family."

Relief spread warmth through Seth's chest. "I appreciate that.

Just...keep the news on the down-low for now. Other than Beck and Heavenly, you're the only one who knows."

"You got it." Matt studied him, his gaze shrewd. "Is the pregnancy news what's got you so twisted up this morning?"

Seth hesitated. The key to the storage unit sat like a boulder in his pocket, pressing against his thigh. For a moment, he reconsidered telling Matt what their dad had left taped to the back of his dresser… then swallowed back the admission. No point messing with his brother's head over what might be nothing. But if he found something, Matt would be the first to know.

"Yeah. Among other things," Seth said carefully.

"Other things?" Matt's eyes narrowed. "Oh, telling Mom about Beck?"

Seth forced himself to hold his brother's gaze. "That's hanging over my head. It's not going to be easy. But I need to get through the next twenty-four hours without fucking everything up."

"You will." Matt watched him for another beat, clearly debating whether to push. Finally, he nodded. "But if something else is going on—"

"I know where to find you."

"You do." Matt nodded. "Good luck."

Seth's mouth twisted into something between a grimace and a smile. "Yeah. Gonna need it."

Matt stepped back toward his car. "See you after you've talked to Mom?"

"Yeah. One way…or the other."

With a wave, Matt climbed into his truck and pulled away from the curb. Seth stood there for a second, watching the taillights disappear, before he slid into his mother's SUV. He slid the key into the ignition and started the engine.

His hands were shaking.

He gripped the steering wheel and forced himself to breathe. The mini-mart was three blocks away. Orange juice. Simple errand.

Except…what followed might answer over a decade's worth of questions…or fuck up his life forever.

Seth shut down that seditious train of thought and pulled out of the driveway.

The mini-mart appeared almost too quickly. He parked, grabbed a carton of orange juice from the cooler, and paid without making eye contact with the cashier. Two minutes, tops.

Back in the car, he set the plastic bag on the passenger seat and stared at it. He could go home now, rejoin what was left of the brunch, look toward the future, and stop giving the black yawning chasm of the past his attention.

Except…he couldn't—not yet.

Seth pulled back onto the road, his pulse picking up again. The storage facility was less than a mile away. He damn near had to pass the place on his way back to the house.

Part of him hoped he'd find nothing but an empty unit. A dead end. That whatever proof his father had hidden was long gone. Then Seth could let it rest, focus on Heavenly and Beck, and their baby. A new house. Hudson. A future that wasn't full of ghosts.

But the other part—the part that still mourned his dad, his first wife, his trusting infant son—couldn't let it go, not if he could finally, *finally* learn who had killed Michael Cooper. And why.

His heart hammered. His hands felt unsteady on the wheel, but he kept driving.

Just grab whatever's there and read it later. No lingering. Get back to Mom's before anyone notices.

The storage facility sign came into view, faded letters on a rusted metal gate. The place had been here forever. Seth had driven past it a thousand times and never given it a second thought.

Today, it might change his life.

At the thought, Seth's stomach plunged, seeming to free fall to his toes.

Anxiety spiked when he turned into the lot and punched in the gate code from the back of the card. Seth half-expected the code wouldn't work after sixteen years.

The gate creaked open, slow and reluctant. A chill went up his spine, but he shoved it aside.

If someone suspected his dad had hidden something here before his death, they would've broken in by now. There'd be nothing left, right?

Right. Besides, almost no one knew he was here. The danger was low.

He could handle this. He wished he had his gun, just in case, but he really shouldn't need it.

In theory.

Thoughts racing, Seth drove through the lot, parked, and used the key to access the door. Again, he was almost surprised when it turned and the lock disengaged.

Swallowing hard, he stepped into the climate-controlled hallway. Surveillance cameras watched from every corner. He walked quickly, counting unit numbers, until he found it.

His heart jackhammered against his ribs. The air felt too quiet. Too empty.

Seth's hand shook as he lifted the key to the lock.

In and out. Quick. Easy. Simple. Jet home.

With that reassurance tearing through his thoughts, he slid the key into the padlock.

Holy shit, it turned.

Mouth dry and nerves singing, Seth's breath caught as the lock disengaged. Its metallic *click* echoed too loudly in the stillness. He yanked the padlock free and lifted the rolling door just enough to duck underneath.

The space was small. Maybe five by ten. Windowless. Empty—except for a single dusty leather zippered pouch sitting in the center of the concrete floor.

When Seth spotted it, he froze. His stomach coiled tight enough to strangle his lungs.

Fuck. After sixteen years, the evidence his father had left was still there.

His dad had been the last person to touch it.

With shaking hands, he crouched and reached for the pouch. The leather was cracked and stiff, the zipper reluctant. When he finally wrenched it open, his breath stuttered.

Inside, a thick binder dominated. Tucked to one side, a gun that looked like his dad's old service piece. Cash, bound with rubber bands that had long since disintegrated. And an unmarked video tape, its plastic case yellowed with age.

The contents alone seemed deceptively innocuous. But people had been *killed* for what might be inside.

And if Nikolai was right, that Seth was being watched, then it was possible he'd just stepped into the shit. Deep.

Fuck, he couldn't stay here. Every second he stayed in this unit he came a second closer to someone realizing where he was and what he'd found.

Before he left though, he had to know for sure what his dad had left…

Seth fought a cold sweat and positioned himself with his back to the wall, eyes on the open door, escape routes already mapped in his head. Then, heart hammering, he lifted the cover of the binder.

Just enough to see.

His father had been a cop, not someone who indulged in speculation or wild theories. He'd been far too by-the-book and steeped in facts to be paranoid. Whatever he'd left as his final message, he'd known beyond a shadow of a doubt to be true.

The binder creaked before it revealed the first page—a list of names. Typed. Clinical. Some familiar. But then…at the bottom, he saw one name circled, written in his father's familiar handwriting.

A name that made his blood run cold.

A name his dad had identified as Specter.

Chapter Twenty Nine

He blinked incredulously.

Gene Hammond.

Seth's world tilted. His stomach dropped so fast he thought he might puke.

Holy shit.

Shock pinged Seth's system. He'd seen the truth, and his brain raced to catch up.

The past sixteen years—every memory, every conversation, every moment—snapped into sharp, horrifying focus.

Gene. His dad's best friend. His partner. The man who'd been a pallbearer at Michael Cooper's funeral and *wept*. The cop who'd saved Seth's life when he was sixteen and hell-bent on wrapping his car around a concrete barrier at a hundred miles per hour. The "friend" who'd checked in and watched over his mother all these years, who'd attended her wedding with that easy grin and fatherly grip on his shoulder.

The man Seth had just told thirty minutes ago exactly where he was going. Who knew Seth was alone and unarmed with sixteen years' worth of evidence that could destroy him. Who was sitting in his mother's family room, drinking mimosas—alone with everyone he loved. Heavenly. Beck. Hudson. His mother. Carl.

He had to get back. Had to act fast. Had to figure out how the fuck to keep them all alive.

Thirty minutes. Not a second more, or I'm coming after you.

What Seth had interpreted as a promise suddenly skidded through his brain in warning. In mere minutes, Gene would come looking for him. How long now? Fifteen? Ten? Less?

Seth's heart lurched. He didn't dare read more now.

Then again, he didn't need to.

Breaths sawing in and out of his chest, Seth slammed the binder shut. His hands shook, and he nearly lost his grip on the goddamn binder as he shoved it back into the pouch, beside the gun, the cash, and the video tape. He zipped it closed and tucked it under his arm, the weight of it both grounding and terrifying.

Then Seth forced himself to move, locking the unit with trembling fingers. When the padlock clicked into place, he ducked back into the hallway, the leather container clutched tightly under his arm.

The building felt too quiet. Too still. He didn't like it. Every footstep echoed. Every camera lens seemed to track his movement.

He was alone.

Unarmed.

And carrying something people had killed for. Something people had died for.

The gun in the pouch might work. But after sitting in a storage unit for sixteen years, it could just as easily misfire. Seth couldn't risk finding out the hard way.

His pounding heart roared in his ears as he forced his legs to carry him toward the exit. He tried to keep his breathing even, tried to keep his unsteady legs from giving out.

Stay alert. Keep your head on a swivel. Get home.

It seemed like half an eternity before Seth pushed through the facility's back door and stepped into the parking lot. The morning sun hit his face, too bright, too normal. The gate was still open. His mother's SUV sat where he'd left it, maybe thirty yards away.

But the hair on the back of his neck stood up. He felt eyes on him.

A sound that didn't belong echoed across the lot—a scrape of gravel, a shift of weight.

Seth's head snapped toward it. He saw nothing except rows of storage units casting long shadows.

Too many places for people to hide. Too many possibilities for this to go sideways. But he couldn't afford to be cautious; he had to get the fuck out of here.

He started moving again, faster now. The pouch pressed against his ribs as he scanned left, right, behind.

Another sound. Closer this time.

His hand twitched toward his pocket—toward his phone. He

couldn't call 911. Anyone—everyone—at the precinct could be dirty. Seth couldn't risk it.

Nor could he text Beck and tell him to get everyone the fuck out of that house. Any contact risked tipping Gene off. One wrong word, one panicked message, and Specter would know Seth had found something damning.

And a cornered man with that much power and everything to lose? He'd go scorched earth, burn it all down.

Seth couldn't risk that, either. He had to get home. Had to walk back into that house and pretend he'd found nothing. That the storage unit had been locked, inaccessible. Empty.

He had to lie to Gene's face and pray the bastard believed him.

Move. Now.

Seth broke into a jog, closing the distance to the SUV. Twenty yards. Fifteen.

Then he heard pounding footsteps. Fast. Heavy. Directly behind him.

Seth's instincts screamed. He twisted sharply, clutching the pouch tighter under his arm, eyes scanning for cover—a corner, a doorway, anything.

But there was nowhere to go.

And someone he couldn't get eyes on yet was coming for him.

Midday sun slanted in through the kitchen window as Heavenly dried another serving platter.

The last few of Grace's friends from church had stopped by after the later mass, staying only long enough to sip coffee and congratulate the newlyweds. Now they'd all gone. Just family remained.

In the family room, Beck stacked the last of the folding chairs against the wall while Hudson sat curled on the couch, thumbs flying across his phone, completely absorbed in whatever game he played.

The house had settled into an easy post-brunch lull.

Heavenly exhaled, but she couldn't seem to settle in the quiet.

She'd finally breathe when she was on the plane. Another eight hours...

Grace sighed contentedly. "Brunch was lovely, but I'm glad it's over. Now I can relax a little."

Carl set more dirty dishes beside her and grinned. "You'll be planning another party tomorrow."

"Hush!" Grace laughed, playfully swatting his arm with her soapy fingers.

Heavenly watched them with a smile, the thought she'd held at bay all morning drifting back in.

Pregnant.

Though Beck and Seth had told her a mere six hours ago, her feet still hadn't touched the ground.

She was going to have a baby. *Their* baby.

The knowledge still didn't feel real. But it was. A tiny life was growing inside her right now, invisible and perfect. And terrifying.

Heavenly's hand drifted toward her stomach before she caught herself. She didn't dare give their secret away, especially with Grace right beside her. Instead, Heavenly pretended to brush a non-existent crumb off her slacks and dropped her hand.

Some part of her wanted to tell Grace in the hopes her face would light up with pure, unguarded joy the way it had when the woman had first hugged Hudson. But Heavenly couldn't. Not until Seth told her the truth.

A truth that might have his mother shunning their child. A truth that might cost Seth everything.

Heavenly's chest tightened, but she did her best to tuck the worry away as she turned back to the dishes.

When she turned, she caught Beck watching her, his gaze steady and warm. When their eyes met, something passed between them—a quiet understanding that didn't need words. A sweetly whispered secret.

We made a baby.

The corners of his mouth lifted. Just barely. But enough.

Heavenly's heart squeezed. She ached to cross the room, wrap her arms around him, press her face into his chest, and just feel this moment with him. Instead, she settled for a clandestine smile in return.

But he understood. She saw it in his eyes.

Despite all the secrecy and uncertainty, their connection grounded her. Steadied her. Beck was her constant. So was Seth, except…

He'd bolted for the stairs when Grace asked him to run out for more orange juice, as if he'd been waiting for an excuse to escape. She hadn't noticed it earlier—she'd been too focused on keeping the fruit and pastry platters replenished—but Seth had seemed a bit off.

Because of the baby?

After he'd lost Autumn and Tristan, she knew he'd carried a mountain of guilt. She also knew that fatherhood still terrified him on some level. She understood why.

Maybe Seth didn't see how good he was with Hudson. Patient. Present. Then again, Hudson was sixteen—nearly grown. A baby was different. A baby was helpless. Vulnerable. A baby would need Seth in ways that Hudson never would.

But Seth *wanted* a family again.

True…but wanting something and being ready for it weren't the same thing.

What if the reality of it was too much? What if his fear strangled his hopes for the future?

Maybe she was borrowing trouble.

Maybe Seth was just anxious about sitting Grace down and explaining that Heavenly was Beck's fiancée, too.

She prayed Grace accepted them, that she wanted to be a part of their lives. Of her grandchildren's lives.

If she refused, that would crush Seth.

Across the room, Gene yanked his phone from his pocket, dragging Heavenly from her musings. He glanced at the screen, then slid the device away. A few seconds later, he repeated the whole process again.

Was he checking the time? Wondering when Seth would be back? Heavenly glanced at the front door, wondering that herself.

Another ten minutes passed. The kitchen was almost spotless now —dishes done, counters wiped down, leftovers tucked into the fridge.

Grace hummed softly as she folded the last dish towel. "You've been such a help, sweetheart. Thank you."

"Of course. Everything was lovely."

"I can't wait to help you plan your wedding," Grace said wistfully. "Have you and Seth talked about what you want yet?"

Heavenly's chest tightened. *You might not care after tomorrow.*

But she forced a smile. "A little. Nothing concrete yet. We're still figuring out a timeline."

"Well, whenever you're ready, I'm here." Grace squeezed her hand warmly.

With the cleanup finally done, Grace flipped off the kitchen light and gestured her toward the family room. "Come on. Let's finally sit down and enjoy the afternoon."

Heavenly followed her to the couch, where Hudson was still glued to his phone, thumbs flying across the screen. Without looking up, he shifted to make room for them.

Grace smirked and leaned closer to Hudson. "What are you playing on that thing?"

"Football," he replied, stare locked on the screen.

Grace arched a brow as she glanced at Carl and Beck, chilling in the recliners near the TV as they watched the Eagles and the Giants kickoff.

Behind them, Gene stared at his phone again.

"Why not watch it?" Grace asked, gesturing to the TV.

"'Cause I'd rather *play*."

Grace nodded. "A doer, like your father. So, how do you play on your phone?"

As Hudson began explaining, Heavenly sank into the couch and tucked her feet beneath her.

"C'mon, where's the flag?" Carl barked at the TV. "That's holding, for shit's sake."

"Carl," Grace chided sternly. "We have young ears here."

Beck snorted. Heavenly repressed a grin. And Hudson smirked as he kept right on playing.

When the game broke for a commercial, a soft buzz echoed in the room. Heavenly looked up to find Gene snapping to attention. He grabbed his phone, his stare glued to the screen.

Instantly, his expression shifted—relief flooded his features, followed by something else she couldn't put her finger on. Resolve?

Heavenly wasn't sure what that was about. A work thing, maybe? A bet on the game? She didn't know Gene well enough to guess.

He pocketed the phone, seeming to tuck away the distraction. Then he turned his attention to the game on the big screen. "I hope neither of you are Eagles fans. The Giants are gonna take it. Their defense is too strong this year."

Beck raised a brow. "You sure about that?"

Gene grinned. "Damn right. If Seth were here, he'd agree with me, too."

He probably would.

Where on earth was he? Since Seth was a huge Giants fan, she knew he didn't want to miss this game. Maybe he stopped to get something besides orange juice? Or maybe he'd run into someone he'd grown up with?

While Carl and Gene talked about players and their stats, Beck glanced at the front door, as if he wondered what was keeping Seth, too.

Heavenly tried to tamp down her concern. If he needed help, he'd call.

As the room settled, exhaustion tugged at Heavenly. Beck and Seth hadn't let her sleep much last night, and after a busy day, her lids felt heavy. She could really use a nap.

It was probably too early to blame her exhaustion on pregnancy, but soon…

She closed her eyes. *Just for a minute,* she promised herself.

When she blinked and sat up a few minutes later, Grace had shifted closer to Hudson on the couch, leaning in as he explained his game in a low voice, play by play, his thumbs pausing every so often to demonstrate. She listened intently. Hudson's face lit up.

Carl and Beck were still glued to the TV, debating something about a defensive formation Heavenly didn't understand. Gene tuned out of their debate.

He was staring at his phone again—scrolling, pausing. He read something.

His expression shifted. He looked more than focused. His jaw tightened, like he was thinking about something that bothered him.

A few minutes ago, he'd been kicking back and joking with the other men about the game. And now, the next play was underway, and he was glued to his phone.

Had he gotten bad news? Or maybe Gene was just wound a little tight. Not hard to believe of a career cop.

She glanced at Grace, who was smiling and nodding, still absorbed in Hudson's explanation. She'd known Gene for something like twenty years, and she didn't seem to think anything was off.

Heavenly thought about grabbing her phone, which was still upstairs, and texting Seth to make sure he was all right. Surely, he'd be back soon…

Suddenly, Gene tensed. He typed something quickly, his thumbs all but pounding on his screen. He waited with a scowl, looking tense, almost…angry.

What was that about?

Heavenly blinked, watching as he typed again, this time even faster, more emphatic.

She sent a sidelong glance to Beck. Despite the game flashing across the TV, he was watching Gene, too.

Their eyes met, and Beck's brow lifted—the silent equivalent of *what's up with this guy?*

Heavenly shrugged back. *Maybe that's just how he is?*

Too bad Seth wasn't here so she could ask. Speaking of… Shouldn't he be back by now?

Rising to her feet, Heavenly stretched. Maybe she'd text him, make sure he was all right.

By the time she went upstairs, took a bathroom break, found her cell, and settled back on the sofa, she found Gene staring at his phone again.

No, not staring. Glowering. He tapped at the screen—once, twice, three times in quick succession. Then stilled. Waiting. His eyes never wavered. Heavenly could feel the tension pinging off him.

Seriously, what was up with him? A glance proved Grace still hadn't noticed anything out of the ordinary.

Suddenly, his whole body went rigid, shoulders pulling back like someone had lifted him upright by yanking on his spine. His brow furrowed with agitation. Fury locked his jaw.

Heavenly's breath caught. If Gene wasn't a cop, she would have sworn he had murder in his eyes.

Then suddenly, his face went blank, his anger disappearing behind a flat, unreadable mask. Except his sharp eyes. They looked hyper-alert. Almost burning.

Carefully, he pocketed his phone and paced, pausing behind Carl's and Beck's recliners. Then he stopped. Stilled.

Braced?

Heavenly's stomach knotted. Everything about his behavior felt off. Wrong. Almost…menacing.

She clenched her hands in her lap. If Gene was upset about something, why wasn't he going outside to make a call? Or leaving to deal with whatever it was? Why stew in anger in the middle of Grace's family room with his face a mask that didn't quite hide the seething rage in his eyes.

Heavenly swallowed, her throat suddenly tight, and glanced at Beck again, who was leaning forward, focused on the TV as the Giants lined up for another play.

Since Gene hovered behind him now, Beck couldn't see the man's face.

Heavenly's pulse kicked up another notch when Gene started typing again. Even faster than before. Aggressive. His thumb stabbed at the screen. Then he stopped.

He stared. Waited. His jaw flexed.

Heavenly's hands twisted tighter in her lap. Her chest felt too tight, her breathing shallow.

She didn't know what was going on. But everything in her gut was screaming that Gene's behavior had crossed a line from odd to…something she was afraid to put a name to.

With trembling fingers, she opened her phone and started to text Seth, ask him about Gene. Tell him she was afraid.

She hoped like hell he'd reassure her with a few simple words. Or better yet, come strolling through the door and restore her sense of safety.

Before she could, Beck and Carl both jumped out of their seats, high-fiving each other. "Touchdown!"

Despite her unease, Heavenly paused mid-text, a little smile tugging at her lips.

Men…

Then she noticed Gene. He wasn't celebrating. He wasn't even looking at the TV. His face was white with rage and a dark determination that terrified her.

And he was holding a gun.

Heavenly tried to process what she was seeing, tried to make sense of the Coopers' oldest family friend pointing a weapon at Seth's loved ones. She couldn't. Instead, she tried to scream, but she only gaped, fear flooding her veins.

"Gene?" Grace sounded confused, her warbled voice detailing her struggle to reconcile what she was seeing with the man she'd known for decades.

"What the fuck?" Hudson shouted, scrambling back against the couch cushion.

Gene ignored them both, his face cold. Deadly. Unwavering.

Carl and Beck stiffened and turned—but it was too late. Gene moved fast, swinging the butt of the gun viciously down onto Carl's head.

The crack was sickening.

The big, burly man dropped like a stone, his body crumpling, his head hitting the hardwoods with a horrible thud as blood ran down his temple. He didn't get back up. Didn't move.

Heavenly yelped, her heart lurching. Fear gripped her belly, stole her breath. Was Carl even alive?

Grace screamed, her worried stare clinging to her new husband as she jumped from the sofa and raced toward him.

"Sit down, Grace!" Gene snarled. "You can't help him now. None of you can."

Then, without warning, he swung the gun straight toward Beck.

Heavenly watched as if in slow motion. Her eyes widened. A warning buzzed through her head.

Before she could spit out the words, Gene fired.

The deafening sound shattered the once cozy home.

Heavenly flinched, her whole body jerking. Her phone fell from her numb fingers, clattering to the floor. Her ears rang. And her world tilted as Beck cried out and stumbled back, gripping a gaping wound at his shoulder.

As the football game droned on in horrific normalcy, blood oozed from between his fingers and bloomed across his shirt—dark, wet, unmistakable.

"Beck!" Heavenly screamed, instinctively lurching forward.

"No!" Hudson roared at the same time, his voice cracking with horror.

"Don't move," Gene snapped as he pointed the weapon directly at them.

She froze. Beside her, Hudson did the same.

Heavenly gaped, barely comprehending. Gene—*Gene*—had a gun. He'd just knocked Carl unconscious. He'd shot Beck. He was pointing the weapon at her now, at Grace, at Hudson.

This wasn't real. This couldn't be real.

But the blood was real. The sound still ringing in her ears was real.

She blinked at Beck, trying to fight off her shock. His face twisted with both rage and pain, but he shook his head at her. Don't help him. Don't be foolishly brave.

What did he expect her to do? She couldn't stand here and just watch him bleed.

Beside her, Hudson grabbed her elbow. For support? The kid must be terrified.

Then she realized he was holding her back.

Gene raised a brow at Beck, the gun steady in his practiced hand. "If you try anything, I'll blow your bitch's fucking head off. And we both know how much you'd hate that."

Beck's jaw clenched, but he didn't move. Didn't make a sound.

Beside Hudson, Grace started hyperventilating, her breath coming in short, panicked gasps.

Hudson took her hand. "Grandma. Grandma, shh. Squeeze my hand. Just like that…"

"Now that I have your attention…" Gene's hard voice boomed through the living room. "I suggest you keep your fucking mouths shut and follow my instructions very carefully if you want to live. Saint Seth is going to try to save you soon. When he does, I'll be ready."

Heavenly's chest buckled. Her stomach flipped. *Seth!* He'd gone on an errand—and if she couldn't warn him, he'd walk right into an ambush.

Thoughts racing, she scanned the room for her phone, but when she'd dropped it, the device had skittered out of reach. She had no idea how to warn him, but she had to come up with something—or they'd all be dead.

Chapter Thirty

Heart thundering in his chest, Seth risked another glance over his shoulder—and finally saw his attacker.

Recognition hit him like a fist to the gut.

Another cop from the precinct.

Bob Ellis.

Seth had known the old-timer most of his life. He'd attended Michael Cooper's funeral, sitting red-eyed with the rest of the guys. He'd been one of Gene's fishing buddies for decades.

And one of Gene's *thugs*.

Bob's face was tight with determination. With murder. He didn't speak. Didn't warn. Didn't even try to negotiate.

Seth was pretty fucking sure that Gene had sent him. And told Bob to silence him…one way or another.

Thank god, he hadn't called 911. He'd be surrounded by more cops on Gene's payroll, ready to finish what Bob was doing his best to start.

A glint of something metallic caught Seth's gaze. He caught sight of the weapon in Bob's hand. It wasn't his police-issue weapon, a less-than-legal street piece, or even a shotgun.

It was something Seth hadn't expected.

A dart-style tranquilizer gun.

Understanding slammed through Seth's brain pan. Gene didn't want him dead…yet. The bastard wanted him incapacitated. Contained. Then…yeah, after enough torture to suit Specter's anger and bloodlust, Gene would off him.

Seth refused to give the motherfucker the satisfaction.

Teeth bared, Bob fired.

Seth feinted hard to the left, diving and rolling, somehow managing to keep the pouch under his arm. The dart whistled past him and clattered harmlessly to the pavement.

Bob's eyes widened with something that looked like panic. Then he cursed and backed away, fumbling to frantically reload the next dart.

Seth didn't give the son of a bitch the chance.

He pivoted and barreled into Bob, who stumbled and tried to regain his footing. But Seth was bigger, stronger, twenty-five years younger, and a hell of a lot more pissed off.

In desperation, Bob raised shaking hands and pointed the tranq gun at him. Seth grabbed the gun by the barrel and shoved it back at him, ramming it between Bob's eyes with a bone-cracking *thwack*. Bob grunted. Blood spurted from his nose as his head snapped back.

As he stumbled unsteadily, Seth ripped the weapon from his grip. His hands shook as he shoved the half-loaded dart into the chamber and pointed the weapon Bob's way. The old cop froze, fear flashing across his face.

"Did Gene fucking send you?" Seth snarled.

Bob hesitated, then nodded. He half expected the old-timer to beg or bargain. Seth didn't have the time or patience for either. Instead, he grabbed Bob's arm, held him immobile, and pressed the barrel against Bob's carotid artery.

Then Seth pulled the trigger.

Bob staggered, his hand flying to his neck. Shock widened his eyes. His legs buckled—just as his goddamn phone buzzed.

Quickly the drug worked its way through his system. Before the bastard passed out, Seth held him upright as he patted Bob down and located his phone.

"Passcode," Seth growled as he held up the device. "Now."

Bob's mouth moved, slurred words tumbling out almost unintelligibly. "Four…seven…two…nine. Please—"

"Shut the fuck up."

Then Bob's eyes rolled to the back of his head. His knees gave out as his consciousness slipped away.

Seth dropped Bob, not giving two shits when he fell to the asphalt in a head-thumping heap. Then, as he pocketed Bob's phone, he glanced up reflexively—a cop's instinct. The wiring had already been cut from the security cameras mounted around the parking lot, their cables dangling loose against the building's exterior.

Bob had prepared this kill zone. No footage. No witnesses. Clean elimination.

Gene's orders. Gene's reach. Gene's professionalism.

Seth clenched his jaw as he glanced back at Bob, unconscious. Vulnerable.

Fuck that. Bob hadn't planned to show him any mercy, and if the asshole came to, the first thing he'd do was call Gene. Then everyone at the house—everyone he loved—would die.

As far as Seth saw it, he only had one option, and he wasn't going to cry for Bob. The fucking bastard had made his choices. And he was about to find out that when you played stupid games, you won stupid prizes.

Without a second thought, he shoved the tranq gun into his waistband, forced Bob face-down against the asphalt, then gripped Bob's head in both hands twisted—hard. Quick. Controlled. Final.

He was dead.

Seth stepped over him and ran for the SUV, refusing to dwell on the fact that he'd just killed a man he'd known since childhood. No time to process it. No time to feel any certain way. He had to get to the house before Gene got suspicious—if he wasn't already. Seth's thirty-minute window was closing fast.

He had to save his family.

And as much as he wished he could, Seth knew he couldn't do that alone.

First, he had to see who the fuck had texted Bob during their scuffle.

As Seth sprinted to the vehicle and yanked the door open, he threw the tranq gun in the back seat and hauled himself behind the wheel. He settled the pouch on the passenger seat, jammed the key into the ignition, and peeled out of the lot. As he pulled onto the street, he tugged Bob's phone from his pocket, entered the passcode with trembling fingers, and saw a text from Specter.

A single question mark.

Seth's gut tightened. Gene wanted confirmation that Bob had offed him, his best friend's son, the kid he'd known since he was eight years old.

Too bad for Gene that the former cop who turned vigilante, who had left his badge behind years ago, intended to both save his loved ones and kill the motherfucker—no matter what it took.

As he drove, Seth skimmed the message thread between Specter and Bob. Short. Clipped. Professional. No emotion, no detail. Just efficient communication between crooked men with a common criminal purpose.

Cursing, Seth typed a response.

Target down. All secure.

He hit SEND without hesitation.

Then he floored it, tires screeching as he rocketed away from the storage facility. Adrenaline spiked through his veins, sharp and electric. His hands shook on the wheel.

Seth forced himself to breathe. Forced himself to focus.

The leather slid across the passenger seat—proof he suspected would take down Gene and his entire organization. Evidence his father had posthumously protected for the past sixteen years.

The text he'd just sent would buy him a little time—hopefully enough to game plan and execute. But Gene wasn't stupid. Soon enough, he'd figure out that Bob was dead, and he'd been played. And once Gene realized that, he wouldn't wait. He'd act—swiftly and brutally.

Fatally.

Because now, Gene had nothing to lose.

Tamping down his panic, Seth grabbed his own phone and dialed Matt.

His brother answered on the second ring. "Hey, what's—"

"Shut up and listen carefully." Seth cut him off. "Gene Hammond killed Dad."

Silence.

"Gene knows I found Dad's evidence this morning. He's been running a criminal organization for decades, hiding behind his badge. That's what had my head fucked up earlier—not the baby. And everyone is still at the house with him."

"Fuck," Matt breathed.

"I just offed Bob Ellis in the parking lot after he tried to tranq me. Once Gene realizes his guy failed, he's going to assume I know everything. And then…" Seth couldn't finish that sentence.

"What do you need?" Matt's voice sharpened.

"Get a gun. Get back to the house. I'll be there. Stay out of Gene's sight."

"I've got one in my car," Matt said immediately. "I was running an errand, so I'm only ten minutes out. Wait for me. Don't you dare be a fucking hero."

Seth ended the call without making promises. He'd do whatever he had to in order to rescue his loved ones from Gene.

He floored the accelerator, praying he wasn't already too late, and hit a number on his phone he hadn't dialed in years.

He also prayed Nikolai Volkov was feeling generous.

The big Russian answered right away. "Seth Cooper. To what do I owe pleasure?"

"This isn't a social call. I need help. I'll repay you in kind, whatever you want."

"Anything?" Nik drawled. "First, you warn me away from woman and now you want help?"

He'd been pissed off that day at the hotel. Jumpy. Overprotective. Nikolai was beyond brutal, but he lived by his own code of honor. He'd never hurt Heavenly.

"Everyone I love is being held hostage," Seth blurted past his panic. "Including her. She's pregnant."

"This is serious problem," Nik conceded. "I may have time. Busy schedule, you know."

Seth gripped the wheel, half tempted to climb through the phone and beat Nik. "Don't fuck with me. In all the years I've known you, I've asked for one name. *One*. And before you gave it to me, I did your dirty work for a fucking year—"

"Tell me what you seek."

Nik was going to play ball. Thank fuck.

Seth let out a breath. "Weapons. Muscle who aren't afraid to kill dirty cops. And I need them now."

Nikolai's voice shifted, turning more calculating. "And for me? I am businessman. Favors require…context."

Seth's jaw clenched. "The person holding my family hostage? Specter. I know his identity. I have proof. You help me…your turf problem goes away."

"I am listening."

"You would have listened anyway. You just enjoy being an asshole."

Nik laughed. "True. But I provide assistance. You have my word. You give me name."

"Gene Hammond, NYPD detective. I'm pretty sure he's been running the organization for close to two decades."

"For long time, I try to identify Specter," Nikolai spit. "Gene Hammond fits profile well. You want him dead?"

"I do, but he's mine. My father was his partner. He built a case against Gene before the son of a bitch murdered him. I just found the evidence this morning."

"Ah, this is personal for you. And now personal for me, too." A pause. "Next time, lead with that. Now I am motivated to help."

Despite everything, Seth's mouth twitched. "Fucker."

That made Nik laugh. "As always. Tell me situation."

Seth gave him the essentials. When he finished, Nikolai let out a low, dark chuckle. "Specter sent man to kill you before lunch? Very rude. Clearly, he must die."

"That's the plan."

"I approve." Nikolai's tone shifted slightly. "What does Specter want?"

"We haven't had contact, but my guess? The evidence. Me dead. And the leverage to disappear."

"He will not kill hostages unless forced," Nikolai mused aloud. "Bodies create problems. Hostages create options."

"Agreed. But I can't leave him any of those options."

"You cannot." A pause. "So you wish to end him and this enterprise. Permanently."

"Exactly. You're in?"

"Of course. And I bring muscle."

"I'm three minutes out from my mom's house. The address is—"

"Do not be naïve, Seth Cooper. I know where she lives."

That took Seth aback…and it probably shouldn't have. "How?"

"It is business to know where important people live. In case they need help." Nikolai's voice was almost gentle. "Like you. So I come. Fifteen minutes. But you wait. You cannot have all fun without me."

"Hurry. My brother Matt is meeting me there. We'll assess the situation and have a plan in place when you arrive."

"Wait for reinforcements. Playing cowboy is bad for health."

It wasn't an order, but advice from someone who knew what cornered criminals did when they panicked.

Seth's jaw worked. "If he starts killing people—"

"Then, yes. Act. But if house is quiet, be smart."

"Hurry the fuck up." Seth exhaled hard. "And Nik? Thanks."

"Save thanks for after killing. We have much to do." Another dark chuckle. "Then? You owe me very expensive vodka."

"Done."

"Good. See you soon, friend. Try not to die before I arrive. Would be very inconvenient."

The line went dead.

His finger hovered over Tony Marconi's contact…and hesitated. He was ninety-nine percent sure his former partner was clean. But his dad had clearly thought the same thing—and look where that faith had gotten him. On the off-chance Tony was dirty, the last thing Seth wanted to do was tip him off. And if his pal was innocent…best not to put him in danger.

With a curse, Seth tossed the phone onto the passenger seat and made the final turn into his mom's neighborhood, hoping like hell he could keep everyone alive long enough to neutralize Gene.

Chapter Thirty One

The football game droned through Grace's family room like it was any other Sunday. The announcers shouted about a fumble recovery as the crowd roared. The jarring normalcy grated on Heavenly's increasingly raw nerves.

Gene hadn't lowered the gun for an instant since he'd shot Beck. He'd simply trained it on her, Grace, and Hudson—steady, unwavering.

A constant, throat-clogging threat.

Across the room, Beck looked alarmingly pale as he slumped against the wall, still pressing a hand against his wounded shoulder. Heavenly watched helplessly as blood seeped between his fingers, trickled down his shirt, and dripped to his lap. With every passing minute, his breaths turned rougher yet shallower.

He was losing too much blood. What if he passed out? What if he bled out and—

She squeezed her eyes shut, unable to finish that thought.

Everything inside her screamed to go to him, to help him. But if she took even one step in Beck's direction, Gene would shoot. And once he started, would he just kill everyone?

Everything seemed so surreal. An hour ago, guests had been here, celebrating Carl and Grace's marriage. There had been laughter, congratulations. Joy and love. Heavenly's biggest problem had been wondering what troubled Seth and whether Grace would accept the fact that he was in a committed threesome.

Now Heavenly feared they might not leave this house alive. Each horrifying moment felt like a twisted nightmare. But it was every bit as real as the gun Gene had no qualms using.

Grace sat rigidly on the far side of the couch, hands trembling in her lap, lips moving silently. Praying. Her face was pasty white, eyes wide and glassy with shock. Heavenly reached over and gave the woman's shoulder a squeeze. Seth's mother must not only be terrified, but grief-stricken. She'd lost one husband to violence years ago. Would she lose the other to the same fate?

Between them, Hudson sat statue-still and angry, his gaze locked on the crooked cop, tracking every shift, every breath, his phone forgotten in terror on the couch cushion beside him.

Gene glanced down at his own device again. He snarled at whatever he saw on the screen. His nostrils flared. His rage spiked. His grip tightened on the gun.

Heavenly's stomach twisted, tangling with her unrelenting fear.

She didn't know what had happened, but it was something Gene hadn't expected. Something that filled him with fury.

Something to do with Seth?

It had to be. Heavenly couldn't think of any other logical reason Seth wasn't back yet. Unless he was already…

She blocked that horrible thought from her mind.

Seth had to be out there fighting back to thwart Gene and his twisted plans. If Seth was dead, Gene wouldn't have sneered minutes ago that "Saint Seth" would be coming to save them. Instead, Gene would be celebrating. He would have everything under control.

His expression very much said he didn't.

Yes, she was guessing, piecing together scraps of logic while terror screamed louder than her thoughts. But she clung to hope. She had nothing else.

Seth must be alive. He'd do whatever it took to keep history from repeating itself. He would risk everything—go scorched earth, burn down the world—to ensure he didn't lose his woman and child again.

Gene's voice cut through her thoughts suddenly, sharp and edged with fury.

"Your precious Seth thinks he's so fucking clever. But I'm smarter. I know he killed Bob." Something cruel flickered in Gene's eyes as he turned the barrel of the gun on Grace. "Did you hear me? Your fucking son offed Bob Ellis!"

Grace flinched.

Heavenly's breath caught.

"Then 'Bob' texted me to say Seth was dead. Does your cocksucker of a kid think I'm a moron?" Gene railed in frustration. "Jesus, how is twenty years of hard work going down the drain in a single goddamn day? I knew your precious Michael had collected evidence against me. Since the day after his funeral, I've looked and looked for it. And nothing. But your motherfucking kid found it less than an hour ago at a nearby storage unit."

Heavenly's gaze flicked to Beck, wide and startled.

How had Seth found out about that? Why didn't he tell us?

Beck's answering expression said he hadn't known, either. Then his expression shifted, as if something clicked into place. Like he finally knew the answer to some question he'd been asking.

"Bob had *one* job," Gene ranted on. "All he had to do was end Seth and take Michael's shit to our safe house. And he fucking failed! He's too loyal to disobey orders, so the fact that his phone is heading straight here means that Seth clocked him and offed him. Motherfucker!"

When he pounded a fist against the wall, Heavenly flinched, watching as he paced, his movements choppy and agitated.

Unfortunately, the gun never wavered.

At least Seth was alive…for the time being. But he was coming here. To rescue them. And Gene knew that. That explained why he was holding them hostage. She, Grace, Hudson, and the others were leverage to bring Seth down.

Oh, god. How could she warn him, stop that from happening?

"Bob's sloppy work made Seth think I'm running amateur hour, but if he's stupid enough to underestimate me?" Gene's smile turned cold. "School is in session, and I'm the teacher."

Heavenly's heart lurched with fear. Gene was both desperate and unhinged. He wouldn't hesitate to kill Seth.

But Seth was smart. Trained and careful. He wouldn't walk in blind.

Right?

Heavenly twisted her hands in her lap, nails digging into her palms. Next to her, Grace's prayers grew louder—barely audible but frantic. Her fingers moved as if she rolled them over invisible rosary beads. And Hudson still tracked Gene with his stare, like a predator watching his prey.

Heavenly did her best to shove down her worries and hold onto hope.

"You." Gene waved the gun in the kid's direction, sending Heavenly's heart jumping into her throat. "Get your ass off the couch."

Hudson's head snapped up, his jaw tight.

"Close those fucking drapes." Gene pointed to the curtains at the front of the house.

Slowly, Hudson stood, fists clenched at his sides. His face was pale, but his eyes blazed with barely contained fury.

"Move!" Gene barked.

Hudson crossed to the front windows, took a regretful last glance outside, then yanked the drapes closed. As he did, the room fell into shadow—heavy, oppressive, suffocating. Everything felt smaller. Scarier.

Fear tightened Heavenly's chest. She felt trapped, as if Gene was sealing them inside a tomb of his making.

"Good." Gene nodded in approval. "We can't let Seth have help, so take Beck and Carl to the basement."

Hudson's eyes widened. "What?"

"You heard me, you little shit. Lock them in. And grab their phones while you're at it. Bring those to me."

"That door only locks from the inside," Hudson pointed out.

"Then wedge a fucking chair under the knob. And stop being a pain in the ass like your dad."

Hudson hesitated, anger rolling off him in waves. His fists opened and closed. His breathing came fast and hard.

Was he considering taking on Gene?

Horror rolled through Heavenly. She shook her head in warning, not even trying to be subtle.

Gene saw. His eyes narrowed, then he swung the gun toward Heavenly. "Step it up, kid. Or she'll be the first to die."

He wasn't kidding. His finger on the trigger, steady and ready, told Heavenly that.

"And you'll be second, kid," Gene promised, his voice cold. "Your choice."

Hudson's face twisted with fury and helplessness. Just when she worried he might take the bullet and go down fighting, Hudson slumped, his shoulders sagging in defeat. His jaw clenched so hard, she saw the muscle tick.

Beck, who sat slumped against the wall, pasty and sweating, groaned as he pressed his palm against his wound. His breathing shallowed. Blood soaked through his shirt, dripping onto the floor.

Worry burned Heavenly's throat. Even in the shadows, she could see the fury in Beck's eyes—the rage at being incapacitated and forced to leave her to Gene's dubious mercy.

Her throat ached with words she didn't dare speak, not that Beck would believe that she was fine, anyway.

Face full of apology, Hudson crouched beside Beck and hauled him to his feet. Her brave surgeon grunted, pain etched deep into every line of his face as he wrapped his good arm around Hudson's shoulders and struggled to stand.

Together, they made their way to Carl, who still lay motionless on the floor, blood matting his hair. Since he'd fallen, he hadn't made a sound. Hadn't moved. Was he even breathing?

Hudson leaned Beck against the opening to the kitchen. Then, with a grunt, he grabbed Carl under the arms and dragged him toward the basement door. Beck stumbled alongside, every movement making him wince. Making him bleed faster.

Terror filled Heavenly as she and Beck exchanged one last glance before he disappeared around the corner. With her heart in her eyes, she silently told him that she loved him. That if this was the end, he'd been everything to her.

Beck paused, his eyes locked on hers. Desperate. Anguished.

He mouthed something. She couldn't hear it, but she knew.

I love you.

Tears burned her eyes. She blinked them back, refusing to let Gene see her break as she mouthed the same words to him.

Beck's jaw clenched. He wanted to say more—promise her he'd keep her safe, that Seth would save them, that everything would be okay.

But he wouldn't lie to her.

Heavenly bit her lip to hold in a sob, but she felt as if her chest was caving in. What if this was the last time she ever saw him? The last time she looked into those dark, steady eyes that had made her feel both safe and dangerously desired?

Please don't let this be goodbye.

She didn't say the words. She couldn't.

Because if she spoke, she'd fall apart.

With a last wrenching stare, Beck disappeared around the corner. Hudson followed suit, dragging Carl behind him.

Gene leaned around the corner to keep watch on the guys while still able to see the women.

Heavenly wasn't sure what was happening, but the scrape of shoes against the hardwoods and the creak of Hudson opening the basement door were unmistakable.

The steep, uneven stairs groaned under the guys' collective weight. A thump. A grunt of pain. Then Beck's low rumble, unintelligible and strained.

Hudson's whispered apologies followed. "I'm sorry. Really sorry."

Another thump. Heavier this time. Carl being dragged down the steps.

Heavenly's nails dug into her palms. She hated feeling helpless, hated that she could only sit here and listen as they endured what might be their final prison.

Suddenly, a sobbing Grace gripped her hand. The woman's trembling fingers were ice-cold, her lips moving with more desperate, whispered prayers.

Gun still in hand, Gene stepped closer to the basement door—and took his eyes off her for just a moment. Heavenly glanced at the front door, mentally calculating. It was so close, maybe ten feet.

She could run…but would she make it?

No. Gene would shoot her before she got halfway there. And even if she escaped, Gene would kill Grace. Kill Hudson. Maybe Beck and Carl, too—if they weren't already dead.

She couldn't risk it.

A flash of metal caught her eye. Hudson's phone still sat on the couch where he'd left it.

If she could just—

"Don't even think about it," Gene growled, his glare landing on her. "Or I'll shoot the kid."

Heavenly froze. Her heart hammered. She held up both her hands.

Gene's smile was vicious. "Smart girl."

Minutes crawled by, each feeling like an eternity. She sat frozen, her heart racing while her brain screamed at her to do something.

But she had no idea what.

Finally, footsteps echoed back up the stairs. Hudson emerged, pale and shaken, a phone bulging from each of his front pockets. He grabbed a chair from the kitchen table, the scrape of it against the floor sounding final. Then he wedged it under the knob of the basement door.

Beck and Carl were locked in. The two men big enough to fight off Gene were neutralized.

Heavenly's panic surged, clawing at her throat. Now, it was just her, Grace, and Hudson.

And Gene knew Seth was coming.

Hudson looked ready to explode as he crossed the room, yanked the two phones from his pockets, and dumped them on the coffee table with a clatter that made her start.

Gene just kept tightening the noose. She couldn't wait anymore. If they were going to survive this ordeal, she needed to think. Needed to find a way out.

But she'd never faced danger like this. She had no idea what to do.

Hudson sank onto the couch, his face devastated. His hands shook with terror and rage.

Gene turned the gun back on the boy, gesturing wildly. "Now the others. Put the rest of the phones on the table."

Hudson slumped. "I don't know where Grandma's phone is."

"In my purse, honey." Grace's voice shook. "In the kitchen, on the counter near the stove."

Hudson hesitated before he got to his feet and retrieved the phone under Gene's hawk-eyed stare. Wrath filled the teenager's face as he carried it back before setting it carefully beside the others.

Hudson looked her way then, his green eyes—his father's eyes—

meeting hers with silent apology before he bent and picked up her phone from where it had fallen on the floor.

As he did, Heavenly noticed his still sitting on the couch cushion. Her heart raced. If she could just reach it—text Seth—warn him somehow…

"I already warned you once." Gene leveled the gun her way. "So help me, bitch, if you touch it, I'll put a bullet in your fucking skull."

Heavenly froze, her fingers halfway to the cushion, then pulled back her trembling hand.

Cruel satisfaction engulfed his smile as Hudson added her phone to the growing pile of technology.

"Now yours, kid," he ordered Hudson.

The teenager paled. Panic flashed across his face before he gritted his teeth, plucked up his device from the couch, and dumped it on the gleaming wooden surface next to the others.

Five phones sat in plain view three feet away, unreachable.

Now they were completely cut off. Every lifeline gone. Every illusion of help stripped away.

Gene had them trapped, and his terrible smirk said he knew it.

Guilt filled Hudson's face, as if he was beating himself up for betraying everyone.

She sent him a reassuring smile. *It's okay. There was nothing else you could have done.*

In that moment, he looked so much like Seth that it almost broke her heart.

"Good job, kid. Now sit down," Gene ordered, gesturing with a jerk of his gun toward the couch. "Next to Grace. Where I can see you."

Hudson obeyed, sinking onto the cushion beside his grandmother.

Gene's message was unmistakable. They were leverage. And they were expendable.

Beside her, Grace blinked, her stare landing on Hudson's tormented face. Then she lifted her gaze to the spot on the floor where Carl had fallen before trailing to the unmistakable stain of Beck's blood. Something inside her seemed to snap.

"What are you *doing*, Gene?" Her voice cracked. She sounded raw and desperate.

He turned his focus on her, his eyes wild with rage. "Michael asked the same stupid question, in that same righteous-ass tone—right before I blew his fucking brains out."

Gene's words landed like a sledgehammer.

Grace gasped, the sound strangled and broken. Disbelief rippled across her face. Heavenly felt the woman's shock blasting through the room in a wave of horror. Grim silence followed.

A moment later, Grace opened her mouth, but nothing came out. She stared at Gene like she was seeing him for the first time—not the man she'd known and trusted—but the vicious monster he'd concealed for decades.

"Why?" she finally managed to choke out. "Michael was your *friend*."

"Michael should have learned to either shut the fuck up or cooperate. I offered to let him in on the business, but no. He had to be a goddamn saint." Contempt twisted Gene's face. "He made his choice. So I made mine."

His words were sharp. Cruel. Like Michael's murder was less important than the weather.

Grace's face crumpled. Her shoulders shook with raw, guttural sobs that tore at Heavenly's heart. She slapped her hand over her mouth, trying desperately to hold in her grief, but it broke through in jagged gasps.

Hot tears stung Heavenly's eyes. She'd never met Seth's father, but she nearly cried with Grace. The woman had spent sixteen years mourning her beloved husband, believing he'd been gunned down in the line of duty by the criminals he'd sworn to stop.

And it had all been a lie.

His best friend—his *partner*—had killed him for a buck.

"I'm trying to think here," Gene snapped. "And I can't do it with you blubbering. So shut the fuck up or I'll do it for you."

Hudson tensed, fists clenched. His whole body coiled in fury.

Heavenly caught his eye and shook her head. Subtle but firm.

Hudson's jaw worked, rage and helplessness warring across his face. Finally, he cursed under his breath and sulked against the back of the sofa, crossing his arms over his chest.

Heavenly sighed raggedly. Beside her, Grace's sobs had quieted to shuddering inhalations. Tears still streamed down her face as she rocked, clearly trying to hold herself together and failing.

Every cell in Heavenly's body hurt for the woman. The shock. The pain. The utter betrayal…

Then she realized… If Gene had killed Michael, he'd also ordered Autumn's and Tristan's deaths. He must have. Seth had been investigating his father's murder, and he'd gotten too close. So Gene had blown away his wife and infant son, then left him to drown in guilt and grief.

Did Seth know? Had he figured it out? Would whatever Michael had left in the storage unit prove how evil Gene was?

Seth must know by now. He had to. Or else…why wasn't he back?

Heavenly felt the screws of danger tighten.

The monster was waiting for Seth to return so he could clean up the last of his loose ends. If he managed to silence Seth, he'd kill them all without a second thought.

She couldn't let that happen.

A whisper of a plan began forming in Heavenly's head, fragile and desperate…but the best she had.

"Gene." She was surprised by how steady her voice sounded. "Can I go check on Beck? Help stop his bleeding?" *Maybe sneak out the basement window and get help?*

Gene snapped his head in her direction, his expression vicious. "Don't fucking move. Your other boyfriend is just fine."

She blinked, his words a paralyzing shock. *He knew?*

Heavenly's heart stuttered as she whirled to Grace, whose brows furrowed with confusion on her tearstained face.

"You didn't know, Gracie? Priceless." Gene shook his head, somehow mocking and pitying at once. "But I'm not surprised. You're just like Michael, too good to see the bad in others."

Grace's lips parted, but nothing came out. Then she turned her questioning stare on Heavenly.

Dread filled her. Humiliation followed. What should she do? Say?

If she wasn't careful, she could mess up Seth's relationship with his mom—if they lived long enough for that to matter.

"Oh, your face... Look at all that guilt." Gene laughed before turning back to Grace. "Bet you don't know that your golden boy is a class-A pervert. Always has been. He used to belong to Graffiti, that kink club in the city. The one where people wear leather and chains and call each other Master. And Autumn wasn't just his wife; she was his slave. Seth controlled her. She couldn't so much as put on a goddamn sock without his permission. The whole precinct knew it."

Grace flinched as if he'd struck her. Then she shook her head in denial, her mouth in a flat, mutinous line.

Heavenly wanted to scream at Gene, but her throat had closed up. Her hands shook. Besides, begging him for any sort of mercy was a waste of breath.

"I didn't think the bastard could get any more depraved." Gene sounded almost conversational now. "But I underestimated him. When he rolled into town with this bitch and the doctor? Beck couldn't take his eyes off her. At first, I thought he just had a stiff cock for her. Made sense—she's young, pretty, and fuckable. But then..." Gene paused dramatically, like he was savoring her destruction. "Then I realized she was eye-fucking him right back—in front of Seth. And instead of losing his shit and beating in his pal's face, Seth smiled, like he was excited knowing another man wanted to rail his fiancée."

Heavenly's stomach churned. He was twisting everything, making the love she felt for Beck sound sick and wrong.

"Stop," Grace whispered, her voice barely audible.

Gene ignored her. "The more I watched them, I realized Seth doesn't just enjoy knowing that Beck wants to fuck her. He gets off on her spreading her legs for him." His gaze locked on Heavenly, cold and calculating. "They both fuck you, don't they, sweetheart? Yeah... Do they plow you one at a time? Or share you like a blow-up doll?"

"Stop." Grace's voice broke, louder now, desperate.

But it was too late. Gene and his nuclear tongue had dropped the ultimate bomb. Now he stood, smiling and enjoying the fallout.

Heavenly's heart pounded so hard she swore it might burst through her ribs.

For a moment, she considered denying Gene's accusations. After all, Grace was worried about Carl. She'd already suffered a massive shock today. She didn't need another. It might even be a kindness to insist that Gene had spewed lies to divide them.

But Heavenly refused to lie when they might all be dead in an hour. Not when this might be the last conversation Grace ever had about her son.

She slowly turned to Seth's mom, whose eyes were red rimmed from crying in a face pale with shock.

"It's true," Heavenly murmured, her words shockingly steady.

Grace's breath hitched. Her hand flew to her lips as if she was utterly speechless.

"But Gene has everything wrong," Heavenly assured, her voice cracking with tears. "I love Seth with my whole heart. He's good and brave and kind. He makes me feel treasured, protected in a way I've never felt."

Grace's lips trembled. "Then why..."

"Because I also love Beck. I didn't mean to. I never planned it. But he challenges me. He makes me laugh. And they—" She sniffled, willing Grace to understand. "They both love me. And they both accept that. No, they're happy about it. Not because they're perverts or broken or wrong. Because we're all just following our hearts." She paused to swallow past the lump in her throat. "We know our love doesn't fit into a neat little box, but together we feel complete."

Grace made a small sound—something between a gasp and a sob.

"Beck and Seth proposed to me together," Heavenly continued, her voice shaking. "And I said yes. Please don't be angry with Seth." She reached for Grace's hand, gripping it desperately. "He didn't want you to find out like this. None of us did. He planned to tell you tomorrow. He waited because he didn't want to ruin your wedding."

Tears filled Grace's eyes. Heavenly wished she knew the woman better. She couldn't tell if Seth's mother was disgusted, just trying to understand, or something else entirely.

Heavenly pressed on. "He's been trying to figure out how to break the news to you for months. He was terrified you'd disown him, like you threatened with the twins. Terrified you wouldn't love him and—"

Her voice broke again as sobs overtook her. "He loves you so much. You're one of the most important people in his life."

Grace's tears spilled over, streaming down her soft face. The woman squeezed her fingers. What was she thinking?

"I'm sorry we weren't honest with you, but I won't apologize for our love," Heavenly whispered, raw and broken. "What the three of us have is real and beautiful. You don't have to accept Beck and me. We understand. But please don't shut Seth out of your life. It would break him."

"Grandma?" Hudson murmured. "The three of them belong together. And before you ask, yeah, I know. I've known the whole time."

With her chin quivering, Grace blinked away fresh tears and stared silently for what felt like an eternity.

Heavenly braced herself for rejection. For the woman's disgust. For her righteous indignation.

Instead, Grace swallowed hard. And then…slowly, she nodded. "I don't care."

Heavenly's breath caught.

"I don't care," Grace repeated, her voice still shaking. But this time, it sounded stronger. Resolved. "It doesn't matter to me who Seth loves. I don't care what your relationship looks like, how many people are involved, or what anyone else thinks. I only care that he's loved."

"He is." Heavenly's chest broke open, a sob tearing free. "More than you can imagine."

Grace nodded, squeezing Heavenly's hand so tight, it hurt. "I want him to be happy. That's all I've ever wanted for my boys. If you and Beck make Seth happy, then that's all I need to know. I accept the three of you, however you want to be together." She drew in a shuddering breath. "Today has taught me what's really important. I just hope we all stay alive so I can tell him."

Heavenly couldn't hold back. Sobbing, she threw her arms around Seth's mother. The woman clutched her back as they shared tears, bound by terror and love and the desperate, aching hope that they'd all survive this ordeal long enough for Grace's acceptance to mean something.

"It's okay, sweetheart. Don't cry," Grace whispered, stroking Heavenly's hair like she was comforting a beloved daughter. "I'm sorry you all felt like you'd lose me if you told me the truth. I'd do almost anything to go back and change that."

Without warning, Hudson leaned in and wrapped his arms around them both. He held them tight, just like Seth would have done. Heavenly's heart squeezed.

They sat together, clinging for long moments—three people in the shadow of a monster's gun, living in the moment and trying to hold on when hope felt impossible.

Heavenly kept the news about the baby to herself. Gene would twist it into a weapon, a bargaining chip, to destroy Seth from the inside out.

For now, she simply prayed they'd all live long enough to tell Grace.

"Jesus, spare me emotional broads." Gene's voice sliced through the moment like an ax. "Dry your fucking tears and shut up. I've heard enough bellyaching, and Seth is almost here."

At that, they jerked apart. Heavenly's heart leapt to her throat. Seth was close?

Scowling, Gene checked his phone. Then he cursed as if he didn't like whatever he was seeing.

Dangerous hope flared as the crooked cop's thumbs flew across his screen.

His phone lit up once, twice. Then the screen lit up again and again with incoming texts.

Gene answered them quickly, his expression shifting from agitation to focus. Then a slow smile of satisfaction spread across his face.

Heavenly's heart threatened to stop.

That expression said that Gene's fate had turned. He'd set his scheme in motion, and it was working. She'd bet he was calling in reinforcements to put down Seth before he could even get near the house. And they were responding.

Gene wasn't working alone anymore.

Horror washed over her. How could she warn Seth, send him some signal that wouldn't get them all killed? Gene had taken their phones, blocked all their exits, and cut them off from the outside world. And Seth was outnumbered, outgunned, and unaware of the overwhelming danger he was about to face.

With a grim expression, Gene pocketed his phone. "That fucking bastard blew up my entire operation in a single morning, and I'm going to repay him by making sure he dies after watching me off each and every one of you." Then he pointed his gun directly at Heavenly. "You first."

Chapter Thirty Two

As Seth approached his mother's neighborhood, he fought every instinct screaming at him to floor it and crash through the front door. But Gene knew he was coming. If he hadn't already, he was calling for backup. He had hostages. He had control.

But Seth had one advantage: he knew the house in a way Gene never would. Every inch of it. Every blind spot, every angle, every way in and out.

He would use that to his advantage—minimize risks as much as possible—then proceed with caution and save his loved ones. He couldn't what-if himself into a mindfuck that would cripple him.

And he sure as hell wouldn't fail again.

Letting out a rough breath, Seth turned onto his mother's street and tucked the SUV behind the neighbor's conversion van three houses down, shielding the vehicle from the front-facing windows of his childhood home.

He killed the engine. Then his stare fell on the leather pouch in the passenger seat. He hesitated. Damn it, he couldn't leave this goldmine of evidence in his car. Anyone, especially Gene's goons, could break in and steal the only proof of Gene's corruption. He had to stash it someplace where Gene couldn't reach it, would never think to look for it.

He'd have to figure something out. One problem at a time.

For now, Seth shoved the leather pouch under his arm and slipped out of the car.

It was a seemingly typical Sunday afternoon, quiet as sunlight filtered through the trees. A couple walked their dog. A few doors down, a man mowed his lawn.

Today, the quiet felt like its own kind of threat.

Seth didn't hesitate. He crouched low to the ground as he cut through the neighbors' yards, using trees and overgrown hedges for cover. Pounding heartbeats later, he advanced, darting for the old oak tree his dad had planted when Seth was five. Finally, he tucked himself behind the thick shrubs he and his brothers had hated trimming every summer.

After dragging in a ragged breath, Seth sprinted to the side of the house without sight lines to the front door and pressed his back against the cool vinyl siding. Then slowly, he inched to the front edge of the house and peeked around the corner.

The family room drapes were closed. Seth's gut clenched. Grace Cooper opened those curtains every morning. She loved the natural light. So seeing them shut this early in the afternoon was like a neon sign flashing DANGER.

Gene had done it purely to lock his loved ones in and to prevent Seth's visual recon.

Fuck you.

Another glance up at the house. The bedroom curtains on the second floor were wide open. That meant Gene had the hostages on the main floor or the basement.

Time to test his hypothesis.

Crouching low, Seth scurried along the foundation toward the basement window, hoping for a clandestine peek inside.

As he neared the small window, it creaked open.

Shit.

With his heart thudding, he flattened himself against the siding again, hoping like fuck that his decision to leave his gun in LA to avoid the hassle with TSA didn't cost everyone he loved their lives.

Seth froze as he waited to see who emerged, coiled and ready to pounce. If Gene stuck his head out, he'd have to attack quickly. Lethally.

He'd only get the element of surprise once.

But it wasn't his nemesis whose head appeared in the opening. It was…

Beck?

The good doctor extended one arm with a grimace, frantically clawing at the grass as he struggled to pull himself out the tiny window.

Seth lunged forward, relief sweeping through him at the sight of his friend alive and fighting. He grabbed Beck's arm and tugged him free.

With a groan of agony, Beck rolled onto his back. He was sweating and shockingly pale. Blood soaked his shirt.

Seth's heart sputtered at the sight. "Fuck! You're shot."

Beck's voice was tight. "Noticed that, huh?"

Despite his obvious pain, the surgeon's sarcasm was unscathed.

"Hard not to." Seth automatically checked the wound on his left shoulder. The entry point was ragged and ugly. As he started to ease Beck onto his right side, the doctor stopped him.

"There's no exit. The bullet is still lodged inside me."

"Did you escape?"

Beck scoffed. "The cocksucker locked me and Carl in the basement."

So the able-bodied men couldn't protect the women or put up a fight. Coward.

"And Heavenly? Is she okay?" Seth demanded. "Has Gene shot anyone else?"

Beck shook his head, his eyes sharp and focused "I haven't heard any more gun shots. Yelling, but that's it."

More relief. But Seth didn't dare relax as he pulled out his phone. "You need a hospital."

Beck's hand shot out and gripped Seth's wrist. "I'm not leaving."

"Damn it, Beck. You—"

"Will be fine. The bleeding has slowed. It hurts like a bitch, but I'm not gonna die. I'll get patched up once we get everyone out."

Seth didn't bother trying to reason with Beck. He'd be wasting his breath. Besides, if the shoe was on the other foot, Seth wouldn't budge either.

With a terse nod, Seth helped Beck sit up, propping him against the house behind a bush. "Tell me what happened. Where is Gene keeping everyone?"

"One minute Carl and I were watching football. The next, the son of a bitch clocked Carl with the butt of his gun. Knocked him out cold. He's got a minor concussion. Then the asshole shot me, no fucking warning. He forced us down to the basement. Before that, Gene had everyone else pinned to the family room sofa."

"Jesus." Seth itched to kill the motherfucker.

"I'm worried about Hudson." Beck's brows furrowed.

Seth felt his stomach drop. "Is he hurt?"

"Not physically. But Gene forced the kid to drag Carl and me to the basement and take our phones. I'm sure Gene took all the others, too. But poor Hudson was freaked out. Kept whispering he was sorry. I told him it wasn't his fault and to stay calm, not to give Gene any reason to shoot him, too."

"How many guns does Gene have? What kind?"

"I only saw one. Looked like a Glock."

Seth's throat tightened. "How's Carl?"

"His head hurts like hell. Minor concussion, but he came to about ten minutes ago. Helped me get to the window, but he couldn't fit through."

The news filled Seth with relief and rage. He tried to calm himself with the reminder that everyone was alive...for now.

"I'll be right back." Seth eased toward the window, then peered inside.

Carl sat on the stool next to the basement workbench, resting his head in his hands. He was pale and shaking, blood caked on the side of his head—completely unlike last night's vibrant groom.

His stepfather lifted his head. The second their eyes met, he jolted and rushed to the window. The tears of fear and fury in his eyes nearly crushed Seth.

"Thank God you're here. G-Gene has your mom and—"

"I know. I'm going to get them out." Seth pulled the satchel from under his arm and held it out. "I need you to hide this in the safe next to the workbench. If Gene gets his hands on what's in there, we're all dead."

Carl took the leather pouch, then peered back up at Seth. "I don't know the combination."

"Sure you do. Or rather, you'd better. It's Mom's birthday."

A flicker of warmth darted over his face. "I'll lock it right up. Just… go save my girl."

"On it. Sit tight. We'll get you out of there as soon as we can," Seth assured before making his way back to Beck.

"What's the plan?" Beck croaked.

"I called for backup. They're on their way."

"Gene knows you're here and that you killed Bob. He's been tracking you on Bob's phone."

"I didn't dump the fucking thing because it's evidence." Seth scrubbed a hand through his hair. "I never thought Gene would be stalking his minion like a helicopter parent."

"Based on Gene's violent outburst, I'm guessing you found something important at your dad's storage unit?"

Gene had fucking told them?

Seth grimaced, guilt searing his veins. "Fuck, I'm sorry. I swore I wouldn't dig again…and I did. But I had no idea until I got to the storage unit that Gene was the one who killed my dad and ordered the hit on Autumn and Tristan. I should have left well enough alone, but…" He sighed. "I couldn't. And now I've brought a world of shit down on all of you because I—"

"Stop. Gene did this. Not you," Beck insisted, gripping Seth's wrist. "We'll hash out the rest later."

Seth hesitated, then nodded. Beck was right; now wasn't the time.

"All that matters now?" Beck muttered, despite the pain etched into every line of his face. "Heavenly and our baby are inside that house. We have to save them."

Our baby.

Those two words hit Seth like a wrecking ball.

This morning they'd woken up as future fathers. If he didn't fucking stop Gene, their future might be dust by sunset.

"We will. And we'll deal with Gene so he can never hurt anyone again," Seth growled.

His stare connected with Beck's. A silent understanding passed between them—absolute, unshakable.

"When your backup arrives, I'm going in with you." Beck straightened, wincing.

"Not with that shoulder." Seth's voice was low and firm.

"Goddamnit, Cooper. I'm not helpless. I can still—"

"No. You're my fail-safe." Seth swallowed the emotion clogging his throat. "If something goes wrong—if I don't make it out—you have to take care of Heavenly, our baby, and Hudson. Make sure they live long, happy lives."

Beck opened his mouth to argue, but Seth held up his hand.

"I'm counting on you to take care of our family. This isn't about pride or ego. It's about their survival."

Beck gritted his teeth, then exhaled a heavy sigh. "If it makes you feel better, fine. But you better not fucking die in there."

"That's the plan," Seth assured as he caught a glimpse of Matt—armed and alert—darting across the neighbor's yard. His movements were deliberate and silent as he innately traced the same path Seth had taken.

Gratitude that the first of his reinforcements had arrived tangled with his guilt for dragging his younger brother into this shit and putting his life at risk. But without help he could trust, innocent people would die today.

Matt rushed to his side, against the house, and wrapped Seth in a fierce embrace. "You doing okay?"

"Define okay," Seth quipped, clapping his brother on the back before releasing him. "You?"

"I'm worried shitless about Mom and fucking furious at—" Matt's words died when he spotted Beck slumped against the house. "Oh, shit." He crouched down beside him. "You've been shot."

"Your observation skills are as sharp as your brother's. It's just a flesh wound," Beck said flatly.

Matt sent him a skeptical stare, but he didn't argue. Instead, he glanced back at Seth and held out a SIG with a suppressor. "Brought you this."

Seth accepted the Glock and gripped it firmly.

"Stay here." Matt clapped Beck on the leg. "Don't die and don't worry. I've got Seth's back."

As Beck nodded, something loosened in Seth's chest.

"How blind are we gonna be going in?" Matt rose to his feet, gaze locked on Seth.

He gave his brother a quick rundown.

Matt's expression turned arctic. "Got a plan?"

"Working on it." Seth's gaze flicked back to the house, to the closed drapes and the unnatural silence.

"Work faster, man. We need to move."

"Not yet. We're waiting for more backup."

Matt frowned. "Who?"

Two vehicles pulled up and parked on opposite sides of the street. The doors swung open and men whose dangerous expressions and tattoos ensured they'd never be mistaken for cozy suburban neighbors stepped out.

Then, from the back of the lead car, another man opened the door to the back seat. Nikolai slowly emerged, doffing his thousand-dollar sunglasses with a raised brow.

Seth watched the big Russian gesture to his men—quick, silent signals. They dispersed, blending into the area and taking invisible positions, tightening the perimeter around his mother's house.

Gene would never see them coming.

"Holy fuck! That's—" Matt blinked. "Nikolai Volkov."

"Yeah."

"The Bratva boss. *That* Nikolai Volkov? You *know* him?" At Seth's nod, Matt's voice dropped. "How the fuck do—"

"Long story," Seth interrupted as he watched Nik approach. "I'll explain later."

Matt was quiet for a beat, still gaping. "Do you trust him?"

"Mostly, but definitely today." Seth shrugged. "Gene's been invading Nik's turf, so our interests align."

"Damn." Something like respect flickered in Matt's expression. "You swim in way darker waters than I realized."

Seth didn't reply. His thoughts were churning. Whatever happened next, there'd be no going back. But that didn't change the facts—or his objective.

He couldn't let Gene escape with a hostage. Or start executing people.

And he couldn't be too late.

Nikolai reached them, moving with a stealth and predatory grace that usually had his enemies scurrying away. Or shitting their pants. He clasped Seth's hand—familiar, solid. "My friend."

"Thanks for coming," Seth said.

"Of course." Nikolai turned to Beck, who wore a guarded expression. "Dr. Beckman, I owe apology for startling your woman at hotel. Was not my intention to frighten."

Beck's jaw clenched. "You were warning Seth. I get it."

"Precisely." Nikolai's gaze dropped to Beck's shoulder. "You need doctor. After this, I take you to mine. He is expert with gunshots."

Beck shook his head. "I'm good. Thanks."

Nikolai shrugged like it was his loss, then shifted to Matt. "Pleasure to meet you, Seth's brother. For record, you are all under my protection now."

Clearly, Matt wasn't sure what to make of that. "Um…thanks."

Seth watched the exchange, trying not to torture himself with what *might* be going on in the house. He had to compartmentalize. Now wasn't the time for guilt—for digging when he swore he wouldn't. Or fear—for Heavenly, their baby, his son, and mother trapped inside the house.

Instead, he focused on what needed to be done: containment, rescue, fallout. Denying Gene an exit.

Seth stood next to Beck, who still slumped against the house. He gestured Matt and Nikolai closer. When they moved in a tight circle around him, he dropped his voice. "We're out of time. Gene knows I've got the evidence to destroy him, and he knows I'm here. I'm sure he's just waiting for backup before he makes a move."

"Specter will wait long time. My men stop them."

Seth raised a brow. "Tell them to incapacitate only. No killing."

Nik pressed a tattooed hand to his chest. "You insult me, Seth Cooper. I am not amateur. Dead cops, even crooked ones, are problem."

"Exactly," Seth agreed. And if the situation wasn't so tense, he'd poke fun at Nik's dramatic flair. Wouldn't be the first time.

"How do we stop him?" Matt asked.

"We've got maybe ten minutes before Gene realizes he's been outplayed and goes off the deep end. Somehow, we've got to get in there, rescue everyone, and neutralize him. If he panics, he'll either start shooting or run with a hostage, probably Mom or Heavenly. Either would be catastrophic."

"Specter will not get far," Nik assured.

Matt nodded, face grim with resolve. "If he fucking tries, I'll kill him."

Seth shook his head. "No. That son of a bitch is *mine*."

Matt hesitated, then nodded.

Nik looked less convinced, so Seth got in his face. "This is just business for you. This asshole destroyed my life twice. He killed people I love, so it's fucking personal for me. I'm the one who ends this. You got it?"

For a moment, Nik glowered. Then he rolled his eyes. "You steal fun."

But the big Russian had given in.

Seth clapped him on the shoulder. "Don't worry. I'll make damn sure he pays, one way or another."

Nikolai's phone buzzed quietly. He glanced at it, then typed something back. He'd barely hit SEND when it buzzed again.

As Nik's thumbs flew across his screen, worry gripped Seth. "Problem?"

He shook his head. "My men intercept Specter's backup around neighborhood. They take nap in trunk of car."

"That was fast." Matt was clearly impressed.

Nikolai flashed his brother a toothy smile. "No one wishes to disappoint me."

Seth knew that was true. "Beck, you up to filling everyone in, like you did me?"

A glance at the good doctor's gray face and jaw clenched in pain worried the hell out of him.

But Beck nodded, clearly determined to help however he could. "Carl is locked in the basement. Gene has Grace, Heavenly, and Hudson in the living room. And as you can see"—he pointed to his shoulder—"he has a gun, and he's not afraid to use it. This was an 'attention-getter.' Spoiler alert: it worked."

"If we're going to get inside the house without more bullets flying, we need a diversion to pull Gene's attention away from the hostages. Then we can rush in through different points of entry, surround him, and free everyone."

Matt shifted his weight. "What kind of diversion?"

Seth shrugged. He hadn't gotten that far. "I'm up for—"

A gunshot cracked through the air.

From inside the house.

The hope that he could extract everyone without bloodshed shattered in that one sound.

Seth stopped breathing. Ice flooded his veins, followed immediately by white-hot terror that threatened to obliterate him.

Heavenly.

The woman Seth loved more than anything. The mother of his unborn child.

If Gene was going to kill someone, he'd choose her first. The son of a bitch knew it would destroy Seth fastest.

He gripped the gun in his fist as his vision tunneled.

The time for talk was over. The time to destroy that cocksucker was now.

"Go. Go. Go!" he roared.

Seth didn't wait for confirmation, didn't look back to see if Matt and Nik were moving.

He ran straight for the door, his boots pounding the pavement. Adrenaline screamed through his system, drowning out everything but the primal need to get inside.

From the corner of his eye, he saw Matt veer toward the side of the house, pointing in the direction of the mudroom. Nik split away, heading for the patio door around back.

Three entry points. Surround the bastard. End this.

Now.

Seth hit the front porch at full speed and, gun raised, kicked in the front door. It exploded inward with a splintering crack, the frame giving way under the force of his boot. He surged into the foyer, every nerve firing as he scanned the family room.

What he saw made his heart lurch.

Hudson—*his sixteen-year-old son*—had slammed Gene flat on the floor. The bastard who had murdered Seth's father and wouldn't hesitate to put a bullet in his son's skull growled threats as he thrashed, trying to strong-arm the kid off him. Hudson bared his teeth and shoved at Gene's shoulders, white-knuckled and straining to keep the crooked cop pinned.

Equally shocking, a flush-faced Heavenly stomped on Gene's arm—the one with his fist still gripping the gun—grinding it into the floor. His proper, very Catholic mother balanced on the same arm, spewing profanity that would have made a sailor blush.

Relief hit Seth so hard his knees threatened to give out. He sent up a silent prayer of thanks.

Though fucking reckless, they were incredibly brave.

And by some miracle, they were all alive.

But that didn't absolve Gene fucking Hammond.

The murderous bastard had threatened to end everyone in the room. If not for Hudson, he'd have killed them all without an ounce of remorse.

Fury crashed Seth's system, spiking with the terror in his veins. He crossed the room and hauled Hudson to his feet with enough force to send the kid stumbling. "Get back—all of you!"

The women scrambled away, wide-eyed and trembling.

Hudson came up fighting, his expression wild, his pupils adrenaline-blown and wide. "Dad—"

"Back!" Seth barked as he bent and slammed the barrel of his gun against Gene's temple.

The asshole froze, his body going rigid beneath the cold steel.

Matt burst in from the kitchen, weapon in hand, and mirrored the threat on Gene's other side before twisting the gun from the prick's hand. The corrupt cop's fingers spasmed, but he knew better than to resist with weapons trained directly on him, controlled by Cooper men with itchy trigger fingers.

Two guns. Two angles. No escape.

"It's over, motherfucker," Seth growled.

Gene's lips curled into a snarl, but he didn't move. Seth almost wished he would. One twitch, one wrong breath, and he'd happily blow Gene's brains all over his mom's hardwoods.

In the next beat, the patio door shattered with a bone-rattling crash. Nik stormed into the room, weapon drawn. He leveled his gun at Gene's face, a slow, predatory grin stretching across the Russian's rugged face.

Gene blanched as recognition dawned. Raw, unfiltered fear followed. "Volkov?"

Nik tilted his head, his gun unwavering. *"Da."*

Satisfaction filled Seth as he lowered his voice to a lethal whisper. "So…you know my friend Nik?" He pressed the barrel harder against Gene's temple. "Or should I call you Specter?"

Gene flinched, jaw flexing. Still, he refused to reply.

"You invade turf." Menace thickened Nik's accent. "Mistake will cost you."

His smile faded. His aim didn't. He stepped closer, never rushing.

Seth's finger tightened on the trigger. His pulse hammered in his ears. Every cell in his body screamed to pull it. To end this son of a bitch right here, right now.

Gene had taken *everything* from him. His father. His first wife. His infant son. Sixteen years of lies. Sixteen years of sitting at family dinners, smiling, pretending to be a friend while he'd been the architect of all the worst moments of Seth's life.

A bullet was too quick. Too clean. Too easy.

Seth's jaw clenched. His hand didn't waver. But he didn't pull the trigger.

Yet.

He'd spent four fucking days torturing Silas Nichols, the assassin Gene hired to murder Autumn and Tristan. Four days of extracting every scrap of information, every name, every detail, except the one he needed most—before he'd finally let the bastard die.

Gene deserved all that and worse.

Seth's gaze flicked to Heavenly—pale, shaken, but alive. Then to his mother, tears streaming down her face.

Both women had been seconds from execution.

Hudson had thrown himself at a killer to save them.

Gene had been willing to murder them all. To take everything Seth had fought to rebuild.

Gene needed to *pay*.

Seth's gaze flicked to Nik. The Russian's expression said he understood. That he'd give Seth whatever time he needed. Whatever tools he required.

"Seth." Matt's voice cut through the silence, tight and controlled. "What do you want to do?"

He stared down at Gene, the man who'd played the role of family friend for two decades while building his empire on blood and lies.

Seth's hand didn't shake. His voice was cold. Final.

Seth straightened slowly, his gun still trained on Gene's skull. His hand was steady. His breathing had evened out. The red haze of fury was still there, but it had cooled into something harder. Colder.

"Nik, stay with this son of a bitch, will you?"

Nikolai's grip on his weapon tightened. "He goes nowhere."

"Matt?" Seth asked.

"On it." Matt kept his gun pressed to Gene's temple, stare locked on the bastard.

Gene lay, back flat against the hardwood, his breathing labored. He didn't speak. Didn't move. Just glared.

But he was defeated, and his face said he knew it.

Good.

Seth refused to give the son of a bitch more of his energy right now. The people he loved needed him, starting with his son.

Hudson stood frozen a few feet away, chest heaving, eyes wild. Heavenly had curled an arm around him in a motherly gesture, whispering soft assurances as tears streamed down her face. His mother held Heavenly's other hand, face ashen with shock.

They were alive. All of them.

Seth was so fucking grateful.

But the terror had taken its toll on them.

Beck stumbled through the splintered frame of the front door, pale and stoic, one hand pressed to his bloody shoulder. His jaw was tight with pain he refused to voice.

Heavenly gasped. "Beck!"

She ran to him, her shaking hands fluttering over his wound. "Oh, my god, you're still bleeding. Let me—"

"I'm fine." Beck's voice was rough as he wrapped his good arm around her waist and pulled her against his blood-soaked chest.

"You're *not.*" Her voice broke as she tried to assess the damage. "The bullet's still in there. You need—"

"I know." He tightened his hold, his face buried in her hair. "But right now, I just need *you,* little girl."

Relief flooded Seth. Beck—even half dead on his feet—was taking care of their girl…making sure she felt safe and loved.

Suddenly, he heard the clatter of a kitchen chair tumbling across the tile and turned to find his trembling mother wrenching open the basement door. *"Carl!"*

Footsteps pounded up the stairs. The burly man appeared, disheveled and pale, but whole. He pulled his mother into his arms and held her close as she sobbed against his chest.

Seth let everyone else have their moments. Right now, his son needed him.

He schooled the violence from his expression as he approached a white-faced Hudson. The teen still stood rooted in place, eyes glassy and unfocused, clenching and unclenching his fists at his sides. His chest heaved like he'd just run a marathon.

Shock. Adrenaline crash. Seth knew the signs.

He slowed his approach to keep from spooking Hudson and cupped his shoulder. "What you did was brave, son. Dangerous as fuck, but brave."

Hudson's breath hitched. He blinked slowly, and when his eyes met Seth's, tears flooded down his cheeks. His whole face crumpled—fear, rage, relief, all of it hitting at once.

"I'm sorry, Dad." His voice cracked. "I didn't know what else to do. That cockbag threatened to kill us all and make you watch." He swiped at his face with the back of his hand, but the tears kept coming. "He grabbed Heavenly. He was going to do her first. I-I don't know what happened. I just lost it. I couldn't let him k-kill her."

Seth's throat tightened. Fear of what could have been threatened to choke him as he yanked Hudson against his chest and held him tight. "It's okay. You did good. You saved Heavenly's life…saved everyone's lives. But seeing you pin Gene down, watching him try to break free and kill you…it scared the hell out of me. I could have lost *you*."

Hudson collapsed against him, his body shaking with raw, ugly sobs.

"I've got you, son," Seth assured, cupping the back of Hudson's head. "You're safe. Heavenly is safe. Everyone's going to be all right."

"Beck?" Hudson demanded.

"Right behind us. He needs medical attention, but he'll be okay. Deep breath."

Hudson nodded, his fists gripping Seth's shirt like he was drowning. "I was so scared."

"I know. But you didn't let fear win. You protected them. You protected *her*." He held Hudson tighter. "I'm so proud of you, son."

"I wasn't trying to be brave. I just…reacted."

Seth understood that perfectly, and that spoke volumes about Hudson's character. Proud was an understatement. "I love you."

Hudson's breath stuttered. He clung harder. "I love you, too."

Seth pressed his lips to the top of Hudson's head, his own eyes burning. Then, because the kid needed it, he pulled back just enough to meet his gaze and forced a crooked smile. "Maybe we don't mention this to your mom right away, yeah?"

Hudson choked out a laugh, swiping at his tears again as he worked to pull himself together. "If ever."

Seth squeezed his shoulder once more. "You good?"

His son nodded. "Yeah. I'll stop crying like a pussy."

"You're not a pussy. It's adrenaline drop. Go check on Grandma Grace. And maybe don't tell her you're a pussy when she asks how you are."

Hudson's smile brightened. "I don't think she'll care. Did you hear the words coming out of her mouth?"

"Yeah. She was once married to a cop." Seth winked.

As the kid crossed the room to where Grace and Carl embraced, Seth turned and damn near lunged for Heavenly. He couldn't wait another second to hold her.

She saw him coming and broke away from Beck to throw herself into his arms. Seth caught her, lifting her off the ground as he clutched her to his chest and buried his face in her neck. She wrapped her arms around him so tightly she nearly crushed him.

Her tears soaked his shirt. "I was worried. He was going to kill you. He said—"

"Shh, angel." Seth's voice was raw. "Everything's okay. You're safe. I'm safe, and I've got you."

He kissed her—fierce, desperate, claiming, fingers tangling in her hair. She kissed him back just as hard.

When they finally broke apart, both of them gasping, Seth looked up to find his mother standing a few feet away, her face wet with tears of both joy and contrition.

She didn't hesitate. She threw herself into his arms.

Seth caught her, holding her tight as she sobbed against his chest.

"I'm sorry," she choked out. "I'm so sorry I made you feel like you couldn't be honest about who you love." She pulled back, her hands cupping his face. "Never again. I love you. I fully accept the people you love. I'll do better. I promise."

Seth blinked, stunned. "You…you know?"

"Gene outed us," Heavenly explained. "And I didn't know if… if—"

They'd make it out alive.

"So I told your mom the truth. I know you wanted to do it, but…"

He brushed pale curls from her mottled cheeks and shook his head with a hint of a smile. "I really didn't, so thank you."

His mother gripped his arm, sniffling. "I feel awful that I caused you so much anxiety. I never want you to think I'd stop loving you for following your heart. I don't care what your love life looks like. If you and Beck are…romantic, that's okay. Great. I just want—"

"We're not," Seth insisted. "We both love Heavenly and want to take care of her…together. That's it."

"And that's wonderful. As long as you're happy, safe, and alive. Nothing else matters."

Seth's chest constricted. He swallowed tightly, his voice rough when he finally spoke. "I'm so damn relieved, Mom. When I thought I had to choose between my heart and your approval, it was killing me. But I chose my heart, because I belong with Heavenly and Beck."

She nodded, her smile trembling but genuine. "You should choose them. Always."

Beck slid his good arm around Heavenly's waist and brushed a kiss across her lips. Then he met Grace's gaze. "Thank you."

She looked at him—really *looked* at him—and after a long moment, she gripped his hand. "No, thank you for trying to protect my feelings."

Seth exhaled. He couldn't quite read his mom's expression, but the weight that had been pressing on his chest for months lifted. Their secret was out. And his mother had accepted them. Deep down, she might not love it. She might be disappointed that they couldn't get married in the church. But she wasn't going to disown him or the people he loved.

For now, that was enough.

Carl approached then, extending his hand. Seth shook it, firm, solid.

Then Carl pulled him into a brief embrace. "Thank you for saving my girl."

Seth smiled, his throat tight. "I told you I would."

"And I'm eternally grateful."

A few feet away, his mother caught sight of Matt, who'd barely moved from his post beside Nik, his gun still trained on Gene's glowering face. Her expression crumpled all over again as she crossed the room to him, arms outstretched.

"Mom—" Matt started.

She was already pulling him into a fierce hug. "You could have been killed. You and Seth both. My boys—"

"We're okay, Mom." Matt's voice was soft as he held her. "We're okay."

Seth smiled despite everything. His mother had both her sons safe and alive.

They'd all survived.

While everyone was wrapped up in reunions and tears, instinct pricked Seth. The hair on the back of his neck stood up as he whirled to where Nik stood alone, gun trained on Gene, without backup.

Fuck.

Seth pushed his way between Heavenly and Beck, racing toward Nik. "Matt, get back—"

Suddenly, from flat on his back, Gene swung his fist into Nik's kneecap with brutal force.

The Russian stumbled as his leg buckled. His gun wavered.

Gene took advantage of the moment and lunged toward his own ankle, yanking a small pistol from a hidden holster.

As fast as lightning, he swung it up and aimed it directly at Seth. Gene didn't stand or even attempt to flee. He just smiled—cold, vicious, resigned.

"If I'm going down, motherfucker," Gene snarled, his finger tightening on the trigger. "Then I'm taking you with me."

Chapter Thirty Three

Seth's world slowed. His thundering heart echoed in his ears.

Suddenly, someone rammed him from the side, shoving him hard. He crashed to the floor as the gun went off—the crack deafening in the enclosed space.

Heavenly's blood-piercing scream reverberated deep into Seth's bones. His mother yelped.

Hudson screamed, "No!"

Heart in his throat, Seth snapped his head up to see Beck panting and ghost-white where he'd been standing a split second ago.

He fucking saved my life.

He took in Beck's ashen face as he swayed on his feet. His hand was still pressed to his blood-soaked shoulder, but his eyes—his eyes were locked on Gene with pure, unyielding fury.

Then Beck's knees suddenly buckled. He dropped hard, catching himself with one hand on the floor. His breathing was ragged and shallow. He looked seconds from passing out.

Seth raised his weapon and aimed it squarely at Gene's skull as he leapt to his feet, voice dropping to lethal tones. "Don't. Fucking. Move."

As Heavenly raced to Beck's side, Nik and Matt lunged forward in tandem, slamming Gene back down. Nik wrenched the small pistol from his hand with a savage twist, then shoved the barrel of his own gun against Gene's temple.

Matt pressed his knee into Gene's chest, pinning him. "Stay down, you piece of shit."

Gene didn't fight, just glared up at them, his breathing harsh, his face twisted with rage and defeat.

The bastard was finally, totally done.

Seth kept his gun trained on Gene, fury and frustration warring in his chest, silently admonishing himself for failing to search Gene. He, Matt, and Nik were professionals; they fucking knew better. But the relief of finding his family alive distracted him. And Gene had done what he did best, taken advantage of the moment. Even in defeat, the lapse had almost cost Seth his life.

It would have, if not for Beck.

Seth's throat tightened. His eyes burned as he turned.

Despite barely being able to stand, Beck had pushed him out of the way—thrown himself between Seth and Gene's bullet. He could have died saving him.

Over their shared love of Heavenly, he and Beck had built a solid foundation of commitment. But now?

Their brotherhood was unbreakable.

"Beck," Heavenly pleaded. "You need to sit. Let's get you to the couch."

"Give me a minute, little girl," he murmured. "Lemme catch my breath."

Seth wanted to rail at the man—tell him he was a goddamn idiot for risking his life. But thankfully, there'd be time for that later.

Seth swallowed hard and rasped, "Thank you, man. I owe you… everything."

Beck lifted his head slightly and managed a weak smile. "I told you not to fucking die."

It was completely out of place, but Seth laughed. "You did. Guess I need to learn to listen."

Suddenly, his mother rushed over, sinking to her knees beside Beck. Tears streamed down her face as she carefully touched his uninjured arm.

"You saved my son." Her voice broke as she cupped his face, her expression both fierce and tender. "You saved his *life!* You're truly a Cooper…now and forever." Her voice softened. "If you want, you can call me Mom, too."

Seth's chest constricted so hard he thought it might cave in.

His mother—his traditional, Catholic mother—had just claimed Beck as her son. Not in theory. Not out of obligation for his role in Seth's and Heavenly's lives.

But because she'd *chosen* him with her heart.

Seth blinked hard, his throat too tight to speak. He met Beck's gaze across the room. The surgeon's eyes were glassy, his expression stunned.

"I'd be honored," Beck said, his voice rough.

Grace pulled him into a careful embrace, mindful of his injuries, as Heavenly wiped tears from her cheeks. Beck sagged against his mom, his face slightly crumpled before he pulled himself together.

Seth looked away, giving them the moment. His hand was still steady on his gun, his eyes locked on Gene.

The bastard wasn't getting another chance to get away. Justice had come for the son of a bitch, and Seth had appointed himself judge, jury, and executioner.

He let the sounds of his family fade behind him. What waited in front of him was unfinished business.

He turned his focus on Gene, his voice cutting through the room like a machete. "Matt. Nik. Pat that motherfucker down. Every inch. I want to know if he's hiding so much as a fucking toothpick."

Matt dropped to one knee. As he began running his hands over Gene's legs, the prick thrashed and kicked at him. Nik growled and put a boot on Gene's forehead, pinning the asshole into place. When Matt started skimming his torso, Nik flashed a taunting smile and aimed his gun straight at Gene's face. The prick glared, but didn't dare move.

"Clean," Matt said finally, stepping back.

"Thank you." Seth turned back to the other men in the room. "Carl. Hudson. Take the women upstairs. Lock the door and turn on some music."

His son looked confused. "Music?"

Seth nodded. "Loudly."

Understanding crossed Carl's face. "On it."

"Hold up," Seth called out, glancing at Nik. "He needs a gun. Got an extra?"

The Russian didn't hesitate. He reached behind his back and produced a Glock 43, offering it to Carl grip-first. "Is loaded. No safety. Point. Shoot."

Carl gripped the weapon, with a nod. "Thanks."

Nik inclined his head.

Seth nodded at his son, then told Carl, "If anyone other than me, Matt, or Nik comes through that door upstairs, kill them. No questions asked. Clear?"

"Absolutely," Carl assured. "Come on, everyone. Let's go."

Hudson started to protest, but Heavenly wrapped an arm around his shoulders and shook her head, guiding him toward the stairs.

But Seth's mom stood like a statue, her furious gaze locked on Gene. Finally, she addressed Seth. "What are you going to do?"

He swallowed tightly. When he'd gone dark and disappeared for a year, she'd never once asked where he'd been or what he'd been doing. Had any of those questions rolled off her lips, he would have lied and taken all the sins he'd committed to his grave.

Now she was asking for the dark truth.

This time, Seth refused to lie.

"As long as Gene is alive, he'll put his criminal enterprise over his badge and keep killing. He murdered Dad to protect his operation. He murdered Autumn and Tristan to cut me off at the knees. He tried to have me killed this morning to silence me. He took you and the people we love hostage an hour ago." Seth's jaw tightened. His nostrils flared. "He even tried to end me after being subdued. As long as he's breathing, he'll keep killing. So I'm going to do what needs to be done."

His mother's lips trembled. Tears filled her eyes. But her voice didn't waver. "Send him to hell."

Seth blinked, stunned.

His devout, Catholic mother—who prayed the rosary daily, who believed in forgiveness and God's will—had just given him permission to execute a man.

Gaze fierce, she stepped closer and placed her hand on his arm. "He doesn't deserve your mercy, Seth. He deserves your justice."

Seth's throat tightened. He nodded once, unable to speak.

She squeezed his arm, then turned toward Carl, who stood waiting at the foot of the stairs with Hudson and Heavenly.

His angel's face was pale, her blue eyes wide and tear-filled. She looked terrified—not of Seth, but *for* him. For what he was about to do. For what it might cost him.

He held her gaze, but didn't speak. He let his face tell her what she needed to know.

When this is over, I'm coming for you.

She didn't ask questions, just pressed her lips together and nodded. Then, with her heart in her eyes, she sent him one last look before turning away.

Clutching the gun in his hand, Carl rushed everyone upstairs. When they reached the top of the landing, Seth winced. "Wait! Mom, maybe you should, um…toss down some towels."

"*Nyet*," Nik insisted, holding up a hand. "I have plastic sheet in car."

Seth turned to him, one brow raised. "Of course you do."

Nik shrugged. "Much cheaper than cleaning crew."

Despite everything, Seth almost smiled, then hollered up the stairs, "Never mind. We got this."

As Nik pulled out his phone and typed a quick message, Seth watched Carl usher everyone inside the master bedroom. Then, with a nod Seth's way, he closed and locked the door.

Less than a minute later, one of Nik's dangerous, tattooed henchmen stepped through what was left of the splintered front door. He silently strolled into the room carrying a neatly folded, dark blue industrial tarp and handed it to Nik before disappearing outside again.

Matt grabbed one end of the plastic. Nik took the other. Together, they spread it across the living room floor.

Seth turned to Gene. "On the tarp. Face up."

Gene didn't move. Didn't speak. Just glared.

Seth bent, muscles flexing and burning, as he grabbed the shitbag by the collar and tossed him onto the plastic. Gene landed hard on his back, the air punching out of his lungs in a grunt.

Seth, Matt, Nik, and Beck stepped in close, forming an inescapable circle around him, glaring at the monster.

Gene's chest rose and fell in labored breaths. Calculating and desperate, his stare darted around the four men hovering over him.

He knew he was trapped.

"So this is it? You're just going to kill me in cold blood?" Gene let out a bitter laugh. "You're no different than me."

Seth crouched, bringing himself eye-level with the bastard. His voice was cold. Controlled. "Oh, I am. The difference is, I protect people. You take advantage of them." He paused for a moment to let his words sink in before an icy smile tugged his lips. "I haven't read it all, but I'm pretty sure I have enough evidence to send you and all your corrupt buddies to prison for life. All those dirty cops—especially a high-ranking detective like you—won't fare well among the criminals they've incarcerated over the years. Then again, being ass-raped is too good for you."

Nik leaned in, his shadow falling across Gene's face. He flashed an ugly smile. "I have many associates in prison. I make sure they take good care of you."

Gene's jaw clenched. His breathing quickened. For the first time, real fear flickered in his eyes.

"Just kill me," he ground out through gritted teeth.

Seth straightened slowly. He looked at Matt.

His brother's face was hard, his jaw clenched so tightly it ticked. He'd been silent through all of this—watching, waiting. But Seth saw it in his eyes. The same grief. The same rage.

Matt had suffered when they'd lost their father, too.

Seth nodded his brother's way.

Like lightning, Matt moved in. He kicked Gene in the ribs. The crooked cop grunted, rolling onto his belly with the force of the blow.

Then Matt lifted his boot and brought it down on the back of Gene's head, slamming his face against the hardwoods and breaking his nose with a sickening *crack.*

Gene howled.

Matt stepped back, his chest heaving, his jaw still clenched. No doubt, he had more liquid violence thrumming through his veins, but he stepped back and nodded Seth's way.

Seth crouched again, this time beside Gene's head. The bastard was wheezing now, blood and spit pooling on the plastic beneath him.

"Beg me," Seth said quietly.

Gene's breath hitched.

"You made my dad beg, didn't you?" Seth's voice dropped to a whisper. "Made him beg for his life? For his family? Before you put a bullet in his skull?"

Gene turned his head just enough to meet Seth's eyes. Blood smeared his teeth when he smiled. "Fuck you."

Seth didn't flinch. Didn't blink.

He rose to his full height, pulled the gun from his waistband, and aimed it at the back of Gene's head.

"No," Seth said, his voice arctic and brittle. "Fuck you."

He settled his boot between Gene's shoulder blades, pressing down just enough to feel the bastard's ribs shift beneath his weight.

In his mind's eye, he saw his father—laughing at the dinner table, tossing a baseball in the backyard, ruffling Seth's hair. He saw Autumn, radiant and beautiful, her hand resting on her swollen belly. He saw baby Tristan, tiny and perfect, his fingers wrapped around Seth's thumb.

This is for you, he thought. *All of you.*

The room went utterly quiet.

Nothing moved.

No one spoke.

Seth squeezed the trigger.

Once.

Twice.

The shots cracked through the air, sharp and final.

Seth didn't look down. Didn't need to.

The bastard who'd destroyed his family was dead.

Seth lowered his weapon, his hand steady, his breathing even as he heard the bedroom door upstairs burst open.

Quickly, Seth gestured to Matt and Nik, who flipped the sides of the tarp over Gene's body, concealing the gore from view.

Satisfied, Seth turned his back on the scene, tucked the gun out of sight, and slung an arm around Beck's waist. The surgeon bit back a grimace and shuffled as Seth helped him across the family room.

Then Heavenly appeared at the top of the stairs, her eyes wide and searching. The instant she caught sight of her men, whole and alive, relief smoothed the fear from her face.

She raced down the stairs toward them, her blinding smile filling Seth's heart with love.

Tears of joy streaming down her cheeks, Heavenly bounded off the last step and flung herself at them, wrapping them both in a warm embrace. She didn't say a word, simply cupped their cheeks—as if making sure they were alive and real—and stared into their eyes before peppering their faces with watery kisses.

Seth closed his eyes and hugged them both tighter.

His past was truly behind him now.

Whatever came next would be the life he'd fought to live—with the people he loved.

Epilogue

Los Angeles
January 1

Heavenly stood in front of the full-length mirror in the master bedroom of their new house and studied her reflection—face bare, hair loose around her shoulders, silk robe tied at her waist.

Today, she was finally getting married, and she couldn't stop smiling. And like everything else in her life, nothing was traditional. So nothing about this wedding would be, either.

To her, that was perfect.

Last night's "bachelorette party" had been nothing like Gloria's Vegas penthouse boozefest with penis-shaped straws and hot male strippers. No, hers had been in her new living room with Grace, Gloria, Raine, and Maggie, watching schmaltzy movies, nibbling saltines and sipping ginger ale, and swapping pregnancy stories.

As gatherings went, it had been small. Full of laughter. Overflowing with sisterhood—all shared with the unlikely circle of women who had become her family. Not the one she'd been born into, but the one she'd found. The one that mattered.

And today, bless them, they would hold her hands and help her take the biggest step of her life.

She would marry Kenneth Beckman and Seth Cooper—the men she loved more than anything.

Her ending might not be a typical fairy tale, but it was absolutely her dream come true.

"Knock, knock!" Gloria called, rapping on the door as she pushed it open. She emerged into the room, her sassy red hair freshly coiffed and wearing a lacy sage green dress that almost made her look like a typical suburban wife. But the big, brash smile that was pure Gloria was her madame-coded bling. "Am I interrupting something? Ken come to give you a quickie before the ceremony?"

Heavenly had to laugh. "Nothing that exciting, I'm afraid."

"Not for lack of trying," Raine snorted, wearing flawless makeup, a gorgeous mauve chiffon dress, and bare feet. She carried in her giant case, full of implements to make Heavenly look more like a bride. "He and Seth were planning an offensive on your bedroom last night, but I made Hammer and Liam cockblock them. You're welcome."

That made Heavenly giggle. "Thank you."

She wouldn't have minded spending her last night as a single woman wrapped in the arms of her men. But that would come tonight, after they'd pledged their lives to one another in front of their loved ones.

Even the thought was going to make her cry.

When she sniffled, Grace bustled in, looking polished in a sedate gray dress. With a concerned expression, she hooked Heavenly's wedding dress on the back of the door, the lace and delicate beading catching the morning light, before reaching for Heavenly's hand. "Oh, sweetheart. Is everything okay? I was nervous on my wedding day. Both of them. It's going to be all right. We're here, and you're beautiful."

She hugged her mother-in-law-to-be, so grateful their relationship had come so far in the past few short months. "I'm happy. I promise these aren't nervous tears."

Maggie, her soon-to-be-sister-in-law, followed Grace into the bedroom, looking lovely in blue, despite the somewhat green tint to her skin. She smoothed a hand down her still-flat belly. "They're pregnancy tears. I should know. It's not even my wedding, and I woke up crying."

Heavenly grinned as she pressed a hand to the slight curve of her stomach and bit her lip. Three months along, and the baby was starting to make its presence known. Not obviously yet, but enough to know the hormones were real. Enough that she'd tried on her dress twice this week to make sure it still fit.

Raine sniffled as she settled Heavenly onto a stool and opened her case of hair implements and war paint. "That makes two of us. Damn hormones." Then she tipped Heavenly's chin in her direction and studied her bare face. "You look way calmer than the rest of us."

Heavenly's smile widened. "Only because I know in my heart I'm making the right choice."

Raine nodded. "You totally are. So glad my brother didn't jump on you when you offered him your V-card."

"Me, too." Heat rushed to Heavenly's cheeks as she slanted a wary glance at Grace and Maggie. "Long story."

Grace squeezed her hand. "Seth told me about your horrible landlord. Oh, sweetheart, I can't imagine how scared you were... And I'm so proud of those men for coming to your rescue. I know it wasn't funny then, but—"

"But it's hysterical now," Gloria piped in. "Ken isn't usually homicidal, but Raine, honey, you wouldn't have a brother left if he'd hustled Heavenly to bed."

"You really wouldn't," Maggie put in, carrying a sleeve of saltines and a ginger ale. "If Beck hadn't ended him, Seth totally would have. I really had no idea what a badass he is."

Heavenly had known almost from the beginning. At first, he'd scared her more than a little. But now she wouldn't want him any other way. His protective ferocity—the one he displayed every day for the people he loved—made her feel so safe.

"And thank god. I'm grateful Seth was there when it mattered," Maggie said softly. "That he saved all of you that horrible day."

Heavenly's throat tightened. Seth's decisive action. Beck's blood. The terror on everyone's faces. But today wasn't about dwelling on darkness. It was about celebrating the light they'd found together.

"We all are," she managed, her voice thick.

"Hey, none of that. Making you gorgeous won't be hard," Raine announced, diving into her kit and immediately circling. "You're always gorgeous. But not if you have swollen eyes and a red nose. I want your grooms speechless at your beauty when they see you, not wondering who to beat the crap out of for upsetting you."

Gloria chortled. "Ken speechless? I'd pay money to see that. He's always got something to say."

Grace joined in. "The more I've gotten to know him, the more I've realized you're right."

"It's okay; you can say it," Gloria encouraged. "He's a smart-ass."

Her mother-in-law-to-be sent her a searching stare, and Heavenly had to laugh. "He really is, and he'd be the first one to admit it."

"True, but I love that about him." Grace both laughed and grimaced. "And believe me, Seth isn't perfect."

Raine almost spit out the tea she'd been drinking. "Um…not even a little."

Heavenly giggled. "I love him, but…no."

Quiet descended as Heavenly watched her bestie prepare for beauty battle.

"Ready to be a bride?"

"Beyond." She reached up to squeeze Raine's hand. "Thank you."

"Oh, sweetie. Of course."

After a shared hug and more tears, Raine got down to work. "Two hours until showtime, ladies. We got this."

"As far as I'm concerned, she's already perfect," Grace said softly, her eyes already misty as she smoothed Heavenly's hair back from her face.

She smiled at Grace, who had been more of a mother to her in the last few months than her own had ever been. "I just don't want to look pregnant in my pictures."

"You won't," Maggie assured her with easy confidence. "First babies take forever to show. I didn't pop until almost six months with Anna. With this one?" She patted her own still-flat belly. "I'm only five weeks pregnant now, and I swear my clothes are already getting tight."

"OMG, right?" Raine agreed, sectioning Heavenly's hair for hot rollers. "I'm showing much earlier with this pregnancy than I did with the twins. Either Hammer's son is massive or my body's a mess. I'm hoping for the latter."

Everyone busted out laughing, then quiet settled as the preparations continued.

Heavenly watched as the four women moved around her with purpose. Grace fluffing her veil and making sure her shoes were pristine. Gloria fussing with jewelry and slipping X-rated lingerie into

Heavenly's suitcase when she thought no one was looking. Raine pulling out brushes and palettes with the hand of an artist. Maggie handing her crackers and a can of ginger ale with a contented smile.

These women were her family now. Her girl posse. And her heart was beyond full.

As Raine attacked her hair—curling, pinning, creating something elegant and soft—Maggie shifted on the bed. "Hudson seems to be doing great. Everything went well—the move, the coming baby, his visit with Laura over the holidays?"

Heavenly's smile softened, thinking of the teenager who'd become such an unexpected blessing in their lives. "It was a lot of change for a sixteen-year-old. He wasn't happy at first, especially about the baby. He thought things would be a repeat of his old life with Laura, that he'd get shoved aside."

Grace made a sympathetic sound. "He told me that you assured him that he was irreplaceable."

Heavenly teared up, earning a scowl from Raine. She sniffled. "It took some convincing, but he finally understands that this baby will never take anything from him, especially our love and attention. We're just giving him more family."

"What about the move?" Maggie prompted.

"He understood the need for a bigger house. Luckily, we found this place. It's perfect for our growing family, but he didn't have to start over at a new school."

"He loves it here. He told me," Grace murmured.

Maggie grinned. "I'm sure the huge pool, game room, media room, weight room, and sauna helped to soften the blow."

They all laughed, and Heavenly felt warmth spreading through her chest. "So did the car Seth gave him when he came home from spending Christmas with Laura last week. It's kind of extravagant, but we wanted him to be able to drive himself to and from school. And he's ready for the responsibility."

In truth, their lives were falling perfectly into place.

"Speaking of new houses…" Grace cleared her throat, her expression shifting to something more somber. "Carl and I are putting both our houses on the market. We were always going to sell Carl's but…"

The room went still.

"Really?" Heavenly blinked. "That's where you raised the boys."

"I know. But now that place is just…haunted. Not by ghosts, but by the day I nearly lost all of you." Grace's voice wavered. "Every time I walk into that family room, I see Carl lying unconscious on the floor, Beck bleeding, and that monster pointing a gun at our heads. I'll miss all the memories of the boys growing up there, but I can't—I can't live there anymore."

Gloria moved to Grace's side, wrapping an arm around her shoulders. "Oh, honey. Of course you can't."

Heavenly stood and pulled Grace into a fierce hug. "I'm so sorry. But you're doing the right thing. You deserve peace."

"Thank you, sweetheart. This spring, Carl will be building us a house on a gorgeous piece of property we found with a lovely view of the Hudson. We're excited."

"That's fantastic."

"I'm jealous," Maggie chimed in. "The neighborhood is beautiful. Wait until you see it."

The chatter and laughter continued as Raine continued her ministrations. Heavenly closed her eyes and took in the moment until finally her bestie sprayed her makeup and swept her hair into an elegant bridal 'do. Then she stepped back with a gasp. "You look gorgeous!"

Heavenly opened her eyes and gasped.

The woman staring back at her in the vanity mirror looked...ethereal. Raine had worked magic, creating soft, romantic waves that framed her face while the rest was swept up in an elegant twist. Her makeup was flawless but natural—dewy skin, rose-tinted cheeks, lips painted a soft pink. Her eyes looked bigger, brighter, shimmering with barely contained tears.

She looked like a bride. Not just any bride, but herself—enhanced, glowing, ready.

"Oh, my god," she whispered, one hand flying to her mouth.

"Right?" Raine grinned, clearly proud of her work. "I told you. Gorgeous."

"I can't believe that's me."

"Believe it, honey." Gloria squeezed her shoulder. "You're stunning."

Raine clapped her hands, bringing everyone back to the moment. "Okay, ladies. We've got forty-five minutes and a bride who needs to get into her dress. Grace, you're on zipper duty. Gloria, accessories. Let's move."

The next thirty minutes passed in a flurry of activity. Heavenly stepped into her dress—the ivory lace hugging her curves perfectly, the beading catching the light with every movement. The zipper closed without incident, much to her relief.

Grace fastened the gift Beck and Seth had given her into place—a simple bracelet with three interlocking circles. Gloria slipped pearl earrings into place. Raine made final adjustments to her hair and makeup, then stepped back with a satisfied nod.

"Perfect," Raine breathed. "Absolutely perfect."

Heavenly turned to the full-length mirror and barely recognized herself. She looked...radiant. Luminous. Like a woman deeply, irrevocably in love. Like a bride about to marry the two men who'd saved her in every way that mattered.

"Oh, sweetheart." Grace pressed a hand to her mouth, tears streaming freely now. "You're the most beautiful bride I've ever seen."

Maggie crossed to Heavenly and pulled her into a careful hug. "You look amazing. I'm so happy for all three of you."

"Thank you," Heavenly whispered, squeezing her tight. "For everything."

"That's what family's for." Maggie sent her a watery laugh. "I'm ruining my makeup. I should get back to Danny before Anna decides the pool is more interesting than his lap. Good luck."

She slipped out, leaving the door open just a crack.

"You look beautiful." Gloria stepped forward next, her usual brassy confidence softened by genuine emotion. She cupped Heavenly's face in both hands, eyes searching hers. "You're going to be so happy, honey. If there's one thing Mama Gloria knows, it's men. And those two you've got worship the ground you walk on. You three deserve every bit of happiness."

"Thank you, Gloria. For everything you've done for me. And especially for Beck. He loves you to pieces."

"I love him, too, and don't you dare make me cry." Gloria fanned her face, then pulled Heavenly into a fierce hug. "And just remember, when you and Ken and Seth need a babysitter…" She paused dramatically. "Don't call me."

Heavenly giggled. "Wouldn't dream of it. Love you."

"Love you, too, honey. Now go marry those men!" Then Gloria swept out, leaving a trail of expensive perfume in her wake.

"Men," Grace echoed with a shake of her head. "A year ago, I never would have imagined saying that and meaning it."

Heavenly met Grace's eyes in the mirror. "Thank you," she said quietly. "For being here. For understanding. For…everything."

Grace lingered, straightening Heavenly's veil with trembling fingers. "Welcome to the family, sweetheart. Officially." Her voice cracked. "I'm so grateful Seth found you and Beck. That you all found each other."

"Me too," Heavenly whispered.

"And for the record, if I'm in town, I'd love to babysit," she said pointedly, shooting a look at the door Gloria had just exited through. "I'm hoping you three are planning for more babies. Lots more."

As enthusiastic as Beck and Seth were about her being pregnant with this one? "We are. You'll have lots of grandkids to spoil."

"I'm so blessed. Now if I could just get Matt to find a nice girl and settle down…" Grace's expression turned wistful as she pulled Heavenly in for a long, tight hug.

It was all the acceptance Heavenly needed.

Finally, Grace pulled back, dabbing at her eyes with a tissue. "All right. I need to leave before I completely fall apart." She kissed Heavenly's forehead. "See you out there."

The door clicked shut behind her, leaving Heavenly alone with Raine.

Her best friend stood, studying her with an expression Heavenly couldn't quite read. Not quite sad, not quite happy—something deeper, more complex.

"Come here," Raine said softly, arms open wide.

Heavenly crossed to her and melted into Raine's embrace. For a moment, they just stood there, holding each other in the quiet room.

"I can't believe this is really happening," Heavenly whispered against her shoulder.

"I can." Raine pulled back and looked into her eyes with a strong, steady gaze. "You know why? Because you fought for this, no matter how hard it got. Even when you didn't think you could handle Beck or Seth, much less both of them. Even when you got propositioned by a sex donkey."

"Don't remind me." Heavenly laughed and shook her head. "But I did give up."

Raine shook her head. "You got scared. You got overwhelmed. Still, you came back, and you loved Beck and Seth through all their damage and fear and stupidity. And they love you right back."

"You showed me it was possible."

Raine smiled through her tears. "That's what best friends do. Remember the day we met? Me on that hospital gurney, blood everywhere, scared out of my mind."

It had been both one of the worst and best days of Heavenly's life. "Of course. You were so strong, even then."

"I didn't feel strong. I felt broken. But you looked at me like I wasn't. Like I was going to be okay. And somehow, I believed you. And now look at us—both pregnant, both married to two incredible men, both building the families we've always wanted."

Heavenly let out a watery laugh. "How did we get so lucky?"

"We didn't. We fought for it." Raine cupped her face. "And you're going to keep fighting for it. When things get hard—and they will, because babies and exhaustion and hormones are no joke—you're going to remember why you chose them. Why they chose you. And you're going to hold on."

"I will."

"I know." Raine kissed her forehead. "You got this."

"Thank you." Heavenly could barely get the words out. "For everything. For being my friend and the sister of my heart."

"That's what family does." Raine pulled her close one more time.

"Now stop crying before we both look like raccoons and I have to redo everything."

They laughed together, holding each other tight, two women who'd found their way from lost to found, from broken to whole.

Finally, Raine pulled back. "I need to get out there before Liam and Hammer send a search party. But first—" She grabbed her phone. "One picture. Just us."

They posed together, Heavenly in her wedding dress, Raine in her mauve gown, both of them teary and radiant and exactly where they were meant to be.

"Perfect," Raine said, examining the photo. "I'm framing this."

"Me, too."

Raine gave her one last squeeze, then headed for the door, pausing with her hand on the knob. "And Heavenly?"

"Yeah?"

"I'm going to sob like a baby when you walk down that aisle. I'm really proud of you." Her voice broke. "And I love you."

Heavenly's eyes stung. "I love you, too, bestie."

The door closed softly behind her, and suddenly Heavenly was alone.

Silence settled around her like a blanket.

Heavenly turned back to the mirror, taking in her reflection one last time. The woman staring back at her looked confident, radiant, ready—so different from the scared girl who'd walked into Beck's penthouse all those months ago, desperate and alone.

She thought about that night. How terrified she'd been, offering herself to River because she'd had no other options. How lost she'd felt, caring for her dying father, drowning in debt, convinced she'd never have anything more than survival.

And now...

Now she had everything.

Two men who loved her fiercely. A baby growing inside her. A home filled with laughter and hope. A family—not just Beck and Seth, but all their brothers, Hudson, Grace and Carl, Gloria and Buddy, Raine and her men—all bound together by choice and love.

She smoothed her hands down the lace of her dress, drew in a deep breath, and smiled before she opened the door and stepped into the hallway, ready to walk toward the men who were waiting for her—and the future they would build together.

Her heart hammered against her ribs as she hurried downstairs, moving quickly but carefully in her gown. When she reached the bi-fold doors leading to the patio, she paused, peeking around the frame.

The sight melted her heart.

The backyard had been transformed into something magical.

White chairs arranged in neat rows faced an archway draped in ivory fabric and winter greenery. Delicate lights were strung overhead, twinkling like stars even in the late afternoon sunlight. White water lilies floated atop the swimming pool's blue surface, while the sprawling grassy property stretched toward the hills.

Nerves humming, heart soaring with excitement, Heavenly stepped onto the patio, casting a quick glance over the small group of family and friends before her gaze landed on Beck and Seth.

Butterflies dipped and swooped in her belly.

They looked so devastatingly handsome in their crisp dark suits, standing side by side beneath the ivory-draped archway, watching her with such raw devotion, fierce possession, and blinding love, that Heavenly nearly forgot how to breathe.

Her impatient, dominant men each lifted a finger and pointed to the empty space in front of them. A wide grin spread across her lips as she began her walk down the aisle, acutely aware of their gazes tracking her every step.

As she moved between the white chairs, she caught glimpses of their family and friends—Nikolai and Jericho in the back row, the unlikely pair looking oddly comfortable beside each other. Zach sat with Hannah, their hands clasped. Matt, Danny, and Maggie watched with little Anna perched on Danny's lap.

But Heavenly's focus kept pulling back to Beck and Seth, mesmerizing and inevitable.

Raine sat between Hammer and Liam in the next row, tears already streaming down her face. River grinned and gave her an enthusiastic thumbs-up as she passed.

In the front row, Grace clutched a tissue, her smile trembling with joy, beside Carl. Hudson sat proudly next to them, flanked by Jack and Connor. Across the aisle, Buddy held Gloria close.

And there, on a pedestal beside the archway, sat the framed photo of her father. Abel Young smiled out at her—that gentle, knowing smile she'd carry with her forever. For a moment, the ache of his absence threatened to crush her. But then she felt it—his presence, palpable and warm, his blessing washing over her like the hugs he'd given so freely when he was alive.

I'm here, sweetheart, she could almost hear him whisper. *I'm always here with you.*

Every person had fought for them, protected them, loved them.

But like magnets drawn to steel, her eyes returned to her men. Her future.

When she finally reached the archway, she turned to face their guests as Beck and Seth moved in beside her. Calm. Confident. Faces etched in love, they each extended a hand. Heavenly drew in a deep breath and placed her trembling fingers in their palms.

The warmth of their touch spread through her while the rightness of their connection settled deep in her bones.

This was where she belonged.

With them.

Between them.

For a long moment, they simply looked at each other with expressions that spoke of everything they'd survived, everything they'd become, and everything they'd share in the future.

Beck cleared his throat, his voice deep, strong, and firm as he began. "Heavenly, when I first met you, I was convinced you were too young and innocent for someone like me. I tried to stay away, god knows—" He shook his head. "But couldn't. Your kindness, your strength, your endless ability to love made the pull I felt too strong to resist. Winning you over took a long time and a tremendous amount of patience—which has never been one of my strong suits."

Everyone laughed, Beck included.

Then he sobered again. "But when you finally let me in, I fell completely and irrevocably in love with you, Heavenly Young."

Tears slipped down her cheeks as she fought the urge to throw herself into his arms.

"So from this day on, I promise to protect you, to cherish you, to honor the gift of your love every single day. I promise to be the husband you need and the father our children deserve. I promise that no matter what challenges we face, I will stand beside you—beside both of you—and fight for the family we're building. You are my heart, little girl. My forever."

The silence that followed was profound, broken only by sniffles from the guests, especially Gloria and Grace.

Heavenly swallowed tightly and sent the men who'd become her whole world a watery smile. Then she inhaled a shaky breath, praying she could keep herself together long enough to recite her vows half so eloquently.

"Beck, Seth...I stopped believing in fairy tales years ago. I was convinced happy endings didn't exist. But then you both walked into my life and showed me what love could be. It started out messy and complicated. Nothing was ever easy, and so many times I nearly let fear win. But together, we worked to make our love real and true. And absolutely beautiful. I would be alone and empty without you."

As the words poured from her heart, they gently strummed their thumbs over the inside of her wrists, silently supporting and encouraging her to continue.

"Beck, you taught me that darkness and light can exist together, that protecting someone doesn't mean shielding them from the world but giving them the strength to face it. You showed me what it means to be cherished, to be pampered, to be someone's priority, and to be loved with an intensity that still takes my breath away."

Beck's smile quivered as he squeezed her hand.

"Seth, you taught me that love can be fierce and protective while still being tender. That broken people can heal. That even when fear screams at you to run, love is worth fighting for. You showed me that vulnerability isn't weakness—but the bravest, most sacred thing we can offer another person. And you gave me hope that family isn't just about blood, but about choosing each other every single day."

Seth's throat bobbed as he swallowed hard.

"I promise to love you both with my whole heart," Heavenly said, her voice slightly cracking. "To be the loving, caring wife you need, a loving, nurturing mother to our children, and the woman who will stand beside you and support you throughout our lives. To choose you —to choose us—every day for the rest of my life. You are my family. My home. My forever."

Seth's jaw tightened for a moment before he found his voice. "Angel, I was dead inside when you found me. Walking through life but not living. I was afraid to feel, afraid to love, afraid to hope for anything more than the next empty day. Then you crashed into my world and demanded I wake up. You refused to let me hide in grief and fear. You pushed me, challenged me, loved me even when I didn't deserve it."

Heavenly's breath hitched on a sob.

"I know I wasn't easy to love," Seth admitted, his eyes glistening. "But you never gave up on me. Never stopped believing that I could be more than my past. And because of you—and Beck—I learned to live again. To hope again. To believe in tomorrows instead of drowning in yesterdays."

When he lifted her hand to his lips and pressed a kiss to her knuckles, she nearly crumpled against him.

"I promise to spend the rest of my life making you happy," Seth vowed. "To be the man you can trust to protect your heart. The father our babies deserve—present, protective, and unafraid to love unconditionally. And to be a husband and partner who is totally committed to you and Beck. You saved me, Heavenly. And I will spend every day of my life treasuring that gift."

Seth reached over to the pedestal beside Abel's photo and retrieved the three rings resting there.

Beck and Seth each took one side of Heavenly's ring, their fingers overlapping as they slid it onto her finger together, settling it perfectly against her engagement ring. The symbolism wasn't lost on anyone—one ring, two men, binding her to both of them.

"With this ring, we choose you, Heavenly Hope Young," they murmured together, their stares full of devotion that nearly made her cry again.

Seth handed her the other two bands.

Heavenly trembled as she took Seth's ring first—a platinum band with Celtic knot work—and slid it onto his finger, her eyes locked on his. "With this ring, I choose you, Seth Michael Cooper."

Then she lifted Beck's ring—dark tungsten with a subtle brushed finish. As she slipped it onto his finger, she repeated, "With this ring, I choose you, Kenneth Edward Beckman."

Beck's thumb immediately went to the unfamiliar weight on his finger, his smile wide and full of joy.

Soft sobs and sniffles echoed through the crowd as Beck and Seth crushed her between them, holding her tightly. Heavenly closed her eyes and breathed them in, her heart soaring to the stars.

Suddenly, Liam's Irish accent rang out, his voice carrying warmth and joy. "Well then, lads, I think it's time to—kiss your bride!"

Beck and Seth didn't need to be told twice.

As laughter, applause, and celebratory shouts echoed across the patio and into the twilight sky, Beck captured her mouth, kissing her with a thoroughness that made her dizzy. Then he cupped her face and turned her to Seth, who claimed her with a spine-bending kiss overflowing with passion and promise.

When they finally broke apart, Heavenly looked out at the faces of their family and friends. Everyone was on their feet, clapping and cheering, celebrating this unconventional union that had been forged in fire and tempered by love.

Grace was wiping tears from her cheeks, her smile radiant. Carl had his arm around her, looking equally moved. The twins were whistling and tossing fist pumps into the air, while Hudson smiled softly as if he finally believed he belonged.

"Let the party begin!" Hammer announced, and everyone surged toward the trio to offer their congratulations.

Minutes later, the reception was in full swing. Laughter and music from the outside speakers filled the air as the sun began its descent toward the horizon.

The trio moved through the small crowd, accepting hugs and well-wishes. Heavenly's heart was so full she thought it might burst.

"Hey, Seth," Hammer called, stepping from the house and hurrying toward them with a package in his hands. "When I went inside to use the john, the doorbell rang. So I answered it. A delivery guy handed me this. It's addressed to you."

"Thanks, man." Seth smiled.

"Hope it's something good," Hammer said, shoving the package in Seth's hand before jogging back inside the house.

"Who's it from?" Heavenly asked, peering over Seth's shoulder.

"Tony." Seth grinned, tearing it open before pulling out a bottle of champagne.

"Oh, there's a note," Heavenly said, pointing to the bottom of the box.

Seth plucked it up and began reading. "Hey, partner. Hope you have a wonderful wedding. Give my regards to your angel. Best of luck. Detective Second Grade, Tony Marconi. Well, I'll be damned, he's been promoted."

"That's great news, right?" Beck smiled.

"Awesome news." Seth nodded. "Jericho told me that the precinct was in flux after they dismantled Gene's operation. Guess they've been busy weeding out the good cops from the bad. And Tony is one of the best."

"I'm so glad you two have remained friends," Heavenly murmured and glanced at the numerous cloth-covered tables near the pool.

Beck joined Hudson, Jack, and Connor who were clustered together, laughing and talking. Not far from them, Matt and River were deep in conversation, while Danny sat beside them, bouncing Anna on his knee. Maggie smiled next to him, sipping more ginger ale.

Nearby, Buddy and Gloria swayed to the music, looking like they'd been dancing together their whole lives while Zach and Hannah, who were giving their relationship another try, talked quietly.

Seth trekked over to join his mom and Carl. Heavenly headed to the bar to grab some water. Off to the side, Nikolai and Jericho had their heads bent close together, talking in low tones.

Suddenly, Jericho straightened and held up his hands. "Don't tell me. I don't want to hear anything about that. It's called plausible deniability."

Nik chuckled, the sound low and gravelly. "You are right, my friend. Better you not know."

Heavenly suspected they were talking about the aftermath of what had happened in New York. Clearly, the fallout wasn't completely over yet.

Memories of that terrifying day crashed over her. Even now, three months later, she could still feel the cold terror of watching Beck bleed, of not knowing if he'd survive.

After Seth had ended Gene, Nik had taken control with frightening efficiency. He'd called his doctor—a brilliant surgeon who'd trained in Moscow before coming to the States—who told Nik to get Beck there immediately. While his men dealt with the crime scene, Nik had promised Seth he'd handle everything: replace the damaged doors, dispose of the body, erase all traces.

At the doctor's brownstone, Boris had worked with steady, expert hands to remove the bullet while his wife, Yulia, fed the rest of them—keeping Grace and Hudson calm while Seth pored over the evidence from Michael's binder. Page after page of corruption. Proof of Gene's criminal empire spanning decades.

Seth had called Jericho, whom he trusted implicitly, before he'd even finished reading. The FBI agent had promised justice would come—and it had.

Boris had emerged hours later with good news: the surgery was successful. Beck would heal completely and his career was safe. The relief had nearly brought Heavenly to her knees.

They'd returned to Grace's house that night, exhausted but alive.

Seth had called in the whole family. Once everyone had arrived, he played the video tape his father had left in the storage unit. Carl had wrapped a sturdy arm around his new bride. When Michael Cooper's face had filled the screen, Grace covered her mouth and silently cried. Michael's voice—identical to Seth's—was steady as he detailed everything he'd discovered about Gene's criminal empire. It had been a message from beyond the grave. A father's final gift to his family.

It had been gut-wrenching and emotionally crushing to watch.

There had been tears—lots of them. Tight hugs, and finally closure that had been sixteen years in the making.

When they'd flown back to LA that Monday morning, Jericho had met them at the gate. He'd assured Seth that no charges would be filed for Gene's death—it was self-defense in the protection of hostages. The fact that Zach had helped them take down The Chosen mere months ago gave Seth a ton of legal leverage.

Seth had given Jericho the satchel and the box he'd kept hidden in his closet...finally letting go of the burden he'd been carrying for half his life.

In the weeks that had followed, Jericho and Nikolai had established what they called a "working relationship"—a delicate alliance between law enforcement and organized crime. It operated in morally gray areas that Heavenly tried not to think too hard about, and it served a purpose. Any members of Gene's organization who, for whatever reason, couldn't be prosecuted through legal channels had met with unfortunate "accidents" orchestrated by Nik. The rest had been arrested and were working their way through the justice system.

Gene's organization had completely collapsed. Specter was gone. Nik had gleefully reclaimed his territory and restored his power in the Russian underworld.

Now, watching the unlikely pair together at her wedding, Heavenly felt a surge of gratitude. They'd saved her family and had helped bring justice and closure.

She approached them with a warm smile. "Thank you both for coming. It means a lot having you here."

Nik's face lit up with his trademark grin, mischief dancing in his eyes. "Thank me by naming baby Nikolai."

Jericho scoffed and shook his head. "Oh, god! Don't do that. Jericho is much easier to say...and spell. Plus the kid won't get his ass kicked on the playground."

Heavenly laughed and rolled her eyes. "I'll take your suggestions under consideration."

She plucked up her water and left them to their cryptic conversation, strolling across the patio to claim a seat at the table with Hammer,

Liam, and Raine. But before she reached them, a hot hand settled possessively on her hip.

"Having fun, little girl?" Beck murmured in her ear from behind her.

"Yes." She sighed, leaning back against his solid warmth. "This is perfect."

"Almost," Seth said, easing in beside her, voice dropping to that low, seductive tone that never failed to make her shiver. "We still haven't had our first dance. Or cut the cake. Or—" His grin turned wicked. "Made good on our wedding night promises."

Heavenly felt heat pool low in her belly despite her earlier nausea. "You two are insatiable."

"Only when it comes to you," Beck assured her, his lips finding the sensitive spot below her ear.

Before they could whisk her away for any of those activities, Seth's expression turned serious. He took her hand, his thumb stroking across her knuckles. "Actually, angel, I have something for you first. Come with me?"

Curious and slightly apprehensive, Heavenly followed him to a quieter corner of the patio, away from the music and laughter. Beck splayed his hand on the small of her back as he walked beside her.

Seth reached into his jacket pocket and withdrew an envelope, his expression carefully neutral. "I found your mother."

Heavenly's breath caught in her throat. She stared at the envelope in shock, her heart racing wildly. "You…found her?"

"Yes. I tracked her down, just in case…" Seth pressed the envelope into her now trembling hands. "If you want to know where she is, how to contact her, or what she's been doing all these years, it's all in here. But Heavenly—" He searched her face, his stare intense. "You don't have to open it. You don't owe her anything. This is your choice, and your choice alone. If you want to burn it without looking inside, I'll light the match myself."

Beck's hand remained on her lower back, steady and supportive. "Whatever you decide, we're with you, one hundred percent."

Heavenly stared at the envelope, feeling the weight of it in her hands. Inside was information about the woman who'd given birth to her, raised her for fifteen years, then abandoned her to chase whatever selfish dreams had been more important than her own daughter.

For a long moment, she wavered. Part of her wanted to know—wanted to understand why. Wanted to ask the questions that had haunted her eight long years. Wanted...something. Closure, maybe. Or answers that would explain why she'd never been enough to make her own mother stay.

But then she looked past her men...

To Hudson laughing with the twins.

To Maggie chasing a laughing Anna around the yard.

To the rest of Seth's brothers, relaxing and seemingly enjoying each other's company.

To Grace and Carl, Gloria and Buddy, Raine and her men—people who had claimed her as their own without hesitation—gathered together, grinning and swapping stories and laughter at the bar.

Unfiltered joy settled over her.

Heavenly finally understood the true meaning of family.

She thought about the baby growing inside her, about the future she and Beck and Seth were building, and about the bliss she'd found in their big, beautiful hearts.

These people had fought for her, protected her, celebrated her, and loved her.

Not the woman who'd walked away without a backward glance.

Not the woman who'd chosen herself over her own child...over her sick husband.

"I don't want to know. She's a selfish woman," Heavenly said firmly, her decision made with absolute certainty. "She chose to leave me...leave my dad. I don't want her in my life." Her hand drifted to her stomach, protective and fierce. "Or our child's life. She made her choice the day she walked out. I've made mine."

Without another word, without a moment's hesitation, she walked to the chimenea and stared at the flames. Then tossed the envelope inside. The fire consumed it eagerly, turning years of potential what-ifs into curling, scorched ash.

She watched it burn, feeling...free.

Seth pulled her into his arms, his embrace fierce and proud. "I love you, angel. So fucking much."

"I love you, too," she whispered against his chest.

Beck wrapped around them both, and the three of them stood together as the smoke of Heavenly's past wafted up into the evening air.

Like Seth and Beck, she'd chosen her future over her past.

As the sun finally dipped below the horizon and the fairy lights overhead glowed bright, the party showed no signs of slowing. Music filled the air, laughter echoed across the patio, and Heavenly felt wrapped in a cocoon of such profound joy it almost hurt.

Raine sidled up beside her at the dessert table, mischief dancing in her eyes. "So," she said, her voice pitched low and conspiratorial, "your men told Hammer and Liam that they're planning on taking you to Shadows soon."

Heavenly felt her cheeks heat, the blush creeping up her chest. "They did?"

"Mm-hmm. And I hereby volunteer to pick out the perfect outfit for you." Raine's grin was pure wickedness. "We both know I'll find something to drive them completely insane. Remember that little pink see-through number with all those bows I found for you? The one they practically tore off with their teeth?"

"Oh, I remember." Heavenly shivered, as that erotic night crowded her brain. "But...I'm pregnant. Can I still go to the club?"

"Honey, you can do almost everything right up until labor. Trust me—Hammer and Liam have tested my limits."

"Really?" Heavenly smiled. "I'm not sure what to expect."

"They'll show you. And they'll be damn happy about it, too," Raine assured her with a wink.

"I hope my stomach settles down before they take me. I'd hate to puke all over Hammer's floor." Heavenly cringed.

Raine leaned in close. "Trust me. Worse things than puke have ended up on Hammer's floor. Don't take a blacklight to it, just saying."

Heavenly tried not to cringe. "Eww."

"You have *no* idea. But I need to get back to the table before Hammer or Liam come and carry me off for being on my feet too long," Raine drawled, rolling her eyes as she plucked up a couple of plates of cake.

"I'll come over and sit with you soon," Heavenly called to her as she strolled away to rejoin her own men.

As a slow, romantic tune filled the air, Beck and Seth hurried her way and escorted her to the middle of the patio. Several couples were already cuddled close together, swept away in the music and their love as Beck and Seth pressed her between them. They swayed together, moving in a rhythm only they understood. Beck's hand settled at her waist while Seth's fingers gently cupped her nape as they moved as one—just like they did everything else.

"Are you happy, little girl?" Beck murmured in her ear.

"Beyond happy," Heavenly whispered, her heart swelling with more love than she could imagine. "I never knew I could feel this much joy."

"Good." Seth pressed a kiss to her temple. "Because we have one more surprise for you."

Heavenly pulled back slightly, eyeing them suspiciously. "What kind of surprise?"

Beck reached into his pocket and pulled out a colorful flyer. Heavenly's eyes grew wide when she read the name on the glossy paper. "Hawaii? You're taking me to Hawaii?"

"For our honeymoon." Seth grinned. "Two weeks in paradise. Just the three of us. White sand beaches, crystal-clear water, absolutely nothing to do but relax and devour you."

Heavenly's throat tightened with emotion. "But...what about Hudson?"

"Mom and Carl are going to stay here with him."

"But we just moved in. There's still so much to do—the nursery to set up, Hudson to settle in, and with the baby coming—"

"All those things can wait," Beck interrupted gently, stroking her cheek. "We promised Abel we'd make sure you saw the world."

"That we'd let you spread your wings and fly, angel," Seth added, pressing a soft kiss to her lips.

"I love you both for wanting to keep that promise," Heavenly said, cupping their faces. "I love that you cared enough about him—and about me—to remember what he'd asked. But I don't need to see the world."

Seth's brow furrowed. "Angel—"

"The only reason Dad wanted me to travel was so I could figure out what made me happy. But I already know what that is. It's not exotic islands, or castles, or even cabins in the woods. And it's not checking off items from some bucket list."

She clasped their hands and squeezed them.

"Beck, Seth, our baby, Hudson..." Her voice quivered with emotion and conviction. "You're my world. My adventure. My everything. I don't need to travel to the ends of the earth because all I ever need is right here."

Then Seth made a sound that was half laugh, half groan as he pulled her against his chest and banded his arms around her as if he'd never let go. "Fuck, angel. You're too good to be true."

"She is," Beck agreed in a dark, hungry voice as he surrounded both of them with his arms.

They stood, wrapped together as one while the party continued around them.

Heavenly closed her eyes and drank in their warmth, their scent, and their love.

She'd finally found the happily ever after she'd never dared to believe in.

The family she'd always dreamed of. The home she'd always craved. And the unconditional love—no longer messy or complicated, but absolutely perfect.

"We're still taking you to Hawaii," Seth murmured in her ear.

"Only because we love watching you strut around in that sexy little pink bikini," Beck growled against her neck.

Heavenly nuzzled against their hard bodies. "What if we don't leave the room?"

"That would be even better," Seth murmured. "Except...before we fly home, you have to marry one of us legally."

"We don't care which. Should we flip a coin?" Beck laughed.

Heavenly laughed. "I love you. Both of you. So much it scares me sometimes."

"We love you, too," Seth splayed his hand over her stomach protectively, where their baby grew.

"You're ours forever," Beck added, pressing a kiss to her shoulder. "And we're yours. And now, our beautiful *wife*, come here so we can prove it."

Did you miss the sizzling, high-drama,
high-heat start to the Unbroken series?

THE BETRAYAL
The Unbroken Series: Raine Falling (Book 1)
by Shayla Black and Jenna Jacob
(will be available in eBook, print, and audio)

Two friends. One woman. Let the games begin…

THE BETRAYAL

The Unbroken Series: Raine Falling (Book 1)
by Shayla Black and Jenna Jacob
(will be available in eBook, print, and audio)

Two friends. One woman. Let the games begin…

Raine Kendall has been in love with her boss, Macen Hammerman, for years. Determined to make him notice her, she pours out her heart and offers him her body—only to be crushingly rejected. When his very sexy best friend, Liam O'Neill, sees Hammer refuse to act on his obvious feelings for her, he plots to rouse his pal's possessive instincts by making Raine a proposition too tempting to refuse. He never imagines he'll fall for her himself.

Hammer has buried his lust for Raine for years. After rescuing the runaway from an alley behind his exclusive club, he's come to crave her. But tragedy has proven he'll never be the man she needs, so he protects her while keeping his distance. Then Liam's scheme to make Raine his own blindsides Hammer. He isn't ready to give the feisty beauty over to his friend. But can he heal from his past enough to fight for her? Or will he lose Raine if she gives herself—heart, body, and soul—to Liam?

5 Stars! "A-maz-ing!! [The Betrayal] will leave you breathless and have you turning pages like crazy fast trying to get to the end! It was so good!! I loved it!" - Amazon Review

PREVIEW

Fuck off, was it? Liam watched Hammer shut himself away and shook his head. Through the past decade, he and Hammer had shared so many good times, so much laughter, untold quantities of liquor, and of course for a time, Juliet. The man was the closest thing he had to a brother. Sure, they'd exchanged a cross word or two, but never anything like this. Clearly, his friend didn't appreciate his interference. But he needed it.

Since Macen had moved to California eight years ago, Liam only saw the man every November seventh, but they'd talked on the phone often. Hammer had acted as if he'd grieved and moved on, and from their conversations, Liam had never imagined otherwise. So when Hammer had invited him to visit after his divorce, Liam had jumped at the chance, eager to avoid the coming winter and painful memories.

An hour after arriving at Shadows, Liam knew Hammer had hoodwinked him. Why the fuck hadn't he realized how truly damaged Macen was? About two minutes later, he'd discovered Hammer was in love with a girl he wouldn't let himself have.

Liam more than saw Raine's appeal. Besides being a striking beauty, she was smart, fiery, good with people. And terribly in love with Hammer. Liam had pulled her aside once or twice to ask about his friend. She'd been skittish but had guarded Macen and his privacy fiercely. They'd suit well.

Getting the thick-headed man to see that, however, was proving difficult.

Tiptoeing around Hammer's issues for the past two months had accomplished nothing. Talking about them this morning hadn't helped, either. Clearly, Macen wasn't ready or willing to exorcise his ghosts.

Running a hand through his hair, Liam paced down the hall. He missed the laughing mate he'd once known, one with life and vigor pumping in his veins. If Hammer didn't know how to move forward, Liam would give him a serious shove—starting with his size thirteen up Hammer's ass.

And Raine would provide the force behind that kick.

About her, Hammer was intensely protective and possessive—in a way Liam had never seen his friend behave. Macen hoarded the lass and snarled at any other Dom who dared to touch her. Liam had every intention of forcing him to choose between hiding behind his walls or watching Raine blossom under another man's dominance.

His own.

He'd been considering this for a few days now and was convinced he stood a good chance of healing not just one heart, but two. Though he hadn't spoken to her about anything other than Hammer, Liam sensed that Raine was broken, like the china she'd carried in her hands. And she was starved for affection. Any idiot could see that she needed caring more than discipline, but she would thrive for the man who gave her the proper measure of both. Granted, Raine might turn him down, but he could be persistent for both their sakes.

Then once she'd gained a bit of confidence and Hammer had pulled his head out of his ass, Liam planned to be on his merry way and let them live happily ever after.

But he had no illusions; the moment he took Raine under his wing, Hammer would see it as a betrayal...

THANK YOU

Thank you for reading *The Commitment*! If you enjoyed it, please review and recommend it to your reader friends. That means the world to us!

If you'd like an easy way to keep up with the latest news, releases, and sales from Shayla and/or Jenna, subscribe to our newsletters for announcements about new and upcoming titles, series' previews, exclusive excerpts, teasers, random stuff about author life, and more!

Shayla's VIP Reader Newsletter or www.shaylablack.com

Jenna's Reader Newsletter or www.jennajacob.com

ABOUT SHAYLA BLACK

LET'S GET TO KNOW EACH OTHER!

With over 25 years in publishing, SHAYLA BLACK is the New York Times and USA Today bestselling author of 100+ novels. Known for her ability to craft rich characters and emotionally nuanced stories, she has won awards, sold millions of copies, and been published in a dozen languages. But it's her spicy, steamy romances that have readers breathless for more. After two decades with major New York publishers, she now enjoys the freedom of being independently published.

As an only child, Shayla occupied herself by daydreaming, much to the chagrin of her teachers. In college, she found her love for reading and started pursuing a publishing career. Though she graduated with a degree in Marketing/Advertising and embarked on a stint in corporate America, her heart was with her stories and characters, so she left her pantyhose and power suits behind.

Shayla currently lives in North Texas with her wonderfully supportive husband, her daughter, and two spoiled tabbies. In her "free" time, she enjoys reality TV, gaming, and listening to an eclectic blend of music.

TELL ME MORE ABOUT YOU.

Connect with me via the links below. You can also subscribe to my YouTube channel and enjoy LIVE, interactive #WickedWednesday video chats full of fun, book chatter, and more! See you soon!

Website
VIP Reader Newsletter
Shayla Store
Ream Stories
Facebook Book Beauties Chat Group

Explore all the rest of the Unbroken series and

Shayla's 100+ titles at ShaylaBlack.com!

ABOUT JENNA JACOB

USA Today Bestselling author Jenna Jacob paints a canvas of passion, romance, and humor as her alpha men and the feisty women who love them unravel their souls, heal their scars, and find a happy-ever-after kind of love. Heart-tugging, captivating, and steamy, her words will leave you breathless and craving more.

A mom of four grown children, Jenna, her husband Sean and their furry babies reside in Kansas. Though she spent over thirty years in accounting, Jenna isn't your typical bean counter. She's brassy, sassy, and loves to laugh, but is humbly thrilled to be living her dream as a full-time author. When she's not slamming coffee while pounding out emotional stories, you can find her reading, listening to music, cooking, camping, or enjoying the open road on the back of a Harley.

CONTACT JENNA:

Website
E Mail
Facebook Page
Jenna's Jezebels Party Page
Instagram
TikTok
BookBub
Amazon Author page
Newsletter
Goodreads

Explore all the rest of the Unbroken series and

Jenna's other titles at JennaJacob.com!

www.ingramcontent.com/pod-product-compliance
Lightning Source LLC
LaVergne TN
LVHW010625110826
845149LV00014B/2783